MISS DEXIE

A ROMANCE OF THE PROVINCES

MORE WILDSIDE CLASSICS

MISS DEXIE

A ROMANCE OF THE PROVINCES

STANFORD EVELETH

WILDSIDE PRESS

MISS DEXIE: A ROMANCE OF THE PROVINCES

This edition published 2005 by Wildside Press, LLC.
www.wildsidepress.com

INTRODUCTORY—1864
AND WAR TIME.

The war between the North and South has sent a wail of grief into thousands of homes throughout the land, and the dreadful death-roll is daily being added to, for battle follows battle, and the slaughter is appalling, even to those who have been hardened to the sight by months of action. No wonder that the faces of wives and mothers are white with anguish—that fearful death-list has carried desolation to their hearts, and others, just as dear, are obeying the command, "Forward to Spotsylvania."

Men stop to discuss the situation at street-corners, or hurry to the telegraph or newspaper offices for the latest news, their anxious faces telling how their lives have been touched by this outbreak of strife.

Among those who pass along the streets of a New England town, is one whose genial countenance attracts attention. He is above the average height, strong and well proportioned, and his quick and energetic step and wide-awake appearance proclaim him of New England birth.

As he nears a house in the suburbs, a shout of welcome greets him, and he lifts his eyes and smiles upon a group of young faces in an upper window; a moment more and the door is thrown open, and childish forms hurl themselves upon him.

As soon as the children's noisy greeting was over, Mr. Sherwood entered the room where his wife awaited his appearance, and drawing a chair near the couch where she was reclining, related the news of the day.

"Yes, I am later than usual, but I received a despatch from mother, and that detained me," said he, in answer to her remark. "I have arranged to run down to the farm tomorrow, as mother says my immediate presence is necessary."

"And is there no word from Charley yet? His name is not in the list of killed or wounded, but I fear the worst."

"His wife was at the telegraph office while I was there," said Mr. Sherwood, as they entered the dining-room. "She expected news every hour, and will send you word directly she gets a message. I tried to persuade her to return with me, but she was too anxious to leave the office until she had some reply to her despatch."

"This is a trying time for wives and sisters, and Charley was my favorite brother. But what new trouble has happened at the farm, that you are needed in such haste?" Mrs. Sherwood asked, as she poured out the tea.

"It seems that mother has heard that I intend joining the new company, if it is called out, and she has objections which she wishes to make personally. You know mother is not a Unionist; her southern prejudices are too strong for that, and the possibility of my joining the northern army has embittered her mind. You might come with me tomorrow; the change would do you good," he added.

"My visits to the farm are doubtful pleasures," replied Mrs. Sherwood, who had but little sympathy with her husband's people, "but any change will be welcome while this uncertainty exists about my brother. Can I trust you all to be good and obedient if I leave you in charge of Nurse Johnson?" she asked, lifting her eyes to the young faces around the table.

The best of behavior being readily promised, Mrs. Sherwood soon left the room to make preparations for the unexpected journey, and early next morning Mr. Sherwood and his wife were on the train bound for Crofton, the nearest station to the old home farm.

While they are on the way, a glance at the history of his parents will explain how matters stand at the homestead.

Squire Sherwood was a well-to-do farmer, who was well known outside of his own village, having held several public offices at various times, but these had been given up in order to superintend his fine farm, which years of toil had brought into a high state of cultivation. Early in life, while doing business in Louisiana, he had married a southern lady; but a few years later he came into possession of the farm, and they moved North.

His wife found the change very great, and often sighed for the luxurious life of her southern home; but she fell into New England ways more readily than might have been expected. When she moved north, she brought Dinah, who was her particular property, with her; indeed, Dinah was so much attached to her young mistress that she refused to be left behind, and life on the farm was made more endurable by her services. When, in the course of time, a son was born, he was placed in Dinah's care, and little Clarence was as fond of his black nurse as was ever the southern-born child of its black "mammy" of the southern plantation.

But Mrs. Sherwood did not lose her individuality by her marriage. The peculiar institution of the South she would like to have seen extended to the North as well, and when the disruption took place her sympathies were with those of her old home; she was heart and soul a southerner. Up to this time the same friendly feeling existed between mistress and maid as when they had lived under a sunnier sky; but the sentiments engendered by the hated Abolitionists, soon found vent in sharp words, and other abuses, that hitherto the faithful creature had never known.

Dinah felt keenly the change in her mistress, but bore it patiently, thinking it would soon pass; but village gossip soon spread the report of Mrs. Sherwood's treatment of her black servant, and the southern sentiments, so openly expressed, caused the family to lose the estimation of their neighbors, and gained instead their animosity. Party feeling ran high, and the villagers declared that if there was another draft made, the son should be made to fight against the avowed principles of the mother, and as the sentiments of both parties grew stronger as the war advanced, it brought matters to a crisis.

Hence the telegram requesting the son's presence at the farm.

When the train arrived at Crofton, the carriage was waiting for the travellers, in charge of the hired man, and they were soon driving along the familiar road to the homestead.

"What is the matter at home, Joe?" said Mr. Sherwood. "Are all well?"

"Yes, all well, sir," and Joe touched the horse lightly with the whip; "but the war news is troubling them, and making your mother very anxious about you."

Joe was an old and trusted servant, having lived with the family for years, and so much confidence was placed in him that he seemed like one of the family. When they arrived at the farmhouse, the son wished to know at once why he was sent for in such haste, but his father replied: "Plenty time, Clarence, plenty time ahead of us to talk about the matter; let us have dinner before we discuss troublesome questions."

But the mother's heart was too full of anxiety to wait, and she asked: "Is it true, Clarence, that you are going to join the Union army?"

"Well, I am ready to do my duty, mother," he replied, in a conciliating tone, "but I have not yet joined the company, so you need not be anxious about me until you have cause."

"But I have cause already! I hear that another draft is soon to be made, and the people around here are determined that you shall be drawn into the fight, if only to spite me, but if you enter the army at all it should not be on the Unionists' side; that would be taking up arms against your kith and kin, and no son of mine must do that!"

A look of terror spread over the face of the son's wife. Was her husband to be torn from her side, as the mother feared?

"I cannot argue this question with you, mother, lest we should not agree," said the son, gently. "It is a pity that as a family our interests are so divided; but others have placed their interests against kith and kin, and, if duty called, I should have to do the same. I own that at present I shrink from the call, as the forces seem concentrated near my sister Annie's home. I wish she would come north, but that cannot be expected while her husband is in danger. He has command of an important position, but Sherman is sure to dislodge him, and I fear the result will be disastrous. But I see you have something else in your mind at present, so what is it that you wish me to do, mother?"

"I want you to leave the country, Clarence. I cannot bear the thought of you being drafted to fight against my home and people, and your own natural affections should cry out against uniting with the slayers of your kindred."

"Oh! this cruel, cruel war!" cried the son's wife. "We are indeed a divided family, for my brother is with Sherman near Atalanta, fighting against my husband's people. Oh! Clarence, do as your mother wishes, and let us leave the country, for my heart will break if you are drafted!"

"You must leave at once, if at all," said the mother; "even a week's delay may be too late, for the neighbors boast that before the month is out I shall see my son march away to Washington! I would give every dollar we possess to help the southern cause, if what they threaten should come to pass!" she added, in an angry tone.

"Well, mother," replied the son with a smile, "my patrimony is too precious to run such a risk, and as I am not very anxious to shoot anyone, or be shot at either, I will do as you wish, and let you live in peace. I feel confident that a few months will end the struggle, or my decision would be different; but where do you wish me to go?"

"Go!" her countenance softening at once. "You can decide that for yourself; as long as you are out of the reach of the Unionists, that is all I ask. So, go to Halifax, if you like!"

"Very well, mother, to Halifax I'll go, but you do not seem to have the welfare of your only son very much to heart, after all, by the way you speak."

"Nonsense! Clarence, you know my heart better than that! I mean that it matters little where you settle, so long as you are out of American territory until the war is over."

"Oh! Halifax will suit me very well, mother. Ever since I can remember you have threatened to send me to Halifax; so now I'll go, and I do not believe I shall find it a place of torment either. Nelson, who was in partnership with me when I was in Augusta, has moved his family there, and I may join him again in business. He is buying up horses and sending them to headquarters. What! you surely would not object to me making some money out of the Unionists?" he asked, in answer to his mother's quick look of surprise.

The discussion lasted some time, but to the relief of the son's wife they decided to return home the following day, that her husband might have an opportunity to settle his business in time to catch the first boat to Halifax.

Becoming aware of the hostility which prevailed among the neighbors, on account of Dinah's presence at the farmhouse, Mr. Sherwood proposed to take her with them to Halifax as their hired nurse. He had a kindly feeling for the good, old woman, who was such a faithful and partial nurse to him in his boyhood, and he could not help seeing that she was less kindly treated than formerly, and to his surprise his mother consented to the plan. Dinah made no objection when the matter was laid before her, for like many colored women of her age she had an intense love for children. This love had grown stronger during the years there had been no children at the farmhouse to lavish it upon, and the short visits that the grandchildren made at the farm were red-letter days to Aunt Dinah.

Mrs. Sherwood found her cares much lessened with Dinah installed as nurse. The care of children was always a wearisome burden to the rather indolent mother, so the irksome duties were readily placed on the willing shoulders of Dinah.

While Mrs. Sherwood awaited her husband's directions, her brother's wife appeared one day, bearing the sad announcement that Charley had fallen in the last battle; and though Mrs. Sherwood had been expecting this from the first, her grief was more distressing to witness than that of the afflicted, sad-faced wife.

But there had been no hope in Mrs. Sherwood's heart since her brother had bidden them farewell, and marched away with his comrades; and her fears being realized, she was more anxious than ever to leave the country that might yet claim her husband also, and when word came from Halifax that a furnished house awaited the family, Mrs. Sherwood easily persuaded her bereaved sister-in-law to accompany them thither.

A few weeks later, the family—consisting of Mrs. Sherwood and her brother's childless widow; Gussie and Dexie, twin girls of sixteen; Louie, aged thirteen, Georgie ten, Flossie three, and a year-old baby in the arms of black Dinah—arrived in Halifax, where this story properly begins.

CHAPTER II.

The new home awaiting the family was situated in the south end of the city. The house, which is still considered a desirable residence, was built in a style very common in Halifax, for the accommodation of two tenants. The owner, a Mr. Gurney, lived in one part of it; he was a native of England, but at the solicitation of his brother, who was an officer in one of the regiments, he had removed to Nova Scotia, and was doing a prosperous business on Granville Street.

Mr. Gurney had a large family. Cora, the eldest, was just out of her teens; then came Launcelot or Lancy, as he was usually called; then Elsie, and so on, till you came to an infant in arms. As the cabs containing the Sherwood family drove up to the house, the nursery windows in the second story of the Gurney household were filled with childish faces, anxious to see what sort of playmates their new neighbors might be; and when the young strangers alighted on the sidewalk they observed the happy faces and smiled back in return, thus pleasantly intimating that they hoped to be friends. But when Dinah appeared with the baby, the faces in the window betrayed their astonishment. "Oh! a black nurse! and the baby don't seem a bit frightened of her!" they exclaimed in surprise.

"I wonder if they love her when she is so *very* black," said little Gracie. "I shouldn't love to kiss her, would you, Percy?" looking at their own fair-faced nurse in loving approval.

Mrs. Sherwood was surprised to find the house so neatly and comfortably arranged, but she soon learned that she was indebted to Mrs. Gurney for this pleasant state of affairs, for she had given Mr. Sherwood much material assistance in making the rooms look home-like and cheerful.

In the evening, when the family were assembled in the parlor, Mrs. Gurney tapped lightly at the door, and her cordial greeting seemed more like that of a friend than the first meeting of strangers, and when Mrs. Sherwood began to thank her for the thoughtful attentions that had made their homecoming so pleasant, she stopped her with a word.

"Do not thank me, I beg of you, Mrs. Sherwood," she said, with a smile. "I have only done for you what I wish someone had done for me when I first came to Halifax. I know by experience," she added, as a smile lit up her motherly face, "what it is to come into a strange place, among strange people, with a hundred things needing to be done at once, and a family of children to attend to besides. I felt sure you would like the place better if you found it a bit homelike and set-tled, but I have come in to explain. I was afraid you might think I was making myself too busy in your affairs. Now, I do hope, Mrs. Sherwood, that you will not make strangers of us after this." Her face beamed with kindness as she spoke, and after a short and friendly conversation she withdrew.

The next day was a busy one in the Sherwood household, but in the afternoon the twin girls were invited to go for a walk with the young ladies next door, while Louie was persuaded to go up to the nursery with the Gurney children.

Louie felt very shy when she found herself among so many little strangers, but the kind, good-natured nurse, in white cap and apron, who presided over this restless brood, soon set her at ease by bidding the children show Louie their toys. And what a store of them there were to be sure. There were several miniature sets of dishes of various patterns, and whole families of dolls, from the aged grandmother in a white frilled cap, to the tiny china specimen that was too small to be dressed. There were Noah's arks that held animals that would have astonished old Noah himself, and rocking-horses in various stages of dilapidation, from the bright new one with only a scratch on his leg, to the headless and tailless steed that rocked in a melancholy way in the corner. Then there was a swing that hung from the ceiling, and a springy teeter-board that could bounce the little ones quite into the air. These and other treasures were duly inspected by the shy Louie, who soon entered heartily into the games started for her amusement.

The twin girls were delighted with their walk. They had viewed the city from Citadel Hill, and had extended their walk to other spots of interest, but it seemed to them that they had moved nearer the seat of war, instead of away from it, for the sword and gun-bearing officers and soldiers whom they met in different parts of the city seemed more warlike than those who had passed through the streets of their old home, as they journeyed toward headquarters.

In a short time the family settled down to the routine of home-life that comes natural in all households, and having secured competent help, Mrs. Sherwood was able to order her household without much exertion on her part; in fact, she began to feel that she might now take life comparatively easy, and, little by little, the duties of housekeeper were laid upon Aunt Jennie.

Dinah found the burden and exactions of her small charges quite bearable, so the not-over-anxious mother was relieved from trouble in that quarter also. But Dinah seemed well satisfied. Her love for the little ones placed under her care had been strong enough to silence the superstitious dread that had filled her heart when she first learned the destination of the family; but in spite of her efforts to please everyone, Dinah could not overcome the strong dislike which Biddy openly and emphatically expressed for all "nagers." Consequently, a wordy warfare spiced the day's doings occasionally, but, thanks to Aunt Jennie's tact and kindness, even this grew less and less, as occasion for them vanished.

A few weeks later, Mr. Sherwood accompanied Mr. Nelson to Prince Edward Island, on a horse-buying expedition, but we will not follow them, as our story has to do with those in Halifax; it is sufficient to say that they secured a number of valuable animals for the

New York market, at a price that surprised Mr. Sherwood until he understood that the Island farmers were ready to dispose of all products "cheap for cash."

As might be supposed, the friendly intercourse between the members of the two families grew stronger as the taste of each became more apparent.

Dexie and Elsie were "chums" at once, though each possessed an opposite nature; one supplied what the other lacked, so they agreed charmingly.

Gussie was older in appearance than her twin, Dexie, and preferred the society of a "grown-up" young lady, and Cora Gurney found her a pleasant companion.

Launcelot Gurney, or Lancy, was the musical genius of the Gurney family, and this soon caused a feeling of friendship to spring up between him and Dexie Sherwood, and few days passed in which they did not spend considerable time in each other's society. But the closest observer could find no fault with this intimacy. It sprang from the similarity of tastes, and the frank, straightforward manner which marked their intercourse denied the existence of any foolish sentimentality. Though younger than Cora, Lancy seemed by his steady ways and manly behavior to be the eldest of the family. Perhaps the fact that his father talked so much with him, and interested him in matters that seldom claim the attention of youths of his age, had something to do with his manner, but behind his usual calm exterior there was an amount of conceit not always apparent to others, a conceit that placed himself above the ordinary High School boys who had been his daily associates. This they had felt intuitively, and with his precise habits and nicety of dress had caused him to be dubbed "the dandy."

Another member of the Gurney household must also be mentioned, for Hugh McNeil belonged to the family almost as much as Lancy himself, seeing that he had been cared for by Mrs. Gurney before Lancy was born. He was the son of a strange marriage, a marriage that had turned out disastrously. His father had been valet to Mr. Gurney's eldest brother, and, while attending his master in Paris, had fallen in love with a pretty French waitress, and secretly married her. On returning to England with his master, the French wife followed him and revealed the marriage, and this so enraged McNeil's master that he discharged him on the spot. Whereupon McNeil, after securing a comfortable lodging for his wife, left for Australia, intending to send for her as soon as he obtained permanent employment. Before he had done so, the French wife died in giving birth to little Hugh; and the matter coming to the knowledge of Mrs. Gurney, she had pitied the motherless babe and had him placed in a comfortable home. As he grew older, Mrs. Gurney became so fond of her young protégé that he was taken into the family, and was given an education that enabled him, in later years, to be of much service to his benefactors.

In looks he favored both parents, inheriting the strong, sturdy frame of his Scotch father, with the dark features and piercing black eyes of his mother. At present, he occupied the position of clerk or general factotum to Mr. Gurney; his quickness and ability to grasp the requirements of business, with the general activity of his movements, made him invaluable, and Mr. Gurney trusted him like a son. Amongst other duties, Hugh frequently attended auction sales, to watch for bargains in their line of business, and it was at one of these sales that Mrs. Sherwood met him. She had accompanied Mrs. Nelson to a sale of bankrupt stock, and wishing to secure some desired articles she asked Hugh's assistance, and he served her so well that he was asked to call, and he was received so graciously by more than one member of the family that the call was often repeated, and he soon had the "freedom of the house," as Dexie laughingly expressed it.

The English custom of playing at charades or tableaux, was much in vogue in the Gurney household, and on rainy days the children were sure to be found in the attic, where a mimic stage had been erected, and drop curtains of a peculiar style and pattern added to the attractions of the place. The young neighbors next door were soon initiated into the mysteries of the "green room," and their added numbers made the audience seem immense, since it took every available box and board to construct "opera chairs" for the crowd; but every chair was sure to be filled when the new "star," Signora Dexina, was announced to appear before the footlights, and if these latter were but candles left from the last Christmas tree, what mattered it?

One day while up in the attic rehearsing a new piece, the idea occurred to them that a private entrance into each other's apartments, by way of the attic, would be a great convenience, so they eagerly searched the partition for a loose board. Finding one that was quite broad, they put forth every exertion, and after much shoving and prying, during which their fingers received many splinters and bruises, they succeeded in getting the board loose from the floor. By shoving it aside, they could squeeze through the opening into the opposite attic, then the board would swing back to its old position.

The "convenience" of this private entrance only children could explain, as it seemed hardly worth the exertion to climb three pair of stairs for the pleasure of entering the house of their next-door neighbor by this narrow doorway, but the children were delighted with it. In after-years others, long past childhood, did not scruple to use this doorway, and silently bless the hands that formed it.

The good old custom of family worship was daily practised in the Gurney household, and appearing suddenly in the dining-room one morning, just as the family were about to "take books," Dexie stayed to prayers, and was so impressed with the charm and simplicity of the devotions, that she asked permission to come again.

The exercises consisted of reading, verse about, a portion of Scripture, then a verse or two of some well-known hymn was sung, after which Mr. Gurney made a short prayer, using simple words within the comprehension of the little ones. Special mention was made of the needs of the family. If any of them were ill, they were mentioned by name, and it gave Dexie a curious feeling the first time she knelt with the family to hear Mr. Gurney ask for a "particular blessing to rest on our young neighbor, who worships with us this morning." The charm of it all seemed to be in the feeling of reality there was about it, the decorous behavior of the little ones showing that it meant more than outside form to them. None of the Gurney family was excused from this morning worship unless sickness made it impossible to appear, and it soon became a regular thing for Dexie Sherwood to make her appearance with her Bible when the bell rang for prayers. Dexie thoroughly enjoyed these exercises, her religious education having been limited to the little she had learned in Sunday School, for the Bible was not a very well read book in the Sherwood household, and its treasures were almost unknown, until they were opened to her eyes by the Gurneys.

Aunt Jennie was much surprised when she learned the cause of Dexie's frequent morning visits next door. The evident desire for instruction which made her niece seek from others what should have been imparted to her at home, came like a reproach to her heart. She had been reared in a Christian home, where Bible truths had been imparted to her from her cradle up, so she now endeavored to supply what was lacking in the religious education of her young relatives. It was done quietly and without ostentation, but the last half hour of the day was given to Dexie, and she spent it with her aunt in the privacy of her chamber, where they studied the Book together. Dexie tried to persuade Gussie to join these readings, but with no success, for Gussie, like many others, "cared for none of these things."

CHAPTER III.

When Mr. Sherwood returned from New York, he was accompanied by a Mr. Plaisted, a gentleman of a speculative turn of mind, who had attached himself to Mr. Sherwood with a persistency that showed he had "the cheek of a drummer," and he had invited himself to accompany Mr. Sherwood to his home in Halifax. Although fond of horses, there was nothing about the appearance of Mr. Plaisted to suggest the jockey: he was what would have been termed in a later day a fair specimen of the genus dude. He was of medium height, and was decidedly foppish in his manner, and with his elaborate neckties and perfumed curls, he was, in his own estimation at least, quite irresistible. His hands and feet were unusually small for a man. The latter he was very proud of, always encasing them in boots of the very latest style; and, no doubt, the "cold cream" and other cosmetics which he nightly used helped to give his hands and face the fair appearance that so delighted himself.

His presence in the household seemed to have an opposite effect on the twin girls. Gussie was delighted with his fine appearance and gallant speeches, but Dexie seemed to see the ignoble nature behind and kept him at a distance.

A few evenings after his arrival, when the family were assembled in the parlor, Mr. Plaisted, who was leaning back in his chair, in an attitude peculiar to Americans, asked: "Have you a son living in Boston, Sherwood? I met a young fellow in a broker's office bearing your name. Any relation of yours?"

"No, neither a son nor a relation; this is my only boy," Mr. Sherwood replied, reaching for Georgie's ear in a playful manner.

"Ah! that's a pity now! a grown-up son would have been some use to you. If one of the twins had happened to be a boy, you would have had quite an assistant by now."

Dexie was sitting behind the window curtain, watching the passers-by. She resented this speech, and the rude way it was uttered provoked her into replying:

"One does not need to be born a boy to be of use in this world, allow me to tell you, Mr. Plaisted! for in all things that he needs help, I am my father's boy—not ghost!" she laughingly added, as Plaisted, startled by her sudden appearance, almost overbalanced in his chair.

"Bless me! I didn't notice you were there, Miss Dexie," said he, regaining his equilibrium with an effort. "Guess you've been studying Shakespeare for my benefit, eh, Miss Dexie?"

"Oh! that's just like Dexie," said Gussie, with a frown. "She always likes to make a scene when she can. She will want to go on the stage, I expect, by and by."

"What nonsense! Gussie," said Dexie, smiling good-naturedly, "when all the theatrical performances we are allowed to attend are those that take place up in the attic."

"Oh! come now, Miss Dexie. How often do you slip off to plays with that young chap next door?" said Plaisted, with a sly wink at Gussie. "I often see you down street together."

"Your eyesight must be remarkably good, then," was the icy reply, "for I think no one else can accuse me of 'slipping off' with any person."

"By the way, Miss Dexie, I have been wondering what your name is, ever since I came. Is it an abbreviation or a nickname?" said Plaisted, anxious to turn the conversation. "I have never met with a young lady bearing your name before."

"And you are not likely to meet one again," was the quick reply, as a flush of anger covered her face.

Mr. Sherwood looked across at Dexie, knowing full well that Plaisted could not have broached a more unfortunate subject. Dexie's full name was her chief annoyance, so he answered in a quiet tone, "Her name is Dexter, but she would like us all to forget the fact, and call her Dexie instead."

"Since Mr. Plaisted is so inquisitive, it would be wise to gratify his curiosity at once, and have done with it," and Dexie turned sharply around and faced the rest. "He had better learn the whole of our names, and the history of them as well, and then, perhaps, he will be kind enough to drop the subject forever. Here is the story: At the time father was married he was doing business in Augusta, Maine; but it happened, unfortunately, that mother was born and brought up in Dexter. For some reason, that I have never been able to fathom, when we twins appeared we were honored by being called after those respective places! Gussie was the smartest and best-looking baby, I suppose, so she was selected to bear the name of the capital city, while I had to bear the burden of Dexter! It is a wonder how I managed to survive the christening, for the very name was enough to finish one! Oh! I have wished a thousand times that the town of Dexter had been visited by a conflagration, and wiped out of existence, before mother's people ever went there! But there! I daresay they would have gone to Skowhegan! Norrigewock! Mattawamkeg! or some other place with an outlandish name, and, of course, I should have been named after it, just the same! Dexie is bad enough, but Skowie, think of it!"

A peal of laughter interrupted Dexter's hot-spoken words; but the mention of her name always touched a tender spot, and she added, in an injured tone, that made her father smile in spite of himself:

"And there is Louie. Everybody thinks her name is Louisa, so she escapes the questions of the curious; but her name is Louisiana, after the State where grandma's old home is. We were there for a long visit when she was a baby, and she is not likely to forget that fact all her life. Then papa has a sister in Georgia; so of course we went to see her, too; but her plantation was so lovely we were all delighted when papa consented to stay there a year or two and help Uncle Edward set out some new groves, and get everything in good running order. We were there when Georgie was born, so he got off comparatively easy; but then! boys always do!"

Plaisted's shouts of laughter forbade further expressions of displeasure, and Dexie turned her back again and looked out the window, while she regained her composure. Nothing so aroused her indignation as the mention of her name consequently few knew what it really was. Louie liked her name, for by bearing it she became her grandmother's favorite, and Gussie could look on the matter with indifference.

"I quite sympathize with Dexie," said Mrs. Sherwood, "but her father has a New Englander's love for novel names, and gives no thought to the unnecessary burden that it puts upon the children, one which they have to bear all their lives."

"Oh! well, Gussie can't complain, I'm sure," said Mr. Sherwood. "No one will become inquisitive over her name," he laughingly added.

"I have no doubt that Miss Gussie feels thankful she secured first choice," said Plaisted, "and that her good looks entitled her to it," and he looked over at Gussie with bold admiration in his glance.

"I don't think looks had anything to do with it," said Mr. Sherwood, "else this curly pate would have had first choice," reaching over to pass his hand over the brown rings of hair.

"Seems to me this conversation is much too personal," said Dexie, rising from her seat. "I think a change would be welcome to one and all," and she sat down before the piano.

Mr. Sherwood smiled his approval. He was very proud of his daughter's musical ability, for she could sing and play to suit the taste of any audience, and could arouse the inner emotions of those who had any feelings that were capable of being stirred at all. One of her accomplishments, which she seldom exhibited before strangers, was that of whistling. Few people have heard the exquisite notes that can be produced by an adept in the art, but there are whistlers and whistlers, whose notes differ as much as those of the linnet and the crow. While accompanying herself on the piano, Dexie could produce such wonderful trills and quavers, with such purity of tone, that she could almost rival the very birds themselves, and she never failed to surprise and charm all that heard her. Wishing to please her father, as well as convince Mr. Plaisted that her name did not make her a "ninny," she selected some of her best pieces and sang her most charming songs; then, after a few soft notes, she broke into a bird-song, whistling the notes so faithfully true that Mr. Plaisted was startled as well as delighted, and the conversation he had begun with Gussie came to an abrupt end.

"Well, Miss Dexie, I must confess that you have surprised me," said he, as Dexie resumed her seat at the window. "I never heard the equal of that from the boards of any concert-room in New York. No one would object to paying 'dear for his whistle,' if that quality was purchasable. You would make a fortune on the stage."

"I hope Dexie will never use her whistle as a money-making gift," said her father; "but I think, myself, it is about as pretty music as one ever hears."

"You can bet your life, Sherwood, she would create such a furore in musical circles that she would make something besides money for you. Bring her out, Sherwood; it will pay you better than speculating with horses."

"Heaven forbid!" replied Mr. Sherwood, extremely annoyed at the way Plaisted spoke of his favorite daughter. "I fancy I can make a comfortable living for my family, without turning my daughter into a public character."

"Thank you, papa," came the clear-cut tones from the window; "but pray do not waste any more sentiment on Mr. Plaisted. He happens to be one of that kind of men who would sell their own mothers for profit! But he can't help it, poor man, he was born that way!" and before Plaisted could recover from his surprise, Dexie had left the room.

"That was a pretty good slap, and no mistake," exclaimed Plaisted as he drew out his handkerchief to wipe his hot face. "I meant no offence, Sherwood, 'pon honor."

"Well, as my daughter did not take it so, be kind enough to be more guarded in your remarks in the future. However, in a battle of words, I fancy she is able to hold her own, and come off victor every time, too."

The matter was dismissed with a laugh, though memory lingered long over the plain-spoken words; but in his secret heart Mr. Sherwood was glad that Dexie had so answered this New York gentleman. Dexie had won her position in her father's heart by her prompt and willing service. She it was who could be depended on to do the numberless little tasks, insignificant in themselves, perhaps, but of the greatest moment when taken together, for the joy and comfort of home-life very largely depends on the way these little things are attended to. Her sister, Gussie, was too fond of pleasing herself to be of much service to others; but Dexie was quick to see another's need, and she found it a pleasure to wait on her dear papa, who, however active and energetic he might be when about his business, dearly loved to be waited on when once he was inside his own home. He always found Dexie willing and ready to give all her time for his pleasure. She had even changed the style of her handwriting so as to help her father with his correspondence, and she proved herself such an able assistant that, on giving her verbal instructions, she could write out his letters quite as clearly and businesslike as if his own hand held the pen. Once, in Dexie's absence, he had pressed Gussie into service, but Mr. Sherwood never repeated the request, for Gussie's writing resembled the "sprawls of a many-legged spider that had fallen into the ink bottle, and then wiped his legs on the writing paper," according to Mr. Sherwood's description of it.

But Gussie was pretty if she was not useful. She was a perfect blonde, with a wealth of yellow hair, which she twisted round her head like a golden coronet. Her eyes were as blue as fresh spring violets, and her slight, willowy figure gave promise of much grace when fully developed. Her twin sister, Dexie, was much unlike her in every way, having dark brown eyes, while a mass of short, light brown curls covered the well poised head, giving her something of a boyish air. She had a clear complexion, but was not so fair as Gussie, and her figure was shorter and more rounded. She was quick and alert in all her movements, and laughed when Gussie called her a tomboy, but she was only thoroughly wide-awake, and enjoyed life with a zest that was but natural in a girl of her years. She scorned the languid air that Gussie affected, and looked with disdain on the one-legged storks that her sister delighted to transfer to canvas, and she wondered how it was possible for anyone to sit for hours over a bit of fancywork the usefulness of which was doubtful; but this was the only kind of *work* that Gussie ever cared to do.

Since Aunt Jennie had taken up her abode in the family, Dexie had found great delight in solving some of the mysteries of cookery, and the toothsome articles she evolved, under her aunt's direction, were exhibited with as much pride as Gussie felt when she adorned the new sofa pillow with such gorgeous butterflies that no one dared use it thereafter. But Dexie was at her best when seated before the piano; then her face glowed with a beauty far exceeding that of her sister's, for the soul shone in her face, and she would make the instrument respond to her feelings like a human being. However ruffled her state of mind might be—for, be it known, Dexie was not blessed with a very even temper—she could pour out her troubles to her beloved instrument, as she would to a dear friend, and she always found peace and consolation there.

CHAPTER IV.

One evening, when Mr. Plaisted was still in Halifax, there was a small party held at Mrs. Gurney's, to which the Sherwoods were invited. Although the party was only for "grown-ups," as Elsie Gurney said, invitations were given to Gussie and Dexie, as company for the young members of the party. Among those present was Major Gurney, and several of his brother officers, whose gaily-attired figures added much to the beauty of the rooms.

During the evening music was introduced, and it need hardly be said that most of the songs sung were thoroughly English, and of course much applauded; but Dexie, in her loyalty to the land she called *home*, though living out of its borders, could scarcely conceal her annoyance, and turning to a table near, she picked up a book of views in order to hide her vexation. Presently she became aware that the book before her was composed of views that were unmistakably English; and no sooner was their nationality noted than she dropped the book as if it had burnt her fingers.

"The idea of that little spot on the earth lording it over all creation!" she said to herself, and her lip curled in scorn.

Just then the young man at the piano struck up the notes of "Rule Britannia," which was caught up at once by all the red-coated gentlemen present, as if the very words were a sweet morsel under their tongues. It ended at last with a crash, and Dexie gave a sigh of relief when she saw the piano stool vacant.

But Mr. Gurney was making his way towards her, and, bending over her, said in a low voice:

"Will you favor the company with some music, Miss Dexie? I have often listened to some very enchanting strains from your fingers."

"Well, I think I can play something that will be quite as enchanting as that we have just listened to," Dexie replied. "I don't believe that piece was ever meant to be sung inside four walls, and those officers shout as if they intended to raise the roof. I am afraid my playing will seem very tame after all that bluster," she laughingly added.

"No fear of that," said Mr. Gurney, smiling. "Try and see if you cannot beat them at their own game."

Dexie looked up quickly, and caught his meaning, and as she crossed the room her thoughts were flying through her brain, trying to bring to mind some song that would answer those "red-coated braggarts." A smile came to her lips, as memory served her. Yes, she could sing something that was quite as musical as "Rule Britannia," anyway, and echo the praise of her own land as well. So when she passed her father she whispered:

"Give me the help of your best bass in the chorus;" and bending over Gussie, who was listening to the remarks of a many-striped officer, who was standing near her chair, she said in a low tone: "Give me your help this once, Gussie, and let your alto be heard clear to the citadel."

Seating herself at the piano, she struck a few chords, and then her rich, ringing voice, with every word clear and distinct, sounded through the room:

> *"Of all the mighty nations in the east or in the west,*
> *Our glorious Yankee nation is the brightest and the best;*
> *We have room for all creation, and our banner is unfurled*
> *With a cordial invitation to the people of the world.*
> *So, come along, come along; make no delay;*
> *Come from every nation; come from every way.*
> *The land it is broad enough; you need not be alarmed,*
> *For Uncle Sam has land enough to give you all a farm."*

An amused look passed over the faces of those present as the sentiments of the singer reached their ears, and Plaisted said, half aloud:

"Good for you, Miss Dexie; I back you there!" and when the chorus was reached, his fine tenor was equal to any that had been heard during the evening, his "Come along" ringing out like a bold challenge.

"Hurrah for the Stars and Stripes!" cried Lieutenant Layton, as he joined in the applause that arose as soon as the song had ended. "Your nationality is quite apparent, Miss Sherwood. That's right; don't let your own broad country be sung down."

Dexie found herself immediately surrounded, and was overwhelmed with entreaties to sing again, for the "back slap" had been as diverting as it was unexpected, and she found it impossible to leave the piano without singing again. But she thought that one song in that strain was enough, though Mr. Gurney came over to her side, saying:

"Give us another like the last, Miss Dexie. It is good for these red-coated fellows to remember that they have not conquered all the people on the face of the earth."

"I am afraid it will offend someone," said Dexie, softly. "I couldn't resist the temptation of letting them know that *I* don't think England is supreme. I am a loyal American, even if I do reside in Halifax."

"Oh! there is no danger of offending," Mr. Gurney replied. "The lion has roared quite enough for one evening, so let the starry flag play awhile in the breeze."

But Dexie did not like to flaunt the flag too near the lion's face, and in his own den, as it were; so remembering some of the beautiful, pathetic songs, that had been inspired by the war, she thought they would be quite as much enjoyed.

Lancy Gurney was seldom far from the piano, and as Dexie finished her song she motioned him to her side. A few whispered words passed between them, then Lancy sat down beside her, when there rang out a symphony that delighted every ear.

In a few minutes, Dexie took advantage of the movement she had brought about on purpose to relieve herself, and rose from the piano, leaving Lancy seated at the instrument.

This musical treat brought Dexie into social prominence, as there were several members of the "Song and Glee Club" present, and she was much surprised to receive invitations for herself and sister to join the club.

This club contained some of the best singers in the city, but had no members so young as those now invited to join them. The invitation was never regretted, however, for they soon acknowledged that the "Sherwood twins" were quite an acquisition.

The pleasant evening was over at last, and the twins had received compliments enough to turn older heads than theirs; but Dexie did not dwell on the flattering remarks as Gussie did. Her singing and playing came as natural to her as it did to talk, and she was not puffed up by the praise bestowed on her for it. But Gussie was always vain of her good looks, and she magnified the remarks that her pretty face had elicited, and when they were about to retire Gussie had quite the air of a society belle as she said:

"I have made quite an impression on Lieutenant Morton. I feel quite sure he is almost in love with me already." But, receiving no answer to this remark, she added:

"I hope you are not jealous, Dexie, because I received so many compliments from those fine-looking officers?"

"Pooh! you silly thing! Jealous! Well, that's rich, I must say," replied Dexie, in a tone of scorn. "You seem to think it is a fine thing to be complimented by soldiers, but not so I. Why, didn't Mrs. Gurney tell us one time that it was not considered respectable to be seen talking to soldiers on the street, and I can't see how it makes so much difference if you talk to them behind closed doors."

"Oh, but there was not one soldier invited to Mrs. Gurney's party; they were all officers, every one of them," was Gussie's reply.

"Pshaw! what difference do a few ornaments on a man's coat make to the man inside of it, I'd like to know? I expect that half of them, at least, were common soldiers once themselves, and were bossed around like the very meanest of them. I declare, I'd rather be a black on auntie's plantation than be under some of those bawling officers we met tonight."

But Gussie did not care to discuss the matter further, as it required some time to think the matter out seriously, if she would discover why an officer should be less open to objection than a common soldier, for it was true enough that many who wore the stripes had stepped up from the ranks; yet how few of the better class care to make friends with the common soldier, be he ever so respectable as a private individual. Was it likely that a cloak of uncommon respectability was put on with the officer's uniform? Hardly; else some of them lost the cloak very shortly after it was put on.

CHAPTER V.

Mr. Sherwood, accompanied by Mr. Plaisted, made a trip to Prince Edward Island before the winter set in, and though they did not make a very extensive purchase, they travelled through the country and learned its resources, visiting many farms where salable horses could be secured in the spring. They took the horses they purchased direct to New York, where they were disposed of to good advantage, after which Mr. Sherwood returned to Halifax and settled down for the winter.

Mr. Plaisted remained in New York, but promised to be in Halifax early in the spring, and be ready for the first boat that crossed to the Island.

The first winter in Halifax passed very pleasantly to the Sherwoods. The winter sports were new, and keenly enjoyed, and the "Sherwood twins" soon became as good skaters as those who had practised the art for years. Yet no one must imagine that everything ran as smoothly as clockwork in the Sherwood household, for there are few families who can boast of such perfect regulations that there is *never* a jar.

Mrs. Sherwood had been only too willing to throw off all responsibility and place her duties on Aunt Jennie's shoulders, but there were many things that must of necessity be left to Mrs. Sherwood herself, and when such things were put off indefinitely they were apt to prove annoying; consequently, when "patience ceased to be a virtue," the domestic atmosphere was sometimes cleared by a small-sized storm.

There are also times when domestic helps are apt to be exasperating in the extreme, and a word of rebuke or remonstrance is like a match to a can of gunpowder; the powder is apt to go off, and the girl just as likely, and both leave an unpleasantness behind them. Queer, too, that both are apt to go off at the most unexpected and inconvenient moment; but so it is.

The Sherwood family were not exempt from this experience, for Biddy raised a storm because Dinah seemed to be made more of than she was herself. No explanations or smooth words would bridge over the difficulty. She refused to stay in a house where "a big nager could stay in the room wid the missus and hould the baby as long as she plased;" so she left the house, and quite suddenly, too.

This disarranged household matters somewhat for awhile, as it was some time before a capable servant could be found, and Mrs. Sherwood was obliged to exert herself a little and attend to the wants of the baby, while Dinah filled the vacant place in the kitchen.

But rheumatism had laid its torturing clutches on poor old Dinah's limbs, and she could not be expected to get through the same amount of work that Biddy accomplished, so the help of the twins was frequently necessary to keep agoing the domestic machinery.

This was no hardship to Dexie; but Gussie, oh dear! it was just horrible to have to wash up the breakfast dishes, and to polish the silver. And the rooms *never* needed to be dusted so often before, that she was sure! and wherever the dusters went to after she was done with them was a daily mystery. Dexie offered to solve this trying enigma, but Gussie's wrath waxed hot when she read the words which Dexie printed in large letters on a piece of wrapping-paper and stuck on the wall, for the moral was obvious—

> *"There is a place for everything;* therefore, *put the dusters back in their own place when you are done with them, and you will be sure to find them again.*
> *"(no charge for this advice.)"*

But things moved along somehow, as they always do, yet everyone was glad when the new Biddy appeared, who answered to the name of Nancy, and the ways of the household fell back into former grooves; while the sigh of relief which Gussie gave as she took up her neglected fancywork again, might have been heard—well, quite a distance away.

As the weeks went by, the enforced idleness became irksome to Mr. Sherwood; and having at one time been on the staff of a leading newspaper, he took up his pen again—or rather Dexie did, as his amanuensis—while he brought forth from memories' halls, things interesting, amusing or instructive. He had travelled extensively, and always saw the ludicrous side of things, so he was able to tell many amusing incidents that to others might have passed as commonplace. His productions were eagerly accepted, and, what is better, liberally paid for as well.

The short winter days passed very quickly. Time pleasantly spent is sure to fly fast, and skating and sleighing parties are always merry gatherings; thus so many evenings were given to Glee Club practice, church socials and other like entertainments, that an evening at home was a delightful change. During the winter the Sherwoods had the opportunity of becoming well acquainted with many of the military fraternity, but Dexie's reserved manner forbade the least familiarity. They were merely friends of her friends, and her dislike to the red-coated gentlemen caused her much good-natured chaffing; but it never annoyed her, for she always had an answer ready for the keenest shaft. Lancy Gurney could always depend on having Dexie Sherwood's company when these little pleasure-parties were made up; and when he brought his sleigh out for a "spin" Elsie and Dexie were sure to occupy the back seat, and the vacant place by Lancy's side was never long empty, for the wit and vivacity of his companion made the seat very desirable.

Hugh McNeil always had a share in the pleasures of the rest of the family, and no matter how many offered to fill his sleigh he always kept a seat for Gussie Sherwood, for he had paid her much attention from the first. Gussie found it very pleasant to have someone to take her here and there, and feed her vanity with admiring looks and soft speeches; but if Gussie had a chance to secure another escort more to her mind, she thought nothing of snubbing Hugh unmercifully, yet was willing enough to smile him back to her side when no other gentleman offered his company. But few men care to be made the plaything of a young girl's caprice, and there came a time when Gussie's smile lost its power to charm. Her pretty face had been the attraction; but having ample opportunity of seeing Gussie under the different light of home-life, he could not help seeing the shallow nature that lay behind her outward sweetness, or that this sweetness was more ready to come to the front when self was to be gratified.

But Hugh's heart had been touched for the first time, and when his eyes were opened he was loth to displace his idol, even though he knew that common clay was its substance. For a long time he gave no sign of the change that had taken place in his feelings; he was to all appearances as devoted to Gussie as ever.

One day, along the first of March, Lancy Gurney walked hastily home from the store, and entering the Sherwood household, inquired for Dexie.

"What is it, Lancy?" said Dexie, peeping over the stair rail at Lancy in the hall below.

"Come down, Dexie; I want to speak to you. Can you come for a drive with me?" he asked, as Dexie reached his side. "Father wishes me to do a little business for him a few miles out of town, and I want company. Will you come?"

"Yes, if you will take Elsie as well," was the reply. "How soon are you going, Lancy?"

"In about half an hour, if we can get ready; but I don't want to take Elsie. We will take the single sleigh, and three in a seat will not be comfortable."

"It will be three in a seat or one, Sir Launcelot; so take your choice. Run in and see if Elsie can go, then I will get ready also. No use coaxing; your half an hour is rapidly passing," she added, smilingly, as Lancy lingered, endeavoring to change her decision.

But "three in a seat" was not so uncomfortable as Lancy had imagined, and they were soon speeding over the road, and in due time reached their destination.

They were detained much longer than they expected, and so were late starting for home, and the snow which had been falling in fine, light particles, soon increased in volume, and it was quite apparent that a severe storm was upon them.

When they reached the open road, they found they were to suffer for the delay, for the sharp wind cut their faces and almost blinded them with the drifting snow.

All landmarks were soon obliterated, and, though the way was familiar under different circumstances, Lancy found it hard to distinguish the road from the open field, as the snow fell so thick they could see only a short distance beyond the horse's head.

The girls were soon so benumbed with cold that they were glad to creep beneath the sleigh robes, and the roads were becoming so blocked with drifts that their progress was very slow indeed. Several times they stuck fast, and Lancy had to get out and tramp down the snow, while, with encouraging words, he urged the horse along; but in one of these heavy drifts, snap! went the shaft.

This was a misfortune indeed, for a thorough search in pockets and sleigh-box failed to produce a string or strap of any kind.

Elsie had been on the verge of crying for some time, and this new disaster brought the tears in earnest.

"We shall all freeze to death here!" she sobbed. "Whatever shall we do?"

"You can stop crying, Elsie," said Lancy, who felt bewildered by this new difficulty. "I am bothered enough already. I suppose it is no use to ask you girls if you have any kind of string in your pockets," he added.

"No, of course we haven't," replied Elsie, quite cross. "Girls don't fill their pockets with trash!"

"Here is my belt, Lancy," and Dexie held up a strap of Russian leather. "Do you think you can bind up the shaft with that?"

After some delay, the shaft was strapped together, and they slowly pressed onward.

"How far do you think we are from Halifax, Lancy?" Dexie asked, after they had travelled some distance through the drifts.

"I can hardly say, Dexie, we have come so slowly; but I fear we are not more than halfway."

This was indeed the truth, and the storm seemed increasing in violence; but if a thought of danger passed through their minds, no voice was given to it.

Presently they passed a farmhouse, and they almost decided to stop and ask shelter; but just here the road seemed better, so they pressed on, knowing that their absence would make those at home very anxious. For some distance the road was less drifted, owing to the shelter of a line of trees that skirted it, but farther on they came to drifts that were high and hard packed, through which the horse gave a plunge, breaking the other shaft, and this brought matters to a crisis.

"It is no use, girls; we can't get home tonight. It is a pity we did not stop at that farmhouse," said Lancy, as he ascertained damages. "We will have to get back somehow, I'm afraid."

But how to get back was a question. They had passed the farmhouse such a long time ago that it seemed as if it must be miles behind. Lancy was almost in despair as he felt the broken shaft. How could they reach the farmhouse in this disabled condition? Although suffering intensely from the cold, he thought little of it, but he began to have serious misgivings as to the safety of the girls.

"I am so sorry I asked either of you to come with me," he said, as he bent his head to speak to the shivering girls. "I shall have to cut the reins and tie up the shaft with them, but I fear it will be slow work retracing our way."

"Oh, Lancy, you can't cut the reins! How are you going to drive if you do that?" said Dexie, in alarm.

"I can walk and lead the horse. There is nothing else to do."

"Wait, Lancy! Here is my silk scarf; it is real long and strong," and Dexie forced her cold fingers to untie from under her wraps, the pretty scarf that encircled her neck, which Lancy found to answer his purpose very well.

The sleigh had become so imbedded in the drift, that Lancy was afraid the shafts would pull apart if the horse put forth sufficient strength to extract it, so he decided to take the horse out and turn the sleigh himself. But when the horse found himself free, he refused to stand still, and Dexie insisted on getting out to hold him. Leading the horse around the drift to regain the road, Lancy found there was a level stretch extending in the same direction, and he concluded to follow it and thus regain the farmhouse. He assisted Dexie through the drifts, and as she held the reins he endeavored to turn the sleigh. But he had not quite accomplished his task when a cry from Dexie came through the storm:

"Oh, Lancy! come quick! I cannot hold him, and I hear water running somewhere! Oh, the horse is in!"

CHAPTER VI.

What new calamity had overtaken them! Their only hope of safety seemed in the horse, and he had disappeared from sight, leaving only his head showing above the white mass around him. Lancy was soon at Dexie's side, and understood the situation at once. The level stretch of snow was but the covering of a frozen stream that here flowed parallel with the road. He had led the horse near a weak spot, and the ice had given away beneath him. The water might not be deep enough to drown him, but Lancy saw at once it would be impossible to get the horse out without assistance. He helped Dexie back to the sleigh, saying,

"You and Elsie must cover yourselves up in the sleigh, and wait here till I walk back to that house for help."

"Oh, Lancy! is there no other way?" Dexie cried, her courage giving way at the thought of him leaving them. "You will get lost in the storm, and we will surely freeze to death before help reaches us."

But there seemed no other way out of the difficulty, and he hurriedly tucked the robes around them, while he tried to quiet Elsie, who was almost wild with terror when she learned her brother's intention.

"Hush! Elsie, dear. If I stay with you we shall *all* freeze. You need not be afraid. I will surely reach the house and send someone to you if I cannot come back myself. Don't cry, dear. See how bravely Dexie bears it."

"But you are not her brother," she sobbed; "she has only herself to think of. Oh, what shall we do if you are lost in the storm! How I wish I had never come!" and she buried her face in the seat before her.

Lancy's heart ached for both of them. Yet to leave them seemed their only chance of life, for it grew colder every moment. He must find help soon, or they would not survive the night. Bending over Elsie, he kissed her tenderly, saying, "Don't be afraid, Elsie. I will find someone to send to you before I give up; so don't fret. We'll see mother again, never fear." And bending over to see that she was well covered with the robes, he whispered, "Good-bye, Elsie; pray for help," and he kissed her again.

Passing round to the other side of the sleigh, he secured the robes around Dexie so that the wind could not displace them; then putting his face down close to hers, said, "I am sorry to have brought you into such danger, Dexie; but you know I did not mean to. Will you kiss me good-bye?"

Dexie lifted her face at once, her heart strangely stirred by the tone in which he spoke; but she realized their danger, and this might be, indeed, good-bye.

"Do not fret about us, Lancy," she said. "Think only of yourself, for I am so afraid you will be lost in the storm."

"Never fear, Dexie. But remember this, girls: Don't go to sleep; keep awake, no matter how hard it may be to do so. Get up in the sleigh and jump and scream rather than run the risk of falling asleep here in the cold. Remember, now! Good-bye, girls; and may Heaven keep you both safe," and Lancy disappeared in the storm, leaving a comforting feeling behind him with his last words.

"Oh, Dexie! do you think we shall ever see Lancy again?" Elsie asked, in a choking voice. "Just think how they will fret at home if anything happens to us!"

Dexie could not control her voice just then, so she made no reply.

"I wonder if the poor horse will drown or freeze to death; but perhaps it is warmer in the water than in the wind," and Elsie's thoughts turned again to Lancy.

Then they put their arms around each other, and talked in a weary, desultory way. But it was hard to talk when there was nothing pleasant in their thoughts, and they were so cold, so very cold.

Presently Elsie's head fell over on Dexie's shoulder, and it aroused Dexie to a sense of their danger. Was she really falling asleep, and allowing Elsie to do so as well, after the caution Lancy had given? She lifted Elsie's head gently, saying, "Sit up, Elsie, dear. I'm afraid you are getting sleepy, and you must not go to sleep, you know."

"Oh, do—leave me—alone! I'm—so tired."

"But I can't leave you, Elsie; you are getting sleepy, and don't you remember what Lancy said?" and Dexie lifted her up and gave her a gentle shake.

"Oh, do stop—just a moment."

"No, not a moment!"

Dexie was fully aroused now, and realized Elsie's danger.

"Come, Elsie, you must sit up, for I do not intend to let you sleep;" and she shook her roughly in her alarm, for Elsie had laid her head on the seat, in spite of all her efforts to arouse her.

"Here, if you don't lift up your head and wake up, I'll have to rub your face with snow; so sit up at once. Oh! do, Elsie, dear."

Elsie allowed herself to be lifted into another position, but she seemed dazed, and Dexie was thoroughly frightened and shook her by the arm, as she cried, "Oh, Elsie, can't you hear me? Don't you know that if you fall asleep you will surely freeze to death?"

"Oh, Dexie, I'm freezing now," was the low reply.

Dexie seized her hands and clapped them between her own stiff angers, which felt like lead, they seemed so heavy, but she succeeded in rousing Elsie so that she would talk to her.

"Let us try to sing," said Dexie at last; "perhaps it will be easier than talking," and she began "Jesus, lover of my soul."

But before the verse was finished she became aware that she was scarcely murmuring the words herself, while Elsie had stopped altogether.

"I'm *not* going to sleep; so, there!" she said aloud. "I *will* stay awake somehow, and make Elsie, too."

She found that the effort she had made to speak aloud had aroused herself. The drowsy feeling was dispelled, and she bent over Elsie and shook her until she received a faint answer.

"Do you think Lancy has arrived at the house, Elsie?" she asked a few minutes later. No answer, for Elsie's head had fallen back on the seat. She was oblivious to all remarks.

"Dear me, this will never do! However shall I keep her awake more than a minute at a time? What if Lancy returns and finds her stiff and cold?"

The thought was awful, and for the next few minutes there were some lively movements under the sleigh robes; but the terror that filled Dexie's heart gave way to a feeling of relief as Elsie sat up and reproached her friend for being "so rough."

"But I shall *have* to use you roughly, Elsie, if you don't stay awake," Dexie answered, as she placed the robes around her; "so keep talking, then I'll be sure of you."

But the intense cold seemed to freeze the words on her lips, and soon an unintelligible murmur was the only answer to Dexie's questions.

"What shall I do? She will be asleep in another minute, if I don't look out. If I could only get her cross she would give me less trouble."

As a general thing Elsie was very easy-going, though she had quite a temper when once it was aroused, but with the excellent training she received from her mother, she seldom lost control of herself. When she did, she was cross clear through, and it took her a long time to get over it. Dexie thought that this was a time when a burst of temper might be justifiable; so she determined to pick a quarrel with her, and hoped the end would justify the means.

Shaking her roughly to gain her attention, a few sarcastic remarks soon started a wordy warfare, and sharp words went back and forth for some time. Presently their situation occurred to Elsie, and she burst into tears of repentance.

"Oh, do forgive me, Dexie; to think I would say such things while we are in such danger! I do not know what is the matter with me."

"It is my fault," cried Dexie, unable to keep up the quarrel under such contrite circumstances. "I have been provoking you on purpose to make you scold me; but I didn't mean a word of the unkind things I said to you. I only wanted to keep you awake;" and thus confessing to one another, they calmed down into a state that was almost too angelic for safety, but before they had time to drop asleep again shouts were heard in the distance, telling of relief close at hand.

CHAPTER VII.

Lancy had a hard struggle to break through the drifts, and began to fear he would sink down with exhaustion before he had secured help, but he reached the farmhouse at last, having walked back much faster than the horse had travelled in going the same distance.

A few words of explanation were enough to arouse the family, and even while Lancy spoke, the two men in the room began to pull on their boots and get into their outer garments in a way that showed that they "meant business."

Mr. Taylor and his big son would gladly have gone alone to rescue the girls, thinking Lancy was not in a fit state to return, but the possible fate of those dear to him filled Lancy with dread; he must return and see to their safety. He eagerly drank the hot mixture that Mrs. Taylor placed in his hand, and when the men declared themselves ready, he felt able to accompany them.

"This is a terrible night to be out-of-doors," said Mr. Taylor, as he pulled his coat collar around his ears. "This is the worst storm we have had for years, and it will be a mercy if your sisters are not badly frostbitten, before we can get them to the house. Push on after Tom, and I will be with you in a minute," and he turned toward the stables.

Lancy found it easier to retrace his steps than when he struggled alone through the blinding snow, and presently Mr. Taylor passed them on the back of a horse, carrying a coil of rope and a bundle of rugs, and he was the first to reach the snow-covered sleigh.

"Are you all right?" he called in a cheery voice.

"We are alive, and that's about all," Dexie answered.

"Well, cheer up; your brother is just behind," and as he spoke Lancy joined him.

"Now, young man," said Mr. Taylor, "Tom and I will see after your horse, while you pilot your sisters to the house. They can both ride back on my horse; he will carry them through the drifts better than they can walk. Here are some rugs. Now, shall I help you to mount?" turning to Dexie.

"We are so cold I fear we can't hold on," she replied, her teeth chattering an accompaniment to her words. "I feel as if I had no feet at all," she added, as they lifted her up and brushed the snow from her garments.

"Oh, Lancy! I can't ride a horse," said Elsie, who was being brushed and rubbed back to life. "I never could sit on a rocking-horse itself. I'll be sure to fall."

"Well, you won't have far to fall, so let that comfort you," said Dexie, who was settling herself to her unusual position. "Lift her up, Lancy. There! now hold on tight, Elsie, for if you fall off we can't stop to dig for you!" and the awkward riders moved slowly through the drifts, while Mr. Taylor and his son disappeared down the bank, and very soon their shouts told that the submerged horse was rescued.

The poor animal was thoroughly chilled, but warm rugs were spread over him, and when, in the shelter of the stable, he was rubbed and doctored, he seemed none the worse for his cold bath. Meanwhile, the women in the house—good Samaritans, if ever there were any—had everything prepared for the comfort of the travellers. Rousing fires were blazing in different rooms, and garments were being warmed before them, while a steaming kettle, containing some stimulating beverage, was waiting on the hearth. When the half frozen girls entered the house they received a warm welcome—warm in more than one sense of the word, for the quick-handed women soon divested them of their wearing apparel and placed warm garments upon them—and before they had time to realize the change, they found themselves seated before the fire, wrapped in warm blankets, sipping hot negus, a delicious sense of warmth seeming to pervade their whole being; but as Dexie possessed the most vitality she was the first to respond to the efforts put forth for their relief.

Elsie did not rally so quickly. Her teeth chattered and her limbs trembled long after she thought she was well warmed, but her heart was full of gratitude as she said:

"I did not know there were such good, kind people in the world. It was almost worth while to be caught in the storm to be treated so well by strangers."

And Dexie, from the folds of her blanket, turned her large dark eyes on the women who were kneeling beside them rubbing their feet, and said in a low voice:

"We could not expect our best friends to treat us more kindly. Everything seemed prepared for our comfort before you ever saw us. I'm sure I can't think of one more thing that could be done for us."

"But there is one more thing to be done, my dears," and Mrs. Taylor smiled kindly into their young faces. "We must put you to bed."

"Oh, dear! I feel too comfortable to move," and Dexie leaned back in her big chair with a sigh of content.

"Well, it *is* a pity to disturb you, but to bed you must go," and, much to Dixie's surprise, a pair of strong arms lifted her as if she were a child, and a moment later she found herself in the next room, where a comfortable bed received her.

"How do you like being a baby again, Elsie?" she laughingly asked, as Elsie was placed beside her.

"I think I rather like it, but we have made trouble enough for these good women without letting them carry us to bed. How is it that you can be so good to strangers?" and Elsie lifted her eyes to the motherly face.

"My dear! have you never read the words, 'I was a stranger, and ye took Me in.' You know there is such a thing as entertaining angels unawares."

"I thought you were that kind of people," Elsie whispered, as

Mrs. Taylor bent to kiss her cheek.

"Did you, dear? Then I need not remind you that your thanks are due elsewhere, for I am sure you both have grateful hearts tonight."

"Will you please tell us how Lancy is before you go? We have not heard his voice since we came in," said Dexie.

"To be sure! but you need not be anxious about him. Your brother is in the kitchen, snug and warm, by this time. I must go and put him to bed; but I don't think I shall offer to carry him there," and she laughed softly, adding, as she reached the door. "Do not get up in the morning till I give you leave. You cannot get home until the roads are broken; so stay in bed till the house is well warmed. Good-night, my dears."

There was an interval of silence; then Elsie said softly, "I wonder if our mothers will be frightened because we are not home. I am afraid mother would cry if she knew we were out in the storm tonight."

"Oh! they'll not fret, at least my mother will not. They know that Lancy will look after us."

"Lancy kissed you tonight, didn't he, Dexie? Do you know I believe he has fallen in love with you," said Elsie, in a confidential tone.

"Oh, Elsie! how can you say such a thing?" and Dexie blushed in the darkness. "He kissed you good-bye, and, considering our danger, it was natural enough to treat me the same; indeed he seems like a brother. Even the people here think I am your sister."

"Oh! you needn't mind me, Dexie. Our folks all like you and would have no objections, for I heard mamma tell Cora that she was pleased at Lancy's choice, and thought you would get on very well together."

"Nonsense! Elsie; you must have misunderstood what they were talking about. Lancy and I have been much together on account of our music, and your mother would rather he spent his time over the piano with me, than with the wild young men about the city; that is what she meant. It is only the music that Lancy thinks of; so don't get foolish notions into your head, Elsie."

"Well, perhaps mamma did mean that, but I'm sure she didn't say it so. I thought she meant—something else," and whatever suspicions had been aroused in Elsie's innocent heart were lulled to rest for the time.

But this revelation aroused various feelings in Dexie's heart. She never thought that the friendship existing between Lancy and herself would be so differently construed. She liked Lancy very much, and never hesitated to affirm it, but it made the blood rush to her face when she thought of Lancy's good-bye kiss in the way Elsie had spoken of it.

"Such silliness! Our good times will all be spoiled if people begin to imagine such nonsense about us. How shall I be able to meet him in the morning? But there! it is only Elsie's foolish mistake; I will not think of it any more," so, resolutely putting the subject from her mind, she fell asleep.

CHAPTER VIII.

It was quite late when the young people opened their eyes next morning, and the unfamiliar surroundings made Dexie lift her head with a start; but the sparkle that came from the glowing wood fire in the old-fashioned grate spoke of friendly cheer, and she turned a bright face to her companion as she asked after her welfare.

"My head aches a little, and I feel stiff and sore, but I suppose you feel the same," was the languid reply.

"Not I. I never felt better in my life. I would like to get up and see what the world looks like around here."

Just then the door opened, and Mrs. Taylor stepped into the room.

"So my snow-birds are awake at last; and how do they feel this cold morning?" was the cheery question.

"I am quite well, thank you; but Elsie feels rather tired, I fear," Dexie replied. "May we get up, please?"

"Well, I'll not punish you by making you stay in bed," was the smiling reply, "but I think your sister would be the better of another hour's rest," then adding a few sticks to the blazing logs, she left the room.

Dexie was soon dressing before the fire, her lively tongue keeping up a pleasant chattering as she glanced occasionally through the frosty windowpanes to the white world outside, and Elsie soon roused from her lethargy and showed some inclination to bestir herself also.

When Mrs. Taylor returned, bearing a dainty breakfast, she found them standing before the fire, their arms around each other's shoulders, and she thought them very loving sisters, though their looks betrayed no such relationship.

They were indeed a contrast as they stood together before the fire. Dexie was all aglow, her cheeks dimpled and rosy, her merry brown eyes full of life and her pretty hair falling in rings about her forehead, making her look much younger than she really was; while poor Elsie's face looked all the paler against the background of dark hair that grew low on her brow, and hung in two long braids down her back. Her grey eyes looked dull and heavy, and she lacked the sparkle that made Dexie so attractive.

"Come now, and have your breakfast," and Mrs. Taylor drew the little table nearer the fire. "I am going to let you enjoy it alone, but when you are ready step into the room across the hall. Your brother is anxious to see how you look after your adventure."

Dexie was just going to explain that she was no relation to Elsie, when the conversation of the night before came into her mind, and while she hesitated Mrs. Taylor left the room. As the door opened they could hear Lancy's voice as he conversed with the family, and for the first time it brought a flush to Dexie's face. She shrank from the thought of meeting him, but this diffidence was owing more to Elsie's remarks than to any change in her own feelings.

"Come," said Elsie, at last, "we don't want to sit here all day. Let us go and find Lancy."

She stepped at once to his side as they entered the room, and gave him a sisterly embrace, making Dexie's quiet "good morning" seem a cool greeting in comparison; there seemed a strange restraint between them that neither had felt before, which forbade any show of feeling on either side. This was noticed at once by Mrs. Taylor, who was brightening up the fire, and she said:

"Seems to me you haven't such a warm welcome for your brother as your sister gives him, yet he has been inquiring very particularly after you."

"He is not my brother, Mrs. Taylor. I do not know how the mistake has been made, but we are no relation whatever."

"Not your brother! Then who are you, my dear?" smiling at Dexie's blushing face.

"Lancy, introduce me properly," and Dexie rose to her feet.

Catching the spirit of mischief that shone in her eyes, he stepped quickly to her side, and with a flourish made the introduction.

"Allow me to make you acquainted with our next-door neighbor, Miss Dexie Sherwood."

Dexie bowed graciously to the several occupants of the room, who rose to their feet, and all embarrassment fled at once.

"Next-door neighbors those two may be," was the whispered comment of the young girls who were stepping back and forth as they prepared the mid-day meal, "but there is every sign of a closer relationship in the future, if their looks do not belie them."

But the only sentiment in Dexie's heart was gratitude and love to a Higher Power. As she turned the leaves of a music-book she had picked up from the table she passed the book to Lancy, saying in a low tone:

"If I were home, I would like to sit down to the piano and play that."

Lancy glanced at the page, and his eyes told her that he understood, for the words of the anthem to which Dexie referred began, "Out of the depths cried I, and thou, O Lord, hast heard."

"Does the owner of these books play?" and Lancy turned to address Mrs. Taylor, a sudden thought like an inspiration coming to his mind.

"Only a little. Our Susan is wild over music; but our little old piano is all she has to practise on, and during the winter she can only go into Halifax once a week for a lesson. Susan, show them into the sitting-room, and perhaps Miss Sherwood will play something for us."

As Dexie entered the room she took in at a glance the many pretty and tasteful things which adorned the walls and brackets, and she wondered if Susan's fingers had accomplished such marvels in autumn leaves and other little adornments.

The fireplace was a thing of beauty, with its polished andirons, and the ruddy tongues of flame that leaped forth from the heaped-up wood made a cheerful picture.

Several big cushioned chairs were drawn near the hearth and a basket of knitting work was "handy" on a table, while in the old-fashioned rocker the family cat peacefully reposed.

Lancy had no eyes for anything but the piano, and as Susan opened it she smilingly exclaimed:

"Confess, now, that you think there is little music to be got out of this ancient-looking thing."

"Well, it is an odd make, certainly, but some of these old pianos have a fine tone. Sit down and play something for us, Miss Taylor," and he drew the music-stool in place.

"Oh, no! I couldn't think of it!" she replied, smiling. "My playing is not of an entertaining kind as yet, for even mother flies to the kitchen when I try a new piece, but you will find me a good listener."

Was that the same old piano? thought Susan, as she stood by the instrument watching Lancy's fingers passing over the keys. Why, it seemed to be a thing of life; and she moved away almost in awe at the sounds that came forth from the hitherto despised keys.

Presently Dexie began to sing, low and softly at first, then her expressive voice swelled forth, thrilling the listeners that gathered at the door. Susan slipped away, her eyes full of tears.

"Oh! if I could only play and sing like that I would wish for nothing more," said she to her sister. "That anthem means more than the mere words and music."

"Yes, it sounds like family prayers," replied her sister. "I declare I don't know what I am crying for. I wonder if it would be a sin to mash these potatoes while that singing is going on; they will be getting cold, I'm afraid."

But the closing words rang out joyously, "But Thou hast been merciful and heard us; therefore Thy name will we praise all the day long."

Not until she had finished did Dexie realize that she had so many listeners, but she turned a bright face to the group at the door.

"I did not know we had such an audience."

"Don't stop, friends," said Mr. Taylor, coming into the room. "Such music is quite a treat. I guess, Susan, there is more in that piano than you ever dreamed of. Let us hear something else."

Lancy rose from the music-stool, saying to Dexie:

"Play 'The Mocking Bird,' and I'll sing to your whistle."

A moment later Dexie's supple fingers were dancing over the keys in a delightful prelude. Then Lancy's voice filled the room as he sang the well-known song, accompanied by the exquisite notes of the southern mocking bird, and the continuous warble that poured from

Dexie's throat during the chorus made her listeners start as if a veritable bird were concealed in the room.

"Well, that spoils the old proverb from this time forth," said Mr. Taylor, as he leaned back against the wall and thrust his thumbs into the armholes of his vest. "Whistling girls and crowing hens will hereafter have a chance to be heard. Old saws ain't always true, eh, Miss Sherwood?"

"Well, I never heard a hen crow yet, Mr. Taylor," and Dexie laughed softly, "and I do not know what is their usual fate, but the proverb does not alarm me in the least."

"Do whistle another piece, Miss Sherwood," said Susan. "It will give us great pleasure to hear you."

Lancy turned over the leaves of a book, then placed it on the piano, saying:

"Try that, Dexie, and I'll whistle with you."

It would be hard to express the pleasure that this exquisite bird-song gave to those who listened. All the songsters in the woods seemed let loose in the room, now singing together in full chorus, then singly or in pairs they twittered and trilled as Dexie's soft whistle followed or joined Lancy's stronger notes, while such birdlike notes came from the keys before her as might have deceived the very birds themselves.

"Nothing will surprise me after this," cried Susan, when the song had ended. "I heard my music-teacher play that once, and I thought it the tamest thing I had ever heard; of course he did not try to whistle it too, but the music itself sounded quite different."

"Perhaps your music-teacher never took the trouble to listen to the birds themselves; that makes a difference, you know," said Dexie.

Just then Mrs. Taylor came into the room, saying:

"I think you must come to dinner, but you must give us some more music afterwards. Really, Susan, that old piano is not such a poor affair, after all; is it, now?"

CHAPTER IX.

As was expected, they found there was much anxiety at home over their long absence. Mr. Sherwood was on the watch when the sleigh drove up, and was beside it in time to help the muffled figures alight, and anxious to hear the particulars of their protracted drive.

"Let me go into Mrs. Gurney's just a minute, papa," said Dexie, "and I will tell you all about it when I come back."

Then they found themselves pulled through the hall by the eager children, who had been watching for their appearance for hours, and into the sitting-room where Mrs. Gurney sat with a white, anxious face, waiting their arrival.

In a few minutes the story of their detention was told, Lancy telling his part and Elsie hers, Dexie finishing the story by confessing to the extreme measures used to keep Elsie awake, not sparing herself in the least when telling of the quarrel she had provoked, and there was a suspicious moisture in Mr. Gurney's eyes as he listened to the story.

"You have been in great peril," said he, as he drew the girls to his side. "Let us all kneel a moment and return thanks for the safety of these dear ones;" and all knelt, just as they were: Mr. Gurney with one arm around Elsie, the other around Dexie; Lancy with his fur coat still on, and the whip in his hand; the little ones, who had pressed into the room, dropped to their knees, their arms full of toys; Mrs. Gurney with the baby in her arms—all knelt, while a few earnest words went up from a father's grateful heart.

Mrs. Gurney insisted that Elsie should go up to bed at once, and be doctored for the cold she had evidently contracted, and pressing a kiss on Dexie's cheek, she followed her daughter upstairs.

But for all their care Elsie was confined to her room for several weeks, and her recovery was slow and tedious. They were all thankful, though, that nothing more serious resulted from exposure to the storm, which was the worst that had visited the country for several years.

Dexie had to tell the story over again when she went home; but she made light of it all, making much more fun out of their grand ride on horseback than either she or Elsie had experienced while partaking of it. But the whole story came out when Lancy came in during the evening, and Mr. Sherwood's look of tender solicitude contrasted strangely with the mother's apparent unconcern, as the story of their adventure was related at length.

"I am forgetting that I was sent in here with a message," Lancy said, a few minutes later. "Elsie has been asking to see you, Dexie, and mother wishes to know if you are too tired to run in a few minutes."

Dexie followed Lancy into his own door, and running swiftly up the stairs was soon bending over Elsie, who was wrapped up like a mummy.

"I did not want to see you for anything *very* particular," Elsie said, in answer to Dexie's inquiry. "But I could not go to sleep for thinking of last night. It seems so good to be in my own bed again, safe, after all my fears, that I wanted to tell you once more how sorry I am for being so cross with you; for I was *awful* cross, Dexie, when you talked so harshly to me."

"Now, Elsie! don't speak as if there were anything for *you* to be sorry for, or I shall have such qualms of conscience as will surely make me ill," was Dexie's laughing reply.

After a few minutes' chat, Dexie left the room to return home, but Lancy was waiting at the bottom of the stairs, and he drew her into the parlor, saying:

"Stay with me a little while, Dexie, do; no one will disturb us here, and I want to have a 'sing.' Your father or Gussie are sure to be in the parlor if we go into your house."

"Well, it will have to be a short 'sing,' Lancy, for the drive in the wind has made me sleepy."

When Mrs. Gurney passed the door a few minutes later, and peeped into the dimly lighted room to listen to the soft strains that met her ears, she smiled and softly withdrew, for Lancy was seated at the instrument, and Dexie stood by his side, her hand resting carelessly on his shoulder, while they sang what Mrs. Gurney knew was their private thanksgiving.

As the last notes died away, Lancy turned on the music-stool and took her hand; Dexie's thoughts had been so engrossed that, for the moment, she let it rest there, when she heard the low-spoken words: "I want to tell you something, Dexie."

Instantly Elsie's words flashed into her mind, and she tried to break away from the arm that encircled her waist.

"Let me go, Lancy," was the startled cry. "It is time I was home."

"I will take you home presently, Dexie; I want to talk to you a few minutes first," and catching her hands in his he held her close.

"But I do not want to be held here! Oh, Lancy! let go my hands. I must go home."

"Be quiet and listen to me a minute, Dexie; only a minute. I want to tell you that, when I left you both in the sleigh last night, I felt far worse about leaving you than my own sister. Do you know why, Dexie?"

"I don't want to know, Lancy. I don't want to hear another word."

"You can't get away from me, Dexie; so don't try. I want to tell you," he added, in a lower tone, "that before last night I never knew why it was that I liked to spend all the time I could with you. I thought it was on account of our music, but as I walked through the storm last night the truth came to me. I love you, Dexie, and that is why my heart kept me up till I found help. I was almost wild with fear that something would happen to you before I could get you safely sheltered.

Yes, darling, I love you; and the thought has made me feel so light of heart that I could sing all the time for very joy."

"Oh, Lancy! how can you talk so. You have spoiled all our good times together, for I'll never come in here again when I know you are home," and she turned her face away from his earnest gaze.

"Oh, yes, you will; you will not be so unkind as that. If you refuse to come in here I will go into your house just twice as often; so you can't get rid of me, Dexie," was the smiling reply.

There was a moment's silence, when Dexie said: "It will be a pity for us to quarrel, Lancy, but you must not talk to me like this any more. Really, I did not think you could be so silly. Think how they would all tease us if anyone should find us here; and you know Gussie would make my life a misery if she guessed you had been talking such nonsense."

"It is not 'nonsense' to tell you that I love you, but my love shall not be a source of annoyance to you; no one need know it. Everything will be as usual, only, Dexie, you will know that I love you, and I will know—well, what, Dexie? You do not dislike me any more than you did two days ago, do you?" he whispered.

"I have not changed in the least, but I shall dislike you very much, Lancy, if you do not try and forget what has been said here this evening."

"I cannot forget it even if I wanted to, Dexie. Do not think that I want to vex you, dear, but I want you to understand me. Now, there is only one thing more, Dexie," and his voice grew tender; "that kiss you gave me last night in the sleigh seems to be resting on my lips yet, and has been a sweet memory all day long. But, Dexie," and he laughed softly, "you know it was a very cold kiss, after all. Give me a warm one to take its place, and I'll let you go."

Dexie shook her head and tried to draw back from him. She felt so distressed that the tears were on the point of falling. She had gone through so much during the last few hours, and this unexpected interview tried her more than Lancy was aware.

"Only one kiss," he urged. "You gave it willingly last night, darling."

"But things are not the same as they were last night."

"No, I love you better, Dexie. May I?" But without waiting for permission he kissed the face so near him, and found it wet with tears.

"Dexie, darling, I did not think you would care so much. Forgive me if I vexed you; you kissed me last night without a word."

"But you are not the same, and there was a reason last night. It is not fair, Lancy. You have quite spoiled our good times for the future."

"No, not spoiled them, only made them dearer. Dexie, you shan't be vexed with me. Come over on the sofa and let me talk to you."

"No; you said you would let me go home, and I want to go now, this very minute."

"Very well." He rose and pulled her shawl over her shoulders, then followed her silently into the shelter of her own door. He would have followed her into the house as well, forgetting that Dexie's face would tell tales, but she stopped him at the door.

"I don't want to see you any more tonight, Lancy; I really don't," she said, as they stood a moment in the front hall.

"You are displeased with me for telling you that I love you. Perhaps I should have waited a little longer before speaking about it; but, Dexie, I couldn't keep it to myself. I had to tell you."

"I would not have been any more pleased to hear it, even if you *had* kept it longer;" and, lifting her eyes to his face for a moment, added, "I am not exactly vexed with you, Lancy, but I'm not pleased either. Now, go home; do." Being thus summarily dismissed, there was no choice left him; but before he turned to obey her command, he raised her hand to his lips, and whispered a tender "Good-night, Dexie."

She stood and watched him down the steps, then turned and went quickly to her own room, and locking the door behind her threw herself face down on the bed, and for a few minutes wept without restraint. She felt completely unnerved; so much had happened during the last twenty-four hours that had tried her strength and courage, that Lancy's declaration had filled up the measure of her strength.

But her thoughts, always rapid, soon worked out a semblance of order from the confusion that filled her mind, and she dried her eyes and began to review her conduct in the light that others probably judged her.

She would not deny, even to herself, that she preferred Lancy's company to that of any of her male friends; but they were both so young that it was ridiculous to even imagine that their intimacy meant more than common friendship. However, if Lancy chose to be silly, that was no reason that she should become sentimental also. She was not obliged to fall in love just because Lancy fancied himself in that condition. It would be horrid not to see him or sing with him again when their voices chorded so well together; and Lancy never misunderstood her, if everyone else did. Yes, it would be very hard not to be friendly with him; but, there! surely one can be friendly with a gentleman without being expected to fall in love with him, and she felt positive that if there were a Prince Charming for her, his name was not Lancy Gurney.

Having thus decided the matter satisfactorily to herself, she rose and quickly prepared herself for bed; for several days after she took good care not to be left alone with Lancy, and she kept him at a distance by her saucy speeches.

But his manner to her was the same as usual. The tender look in his eyes, when they met hers, was the only reminder of his words. The knowledge of his love, too, ceased to annoy her, or it was crowded back by the many incidents that filled her life at this time; but it was there, ready to spring up at the slightest touch.

CHAPTER X.

The first day of April dawned brightly. The warm rays of the sun seemed doubly welcome after the cold, stormy weather of the previous month, and the streets were filled with people, who were out enjoying the sunshine regardless of the mud that covered their feet at every step.

But Nova Scotians are a courageous people the whole country over, as witness the intrepidity with which they walk to and fro, year after year, through mud that seems in some places almost bottomless; for, strange though it may seem to outsiders, who cannot expect to learn the secrets of the learned road commissioners, the more time and money spent on a road the softer and muddier it seems to become.

It is a fact that can be vouched for by many responsible persons, that once, while a poor man was walking along one of the country roads in early spring, he sank so deep in the mire that, on putting forth his strength to lift his leg, he pulled it apart above the knee, leaving the lower half sticking in the mud! Fortunately he was carrying a strong cane, and by leaning upon it he managed to keep upright until help arrived, when he was rescued from his perilous position. After much difficulty, the imbedded limb was extracted from the mud, and safely fastened again in its place—it was made of wood!

But, leaving facts for fiction, let us step into the Sherwood household, and we will find Mr. Sherwood busy preparing for another trip to Prince Edward Island.

Mr. Plaisted had arrived from New York a few weeks previously, and was to accompany him, though the departure of this gentleman would cause no regrets in the household, for his true nature had been revealed during his stay amongst them. His bland and courteous manner was not inborn—it had but a surface character; and if "to know a man you must live in the house with him," then it took but a short time to become thoroughly acquainted with Mr. Plaisted. If he had not been so puffed up with conceit, he would have felt the altered atmosphere around him; but he was not sensitive—not in the least—and he could stand an unlimited amount of snubbing without being touched. His familiarity had indeed "bred contempt," and the hope of his speedy departure alone kept back the threatened storm. Even Nancy in the kitchen had been heard to say that, "if the scented dandy didn't kape out ov her kitchen wid his imperdent speeches, she would give him wan blow wid her fist that would spoil his beauty for him," and threatened to "give warnin'" if the mistress did not keep him to his own quarters.

Mrs. Sherwood was more than satisfied to leave all unpleasant things for Aunt Jennie to settle. It was quite convenient to be an "invalid" when there was trouble below stairs, and it required more than a hint to make Plaisted see that he was transgressing all rules of hospitality. When Mr. Sherwood announced that the Straits were opened, and they would leave at once to catch the first boat, they were all willing to "speed the parting guest," even though he would take Mr. Sherwood away with him also.

Strange though it may seem, Gussie was the only one who saw no fault to find in Mr. Plaisted. He was too free with his compliments to be anything but pleasant company to her. She was willing enough to listen to his soft speeches, for in her eyes he was a hero of romance, and the warning words and admonitions of Aunt Jennie only served to exalt him higher in her estimation.

Dexie treated him with such frigid politeness that he did not care to meet her cold stare more often than necessary; so, when he sought Gussie's society, Mr. Sherwood or Aunt Jennie were the only ones likely to interrupt the *tete-a-tete*.

But things were not always to run so smoothly for Mr. Plaisted, and this first day of April brought such discomfiture that his fastidious feelings were very much upset. About noon, when the streets were thronged with pedestrians returning from work or school to the mid-day meal, Dexie noticed Mr. Plaisted sauntering toward the house, twirling his light cane and looking as if he thought himself the pink of perfection. But what was it that was fluttering in the breeze behind him? Some urchin—exasperated, no doubt, by Plaisted's immaculate appearance—had fastened to his coat-tails a bunch of dirty rags, and as Dexie watched him from the window, she was convulsed with laughter as she saw him lift his hat and bow profoundly to the two Desbrasy girls on the opposite sidewalk, who immediately pulled out their handkerchiefs and applied them to their faces; but he walked on, unconscious of the diversion he was causing to the passers-by. As he came into the house, Dexie struck an attitude, and exclaimed, in a tragic voice, "I could a tale unfold!"

Plaisted stood in the doorway, and looked at her in amazement.

"Dexie, don't be a fool," said Gussie, looking up from her wools, and frowning at her sister's strange behavior.

"No, Gussie; I don't intend even to *try* and be one, for when Mr. Plaisted assumes that character, no one else has a possible chance either as court fool or April fool."

Plaisted was too surprised to speak, and Dexie took no heed to his darkening brow, but continued, "So *you* have been studying Shakespeare, and this is a practical illustration, I presume; or possibly you are posing as a disciple of Darwin, and, to prove his theory, have unfolded your tail to the public gaze. I have often wondered what it was you needed to make you a perfect specimen of what Nature intended you to be." Then, catching his arm, she turned him about that Gussie might see, adding, "He is quite complete now, Gussie—see! This is a specimen of the species known as the 'missing link.'"

"For goodness' sake! how long have you been carrying that?" cried Gussie, quite horrified at the sight.

Plaisted turned his head, and understood at a glance the meaning of Dexie's words. Then, angrily grasping the cause of offence, he endeavored to remove it, till an ominous sound of tearing cloth caused him to desist.

"Take it off! take it off! You, Dexter!" he cried, backing around to her. "Take off that trash, I say!"

But that word "Dexter" sealed all chance of help as far as Dexie was concerned, for she put her hands behind her back and surveyed him scornfully.

"Not I! I wouldn't disfigure you for worlds; it quite completes your appearance. It would be a sin to remove what Nature seems to have forgotten in your make-up."

"Do take it off for him, Dexie," said Gussie, coaxingly. I would myself, only I don't want to dirty my hands."

"And do you think that *Dexter* is going to soil her beautiful hands by touching the dirty rags? No; Dexter is not! There might be smallpox on them for all I know; I'm sure they're spotted enough."

Plaisted turned and twisted himself this way and that, in vain endeavors to reach the back of his coat, but could not manage it; and as he stood for a minute, his hands held out in front of him, while he looked over his shoulder at the unwelcome appendage, he did indeed present a woful figure.

"Why don't you take your coat off?" Gussie said at last.

"Oh! confound it; I never thought of that," as he twisted himself out of his coat.

"Why, of course you didn't think of it," retorted Dexie. "How could you be expected to? Everybody knows that creatures with tails are not supposed to think at all."

"Dexie, I'll tell papa if you won't stop; you are impudent," Gussie said, sharply.

"Do tell papa, Gussie. I only wish he were here to see the sight himself. He does not know what he is missing by being late for dinner. It is too bad that he must get the story second-hand, when he might have enjoyed the edifying sight himself if he had only been on time."

"I'd like to see the wretch that put that trash on my coat," said Plaisted, as he flung the mass into the grate. "By George! I'd fix him."

"I'd give a lot to see him myself," said Dexie, exultingly, from the other side of the table; "and he should have at least a quarter for that piece of work, though I'm sure it was worth a whole dollar to see you strutting up the street with signals of distress waving in the breeze behind you. Ha, ha!"

"I believe you did it yourself before I went out," he said, white with rage.

"Oh! I do wish I had! How I do wish I had thought of it! How proud I should feel if *I* had been the one to give the citizens of Halifax such a grand idea of what the lost species are like; and how generous of you, too, to give a free exhibition of yourself, in your proper form, when you might have gone to the dime museum and earned a fortune!"

Plaisted felt too wrathy to reply, but he gave her a look that was meant to annihilate her; then turning to Gussie, who seemed to sympathize with him, said,

"I met those Desbrasy girls as I was coming up the street, and I do believe they saw it. Confound the thing! I remember now that they pulled out their handkerchiefs directly I bowed. I daresay they were laughing at me!"

"Laughing! not they!" put in Dexie. "They happened to see your feet, and were weeping with envy because theirs were so much bigger! Don't fret, Mr. Plaisted, you are not worth looking at without this finishing touch," and with a scornful laugh she passed out of the room, slamming the door behind her.

Plaisted drew a sigh of relief when his tormentor vanished.

"Bless my soul! what a tongue that girl has," and he wiped the perspiration from his brow. "I hope she don't often let her temper loose like that."

"Well, no; but you have only yourself to blame for it, and I was almost going to say that it serves you right, too."

"Why! how's that?" said Plaisted, in surprise.

"Well, you know very well that you have tormented Dexie about Lancy Gurney till you have aroused her temper quite often; but you might have escaped if you had not insulted her just now."

"Insult her! How, pray? I'm sure I did not."

"You called her 'Dexter,' and that is a name she can't stand from anybody. I believe she would have taken off those rags for you if you had spoken to her as 'Dexie,' for she really is obliging, you know, though she did enjoy seeing you made an April fool."

"Bless my soul! I never noticed that I called her Dexter; and so that was the spark that caused the explosion? Well, I shall not forget it in a hurry."

"She generally succeeds in paying back, with double interest, anyone who uses that name to her, as I know to my sorrow," said Gussie, with a shake of her head. "Yet, after all, I don't blame her much, either; but it is the one spot in her make-up that seems vulnerable."

"Well, it is a good thing that I am going away so soon. I expect she will make it hot for me while I am here."

"Oh, no! I guess you are safe, Mr. Plaisted. The storm is over for this time, unless you care to brew another like it; the one word will do it, you know," and she looked up with a smile.

"Thanks; I beg to be excused! That one experience is enough to last me for one while. Ugh! I wonder if there was any disease on those dirty rags," looking at his fingers and then on his coat, as if in doubt which would be the first to break out with it.

As he left the room to smooth out his ruffled plumage, holding his coat at arm's length before him, the sounds of laughter in the next room greeted his ears. As he listened a moment he heard Dexie relating the particulars of the scene in the parlor, and he shook his fist in the direction of the sound. This relieved his feelings somewhat, and he vowed a hasty vow that, for the future, he would leave Dexie Sherwood and her doings alone. He would have spared himself many unpleasant moments if he had kept his vow.

During the time that Mr. Plaisted was staying with the Sherwoods, Gussie had been very cool to Hugh McNeil. As the former was about to leave the city, Gussie thought it time to recall her old "stand-by," and was surprised to find that Hugh was less ready to return to her side than formerly. A feeling of jealousy arose in her heart when she saw that Hugh's attentions were transferred to Dexie.

Hugh had not ceased to come in during the evenings, as usual, even though Gussie was cool and abrupt with him. Not wishing Hugh to feel hurt by the change in her sister, Dexie had talked to him, and had played and whistled for his amusement, till the little spark of kindly regard which had formerly represented his feelings for Dexie was fast being fanned into a flame of passion by these little attentions, which were bestowed in a friendly way, and for her sister's sake.

Dexie was not aware of the change in Hugh McNeil until Mr. Plaisted had left the city, and she was surprised and displeased to see that Hugh now ignored Gussie's presence almost as much as Gussie had his when Mr. Plaisted was near, and turned to her instead.

It was hard to define her true feelings, but when she understood that Hugh had mistaken her friendliness, her whole being seemed to rise up in a vigorous protest. As it is "an ill wind that blows nobody good," Lancy was made happy again by Dexie's presence. She no longer sought to evade him, and her soft, rippling laughter, mingling with the low tones of Lancy's voice, was again heard as they lingered over the piano together.

This made Hugh mad with jealousy, and the fact became so plain to Dexie that her manner was even more gracious to Lancy when Hugh was by to observe it.

But Hugh's sturdy Scotch nature came to the front, and he made a mental resolve to win her in spite of everything; even his master's son should not take Dexie from him. He would wait, but would not vex her by pressing his suit at present when it seemed so distasteful to her; she might smile on someone else instead of Lancy, then he could watch her less easily. He would not meddle with the existing state of things.

Yet he had one bit of comfort given him. He it was who hastily appeared in the Sherwood household one morning with the startling intelligence of the assassination of President Lincoln.

The events "at home" were closely watched by all the family, and this unexpected calamity, just at this time, was as much of a blow to them as to those nearer the scene of strife.

Hugh had always been "Mr. McNeil" to Dexie. She had never used the more familiar name, as the rest of the family were in the habit of doing; but when she heard him tell his news, she caught his arm, and exclaimed:

"Oh, Hugh! do you think it is true, or only a report? Tell us, quickly!" and she looked eagerly into his face, as if to read the truth there.

Hugh longed to clasp the hand that rested on his arm for a moment, for during all their intercourse she had never called him "Hugh," and it thrilled his heart as it fell from her lips. He wished that he might be the bearer of any news, however unwelcome, if it would cause her to forget her reserve and repeat again that little word "Hugh."

But nothing happened, and matters went on about the same during the weeks that followed.

Mr. Sherwood did not return home for some time, for, after selling his horses, he made a lengthy visit to his mother, who was not in the best of spirits at this time. She was alarmed at his boldness in coming to see her, though he assured her he had taken all precaution, her old enemies need not hear of his presence. His visit so cheered her that he saw she needed something to take her thoughts away from herself, and from the conflict that engaged her mind.

Having expressed a desire to have one of her granddaughters come and live with her for a season, and having a preference for Louie, who seemed to be a part of the dear old southern home whose name she bore, it was decided that Mr. Sherwood should bring her to the old homestead for a long visit.

Dinah had been sorely missed by her mistress, though she was slow to acknowledge it; but, at Mr. Sherwood's suggestion, it was decided to bring her back with Louie, that the faithful old nurse might spend her last days with those she had known and loved all her life.

CHAPTER XI.

The influence which a family like the Gurneys unconsciously exert over those brought in contact with them, was not without effect on the lives of their next door neighbors. As Dexie was so intimate with the family, and spent so much of her time amongst them, she was the first to feel it, and the controlling power which governed the Gurney household was finding root in her heart also. She did not realize this herself, but the signs were apparent to those accustomed to look below the surface for the motive that governs all actions.

Aunt Jennie saw more of Dexie's inner life than did her own parents. To them she seemed the same good-natured, light-hearted girl, growing, perhaps, a little more thoughtful and attentive than they could have expected, considering her active nature; yet, if they had thought to compare even the Sunday life of the household with what it had been when they first came to Halifax, they would have been surprised at the change in themselves.

Formerly it was the custom to spend the greater part of the Sabbath morning in bed, and, after a late breakfast, Mr. Sherwood read the American papers until dinner was served. In the evening a walk was indulged in, or, if a popular preacher was announced to appear in any of the churches, he would attend, taking some member of the family with him; but it was seldom that Mrs. Sherwood attended public worship. As the head of the house passed the Sabbaths in this careless fashion, the rest of the household felt free to spend it as it pleased themselves also.

No one seemed to hold the day any more sacred than the other six, except Aunt Jennie; but as Dexie came to note the difference in the Sunday life of her next-door neighbors, and mentally compared it with how the day was spent at home, she inwardly resented the feelings that would intrude themselves, for they pointed out the fact quite plainly that there was something needed in their lives at home which was engrafted in the household next door; and, though she scarcely knew what to do to remedy a difference she did not care to define even to herself, yet she silently resolved that an outward form at least, similar to what she saw next door, should yet be practised at home, for she could not bear the silent reproach any longer.

When Dexie opened her heart to Aunt Jennie about it, she found that the same thing had troubled her quiet auntie for a long time; so together they laid plans that eventually brought about a different Sunday life from that the family had hitherto known. Yet the change began in a very commonplace way, too; for instead of enjoying the extra sleep that the family usually indulged in, they were aroused one Sunday morning by repeated calls to breakfast—calls which were hard to resist when the opened doors let in such appetizing odors from the kitchen, where Aunt Jennie was superintending the morning meal. And if their olfactories were closed to this appeal, their ears were not so easily shut to the sounds that Dexie was bringing forth from the piano, as hymns, anthems and psalms followed in succession, and made further sleep impossible.

"What has got into you all this morning? Have you forgotten it is Sunday?" said Mr. Sherwood, appearing at last. "How can anyone sleep with all this racket going on, Dexie?" he added, stepping into the parlor. "What on earth made you rout us out of bed at this hour? Why, it is not nine o'clock yet!"

"Oh! you slept long enough papa. I am sure we don't need more sleep on Sunday morning than we do any other day. You'll not be sorry you got up when once you have tasted some of the good things auntie has made for breakfast," and she raised her mouth for a kiss, then led him to the table.

Gussie made her appearance in time to sit down with the rest, but she looked cross at Dexie for having disturbed her.

"This is the first Sunday morning we have all met at the breakfast table for months, I do believe," said Mr. Sherwood, leaning back in his chair, as he finished the meal. "But where are the papers this morning? What! still in the office? However am I going to pass the day without my papers? Strange that no one thought of going for them last night."

Someone had thought of it, but had purposely forgotten again, hoping that he might be induced to attend some place of worship in the morning, if for no better reason than to pass the time away.

The Gurneys were members of the Episcopal Church and attended at St. Paul's. Dexie had often accompanied them on Sundays, and had grown familiar with the service that was, in after-life, so dear to her; but, knowing that her father disliked that form of worship, she intended to persuade him to attend St. Matthew's (Presbyterian), as she knew he had a great respect for the officiating clergyman.

"Well, papa, since the time will seem long to you with nothing particular to do, why not come with Gussie and I to hear Dr. Grant? They have a fine choir at St. Matthew's; so we will be sure to enjoy either the sermon or the singing, if not both."

"Oh, I'm not going out this morning, Dexie, so speak for yourself," said Gussie. "It is a horrid bother to dress up so early in the day. I have a nice book to read, so, if you want to go out, you can go with the Gurneys, as usual."

"But I would rather go some place with papa," said Dexie; "and it will be nicer to make a family party of it. Besides, I want to hear what the new singer is like, and of course I can't go alone. You remember Cora Beverly was talking about her, and says she has the sweetest voice she ever heard. You will come with us, won't you, papa?" she asked, coaxingly, as she went behind his chair and stroked his hair.

"Well, I'll see, by and by," Mr. Sherwood replied. "I may go with you this evening, though."

"Now, papa, what will prevent you from coming this morning? I do think you will be most unkind if you refuse, for I have set my heart on hearing that singer. Now, do say 'yes,' papa."

"Well, you little torment, yes, then! Now, leave my hair alone, or you'll have my head as bald as the back of my hand," holding her away at arm's-length.

Dexie bent over and gave him a final kiss; then, turning to Gussie, said:

"Did you see how nicely I have done up your frills and laces, Gussie? That pretty cream lace will look lovely with your new dress, if you frill it around the neck."

"New dress, indeed! Old made over thing, you'd better call it!" was the scornful answer.

"Well, it is too bad that it was not made up to suit you at first. Now that it has been altered, it looks quite stylish, and becomes you splendidly, and this is just the day to wear your new hat."

This bit of flattery had the desired effect. Gussie decided that it really was too fine to stay indoors, so she rose from the table to begin her preparations for church.

"Seems to me you have taken to psalm-singing very suddenly," said Gussie, as Dexie accompanied her preparations with some song of David that was unfamiliar to Gussie's ears.

"Oh, no! they sing psalms every Sunday at the Episcopal Church," and Dexie hummed away with a light heart.

"But not to such tunes as that! They go hopping along on one note, like a hen with a sore foot, and then end up altogether differently from what you expect. Chanting is not singing, and I think it sounds ridiculous."

"Well, a hen with a sore foot would sing a mournful song, I fear; but if you would come to St. Paul's some morning and hear them sing the *Te Deum*, you would not think there was anything mournful about it. It sounds just glorious! Everyone might not think so," she added, noting her sister's scornful look; "but everyone does not admire psalm-singing after the Presbyterian style, either. However, chant, psalm or hymn, it's all one to me so long as I know the tunes, for I hate to stand as dumb as a post when I go to a place of worship. Some people are content to have nothing more to do in the service than say 'Amen' at the close of the benediction, but I think a responsive service claims the attention of careless churchgoers, and gives people something else to think of besides the style of the garments of those around them."

"Well, I enjoy looking at the styles when I go to church, and I hope people will think my hat is becoming," said outspoken Gussie; "I believe other people put on their fine feathers on Sunday with the same object. However, I do believe that an ugly hat is as conspicuous as a handsome one."

"Well, I suppose it is! I wonder if there is such a thing as a 'happy medium' in trimming a hat. Dear me! what a lot of things a person has to think of in this world!" and with a sigh she followed her sister downstairs.

Aunt Jennie watched them depart with a prayer in her heart that some message might reach the heart of her careless brother-in-law, and she seemed to have had her prayer answered, for he was willing enough to attend the same church the following Sunday.

But Gussie was not attracted either by the sermon or the singing. Something else had to be the attraction to draw her out of a Sunday morning, unless she was urged with a persistency that would have moved a mule in the tantrums.

But when Mrs. Sherwood announced, one Sunday morning, that she would accompany the rest to church, Dexie felt that her happiness was complete. She knew it was owing to Aunt Jennie's influence that her mother had put forth this extra exertion, and though it was Sunday, Dexie felt like dancing a jig around the floor, for her mother had become even more indifferent than her easy-going father in matters pertaining to religion.

In the Gurney household there was no day in the week so gladly welcomed as the Sabbath, and of a family containing so many young children this is no light thing to say.

In the first place, the little ones were so anxious not to lose any of the many extra treats that this glad day afforded them, that they put on their best behavior with their Sunday garments—and where is the person, little or big, that does not feel more important in his best clothes, and act accordingly.

Then instead of having breakfast in the nursery, with nurse at the head of the table, the family met around the one table, below stairs; and to the little ones this was a treat indeed. Having the children around him only one day in seven made it quite a change for Mr. Gurney also, though it wearied while it delighted him; and each succeeding Sunday he more fully realized the blessing he possessed in his good wife, for he had none of that patience and tact that is required to keep such a family in order.

Then on fine Sundays all the children went to church, except the two youngest, and the advent of a new member in the family was hailed with delight by one of the family at least; for of course a baby, however new, counted one, and it was warmly welcomed by the one who was thus raised to the dignity of a church-goer.

We must not forget the treat that was reserved for Sunday afternoons, for directly after Sunday-school there was sure to be in readiness for each member of the family a plate containing what the children called "goodies." This was a mixture of confectionery, dates or figs, apples, nuts, pears or oranges, or other fruits as the season might be. As Dexie Sherwood was expected to spend this part of the day with the family, her plate was regularly prepared with the rest; and until the time that Lancy had made known his feelings for her,

Dexie had enjoyed the *tete-a-tete* which he always managed to arrange in some quiet corner. Even now she was not always able to avoid it, without being positively rude, for she could not make Elsie see that her presence was necessary when Lancy managed to give his sister the impression that it was otherwise; it was quite clear that Mother Gurney saw nothing amiss in Lancy's desire to take Dexie "somewhere out of the noise," for the little ones made much of their Sunday freedom.

It was during one of these Sunday afternoon chats that a better understanding was arrived at between Lancy and Dexie. They were sitting in the parlor, with a screen drawn between them and any chance observer, their plates on a small table near them, when Dexie playfully tossed over a piece of confectionery bearing the words, "You look unhappy."

Lancy looked up with such a tender look in his eyes that Dexie instantly repented her action, but it was too late, and she dropped her eyes to read the sweet messenger that fell in her lap, "You have my heart."

Dexie had no answer except, "Do forgive me," and she tossed it over with a look in her eyes that filled Lancy with an unutterable longing to take her in his arms.

"What shall I forgive you for?" he said, laying his hand on hers. "I am not unhappy, only when I see how you try to avoid me. I have kept my promise, and have not spoken a word that could annoy you. Why do you try never to be alone with me? It is hard to forgive you for that," he said, in a low tone.

"I did not mean anything by those silly candies; I was only in fun."

"Then you don't want to be forgiven, is that it? or do you mean that you are going to be good to me in the future?"

"I don't know what 'being good' implies, so I won't promise," she replied, smiling.

"It means that you will not act as if you were afraid to be alone with me a minute, and to talk to me as freely as you did before, well—before that snowstorm. You have never put your hand on my shoulder, and asked me to take you any place since then. You don't know how I miss the pleasant hours we used to spend together, or the delight I felt in the pressure of the hand that has never willingly touched mine since I spoke to you here in the parlor. The Dexie I knew a few weeks ago seems to have gone away, and I miss her very much, indeed."

"I can't be the same as I used to be, Lancy. Something is different, and I'm so afraid someone will make remarks about us if we are so much together as we used to be."

"What kind of remarks? tell me, Dexie. Something we would be ashamed to hear?" and he smiled into her distressed face.

"You know what I mean very well, Lancy, and I couldn't bear it."

"Did you ever hear any remarks before—before that snow-storm?"

"No! I never thought there was anything to make remarks about, but I have been looking at things differently lately."

"In what way, Dexie? Do tell me?" and he caught her hands in a firm clasp.

"Don't, Lancy! Please stop! There has been enough said and done already to make people talk if they knew about it."

"Only a few words, and one little kiss, that was all, Dexie. If the thought of what people might say keeps us apart, you are very foolish, for if we were never to speak to each other again we would be accused of having had a 'lover's quarrel,' so don't keep me at a distance any longer on that account. You are making us both miserable for nothing; for I don't believe you are enjoying yourself a bit under the new rule that you have set up. Confess now, are you? honor bright, Dexie?" and he looked eagerly into her eyes.

"Well, no, Lancy," and she looked up with a smile. "It isn't quite so nice as it used to be, and I have stayed home several times when I wanted to go out. I am not shy, naturally, you know, and I would have asked for your escort if there had not been reasons to prevent me. Hugh has been very anxious to show his gallantry, but nothing would tempt me to go three steps with that big Frenchman."

"Well, I wish Hugh could hear you say that, Dexie, for I was beginning to feel jealous. He talks so much about you I was afraid he had entered the lists against me."

"Lancy, what nonsense you talk! Hugh is Gussie's particular property. What made you fancy that I had stepped into her shoes?"

"Nothing that need vex you, Dexie, so don't frown; but he told me in confidence, you know, that you were—but there; it was in confidence, so I won't repeat what he said. I know he cares more for you than for Gussie, and the fact don't please me very well."

Dexie was silent for some minutes. The remembrance of certain looks and speeches that Hugh had lately addressed to her were now explained; he thought she had quarrelled with Lancy, and he was anxious to take Lancy's place. She lifted her eyes, saying:

"Hugh shall have no chance to think any such a thing. But I know how it has happened. Gussie had no eyes for anyone else while that Plaisted was here, so I had to entertain Hugh occasionally; but dear me! how soft he must be, if my foolish songs have turned his brain."

And then, looking shyly into his eyes, she added, "I won't run away from you any more, Lancy. We will go back to our old ways, but don't talk any more nonsense to me, and we will be chums again. Is it a bargain, Lancy?"

Lancy bent nearer to the curly head that was bent to hide her blushing face, then, seizing her hands, held her close as he whispered, in a tender voice:

"That's my Dexie back again! I won't annoy you with words, but you know what my feelings are for you all the same. Now, seal the bargain, Dexie," and he turned her face to his.

Well, the perversity of girls! is there anything equal to it? Must it really be confessed that the girl who thought that one little stolen kiss was worth crying over should raise her pretty mouth to receive a much longer caress; yes, and enjoy it, too! But there! come to think of it, that first kiss in the parlor was a one-sided affair, reluctantly received; and a one-sided kiss is like—is like—well, whatever is it like? We give it up!

CHAPTER XII.

Returning home by way of Eastport, Mr. Sherwood took passage in a vessel bound for Londonderry, a small seaport on the Bay of Fundy, and from there he travelled by stage to Truro, where he took the train for Halifax.

While on the train an incident took place which, while affording amusement for the passengers, led to after-results that were quite surprising to the Sherwoods.

It seems that a countryman, hailing from Prince Edward Island, had accompanied the vessel in which he had shipped the surplus oats and potatoes that had grown on his farm, and the vessel had arrived in Halifax a few days previously. This being his first trip "abroad," he had determined to see all the sights which the city of Halifax afforded while he waited for the vessel to discharge her cargo and prepare for the return trip to Charlottetown.

His innocent air soon attracted the attention of some sharpers, or "confidence men," as they would have been termed in a later day, and thinking he had met the "gentry for shure" in the well-dressed scamps that were so friendly to him, the countryman willingly accompanied them to an uptown resort, where he was treated to drugged liquor, and then robbed of the tidy sum that the sale of his produce had brought him. Then, adding insult to injury, they had taken him to the depot, and, placing a ticket for Truro in his hatband, they put him on board the cars and left him to his fate.

He was put off the train at Truro in a dazed condition, and passed the night in some out-of-the-way corner of the freight house, where he slept off the effect of the liquor.

His alarm and astonishment when he came to himself and found he was alone and in a strange place, and with empty pockets, was both painful and ludicrous to witness. His distress seemed all the greater in that he had not the faintest idea where he was or how to get back to his vessel waiting alongside the wharf in Halifax.

It took some time to make his story understood, but when it became known to the men about the depot they gave him a good breakfast, and determined to get him "dead-headed" to the city, as the farmer felt sure he could easily find the thieves and recover his money if he once got back to Halifax. He had never seen a train of cars in his life, being too drunk the night before to know how he was travelling; so when the train steamed into the depot next morning, after announcing its approach by ear-splitting shrieks, he dropped out of sight behind a pile of boxes, thinking that some wild creature was let loose upon the streets. Before he could collect his scattered senses he was seized by strong hands and stowed away in a corner of a freight car, where, upon bags of potatoes, he was told to "sit down and keep out of sight." For the first few miles he literally obeyed the injunction, for he shook and trembled with fright, and with every shriek of the engine he ducked his head, thinking his very life was in danger; but as time went by and he still found himself whole and uninjured, he took courage, and sat up and looked about him as well as the dim and close car would permit. By and by the motion of the car caused the door to slide open a few inches, for, fortunately or unfortunately, the door had been left unlocked, so he crawled cautiously forward and peered through the opening, wondering greatly at the frightful speed of the "animal" that was drawing them along, but he concluded that it was "michty encouragin'," for at the pace they were going he would soon be within reach of the rascals who had emptied his pockets.

Not content to let well enough alone, he disregarded the injunction given him to "stay there," and when the train stopped for a few minutes at Shubenacadie, a station on the line, he stepped out on the platform to have a look about him; but not being quick or daring enough to step back on the moving train, he came very near losing his ride.

Fortunately, one of the train hands who had befriended him at first, saw him as the train moved along, and pulled him aboard the second-class car as it passed them.

Having previously been stowed away among the freight, he had no idea of the accommodation for travellers behind him, and the sight of so many people, sitting quietly on the seats, filled him with awe.

But the good-natured brakeman now drew him inside the car, intending to place his wandering friend back into his former quarters as soon as the train stopped at the next station.

When the eyes of the countryman had taken in the scene, the thought immediately suggested itself that this must be some sort of a meeting-house or chapel that was travelling along.

He stood for a few minutes regarding the people before him; then turning a solemn face to the brakeman asked, in a properly subdued voice, as became the situation:

"Is there preachin' here the day?"

Not comprehending the meaning of this question, but thinking the countryman meditated a religious attack on those who were present, the brakeman replied:

"Not today; these are good Catholics."

"Ye dinna tell me!" and his eyes and mouth expanded in surprise. "An' are they repeatin' their prayers?" he innocently asked.

"Oh, yes, everyone of them," was the reply.

"Then let me oot o' this!" he cried, reaching for the door. "It's to Halifax I want to go, so open the door an' let me oot o' this."

"There! sit down and be quiet, or you'll get put out fast enough," replied the brakeman, giving the man a shove into the seat. "You sit still where you are, mind, or you'll get into trouble," he added, as he turned to attend to his duties outside.

Here was his chance. Our friend from the country felt that he was in trouble already. He had no intention of joining the worshippers, for he was a member of the good old Scotch Kirk; so he opened the car-door, and stepped out to the platform outside.

The swift, sidelong jerks almost took him off his feet. Grasping the hand-rail, and looking around for some means of escape, he cautiously stepped across into the better furnished first-class car behind.

"Bless me, but I'm in luck!" was his inward comment, as he beheld the comfortable seats. Taking the first empty one, he sank down on the cushions with evident delight shining from his eyes at his blissful surroundings.

But the argus-eyed conductor soon spied him, and not recognizing him as a ticket-holder, swooped down upon him at once.

"Your ticket, sir."

"The same to yersel', ma frien'!" was the courteous reply, thinking this some new form of salutation.

"Here! no nonsense! where's your ticket? let's see where you're going."

"Weel, sir, I'm hopin' to get to Halifax some time 'fore long. We seem to be gaun as the craws flee, so nae doot we'll soon get there. Does this—er—buildin'—stop there for victuals or—or onythin'?"

The conductor, thinking him out of his mind, said more mildly:

"Who came with you? Who is looking after you aboard the cars?"

"Oh! a nice young chiel yonder; but he left me alane there, so I stepped oot withoot his kennin' an' popped in here."

"Ah, yes; just so. I've no doubt there is a spare room in one of the public institutions awaiting you. What sort of a looking man has you in charge?"

"Oh! he's a clever young chiel, wi' a door-plate on his bonnet; the sexton, I tak' it."

Not making much out of this information, the conductor left him to make inquiries ahead, tapping his forehead significantly to some passengers near, who had overheard the conversation, and who, as soon as the conductor was out of sight, began to question the "harmless lunatic."

His answers to their inquiries were not more clear than those the conductor had elicited, and Mr. Sherwood, who sat a few seats behind, becoming indignant at the rude jokes that were being made at the expense of the unfortunate man, stepped forward to interfere.

Surely he had seen the man before. He gazed at the man's distressed face, but could not place him.

"What's the trouble, my friend?" he asked, sitting down in the seat behind and leaning over to speak to him.

"I'm shure I dinna ken, sir, at a', at a'. There's a mistak' afloat somewhere. I never was in sic a fix afore. This is a queer kintry, I tak' it."

"Where are you from?"

That question set him on the right track at once. He could tell his story if once he started at the beginning, though he found it impossible to make these strangers comprehend his present dilemma; so beginning from the time he left his own dooryard with the last cartload of potatoes, he gave them a detailed account of his wanderings up to the time when he met the fine young gentlemen in Halifax. But he had no idea how he got to Truro; that was all a blank to him. When Mr. Sherwood explained that the train on which he was riding was a public conveyance which went back and forth daily to carry passengers and freight, he could scarcely believe it. His own explanation seemed the more plausible, for did it not agree with what the young sexton told him? He had been befooled once too often to listen to the many explanations of those around him.

But the conductor now appeared, having found out all there was to tell about the man, and feeling annoyed at his mistake, now demanded of the countryman either his ticket or his fare, and threatened to put him off the train at the next station if he did not produce either the one or the other.

"But, ma guid man, I haena a copper aboot me, or it's wullin' enough I'd be to gie ye a shullin' or so for this fine drive."

"Well, off you get then the next time we stop."

"But shurely ye wadna be pittin' a puir man oot o' yer waggon, or chapel, or whatever ye ca' it, whan there's sae mony empty pews? I'm no croodin' onyane, an' I'm wullin' enough to sit onywhere."

"We don't take people on the cars for nothing," said the conductor, decidedly. "If you can't pay, you can't ride."

"Weel, it's the rich anes that's aye the stingiest, shure enough," replied the man, more to himself than to the brass-buttoned figure before him. "But ye widna fin' the like o' yersel' owre in ma kintry, let me tell ye! The puirest farmer widna refuse to gie a stranger a lift if he was gaun the same way as himsel', even if it was only a kairt that he had, an' it loaded to the brim."

"Can't help it," replied he of the buttons, with a grin. "Off you get at the next station, or we'll put you off without ceremony."

"But I'll no gang aff, if I may be sae bold as to tell ye!" said the now angry farmer. "Ye took me to Truro against ma wull, for why did I want to gang to a place that I never heard o' afore; so, then, ye'll tak' me back to Halifax again, wullin' or no, an' whan I get my money back I'll sen' ye the price o' the drive. If ye think I'm croodin' the gentlemen, I'll gang oot an' sit on the steps o' yer backdoor, but, guidness only kens! there seems room enough in these empty pews for a dizzen o' ma size."

"Here, conductor, I'll pay the man's fare," said Mr. Sherwood, who had listened to the conversation with ill-concealed amusement.

This being satisfactory to the conductor, the man was allowed to keep his seat in peace, and, engaging him in conversation, Mr. Sherwood discovered that he had been the guest of the man's brother during one of his trips to Prince Edward Island. His home was on the north side of the island, and the farm of Roderick McDonald was well known as one of the best-paying places on the "Garden of the St. Lawrence."

On finding that the man beside him was the Yankee horse-buyer, Mr. McDonald rose and shook his hand with a warmth that showed his pleasure at the meeting.

This unexpected kindness from one whom he had learned to consider as a man of unlimited means and unusual smartness, quite set him up in his own estimation.

He began to feel quite elated at his present position, and felt himself a hero as he related to the attentive strangers the many strange things he had seen since he left home, quite ignoring the fact that some of his listeners might have been "abroad" as well as himself.

But it was impossible to put a damper on this loquacious countryman, even though he loudly set forth his own ignorance.

"Oh! but I'm a great traveller!" said he. "There's nae kennin' hoo mony miles I've travelled since I left ma hame on the north side o' the Islan'! Let's see; it's thirty miles frae there to the toon, an' it tak's a hale day to cover the distance wi' a loaded kairt o' tawties, let me tell ye! Then, whan we were snug aboard the vessel, guidness only kens hoo mony miles we went afore we cam' fornenst the city o' Halifax, for we were three days on the michty ocean, at the mercy o' ony storm that micht come alang unawares. Yes, indeed, an' we travelled alang through the dark nicht as weel, they tell me, though that I'm no prepared to say, seem' that I was fast asleep in the hold," and he looked around to see if any of his hearers doubted his word. "Then, whan we got to the wharf in Halifax, an' I selt ma tawties an' oats, I cam' ashore an' tramped the streets o' Halifax, up hill an' doon dale, till ma new buits are a' worn oot behin', as ye can see for yersel's," and he lifted up his feet, one after the other, that the truth of his words might be verified; then continuing: "It was whan the thiefin' scoon'rels met me an' made ma acquaintance that I gaed wrang; but I never suspected they'd start me on ma travels again, an' withoot ma kennin', tae—ay, an' sen' me aff withoot as muckle as a copper in ma pocket, at a', at a'! no even as muckle as wad buy me a bit o' breakfast, which the guid folk at Truro gied me for naethin', an', if it hadna been for them, I don't think I wad ever hae been able to fin' ma way back to ma hame on the farm. But here I am, richt amang the gentlemen an' ladies, travellin' alang like the Queen hersel' micht be prood to dae. Ay, but it's a long story I'll hae to tell them at hame whan ainst I get back to ma ain kintry again, an' it's themsel's that'll be dum'foon'ert to hear me tell aboot the mony kinds o' folk ain meets whan they gang abroad!"

"Have you met any naked savages since you left your distant country?" asked one of the sports, with a wink at his comrade.

"Naked savages, is't, you mean? Ay, that I hae, or nearly naked anes," was the quick reply. "On the streets o' Halifax, sir, near the wharves, sir, that's whaur ye'll come across them, but, dae ye ken noo, I aye thocht that savages were black, made sae I mean whan they were born into this worl'. But, dae ye min', it's masel' thinks that some o' them could be made white, if only ane had soap an' water enough to dae't. No that I didna see ony black savages roamin' roon' as weel; but maist o' them had some claithes on, like decent Christian folk. Some hadna come to that knowledge yet; but the nakedness o' black skinned savages isna sae noticin' as that o' white savages, I tak' it."

A hearty laugh followed this last remark, and the conversation became general, until the train arrived in Halifax.

Mr. Sherwood took the countryman to the police headquarters at once, where the story of the theft was told at length, and as he could give a good description of the men who had robbed him it was thought that they might be captured.

As Mr. Sherwood had received such kind treatment from the man's relations in Prince Edward Island, he thought it but fair to repay it by looking after the farmer during the rest of his stay in the city.

To satisfy the man that the vessel had not sailed during his absence he took him down to the wharf, and, after explaining to the captain the cause of his detention, Mr. Sherwood insisted on taking him up to visit his own family.

The farmer demurred at this, saying that his clothes were not in a fit state to visit anywhere.

This fact was evident, but Mr. Sherwood intended to visit a ready-made clothing store on his way up town, and make his friend presentable.

This was rather a delicate matter to accomplish without wounding the man's feelings; but the native tact of the Yankee served him well here, and when the farmer stepped before the large mirror in the back shop of Silver's clothing store and saw his own reflection, he hardly knew himself.

"But hoo am I ever gaun to repay ye?" he asked. "If I shouldna get ma money back I'll be in a bad fix."

"Not at all, Mr. McDonald. I'll buy the best horse you have got, if you will sell him to me, and we can settle this little matter then; but I made enough on the big black horse I bought from your brother to give you this suit and still have a good profit besides."

"Weel, ye're an honest man, for ye paid a guid price for the beast, an' paid it in cash tae."

"Thank you for your good opinion; but in case the police should not find those rascals before the vessel sails, it will be rather hard on you to return home with empty pockets, so let me pay you in advance for that horse."

It was quite a different-looking man that came out of the store a few minutes later, for he had been refitted from hat to boots, and he looked the well-to-do farmer to the life, even the well-filled purse was not lacking, for Mr. Sherwood had given him the horse's value instead of the modest sum the farmer stated as the selling price of his animal.

The polite store-keeper promised to send the farmer's cast-off garments to the vessel, and Mr. Sherwood was soon introducing his friend to the members of his household.

Mr. Sherwood's unexpected arrival made a joyful excitement, and the farmer mentally resolved that an account of the happy meeting between the Yankee horse-buyer and his family should be added to the rest of the story he had to tell when once he arrived home.

When Mr. Sherwood had privately explained to the family the present position of his new friend, together with the respectability of the family and the kind treatment he had received from their hands, he was treated as an honored guest, and Dexie had never been so gracious to the fastidious Plaisted or treated him with half the courtesy as she now bestowed on the honest, kind-hearted, though ignorant countryman.

That this kindness was appreciated was quite evident from the satisfaction that beamed from every wrinkle on his honest face; and when he found himself seated in the most comfortable chair in the parlor, listening to the music that Dexie was bringing forth from the piano for his pleasure, he doubted in his mind if even the Governor himself was as happy and fortunate as he.

As the vessel was to sail the next day for Charlottetown, he had to leave the pleasant rooms for closer quarters on board the vessel; but before he said farewell he exacted a promise that, should any of them ever go to the Island, they would visit his home on the north shore.

As the vessel was about to leave the wharf Mr. Sherwood appeared, accompanied by a member of the police force, who gave over to the hand of the farmer about half the sum which had been stolen from him, and the man actually felt richer than when the whole amount had lain in his pocket. He pressed Mr. Sherwood to accept payment for the drive on the train and for his new suit, but Mr. Sherwood reminded him of the horse he had purchased, saying:

"Look well after my horse, McDonald, and if you will find out where I can get some more good animals I will be glad to pay you for the time and trouble expended in doing so," and with a hearty hand-clasp Mr. Sherwood stepped ashore.

In a few minutes the vessel's cable was shipped and she slowly passed down the harbor, bearing on her deck one who had a heart full of gratitude for kindness shown a stranger in a strange land.

CHAPTER XIII.

Mr. Sherwood's presence at home seemed to infuse new life into the household, and the following weeks passed very pleasantly to Dexie, for her father needed her services again, and for that reason she was excused from much of the endless sewing that seemed necessary in making up Louie's outfit.

Sewing machines were not so common at that time as to be considered a necessary household article, and Mrs. Sherwood was slow to take advantage of the new invention, preferring the use of fingers instead of feet for articles that required a needle and thread to fashion them; consequently Louie's wardrobe took some time to set in order.

Dexie was willing enough to change the needle for the more congenial pen and ink, and Mr. Sherwood insisted that Gussie should put her needle to more practical use. Now, while Gussie liked well enough to handle a needle and thread when something showy and fanciful was to be evolved thereby, she almost rebelled against the plain sewing, it was such dull, uninteresting work; it made so much difference if the sharp little instrument held Berlin wool, floss, etc., or the common cotton thread, which, though so useful, was too prosaic to suit Gussie.

Do not let this convey the idea that the time was all spent indoors, at some employment or other, for never were outings so frequently enjoyed. There were excursions down the coast to Cow Bay, and picnics to various points of interest, which, in the vicinity of Halifax, are innumerable and within easy-reaching distance to dwellers in the city.

Mr. Gurney owned a small boat which carried a sail, but there were plenty of willing hands to row it when the wind failed, and before the summer was over, Dexie could handle an oar with the dexterity that only practice can give.

It was very pleasant of a warm summer evening to glide along the waters of Bedford Basin, through which the boat cut her way as if through molten silver, and there was many a time when the little craft held but two persons, one being Lancy Gurney, and the curly head of his companion was very like to that of Dexie Sherwood's!

The early days of October were marked by the departure of Louie and the kind old nurse Dinah.

Poor Louie! her heart was rent with conflicting feelings. She had been wild with delight to think that she had been the one chosen to spend the winter with her grandma, and, though the journey thither was a pleasure she had long looked forward to, the final leave-takings were so much harder than she had anticipated that she felt almost tempted, at the last moment, to give it up, and stay with those she had never loved so much as she did now, when prepared to leave them.

We must not stop to tell of all the changes which took place in the old homestead when it was decided that Louie was to spend the winter there. The eyesight of the grandparents became so much better as they thought of her coming, that they noticed with startling clearness how dingy the old farmhouse had grown. Their brightened vision regarded the faded carpets with aversion, and when they had given place to new ones the curtains looked positively shabby, and they were astonished to find how much difference a little paint on the house and out-buildings made in the look of the place.

Without chasing away the *homey* took of the low, comfortable rooms, they were made brighter and more cheerful, as if rejoicing with the grandparents in their joy, and joining in the attempt to make the little grand-daughter feel at home.

Unconsciously, the old folks grew brighter themselves, and Grandma Sherwood even went so far as to lay aside the cap she had worn so long that it seemed to belong to her head quite as much as the beautiful grey hair beneath it; and after putting it away reverently in the bottom drawer of the bureau, she took out instead her "best cap," and wore it daily, in anticipation of her grand-daughter's arrival.

The pretty room that had been fitted up for Louie's use lacked nothing to make it perfect except its occupant, and if Louie needed anything to reconcile her to a winter's stay in the quiet farmhouse, this pretty room contained it.

Neither were its treasures revealed in a day, for, weeks after she arrived, grandma would bid her search for some secret drawer which contained something that she would like; and Louie's curiosity would be stimulated by this admission, so that many a stormy day flew rapidly away while she searched with the ardor of an Arctic explorer for the secret spring or knob which, pressed at last, revealed delights that only a young girl's heart can fully enjoy.

Occasionally mysterious packages from the city arrived at the farmhouse bearing Louie's name in full, and the delightful excitement of untying the string and removing the wrappings, was entered into by the grandparents with as much ardor as by Louie herself.

But grandma's heart seemed to grow young again. She knew what would please her little favorite, and she spared no expense if pleasure and happiness were procured with the purchases, and thus passed away the pleasant winter, bringing only that which seemed good into the storehouse of Louie's life and heart.

Louie was destined to see but little of her own family hereafter, for during the following summer the grandmother's health became feeble, and she would not listen to the suggestions that Louie should return home. A few months later Dinah had the melancholy satisfaction of hearing the last words of her dying mistress, who passed away in her arms.

Louie was willing to listen to the entreaties of her grief-stricken grandfather, to remain his little companion a while longer.

The charge of the farmhouse now fell into the hands of Mr. Sherwood's widowed daughter. She had possessed a fine estate in

Georgia, and had lived a life of ease until Sherman's march to the sea, when her plantation was devastated, and her well-kept slaves had joined in the destruction of her property. When her husband's body was brought home for burial, the result of a distressing accident, there seemed nothing else left to do but to return to the home of her childhood, reaching it in time to hear her mother's last request with respect to Louie's future.

Aunt Annie promised to consider the child as her own if she could get the parents' sanction as well as Louie's free consent. The latter was freely gained, as Louie was far happier in her present home.

Mrs. Sherwood saw no obstacle in the way when the matter was laid before her, and she gave up her rights with so little manifestation of regret that even those who knew her best were astonished, and from that time Louie ceased to be a member of her father's family.

The second winter in Halifax was even more pleasant than the first had been, for the Sherwoods had extended their acquaintances, and there seemed always some new pleasure to look forward to.

The Song and Glee Club started up afresh as the winter evenings set in, and with a concert in the perspective the rehearsals were frequent and well attended.

Dexie's fine voice caused her to be given a more prominent part than she thought was her just due. She had no wish to be thrust forward into notice when there were older members of the club who were better entitled to her place, but she had no objection to being accompanist, for in that position she felt at home. But she was destined to come before the public in a more conspicuous manner.

One evening a member of the club brought in some new music, and the few who had heard it were so delighted with its melody, that they eagerly urged its performance at the approaching concert. A copy of the music being handed to Dexie by Lancy, she began to hum it softly to herself, but becoming enraptured with the bewitching strains of the composition, she unconsciously changed the low hum to a soft whistle, which grew louder as she proceeded. Sense of time and place disappeared, and she was unaware of the delight of the little group around her, until the unusual silence caused her to lift her eyes and understand the meaning of the sudden hush that had fallen on those present. A burning blush covered her face as she stammered out:

"I beg your pardon, ladies and gentlemen; I forgot where I was," and then sank on a seat near and hid her burning cheeks behind her book.

Lancy was at her side in a moment.

"Never mind, Dexie. You can't think how well it sounded. They were delighted."

"Oh, how *could* you let me go on, Lancy? You might have stopped me, I'm sure," she said, indignantly.

But she was immediately surrounded, and praises and interrogations poured forth from every side, making Gussie, who stood apart, turn pale with jealousy.

"Why did you not tell us that you could imitate the birds?"

"I never heard anything so perfectly sweet," said a lady member, pressing forward to speak to the blushing girl.

Dexie wished the floor would open and let her drop out of sight, but she gradually regained her composure and listened with displeasure to the general conversation, during which this new element of music was discussed at length.

"Miss Sherwood, do come to the piano and try that again with the accompaniment," said the leader, Mr. Ross. "You really must give us the benefit of that flutelike whistle; it is perfectly irresistible."

"Please excuse me, Mr. Ross; I really cannot," replied Dexie.

"But we can take no excuse. After hearing you once, nothing but a repetition will satisfy us. Mr. Gurney will play for you," was the eager reply.

But Lancy kindly came to her aid, and by a few whispered words succeeded in drawing off the attention from Dexie, by suggesting that if they would try the opening piece first and give Miss Sherwood time to reconsider her refusal, she might whistle later on; and Lancy was rewarded for this short respite by a grateful look as he passed her the open book.

Dexie felt angry for bringing this embarrassing position upon herself, and she was wondering if it would be possible for her to slip away unperceived, when Gussie leaned over her shoulder.

"Well, you did make a show of yourself, you great tomboy! It is a pity that you can't keep your bad manners out of sight, before strangers, anyway!"

This taunt acted like the prick of a goad, and made Dexie determine to stay and show Miss Gussie whether her "bad manners" had placed her lower or higher in the estimation of her friends. When the piece was rehearsed in which she sang the solo, she put forth her best efforts, and rendered it with such pathos and feeling that when it was ended, one and all, with the exception of Gussie, were loud in its praise.

As she lingered a moment beside the piano talking with a member, Mr. Ross stepped over to her side and begged her to try the new piece, and she silently bowed in answer; but the hunted look in the dark eyes might have told how hard it was to nerve herself for this ordeal.

The memory of Gussie's sneering remarks filled her with the needed courage, and when Lancy sat down and passed his fingers over the keys her heart ceased to throb; the very chords had a soothing power, and when Lancy lifted his eyes to her face she replied with a look that she was ready.

The first notes of the piece sounded from the piano, but brought no response from Dexie's lips. Lancy looked up quickly.

"Oh, Dexie, don't disappoint me!" he whispered.

Softly the birdlike notes ascended, fluttered and quivered, then slowly gained strength, then the clear, full notes rang through the room, charming every ear.

Those present listened in breathless silence. It was so faultlessly rendered that it was hard to believe that weeks of practice had not been given to bring such perfection of tone; but Dexie whistled for an object, and that was respect and honor from those present in the face of her "tomboy accomplishment."

It is not everyone who can whistle for a thing and get their wishes gratified; but, to the honor and respect which Dexie desired, was added the praise and approval of the delighted listeners. She felt proud to receive it, for it would forever silence Gussie as to how her "bad manners" were regarded.

Dexie was satisfied with her victory, and would not be persuaded into repeating the piece, though, at the close of the rehearsal, she consented to accompany Lancy in giving an exhibition of a bird-song.

It was the same chorus that had delighted the listeners the morning after the adventure in the snow-drifts, and the rendering of it was greatly enhanced by the better instrument before them.

Lancy played the accompaniment and whistled with her, and their voices seemed transformed into veritable song-birds, as they joined or answered each other's call.

"We must have that at our concert, Miss Sherwood," said Mr. Ross. "We cannot afford to miss it. How is it that I never had the pleasure of listening to this sort of music before, Mr. Gurney? You should have told us of this new accomplishment, Miss Sherwood."

"Indeed! you never would have heard it at all, if I had not forgotten myself so completely," said Dexie, smiling; "but as to whistling at the concert, that is out of the question. It is distressing enough to show my tomboyism before the members here."

"Nonsense! there is nothing of the 'tomboy' about that kind of whistling," said one of the members. "It is an accomplishment few possess."

"Well, it is fortunate for us that you made us aware of this talent of yours, even though it was unintentional on your part, Miss Sherwood," said Mr. Ross. "We must persuade you to give others the pleasure of hearing you. It would add much to the attraction of our concert."

"You are most kind, and your remarks most flattering, but I must be excused," said Dexie, turning with a smile to those who had addressed her. "I do not forget that 'whistling girls' are generally frowned down."

"But there is no comparison between the usual tomboy whistle of girls, and those bobolink, canary-bird notes that come from your lips," said an enthusiastic member.

"Miss Sherwood, I am going to place that piece third on the programme, and will call around tomorrow and see you and arrange for these extra pieces. We can leave out some of the songs rather than miss the treat you can give to those who will be eager to hear you," said the leader, persuasively.

"Indeed, Mr. Ross, I could not think of whistling before the audience we hope to have, so I will excuse you from calling upon me, if that is to be your errand," said Dexie, hurriedly. "I am doing my share as it is."

"Well, if you think it will be too much for you, someone else might take your solo; but that seems a pity, when you are so well prepared. Do you find it tiresome to whistle?"

"Oh, it is not that; it would not tire me if I whistled all day. But I cannot face a hall full of people and whistle to them. It would be dreadful!"

"I would not urge the matter if I did not feel positive of your success. I am sure the members of the club have the average intelligence, and, seeing that you have charmed us all by your unique performance, you need have no hesitancy in trying your powers before a Halifax audience," was the reply.

"Don't think of it. Oh, I never could do it, Mr. Ross. I should be hissed off the stage."

"No danger of that, Miss Sherwood," said Mr. Markman, the best tenor of the club. "I'll answer for it that you will so electrify the audience that they will demand an encore. Don't hide your talent from those who would be so sure to appreciate it."

"Give the matter serious consideration," said Mr. Ross. "I will run in tomorrow and see you, even though I may run the risk of a cool reception. What time shall I call?" he added, with a smile.

"Well, if you must call and see me, I hope it will be on some other errand; I will be at leisure any time in the afternoon, say three o'clock." Then, looking up with a smile, added: "Don't imagine I shall reconsider the matter; I simply could not do it."

"I'll hope to find you in a better frame of mind tomorrow, Miss Sherwood," he replied, giving her hand a cordial grasp. "May I ask permission for Mr. Gurney to be present at the interview?"

"Oh, certainly. I think you can safely venture to do so, seeing that he will probably come in of his own accord, if you don't ask him," and Lancy joined in the laugh raised at his expense.

"Well, that settles it, Mr. Gurney, I shall depend on your support in this difficult matter. Now, before we separate, I think I am voicing the sentiments of the members here when I ask for one more song. Now, Miss Sherwood, you have acknowledged that it does not tire you to whistle, so you will send us home in the best of spirits if you will favor us once more."

Dexie placed her hands over her ears at the applause that greeted these words, and amidst the general laughter Lancy drew her to the piano.

"I am going to sing 'The Mocking-Bird,' so you must whistle," he said. "Come, Dexie, there is no backing out," as she tried to escape him.

"Well, get Gussie to sing with you, and I will; perhaps it will help her good-nature a little—it needs help," she whispered, laughing.

On being sufficiently urged, Gussie stepped over to the piano beside them, and joined her alto to the chorus.

Dexie played and whistled, and, as the members listened, all joined Mr. Ross in thinking that their programme should hold this song also.

"Well, Miss Sherwood, I think you have kept the best to the last. I have heard that song several times, but never 'listened to the mocking-bird' after all. The song in itself is beautiful, but, after hearing you whistle, I see that it is imperfect with the mocking-bird left out. This is rather a cold climate for that species of bird, Miss Sherwood, but I shall give a Halifax audience the pleasure of hearing one, if I have to import one from the South on purpose for the occasion. Tomorrow at three o'clock, remember, Mr. Gurney, and may the fates be propitious!"

When Mr. Sherwood learned of Dexie's refusal to whistle, he was as eager to change her decision as any member of the club.

For once Gussie sided with Dexie, and said all she could to influence her against it, but her motive was so apparent that her father reproved her sharply.

When Mr. Ross and Lancy made their appearance, Dexie had to listen to the expostulations of three very urgent gentlemen; and though she held to her refusal for some time, she was obliged to capitulate at last, stipulating that she should only be asked to whistle one piece. Mr. Ross was obliged to be content with this, but he found it hard to decide which of the pieces he would put upon the programme.

But a thought occurred to him, and he smiled as he considered it. Yes, he would set down the new piece; and if he knew a Halifax audience, and he thought he did, one piece would not content them. The others would do nicely for the "encore" which he knew would be demanded.

He smiled with pleasure as he rose to depart.

"I will set you down for the new piece you were running over last evening, Miss Sherwood," said he, "and Mr. Gurney will play your accompaniment. If you do as well at the concert as you did last night when you first saw the music, I shall be well satisfied."

"But what if I should fail, papa?" said Dexie, when she found herself alone with her father. "How can I stand before so many strange people and whistle? Oh! I'm sure I cannot. No young lady whistles in public, and I feel sure they will hiss me off the stage!"

CHAPTER XIV.

The time slipped by bringing the eventful evening. In many homes nimble fingers had been busy for days fashioning certain garments that were to make the wearers quite fascinating to beholders. But Dexie declared that as her best gown was very becoming, she had no intention of getting a new one on purpose for the occasion, a few extra touches would make it quite presentable. On the morning of the concert, she found there were still some minor things needed to complete her toilet, so she went down-town to do a little shopping.

As she stood in a store waiting for her parcel, her eyes rested on a handbill lying near, and as she read it her face flushed angrily, then turned pale to the lips, for those great, staring letters announced the evening's performance, and she was referred to as one of the chief attractions, but in terms that aroused her temper to its highest pitch.

Who could have worded that awful handbill? She longed to stamp her foot, or scream, or give vent to her angry feelings in some way. How dared they single her out by such a nickname? She snatched the parcel from the hands of the astonished clerk and left the store with more speed than grace.

While she is flying homeward, her angry eyes shining like stars from her pale, set face, let us read the cause of her displeasure.

"Temperance Hall. Temperance Hall.

Tonight.

The Halifax Song and Glee Club will give their
Annual Concert
In Temperance Hall Tonight.

Full Opening Chorus by the Members.

First Appearance of
The American Warbler,
The only songster ever known to whistle popular airs to
piano accompaniment.

Don't Miss It.

Programme to consist of Solos, Duets, Quartettes
and
Full Choruses.

God Save the Queen."

When Dexie reached home she flung open the door and rushed up the stairs to her own room in a perfect fury.

Gussie had watched her swift approach from the window, and fearing that some awful calamity must have happened, followed her sister upstairs, and found her walking the floor like a caged tiger, her eyes positively fierce as they looked straight before her, though seeing nothing.

"What is the matter, Dexie?" she asked in alarm.

Dexie turned and motioned imperiously for her to leave the room, then shut the door with a slam that shook the house. Gussie hurried to her father, saying:

"Oh, papa! do go and see Dexie. I believe she is going to have a fit, for she looks awful."

"What's that?" and Mr. Sherwood looked up from his paper. "Did you say something the matter with Dexie?"

"Yes, do go and see what it is, for she turned me out of the room."

"Have you been teasing her again about whistling?" he asked, looking at her sharply. "I told you to let your sister alone."

"Oh! it isn't that, papa. I have not offended her. She has only just returned from the store, but there's something the matter with her, for her very looks frightened me."

Being thus admonished Mr. Sherwood was soon in Dexie's room, and he was startled at the intense expression of his daughter's face.

"My dear girl! what has happened to you?" he tenderly asked, as he took her hands and drew her to his side. "Try and tell me." He stroked her ruffled hair, and spoke in soothing tones, but it was several minutes before she could utter a word.

"Dexie, my dear, calm yourself, and tell me what is the matter; you will make yourself ill. What is it all about, my dear?"

Dexie pointed to the crumpled handbill that she had tossed under the table as she threw off her wraps, and her father stooped and picked it up, then smoothing it across his knee read the cause of offence.

"Why, you foolish girl! surely it is not this that has put you into such a passion?"

"I won't have it! How dared they! The 'American Warbler,' indeed! Do they think I will overlook such insolence and go to their old concert after that public insult! No, I won't put up with it, so there!" and a flood of tears brought relief to the overcharged heart.

"Dexie, they never intended to hurt your feelings; it is only a mistake on your part to think so for a moment. Why, it is quite a joke, one that the audience will not be slow in appreciating, I'll warrant. Come, dry your eyes, and never mind this announcement."

But Dexie flung herself on the bed, sobbing through her tears: "Oh, papa, what made you make me say I would whistle when I did not want to from the first. I did not think they would treat me so meanly, or I never would have consented. But I won't go near the old hall tonight; no, not a step!"

Her father sat down on the bed beside her, and pushed away the hair from her hot face, saying: "You are quite mistaken, dear, in thinking they meant anything but praise in announcing your part of the programme. If you will just think a moment, you will see it yourself."

"Praise, indeed! They have insulted me in a most public manner. How dared they take such liberties with my name, when it was only as a special favor I consented to whistle at all! Oh, it was such a mean, shabby trick!" and the tears fell in showers.

"Come, Dexie, I can't let you cry like this," and he lifted her gently and placed her beside him. "You will surely be sick if you do not control yourself, my dear. It was too bad to vex you when there is so much depending on you; but it was done unintentionally, I know, and they will soon apologize when they know that the announcement has annoyed you."

"But what will be the good of that? An apology will not recall those handbills, which, I daresay, are all over the city. But I'll make them repent it; they'll find that even a worm will turn if trampled on."

"Tut, tut, what nonsense! You are not a worm nor the kind of bird that eats the worm either—but here's Aunt Jennie. Auntie, can't you help me put a grain of sense into this silly girl's pate? She imagines she has been insulted by this bit of flattery, hence these tears," and he held out the handbill for inspection.

"Why, Dexie, this will never do. You will spoil your eyes for tonight, dear. Nothing so very dreadful has happened, after all. I was quite alarmed at Gussie's account, and feared something serious had occurred. Don't be so foolish as to mind this bit of paper."

But Dexie buried her face in her father's shoulder and cried the more.

"Oh, it is too bad of you, auntie. I thought you would care if I was abused, but nobody does, not even papa; but I'll make somebody sorry, for I won't go near their old concert," and she jerked away from her father's arms, and threw herself back on the bed.

Aunt Jennie motioned for Mr. Sherwood and Gussie to leave the room, thinking she might manage Dexie better alone, for this hysterical crying needed to be checked at once. She sat down beside her and stroked the hot face until Dexie's sobs had somewhat ceased. Her gentle voice did much to soothe the tempest in Dexie's breast, but she seemed to have lost her persuasive power for the time.

Mr. Sherwood went at once to his wife's room to explain the cause of the disturbance.

"How inconsiderate of Dexie to cause so much annoyance!" was her fretful comment. "I am quite sure I shall have the headache, for the way she slammed that door was enough to upset the strongest nerves. I thought of going to the concert myself if I finished my book in time, but it seems my fate to be robbed of all pleasure. Why don't you use your authority, Clarence, and make her behave herself?"

"You must make some allowance for her, wife, for she feels much hurt over that announcement. But the trouble is, what's to be done if she persists in her determination not to appear? I might insist on her going to the hall, but I doubt if I could make her whistle after she got there."

"Well, if you do not use your authority you need not ask me to interfere. She has quite upset me as it is."

"It is not very often that she gets worked up like this. I believe she controls her temper about as well as any of us. She seldom lets her tongue loose as she used to do when things went wrong, but flies to her room and fights it out alone. I expect those Gurneys have a good influence over our wilful Dexie."

"Well, I suppose she does not see those mild, quiet girls fly into a passion very often, and this tiresome concert is to blame for this disturbance. I fear if she has made up her mind not to go, you may as well leave her alone; so let the matter rest, it disturbs me," and Mrs. Sherwood closed her eyes as if the subject had passed completely from her mind.

But Mr. Sherwood could not let the matter rest so easily, and his wife's indifference annoyed him exceedingly.

"Confound their stupidity!" he exclaimed at last, beginning to see it with Dexie's eyes. "They might have known that she would object to such an announcement, but it will be an awkward thing if she does not appear after all. I hope Aunt Jennie will bring her to reason."

"I hope so too, I'm sure," answered the wife with a sigh; "but Lancy Gurney is as much interested in the matter as herself, and I believe he would make her change her mind if anyone could."

"Well, I think I will run in and see if he is at home, but I'm afraid it will make a bad matter worse."

A few minutes later Mr. Sherwood was standing in the parlor next door, shaking hands with Mrs. Gurney.

"We don't seem to meet very often, do we, though we are such near neighbors," she said, with a smile, when the usual greetings had been exchanged, "but you look worried. Are all well at home this morning?"

"We are all well disturbed, certainly," he answered, with a short laugh. "I have just come in to see if I could get someone to help me about Dexie."

"Why? what has happened her? She is not hurt, I hope!"

"Well, her feelings are, tremendously, I can tell you;" and pulling out the objectionable handbill from his pocket, added, "she came upon this down in some store, and has come home as mad as a hatter, declaring she has been insulted, and she vows she won't whistle or go near the concert at all tonight."

"Well, that *would* be rather serious, wouldn't it?" was the mild reply. "Poor girlie, so she don't like to be called the 'American warbler.' It is the publicity of it, I expect, that has hurt her. Where is she now?"

"Up in her room, crying her eyes out. The more we try to reason with her, the worse she is; even Aunt Jennie has failed to quiet her."

"Now if you will let me advise—you know I have more experience with rebellious children than most women," and she smiled up into the anxious face above her, "let her have her cry out, and say no more to her about it just now, and, if you care to turn her over to us, I think I can promise you she will be all right by and by."

"Do you mean that you are willing to take her off our hands for the day?" and he looked eagerly into her face.

"Yes, if we may. I will send one of the children in to ask her to dinner, and we will not let her suspect that we know anything about it until she speaks of the matter herself. We will find something pleasant to take up her attention until Lancy comes home, and by that time she will have had time to think of the matter in a different light."

"But do you think she will consent to whistle after all, Mrs. Gurney? That is the main thing."

"Certainly; I have no fear. If the matter is put before her in a serious light, she will be sure to do what is honorable. Of course, I quite understand that until her temper cools off she will be immovable; those determined natures always are. I have brought up one hot-headed person, and I think I know the weak spot; and Hugh McNeil was never *quite* unmanageable. Do not fret about Dexie, I feel sure she will fulfil her part tonight, and do us all credit."

"Thanks, Mrs. Gurney. You cannot think what a relief it is to hear you speak so confidently about it. I should feel very much aggrieved if she persisted in her refusal, for I urged her to whistle, much against her will, and I feel responsible for her appearance. I think, myself, that it was not just the fair thing to send those handbills broadcast without making her acquainted with the contents beforehand."

"Yes, they might have consulted her; but, of course, it never occurred to them that she would feel offended, and really I wonder that she is myself. Still, I can quite understand it when I consider how uncertain she must feel about her reception as a whistler."

"Yes, that is the trouble, but she went out on purpose to buy some little things to wear tonight, and I would like to know if she has everything ready. But I daresay it will not be wise to refer to the matter while she is of the same mind. Yet I want her to look as well as the rest of them," said Mr. Sherwood, in an anxious tone.

"To be sure. Well, her dress must be prepared for her. It would be a great disappointment to Lancy if anything should happen to prevent her going; so we must unite our efforts and carry the day, in spite of this little freak of Dexie's. Now, I expect my girls know what Dexie's plans were for tonight; and as my dressmaker is here finishing Cora's dress, I will have her attend to Dexie's also; so let Gussie bring in what materials she purchased while out this morning, and we will hold a consultation on the matter. Now, do not be alarmed, Mr. Sherwood," she added, seeing his look of concern. "I will promise to send her to the concert in good trim, and in good temper too," and she smiled pleasantly as she bade him "Good morning," as if it were an everyday affair to bring refractory girls to terms.

CHAPTER XV.

Mr. Sherwood returned home feeling much relieved, and meeting Aunt Jennie on the stairs, asked after Dexie's present condition.

"She is crying still, though not so violently. I fear she has fully determined not to take part in the concert tonight. I have done my best, but I cannot shake her determination, so I have left her to herself to think it over."

"That's right. I have just been in to Mrs. Gurney's, and she has offered to settle the difficulty and be responsible for her appearance tonight."

"That is good news, indeed. I have perfect trust in Mrs. Gurney's ability to succeed where the rest of us all fail; but the next trouble is, I haven't the least idea what Dexie intended to do with the yards of lace she brought home this morning, unless she intends to drape it over her dress in some way."

"Mrs. Gurney has promised to relieve us of that trouble also. She is quite as anxious as we are that Dexie shall make a good appearance, and if you will collect the fixings and take them in, Mrs. Gurney says her dressmaker will do what is necessary."

"Then the trouble may be considered over," said she, with a relieved sigh.

"I will run into Mrs. Gurney's myself, and see what I can do for the general good. How nice it is to have *real* friends so near!" she added, as she followed Mr. Sherwood into the sitting-room.

In about half an hour, Elsie Gurney came running into the house, and as she came through the hall called, "Dexie, Dexie, where are you?"

Aunt Jennie opened the door, saying: "She is up in her room, Elsie; run right up."

Dexie heard the call, and, hastily rising, poured some cold water into the basin, and began to bathe her face. Her head was bent over the basin when Elsie entered the room.

"Oh, here you are! What on earth are you poking up here for at this time of day?" was the matter-of-fact greeting. "You are to hurry up and come into our house and stay to dinner. Mother said you are allowed, so you needn't stop to ask permission; and, just think, the box that grandma sent from England has arrived, and it is full of all kinds of finery. You know we always have a box sent us at Christmas time, but this one was delayed somehow," and she looked curiously at the flushed face that was buried in the brimming hands. "There is always something for everyone of us in the box; but do hurry, Dexie, your face isn't so dirty that it needs soaking, I hope."

"Well, hardly," was the reply, thankful enough to be given so much time to recover her composure; "but I may as well tell you before you find it out yourself that I have had a bad attack of the pouts, and the effect is not so easy to get rid of. Now, you needn't ask what's up, for I don't intend to tell you."

"Pshaw! who cares about your pouts? Not I, anyway," was the reply, in a high and mighty tone. "Come along, if you're coming, and if you're not, then stay home. I can't wait, for I want to see what is in the box for me."

This unceremonious manner of treatment made Dexie come down somewhat from the pedestal of injured greatness, and she forced herself to talk to Elsie to keep her waiting, while she made a fresh toilet.

"Now, do I look a fright?" Dexie asked, as she prepared to follow Elsie downstairs.

"Well, I can't say that you look much worse than usual, but you certainly don't look any better. Your nose looks swelled. Shouldn't wonder if you had it tweaked; but, then, what odds how it looks? Hurry up, and come along. We have apple dumplings for dinner today. Do you like milk or sauce on them best?"

Dexie did not answer; something of more consequence than dumplings was troubling her just then, and as she followed Elsie into the front hall, she was tenderly feeling her nose and mentally comparing it with its usual proportions, inwardly calling herself all sorts of hard names for being so silly.

"But I won't whistle tonight, so there!" she kept saying to herself, as if she needed to keep her determination constantly before herself in order to back it up.

Elsie rushed up the stairs at once, eager to enjoy the delights that an English box always contained; but for once Dexie's interest was centred in herself. Her nose could not be forgotten; in fact, she was trying to reduce its proportions by pressing it between her thumb and finger. She wondered if the rest of the family would notice it and make remarks thereon. Lancy would be sure to know at once that something was wrong; but she would keep out of sight, for she would *not* whistle; no, indeed.

"Oh, Dexie, how you do poke along!" Elsie remarked from the top of the stairs. "I declare, you are enough to try the patience of a Job. Come along, or I'll rush into the room first, manners or no manners; then mother will be displeased."

Dexie was up the few remaining steps before Elsie had finished speaking. She was just as anxious to see the English presents as if half of them were meant for herself. Her swelled nose was instantly forgotten, and she passed through the door that Elsie held open for her, and was soon bending over the treasures with the rest. The room was soon in confusion, as dress patterns, laces, ribbons, gloves and fans, and trinkets in endless variety were strewn over bed, table and chairs. The swelled nose could not hide the beautiful things laid out for her admiring eyes, and she watched with smiling face as Elsie adorned herself with finery without regard to number or suitability.

"Oh, what a fine Indian brave am I!" sang Elsie as she danced before the mirror, her arms adorned with three sets of bracelets, and her neck encircled with ribbons and lace, while several lockets and charms attached to velvet bands added to her glory. "Now, with a few of those ostrich tips in my hair, I shall be ready to start for the Governor's ball," she added, dancing around the room, sending the ribbons and laces gaily fluttering behind her.

"You'll bawl at home, my lady, if you spoil anything with your capers," said Cora. "Take off those things at once, Elsie; some of them are mine, I know. Oh! here is a note, mother. The coral set belongs to Elsie, and is presented by her godmother, and this bangled set is mine. Do you think they would be too showy to wear tonight, mother?"

"Oh! what is this beautiful thing?" Dexie exclaimed, as she lifted a handsome lace bertha. "My! isn't it lovely? How do I look in borrowed feathers—or laces, to be more exact?"

"Oh, fine!" Elsie replied. "I wonder who it was sent to—not me, I hope; it would make me look like a fright, while it makes you look like a fairy," and Elsie turned to examine another parcel.

But Cora had decided in her own mind who it was that should be the first to wear the pretty lace affair, for as she looked at Dexie with the fluffy thing around her neck and throat, she seemed to suggest the very character she was to fill in the evening, and, as she removed it and laid it gently aside, Cora whispered to her mother:

"It will suit her nicely, don't you think? What else would do to go with it?"

"Those ribbons and gloves match it perfectly; they were meant to go together, I expect, for an evening costume. Just see what she takes a fancy to, and lay it aside; then use your own judgment."

A little scream of delight from Elsie betokened another pleasant discovery.

"Gloves! boxes of gloves, and handkerchiefs by the set, and all hemmed, too! Oh! and marked; see, these are my initials. Blessings on the thoughtful person who sent me those, for my handkerchiefs disappear as mysteriously as ghosts. Now, if I only unearth a box of shoe-laces, I'll think my cup of joy quite full."

"Shoe-laces! and they so cheap!" Dexie exclaimed in surprise.

"But I have to buy mine with my pocket-money. I break so many of the tiresome things, that mother thinks it will make me more careful if I have to replace them myself. But they are always in knots, and when I have to keep them neat and tidy at my own expense it leaves me little enough for chocolate creams. Dear me! I think they might have sent me a few dozen, so that I might get a chance to have one good 'tuck in' for once, as the street arabs say."

"Why, Elsie, I am surprised at you," was the mother's mild rebuke. "Surely you can feel grateful, without requiring shoe-laces to 'fill up your cup with joy,'" and there was a faint smile around the mouth that reproved in such quiet tones.

"Ah! I know what ails me, mother dear. 'From all selfishness, envy, uncharitableness,—and all the rest of it, good Lord, deliver me.' I'll say it next Sunday with a different meaning to it, particularly if I get the shoe-laces."

"Why, Elsie Gurney! how dare you speak those words so flippantly!" said Cora severely, looking at her sister in surprise and displeasure.

"I wasn't *thinking* flippantly, if I did speak so. I wasn't, truly, mamma," said Elsie, in a contrite tone. "I never thought I was selfish and—and all the other things when I said it over in church, but I do believe I am—some—anyway. After this I will say 'deliver me' instead of 'us.'"

"Hasty speeches often lead to thoughtful acts. I will be very glad if the missing shoe-laces make my daughter a little more thoughtful about things of greater moment. Do not look so shocked, Cora; it did not *sound* well, I know, but she did not mean it irreverently, I'm sure. I remember when I was a child at home we all had to learn the fifty-first Psalm as a Lenten lesson, and once my little brother came through the rooms, singing it to the most rollicking tune that was ever danced by; but the very contrast between words and tune made the words sink into my heart as nothing else could have done, for I did not learn very readily. Of course, dear, I do not approve of it; but children are children, and the longer they remain so the better, I think," and with a little sigh Mrs. Gurney left the room, laying her hand lovingly on Elsie's head as she passed her.

More than an hour passed before the contents of the box had been examined, then with Dexie's assistance the wrappings which covered the floor were picked up, tables were tidied, and the room put in order.

Mrs. Gurney drew Lancy aside as soon as he entered the house, to explain the difficulty about Dexie.

"What! Not whistle or go near us!" he cried. "Why, she'll have to! Everybody is talking about the concert, and inquiring about our 'warbler.' Those handbills were the greatest success. Not whistle, indeed, when the crowd will be there on purpose to hear her. Why, mother, she is the chief attraction! Where is she? I'll show her very soon that she *can't* back out. They would mob us if she failed to appear. Why, I couldn't go either if she did not."

"Softly, softly, my son," laying her hand on his arm. "Wait a moment till I explain further. Dexie is not one to be forced into doing a thing she does not like, and if you talk to her in that strain you will only strengthen her determination to stay at home. She must be treated differently if we would gain her full consent, and nothing short of that will do. I have watched her face, and I know that unless quiet measures are used she will resist to the last. My boy, I am quite as anxious as you are about it, so do not look so wild. Listen to my plan."

Lancy's excitement cooled down as he listened to his mother's advice, and he promised to do his part if sufficient self-control were granted him.

CHAPTER XVI.

When they met around the dinner-table Lancy was strangely silent, though his eyes shone with suppressed feeling, and Dexie began to hope that the subject of the concert would not be broached; but her hopes were rudely shattered as Mr. Gurney turned his smiling face and said:

"So you have honored us with your company today, Miss Dexie. Are you aware, wife, that our young neighbor has found a place in the hearts of the public, though her identity is hidden as yet under the sweet sounding title of 'American Warbler?' Every one is asking, 'Who is it?'"

Some commonplace remark from Mrs. Gurney, followed by a warning look, caused the subject to be suddenly changed, and in the conversation that followed, the angry flush faded from Dexie's cheeks, the firm shut mouth relaxed; but the workings of her mind were not quite hidden from the motherly eyes that watched her so closely.

Dexie was fully determined not to go to the concert, yet she would not have cared to confess it to those around her, knowing how shocked they would be at such a resolution. Somehow the matter looked different while she was among them as one of the family. She was sure that the high sense of honor that prevailed among the Gurneys would be sufficient to make any of them fulfil a promise once made, even at a great sacrifice to themselves.

But she would not. No! not if they despised her for it! She would not put up with that impudent advertisement, and she laid down her knife and fork quite suddenly, and clasped her hands in her lap in that close grasp that always told when her feelings were stirred.

Mrs. Gurney watched the expressive face, and returned Lancy's look with one of sympathy.

"Lancy is going to drive to the Four-Mile House this afternoon, Dexie," said Mrs. Gurney. "Would you like to go with him?"

"Oh, yes, indeed," was the quick reply, delighted to escape further questioning.

"Then he will have the sleigh ready as soon as you are. Be sure and wrap up your mouth and throat. It never do to catch cold, you know."

Dexie lifted her eyes for one brief moment to the smiling face of the little mother. The reference to her throat brought back the troublesome resolution that would not stay resolved, try as she would. She longed to throw herself at her feet and confess the whole hateful story, but she dared not. That resolution would fall to pieces like a house of cards, if once the story were told to Mrs. Gurney. But she hated herself for the deceit she was practising. How would it end?

As Lancy drove round to the front door Cora ran out and whispered:

"Don't speak hastily to her, Lancy. Remember how much depends on the way you put it. But be sure and get her full consent."

"What time am I to bring her home?"

"As early as possible; if she has not consented by four o'clock, bring her home to mother. You know we have to dress and have tea."

"And what about Dexie's fine feathers?"

"Only get her consent to go, and we will make a perfect fairy of her. Grandma's box just came in time."

Just then Dexie appeared, and was quickly tucked under the robes.

"Wish us good luck, or fling a slipper, do, Cora, for we are going to elope!" Dexie laughingly exclaimed.

"Good luck, then, and with all my heart I wish it; but slippers are costly, and mine are new," was the laughing reply.

"What happy fortune takes you out of town this afternoon, Lancy?" said Dexie, a few minutes later. "Make it forty miles, instead of four, if you wish to earn my everlasting gratitude."

"Any other day, Dexie, I would feel like taking you at your word," and a look full of meaning flashed from his eyes, which she understood.

By and by they passed a fence that was covered with posters, and in the most conspicuous place Dexie saw the obnoxious handbills with their great, staring letters.

"Did you see that?" and Dexie flushed angrily, as she pointed at the announcement.

"Why, yes! and everybody is coming to the hall to hear you tonight."

"Are they, indeed!" drawing her head back stiffly. "Then they might save themselves the trouble, for they won't hear me."

"Dexie, you are not in earnest!" and Lancy tried to repress the hot words that rose to his lips. "You surely would not refuse to whistle after giving your word, and the posters all over the city?"

"Why was I not consulted about the announcement, if I am of so much importance? Who was it that dared to use my name in such a manner? If you know, you can go and tell them that I resent the insult, and will not appear before an audience under such a nickname!"

"Some people would think the title very complimentary, Dexie."

"Those who do can earn the title and enjoy the compliment, then, for it won't be me," was the firm and angry reply.

"Dexie, I can't think you mean all your words imply. If you knew how highly Mr. Ross speaks of your whistling, you would know that he would be the last one to offend you. Indeed, he is so assured that your performance will be the chief part of the concert that he gave it the special mention that has offended you, and he has gone to the expense of fitting up the hall away beyond anything ever seen in Halifax. He is so lifted up you would think he was walking on air."

"He will find solid ground under his feet about eight o'clock this evening, I fancy! for he will find that his 'warbler' has flown to parts unknown."

"Is it possible, Dexie, that you have it in your heart to so disappoint the members of the club, and the public as well? As for the name he has given you, what matters it? I have been called 'The Dandy' for years, but I have as much respect from my friends as if the term were complimentary. Dexie, I can't think you intend to go back on your word."

"Dexie felt the reproach, but would not relent.

"Mr. Ross had no right to announce my part of the performance at all; it was only as a favor I consented to whistle. If I am his 'drawing-card,' it was only fair to consult me about publishing the fact. I feel positive that, after such an announcement, I will be hissed off the stage before I utter a dozen notes. Who ever heard of a girl whistling in public before? It is considered vulgar enough if she is caught at it in private! I cannot face them, Lancy; I truly cannot."

"If it is your reception you are afraid of, Dexie, then set your mind at rest. Even the rougher element would as soon think of hissing a canary."

"But you forget, Lancy, that to be the first to appear in a part so unusual is of itself a risky thing. Had it not been announced I would not mind it so much, as it would be unexpected by the audience, and the very audacity of it would have won to my side the rougher element. As it is, the audience will expect something beyond my power to give them."

"Looking at it in that way, I admit that the announcement was a mistake, Dexie, since it has made you apprehensive of your power to charm; but no one else doubts it, dear, and I feel sure that my Dexie will not put her friends in the embarrassing position that would arise if she purposely stayed away from the concert tonight. I grant that the announcement was a mistake, as you look at it, and that it was very thoughtless of those who got it up to send it to press without submitting it to your inspection; but having done so, and sold hundreds of tickets on the strength of the announcement, common honesty should make you fulfil your part. If your absence only affected the members of the club, it would not matter so much, but hundreds of outsiders would blame the club for obtaining money under false pretences; so you see, Dexie, you really cannot stay home. Do be reasonable, darling."

A deep blush tinged Dexie's cheeks, brought there by something else than the frosty air, and for a few minutes there was silence between them.

Meanwhile, Mr. Sherwood had started out for a walk in order to quiet the anxiety that filled his mind, and meeting Mr. Ross down by the Grand Parade he astonished the man by telling him of Dexie's determination.

"But, Mr. Sherwood, she *must* come," he cried aghast. "Her performance has been announced and is the talk of the city."

"Can't help it, Mr. Ross. I am extremely sorry, but it was that very announcement that has caused the trouble. She says you have insulted her, and she has cried and scolded ever since she set eyes on it."

"Yet I expected the reverse. What's to be done?"

The question was as helpless as the man's face was hopeless.

"Well, I can't say. I can use my authority and insist on her going to the hall, but you know the old saying, 'You can drive a horse to water, but you can't make him drink.' It was only this morning that she came across a handbill, and she flew home in such a temper that it put the whole house in an uproar. I can truly say it has quite upset me, for I was anxious to have her do her best tonight."

"But if I go and apologize, and assure her of my unwillingness to cause her a moment's annoyance, surely I might make amends for my unintentional mistake. I will do anything, everything, Mr. Sherwood, that you can suggest."

"Believe me, Mr. Ross, everything possible has been already done to make her see that you had no intention of 'insulting' her, and we have had to pass her over to our next-door neighbors. If they fail, you can try your persuasive powers. She is out driving with young Gurney just now, and we are simply living on our hopes."

"I trust he will succeed. I would hardly dare to face the people tonight without her. Come and see how well the hall looks while we await her return; then I must see her and explain."

"Better not, Mr. Ross, unless you have some other excuse for calling. If young Gurney gets her to change her mind, you had better make your peace with her after the concert is over, instead of risking it beforehand."

"Very true; but I might call with a bouquet for both of your daughters, and I need not refer to the matter if her consent has been already secured."

"Such an errand would seem natural and should do much towards earning forgiveness," was the smiling reply.

A revolution was going on in Dexie's mind as the sleigh flew over the level road, and Lancy watched the varying expressions, for he had learned to read her face like an open book. Checking the speed of his horse, he turned to her and asked if she felt the least cold.

"Not at all, Lancy; the air is just frosty enough to make it enjoyable."

"The roads are somewhat better than they were last winter when I took you out in the storm. Will you ever forget it, Dexie?"

"I am never allowed to, it seems; but I wish I could drop that twenty-four hours out of my memory,"—annoyed that Lancy referred to the time that was associated with his declaration of love. "I wish you would forget that unfortunate drive and all connected with it. It is no pleasure to remember how near we came to freezing to death," she added.

"Well, Dexie, if you will only look at that side of it, why not repay me for the trouble I took for you that night, and do me a favor in return?"

"If any favor I can do will forever relieve me of any obligation I may be under, you have only to name it," said she coolly, "providing the favor is within reason, though."

"No, I'll not ask it, nor put it that way; not for all the concerts that will ever be held!" he hotly answered. "But, Dexie," and his voice grew tender again, "if the same motive would move you to grant me this favor that impelled me to save you that night, you would make me very happy."

"And this favor, Lancy?"

"Remove the anxiety you have caused us all, and overlook what has vexed you, and come with me to the concert. You know I can't go without you, and our absence will spoil it. My wilful Dexie, don't you think you were rather hasty in your judgment this morning?"

"My judgment don't amount to much when once my temper is up, as you know very well, Lancy; but I'll acknowledge that I do feel rather ashamed of myself, for making such a fuss, though I still think it was a shabby trick to advertise me that way."

"So it was, Dexie; but will you make one shabby trick the excuse for a second? You will take back your refusal, my Dexie?"

"Well, Lancy, perhaps I would, if it were not too late; but it is too late to repent now, for my dress isn't ready, and there are endless other matters to see to that would have kept me busy the whole day, so my repentance will do no good. In fact I haven't the faintest idea what I did with the purchases I made this morning, unless I flung them into the street as I rushed along. What a fright I must have looked! But I don't believe I met a soul that knew me; that's one comfort, anyway."

"Then you would whistle tonight if only your dress were ready?"

"Well, I hate awfully to say it, Lancy, but I do believe I would, for I did not think that my absence would spoil your part of the performance when I spoke so decidedly."

"Then we will consider the matter settled, for your dress will be ready when it is time to put it on," and a look of relief spread over his face. "Mother said she would see about it if you would only go."

"Oh, dear! Does your mother know how silly I have been? Who could have told her?"

"Never mind, Dexie. She knows you won't come back as naughty as you went out. She felt sure of that."

"Lancelot Gurney! Did you take me out on purpose—on purpose to make me change my mind? Well, well! how eagerly I ran into the trap that was set to catch me," and a smothered laugh rang out on the frosty air.

"All's well that ends well, you know. Your father was in despair when your Aunt Jennie could not manage you, so he turned you over to us. Since I have proved myself so capable, that ought to speak well for me in the future, eh, Dexie?" and he smiled mischievously into her eyes. "But I'm not quite sure of you yet, Dexie. Give me your word that you will whistle tonight—honor bright, mind."

"Yes, *honor bright*, Lancy. I'll whistle, or try to, if they don't hiss me when I begin. Now, turn back, and let us get home as quickly as possible; there will be a lot of humble pie waiting for me. I may as well eat it and have it done with. I feel worse to meet your mother than all the rest."

"You forget that I have an errand at the Four-Mile House. That will give us a chance to get warmed, and then for a wild drive home."

When they arrived at the hotel they were glad to find the parlor vacant, for they could monopolize the fire that burned so brightly in the grate, besides enjoying the liberty of free speech.

"You may as well lay aside your wraps, Dexie, as we will not start for home for half an hour," said Lancy, as he returned from an interview with the landlord.

When the sleigh was again brought to the door, there was a triumphant look in Lancy's face that contrasted well with the rosy cheeks of his companion.

"We will have the wind in our faces going home, Dexie, so be sure and wrap up your mouth and throat. It will never do to spoil your whistle after all. I tell you what, Dexie," he added, as he helped her adjust the fleecy scarf, "I feel myself quite a diplomatist, and I shall claim remuneration for this afternoon's work. Do you know what will square the bill?"

"Possibly I may guess your terms, sir, but I shall claim the usual three months' credit," and a saucy face was lifted to his.

"Not three hours shall I wait," he laughingly replied, as he followed the figure that passed so swiftly from his arms. "I have a good notion to claim 'cash on delivery,'" helping her into the sleigh.

"I fancy you would not find it easy to enforce your claim, sir."

"Don't be too sure of that, my Dexie. I have had too hard an afternoon's work to do it for nothing, and 'kiss number two' would settle the account."

There was no chance for further conversation, for Lancy needed to give his attention to the spirited animal before him. It was generally a "wild drive" when Bob wore the harness, unless he were kept well in check, and to those who hastily took the side of the road as the sleigh flew by, it did indeed look like a "wild drive," for the pace never slacked until the house was reached.

There were many anxious eyes on the lookout for their arrival, as Dexie noted with shame, but she determined to face the matter boldly, and if possible make some amends for the trouble and anxiety she had caused.

The front door of both houses opened simultaneously as the sleigh drove up, Mr. Sherwood appearing at one and Cora at the other, and a hundred questions could not have asked more than the one word which fell from the lips of both—

"Well?"

Dexie sprang out on the sidewalk, and with a wave of her hand in Lancy's direction, answered the question in dramatic tones:

"See! the conquering hero comes!"

That was enough; they all understood her, and Elsie, who was standing on the doorstep, flew into the house where the busy needles were flying, shouting as she ran:

"Yes! she is going! Lancy has managed her! She is all right again!"

"There, save that little comedy till by and by, and come in here," said Mr. Sherwood, smiling, in spite of himself at the way Dexie had announced her surrender.

"Come into our house as soon as you can, Dexie," Cora called after her retreating figure. "We want you for something."

What a feeling of relief her arrival caused! They had scarcely realized how great was the tension until their anxiety was removed. But all seemed to breathe more freely, and the preparations for the concert went briskly on.

Dexie threw off her wraps in the hall, and followed her father into the sitting-room, where Aunt Jennie sat waiting.

"You are back, my dear," was the aunt's quiet greeting.

"Yes, auntie, and ready to eat all the humble pie you have prepared for me."

"I have prepared none, my dear, but I am pleased to see that you are ready and willing to eat some. Your father has passed a miserable time waiting for your appearance."

"Poor papa!" and Dexie threw her arms around his neck. "How horrid I have been, to be sure. Now, lay on the stripes easy, and I'll promise not to do so any more," and she playfully held out her hand.

"You had better not, you little tyrant," drawing her to him. "I believe my hair has turned grey with the anxiety you have caused me."

"Oh, so it has! here is one hair quite grey; yes, actually two of them! I'll show you," and a couple of hairs were withdrawn with a jerk.

"Stop! you torment," catching her by both arms. "Isn't it enough that my hair has turned grey? Must you make me bald as well? I thought Lancy was going to sober you down before he brought you back. I'll have to call him in to finish his job."

"No, I'm going to be good, I really am; so say you are not cross with me any more, then I must run off and see about my dress."

"Well, I'll forgive you this time; but if you cut up any more such capers, I'll hand you over to young Gurney for good."

"But I won't be handed over, you dear old papa," giving him a squeeze that almost choked him. "I will not exchange my papa for the best-looking young gentleman you can find in the city. But, papa! do persuade Gussie to leave my shortcomings alone, for the next few hours at least," she added, in a low tone.

"I will see that she does not annoy you. Now, don't you think you had better go and practise awhile?"

"Couldn't think of it, papa mine!" Then, taking her father's face between her two hands, she looked earnestly into his eyes, saying: "Do you think there is the *least* danger of me breaking down tonight? Do you? Confess the truth, sir!" she laughingly demanded.

"Well, no; I don't think there is."

"Neither do I. Trust your naughty tomboy; she is going to 'eclipse all her former efforts and cover herself with glory.' But, wait you till I see Mr. Ross," and she shook her head. "I will forgive him for *this* night only, and then—well, never mind! How is mamma? Is she very angry with me?" she added, presently.

"Not so much as might be expected. You must let her see you when you are dressed."

"Oh! Aunt Jennie, *did* you see anything of a stray parcel, with some lace and other things inside of it? or have I really tossed it into the street?"

"It is in at Mrs. Gurney's with the rest of your apparel for tonight. I have just finished Gussie's suit, and she is all ready to dress. Gloves and all are waiting upstairs."

"Oh, dear! what shall I do, auntie? I completely forgot the gloves. That abominable handbill turned my brain, I do believe; and I thought I was learning to control my temper! Oh, dear!"

"Don't fret, my dear! The best of us are put out sometimes. But everything has been prepared for you in at Mrs. Gurney's; for Lancy's success rests on your appearance, and they were all anxious on his account as well as your own."

"Well, I suppose I must go in next door and apologize; but I would rather get a switching than see Mrs. Gurney."

Dexie's appearance was heralded by a number of little voices, as she made her way to the sewing-room with heightened color and eyes bright with unshed tears.

"I beg pardon of each one of you, separately and collectively," Dexie began. "I never dreamed that my fit of temper was going to affect both households. You are more than kind, and I have no words to thank you."

"Well, don't do it, then," said Elsie; "save your breath, and run upstairs and see your dress, instead. Come, let me show you the finery."

"Where is your mother? I must see her a moment. How does my nose look now, Elsie?" she added, as they went through the hall.

"It looks as if it ought to be tweaked again, you bad girl! But oh, Dexie! your dress is lovely."

And so thought Dexie herself as she stood by the bed whereon it lay, and she bitterly reproached herself for the anxiety her waywardness had caused.

Tears were in her eyes as Mrs. Gurney came quietly into the room.

"Dear Mrs. Gurney—" She could say no more, but the eloquent eyes told the story quite as well as if it had been spoken by the quivering lips.

"There, my dear! There! never mind. It was only a mistake, and we all make mistakes sometimes; so don't fret any more. See how nicely we have managed. Do you like it, my dear?"

"So very much that I feel I shall never be able to repay you for the trouble"—her eyes still full of tears.

"Oh, yes, you will, I expect payment this very night," and the firm, cool hand was laid lovingly across Dexie's shoulder. "When I hear that you have overlooked the cause of the trouble, and have sung and whistled your very best, and to Lancy's satisfaction—when I have heard this, I will consider the debt well paid," and she bent over and kissed the wet cheeks. "You had better try on the gloves, dear; then see if we have forgotten any one thing."

The face was soon wreathed in smiles. The many things made ready for her use by her dear friends made her realize how much they cared for her, and her girlish heart beat fast as she thought of the triumph she was determined to win, if only to please them.

"We are going to have an early tea, and then we will begin to dress," said Cora, making her appearance in the room. "You must put yourself into my hands tonight, Dexie, so be passive and obedient. We have all set our hearts on your success, Dexie, dear."

"And I will not disappoint you, I promise. I would be a monster of iniquity if I did not do my best, after making so much extra trouble for everybody today."

"Ask Gussie to come in with you for tea, Dexie," said Mrs. Gurney, "and if she will bring in her dress, one can help the other get ready."

"Oh, that will be splendid! But I don't want any tea; we had a nice lunch at the Four-Mile House, and I won't eat anything more till after the concert. So you can leave my share till then," she said with a smile. "What new whim possesses you now, Dexie?" asked Elsie.

"It is not a whim. I am going to put forth my best efforts tonight, and I can whistle better if I do not eat."

"What nonsense! did you ever try it?"

"Not purposely, but I know I can."

"That is right, Dexie; use every means to enable you to appear at your best."

CHAPTER XVII.

Mr. Ross had lingered near the house ever since he had parted from Mr. Sherwood, so anxious was he to hear the decision of his erratic "warbler," and he was much relieved when he saw the sleigh drive up to the door at a much earlier hour than he had dared to hope.

Feeling quite sure that she had reversed her hasty decision, he turned his steps to the nearest conservatory, from which he emerged later on bearing a box which contained what he hoped would prove his "peace-offering."

He was received by Mr. Sherwood, who had observed his approach from the window, and his smiling face told the story before there was time to exchange words thereon.

"Can I see her?" asked Mr. Ross, as he heard of Lancy's success.

"Well, I'm afraid not; she is engaged, I believe. I suppose you wish to hear her rehearse?"

"Yes."

"Well, I'm afraid you will have to be content with the promise that she gave to me, that 'she would do her best.' Depend on it, she will not disappoint any of us tonight. I'll answer for that."

"But I should like so much to see her. I would like to apologize for my unintentional mistake. Will you take this bouquet to her with my compliments, and ask if I may see her for a few moments?"

"She is in Mrs. Gurney's at present," said Mr. Sherwood, "but if you will wait here I will step in and see her; but I do not think it will be wise to insist on an interview. My daughter has a temper of her own, and that announcement has provoked her in a way I never saw equalled, so unless she seems perfectly willing to see you, she should be let alone, until after the concert any way."

Mr. Sherwood was soon in the next hall inquiring for his daughter, and she came down the stairs behind Mrs. Gurney, who also stopped to speak to her next-door neighbor.

"Dexie," said Mr. Sherwood, "Mr. Ross sends his compliments with this bouquet, and wishes to know if you will see him and allow him to explain, or apologize, whichever you choose to call it," and he handed her the fragrant flowers.

Instantly they were flung to the end of the hall, and an angry flush rose in her cheeks as she exclaimed, hotly:

"Tell Mr. Ross that I—"

"Dexie, my dear, your promise," came the quiet words from Mrs. Gurney.

"Oh! do forgive me, this once more, Mrs. Gurney," and Dexie rushed after the ill-used flowers; then, in a changed voice, gave the message:

"Tell Mr. Ross that I appreciate his compliments—oh! highly," and she made a grimace, "also his flowers. They smell nice—what is left of them; but I—oh, papa!—I can't see him. Must I go and hear him talk when the very thought of him makes me angry? Make him go away and leave me. I have promised to do the best I can tonight. What more can he ask?"

"You need not see him unless you choose; I will take him your excuses," and he left the house, and returned to Mr. Ross.

"I have brought her excuses in place of herself, and you must rest content with that, Mr. Ross. I think it will not be best to risk the chance of a second refusal, and but for Mrs. Gurney's interference I would have had to bring it, I fear. Let it pass till some other time and take no notice of any coolness she may show tonight, for that public announcement has cut her deeply."

"I am grieved to hear it, Mr. Sherwood; I will endeavor to atone for it at some future time," and with a few parting words he left the house. Very pretty was the picture that the young girls made, as they fluttered about the rooms helping each other to put the finishing touches to their toilets. Gussie's pink and white complexion looked lovelier than ever when set off with a suit in which pale blue and white lace formed the chief parts. Dexie seemed like a gleam of summer sunshine as she fluttered here and there; her pretty suit had been draped with some gauzy material, that glistened and sparkled as the light fell through its folds. The long sleeves had been replaced by short lace ones, trimmed to match the pretty lace bertha, and the long handsome gloves quite completed her costume.

"There, I believe we are all ready at last," said Dexie, as she picked up her neglected flowers. "Let me fasten this cluster of rosebuds in your belt, Cora, as the finishing touch; then I will make a *boutonniere* for Lancy's coat."

"Why, Dexie, you are spoiling your bouquet!" and Cora seized her hand. "I cannot rob you of your flowers."

"But you will take them as a gift, Cora, since they are so beautiful. It would be a pity not to use them. I do not intend to carry them, for I want no flowers from Mr. Ross."

"But perhaps Mr. Ross will not be pleased if you give your flowers away," said Gussie, holding her own bouquet daintily to her nose.

"I fancy that his pleasure or displeasure will not affect me," and an angry gleam brightened her eyes. "I merely accepted them as a peace-offering which binds me for this night only. If the flowers help to make someone else entrancing, they will fulfil their mission as well as if I carried them."

"Well, if we are all ready let us go down and show ourselves to our private families before we try to charm the eyes and ears of the public," said Cora. "Your parents are in the parlor, Dexie; go and make your best bow, before you put on your wraps; Gussie, do like-wise," and Cora gave a sweeping look over their figures. "Why, Dexie!" she added, "are you not going to wear any jewelry after all?" and she pointed to the case she had opened for Dexie's selection.

"Please, if you don't mind, I would rather not. I feel dressed enough."

"So you are, Dexie," Lancy exclaimed, coming to the door at this moment. "Flashing jewels could not improve you, for you look stunning already. But the horses are waiting in the cold, while you girls are admiring yourselves."

With that they ran down the stairs, all except Dexie, who turned to the dressing-table in search of a pin, and as they left the room Lancy came hastily towards her.

"Oh! is it you, Lancy? I have saved some flowers for you. Shall I pin them on?"

As she did so, Lancy slipped his arm around her, and his admiring eyes confirmed the words that fell from his lips. "You are beautiful tonight, Dexie. You need not fear any audience with those brilliant eyes and cherry lips. You will win all hearts, as you have mine."

Dexie lifted her eyes in surprise, and saw a lover's face very near her own, and before she could retreat he had pressed her to his heart, and kissed her on both cheeks.

"For shame! look!" and she pointed to a mirror where their images were reflected. "What would your mother say to such rudeness, sir?"

"I think she would say, 'Dexie, give Lancy one kiss for his trouble this afternoon.' Don't you think I deserve one, my Dexie?"

But Dexie flew past him and downstairs to the parlor, where her parents and Aunt Jennie were awaiting her.

"How do you like my looks, mamma? Am I not pretty, for once?" she asked.

"If you had behaved as well as you look I would see no cause for complaint," said her mother coolly; "but a 'daw in borrowed feathers' is never a pretty sight."

"But, mamma, I am going to be just as good as I look, for this evening anyway; and I am sure, if my eyesight does not deceive me and my friends do not flatter, that I never looked better, so I'm content," and she left the room to put on her outside garments.

She meekly submitted to the extra wraps that Lancy insisted on placing round her face, and she felt, as she stood beside him, that Lancy's tenderness and love added not a little to her daily happiness, even though she had not just the same regard for him as he professed to have for her.

"I think I'll drive down with Hugh," she said teasingly, as they came down the steps to the street, where both sleighs were waiting.

"But I won't let you," said Lancy quickly. "You are mine for this evening. I have earned that much, surely. I can't spare you to anyone else, my Dexie," and he lifted her in beside himself.

They drove quickly to the hall, and were soon in the dressing-room, among the bevy of young ladies who were to take part in the concert. Gussie's heart was pierced with envy as she noticed how much attention was bestowed on her sister, and she heartily wished that Dexie had kept to her refusal of the morning.

Mr. Ross noticed that his peace-offering was not appreciated, and wisely refrained from further remarks, giving the necessary directions in as few words as possible.

Very gay did the Temperance Hall look that evening, with its walls draped with bunting and its stage decorated with palms and other ornamental plants; and it never held a larger audience than now awaited the opening chorus, while the applause that filled the house at its close seemed to make the rafters ring.

The first selections were admirably performed, and were fully enjoyed by those present, but when that part of the programme was reached in which the "American Warbler" made her first appearance, the enthusiasm reached its height, and found vent in round after round of applause.

Lancy made his appearance first, taking his seat at the piano. This intimated that he was not the "Warbler," and the audience looked around in doubt, as if asking each other what next to expect.

A moment later Dexie appeared, and the sea of expectant faces made her tremble. What if she should fail?

The appearance of this bright young girl, bowing before them, caused a moment's hush to fall upon the people. Was she the "warbler," and what was the character of the performance that was rated so highly? After an exquisitely rendered interlude, Dexie's clear whistle joined the accompaniment, and seemed to hold the listeners spell-bound. At its close a moment of silence followed, but when Lancy rose from the instrument the applause began, and grew louder and more deafening, and Mr. Ross hurried to Dexie's side as she left the stage.

"You must come forward again, Miss Sherwood; that encore is not to be resisted," as the thunderous applause grew in volume.

She took Lancy's arm at last, and stepped forward and bowed her acknowledgement. But that was not enough; nothing but a repetition would satisfy the enthusiastic audience, and when Mr. Ross asked her to give "The Mocking Bird" she felt obliged to consent. Mr. Ross had rightly judged a Halifax audience when he said it would not be content with one performance, and not till the strains from the piano rang through the building, followed by the appearance of Dexie, did the uproar cease.

Lancy played a long interlude to give Dexie time to compose herself, then the first strains of the familiar song floated softly through the hall, and very tender and touching did the words sound as they fell from Lancy's lips, for genuine feeling was behind them. It was like a passage in a love-story, and where is the person that does not enjoy the repetition of some passages, even though they may, at the same time, pronounce them silly and sentimental in the extreme?

Dexie stood near the piano. Her soft, low whistle seemed to come from a distance, then floated nearer and nearer, gaining strength and volume as the song progressed; and when Lancy sang "Listen to the Mocking Bird," the joyous, bewildering notes of the birds she was imitating seemed floating directly overhead, then receded as the next verse was sung, returning fuller and sweeter to accompany the chorus, each verse seeming to grow more tender and beautiful, and, when it ended, the enraptured audience showed their appreciation by applauding with all their strength.

"No; I cannot go out again," Dexie said, as Mr. Ross urged her to appear once more in answer to the call. "It is not fair to the rest, for there are other things on the programme much nicer."

"Just this once more," Lancy pleaded, his eyes shining with satisfaction.

"Come on to the stage, at least, Miss Sherwood," said Mr. Ross, "or they will have the house down over our ears. May I announce that you will whistle again at the conclusion of the programme?" and Dexie had to consent. Mr. Ross led her to the front of the stage, and the audience, expecting another repetition, subsided into silence; but it was soon broken when the announcement was made that they should have another selection later on.

Mr. Sherwood found his way to the dressing-rooms, and received Dexie with open arms, while numbers gathered around to congratulate her on her success.

"I am proud of you, Dexie," her father said, as they stepped aside. "I was down among the audience while you were whistling, and on every side I heard words of warmest praise. Your fear of being hissed was a foolish fear, after all. I am sure you are not sorry that you came here tonight."

"No, papa; but I do hope that Mrs. Gurney will be pleased. I whistled for her and Lancy tonight, and if they are satisfied, that is enough. But, listen! That is Gussie's voice; that is the duet between her and Miss Burns. Oh, I do hope they will applaud her heartily!"

But no such feeling had dwelt in Gussie's heart when Dexie was before the audience. If she had failed, had completely broken down or been hissed off the stage, as Dexie herself feared, Gussie would have exulted in her failure; yet if Gussie had faltered in the least, none would have felt it so keenly as her twin sister Dexie.

"Did you see Hugh among the audience?" Lancy whispered from behind her chair.

"Yes; how savage he looked! Such a scowl does not improve his handsome face, if he only knew it. I never saw him look more fierce."

"I expect that he did not like to see you leaning on my arm before them all," he whispered. "He is fearfully jealous, Dexie, so do not flirt with him any more when he goes in to see Gussie," he added, as he stroked his growing moustache.

"I am not likely to flirt with Hugh McNeil or anyone else," she said, with some spirit; "but judging by the looks cast in this direction,

I am under suspicion already, so please leave me, Lancy."

The several selections on the programme were performed to everyone's satisfaction, but every time that Dexie appeared, either as a singer or accompanist, she was received with such marked favor that it was plainly to be seen who was the favorite.

"Now, Miss Sherwood," said Mr. Ross, as the last piece ended and cries for "the warbler" arose in the hall, "send them home so well pleased with our entertainment that they will all be eager to attend our next."

"There is to be no repetition this time, Mr. Ross," said Dexie, decidedly. "Let Mr. Gurney play the National Anthem directly the piece is ended."

"Very well. I will direct the members of the club to be ready to step forward the moment your piece is finished, and we will dismiss them with 'God Save the Queen.'"

As Lancy and Dexie made their appearance the clapping of hands arose again, and, under cover of the noise, Dexie whispered a few words to Lancy, who immediately secured another piano stool. Then they both sat down before the instrument and waited for the signal to begin.

A moment later and the outburst of melody that filled the hall seemed to come from a multitude of song-birds, and the peculiar, birdlike whistle never sounded sweeter or clearer as it rang out in answer to Lancy's more powerful notes, their fingers meanwhile flying over the keys in delightful harmony. Dexie forgot the hundreds of eager listeners. She seemed to have partaken of the free, joyous nature of the birds she was so cleverly imitating, and when the last notes had died away the applause that greeted their ears seemed to shake the building.

It was a decided relief when the notes from the piano overruled the uproar. A moment later and the stage was peopled by the members of the club, the notes of the National Anthem sounded through the hall, and the audience below rose to their feet at this the closing signal.

As the crowd passed out the door, Hugh McNeil made his way to the front; and as he went at once to help Cora Gurney, and gave Gussie the assistance she asked for, Dexie thought nothing of his sudden appearance amongst them until he bent over her and hissed in her ear:

"I could have killed the both of you as you stood there making love to each other before them all, as if you belonged to him already! You shall be mine, not his! I swear it! so take care how you trifle with me!"

Dexie, terrified by his angry looks, hurried away, and Lancy, noticing her white face, asked anxiously:

"What has happened to you, Dexie? You are as white as a ghost."

"Oh! that big Frenchman has frightened me. Didn't you see him talking to me just now?"

"Yes, but I supposed he was congratulating you on your success."

"It is a pity you could not have heard his congratulations, Lancy. I fancy you would not consider them complimentary," and they hurried homeward.

Mrs. Gurney had arranged a little supper for those of the household who attended the concert, and if anyone noticed Hugh's absence, no one dreamed of the cause thereof.

The skill that was required to keep out of Hugh's way during the weeks that followed, might have raised Dexie to an eminent position if it could have been turned into another channel. Such a sharp lookout lest Hugh might find her alone, such a dodging through doors when his strategy had almost succeeded in bringing her face to face—really it was a marvel how skilfully she avoided him. Yet the fact that she did avoid him gave him a false hope, and he thought if he could once lay his heart before her the battle would be his.

CHAPTER XVIII.

Winter changed into spring slowly yet surely, and the almanac declared that summer was nigh long before people were prepared to accept the assurance.

To Elsie Gurney the spring had been particularly trying, and her mother began to feel anxious as day after day found her lying on a couch, listless and weary. The doctor advised change of scene as the best means to recover health and spirits, and Mrs. Gurney decided at last to accept the kind and repeated invitation of a dear friend living in Charlottetown, and send Elsie thither under Lancy's escort. Mrs. Gurney wrote to her friend explaining Elsie's condition, and the kind letter that came in reply caused preparations to be made at once for the visit.

"My guest chambers are all vacant," wrote Mrs. Fremont, "and my girls are delighted with the prospect of having someone new to the place to show around and gossip with. But, with your houseful, surely you can spare more than two of your family. Remember, I have not seen any of you since we came to Charlottetown, so be generous. Launcelot must not think of returning for some weeks, and he must come prepared to see a deal of service, for my girls have already planned drives and picnics that he must lead to success, for Huburt has not yet returned from abroad, and an elder brother is sadly missed in these little pleasure-parties. Elsie shall have the best of care, and I feel safe in promising that when she returns home all trace of her illness will be dispelled."

But Elsie shrank from this visit and begged to be allowed to stay at home. She was naturally shy and reserved, and to go among new faces, and into strange places, and be expected to take part in the pleasures that were being prepared, oh! this was worse than being ill at home, for then her own dear ones would be near her.

But the visit, like the big doses of medicine that the doctor ordered, had to be taken, whether she liked it or not, and the preparations went on, though it grieved her mother to see how Elsie shrank from the visit.

One day when Elsie was crying about her "banishment from home," Dexie Sherwood came into the room, and learning the cause of Elsie's tears she frankly stated her mind as follows:

"Well, if you are not a baby, then I never saw one! The idea of you lying there crying until your eyes are red and swollen because you are going off on a fine cruise! I declare! if I thought I should be treated half so well, I'd fall sick this very day, and you may be sure I would select some complaint that required a change of scene to restore me," and, assuming an expression of extreme woe, she added:

"Your kind friend in Charlottetown didn't say that any sick neighbor might join you, I suppose? for, ah me! I am beginning to feel awfully bad already. Where, oh! where can I go to regain my shattered health?"

Elsie's tears of grief changed to tears of laughter, and she replied,

"Well, I suppose it does look silly for me to be fretting because I have to go away, but I hate to go among strange people. If Cora could come with me I would not mind it at all."

"But Lancy is going with you," said Dexie, "so you cannot come to any great harm. The people over there are quite civilized, I'm told, so they won't likely eat you; not till you get a little more flesh on your bones, anyway."

Mrs. Gurney, who was in the room, lifted her eyes to Dexie's animated face, and said in her gentle, motherly tone,

"Dexie, my dear, why couldn't *you* go with Elsie? I was stupid not to have thought of it before."

"For my health, do you mean, Mother Gurney? But I am afraid I have recovered it already. I have made Elsie laugh, and the unusual sound has cured me like a charm."

"Well, not exactly for *your* health, my dear, but for Elsie's," she replied, as she looked into the laughing face before her. "When I think of the double benefit your companionship would be to her, I wonder that the thought did not occur to me before."

"Oh! Mrs. Gurney, I feel so ashamed," and Dexie covered her hot cheeks for a moment with her hands. "I never intended to suggest such a thing when I made such a thoughtless remark. Oh! what can you think of me! Indeed I only said it to make Elsie laugh."

"There, there; of course I understood your bit of fun," and Mrs. Gurney patted the blushing girl on her shoulder, "but when a suggestion made in sport brings such a change in Elsie's looks, how much good would result if the jest were turned to earnest."

"But imagine me going to Mrs. Fremont's when she is not aware of my existence! I couldn't pass myself off as Cora, for I am too unlike any of the family. Indeed, I fear my wickedness would soon betray me," her embarrassment giving place to a mischievous air.

"If I write and introduce you, you can feel as sure of as hearty a welcome as if you were one of my family. But we must not make plans till we consult your parents," said Mrs. Gurney, turning to leave the room.

"Oh! Dexie, if you only *would* come with me, it would make all the difference in the world," said Elsie. "A weight seems lifted off my heart at the thought."

"Yes, but look at all the nice dresses you are getting made. You would find me a very shabby companion, for I never dare ask mamma for a new dress unless Gussie is in need of one also; but now that papa is home I might manage that difficulty, and I am quite sure of Aunt Jennie's help."

Mrs. Gurney was soon discussing the matter with the parents next door, making much of the great favor it would be to herself if they would spare Dexie to accompany Elsie to Charlottetown. Consent was readily granted, though Mrs. Sherwood could not refrain from expressing a fear that the necessary preparations would be rather troublesome, as she did not feel able to make any extra exertion herself.

Mrs. Sherwood was quite an invalid, or at least she thought she was, which amounted to about the same thing. Necessity did not compel her to bestir herself very much, so she began to think she *could* not, and she was generally found lying on a sofa with a book as companion.

Dexie's absence from home would be rather a pleasant relief than otherwise, as she had an unpleasant way of finding unfinished work and laying it in a work-basket by her mother's side for completion. Dexie's brisk ways and ceaseless activity were extremely annoying, as it seemed a continual reproach to Mrs. Sherwood, who preferred the easy, languid movements of her twin sister.

No one raised any objections to Mrs. Gurney's plans except Gussie, and her objections were many and loudly expressed.

It was shameful of Dexie to thrust herself into the Gurney family as she was doing. Anyone could see that it was more on Lancy's account than Elsie's that Dexie was so delighted to accompany them. Why didn't she go and live with them at once? She might as well, seeing that so much of her sewing was being prepared in Mrs. Gurney's sewing-room.

This, and pages more, was reiterated daily, till Dexie would snatch up her work and run to her aunt's room, and she was heartily glad when the time came to leave Gussie and her unkind words behind her.

Yet it was not only on Gussie's account that she felt so glad to be off, for, when Hugh McNeil heard of her intended departure, he added his persecutions also. At first, when he learned that Lancy was to accompany Elsie, his heart beat high with hope. Dexie would be free from Lancy's influence, and he hoped much from a few weeks of uninterrupted intercourse. His passion for Dexie had grown as the weeks went by, and when the one obstacle, Lancy, was removed, all would be well. His visits to the Sherwoods were more frequent than ever, and he openly showed his preference for Dexie's society.

But Gussie had no other admirer just then, and she accepted the attentions meant for her sister as if they were her own just due. This was so exasperating to Hugh that, when Dexie turned away from him, he would take his hat and leave abruptly. This strange behavior Gussie set down to everything except the true cause, for she did not dream that Hugh's affections had been transferred to her sister, for Dexie openly snubbed him.

But, when Hugh learned that Dexie was preparing to accompany the others, he was almost beside himself with rage. He refused at first to believe it—the idea was too preposterous! Well it was that the announcement was not made to him before the assembled household, for his face revealed the fierce conflict within, and he had quite as many objections to make as Gussie, though they were not so openly and freely expressed. Chancing to meet Dexie in the hall, after repeated efforts to catch her alone, his bitter disappointment was so touchingly expressed that, for the first time, Dexie felt a sort of pity for the man, though she could not understand the intense feeling that seemed to possess him.

"Promise me five minutes alone! only five minutes!" he begged, as Dexie tried to pass him. "You will surely grant me that small favor before you go! I must speak to you, Dexie, even if you refuse me a private interview."

"I have no right to grant even 'five minutes' interview' to my sister's lover," was the cool reply. "You can have nothing to say to me that might not be said before the whole family."

"Am I your sister's lover? You know better, Dexie! I have been blinded by her pretty face, but my eyesight has returned to me. I want something more than beauty in my future wife," and he tried to catch her hand.

But Dexie was too quick for this movement, and she hotly replied:

"And I hope you may get it! May she be blessed with a temper hot enough to make even a Frenchman tire of dancing to the music of her tongue!" and with this retort she flew past him, and the door slammed behind her.

Hugh stood for a moment and gazed after her; then, turning on his heel, pulled the ends of his long moustache into his mouth as he muttered to himself:

"Not so bad, my little girl! The hot temper is there fast enough, but it won't make me dance, unless it will be for joy at getting the owner of it."

This happened just the day before they started on their journey, and, through the hours of that busy day, Dexie kept wondering what Hugh wished to tell her. Should she see him and be done with it? No; for his earnest looks and half spoken words told all too plainly the nature of the interview. Dexie never could explain, even to herself, why she disliked Hugh so much; but his very presence seemed to raise up all the opposition there was within her. To a stranger, he would have seemed more attractive than Lancy Gurney. His figure had attained to manly proportions, and his manner had a charm that was quite pleasing. His dark, handsome face and brilliant black eyes seemed to tell of southern birth; and the heavy, upward-curling moustache added much to his attractions. Dexie had looked upon him with favorable eyes when she first came to Halifax. He had formed a striking contrast to Gussie's fair beauty, but the memory of his handsome face was far from pleasant as Dexie thought of the words he had spoken to her in the hall.

Yet Hugh succeeded after all, and the five minutes he asked for thrice repeated themselves before Dexie could escape from his presence.

The back of the house, or ell, which formed the kitchen, was a story less in height than the main building, and its flat roof was often utilized by both families as a drying-ground for small articles of clothing, and Dexie had stepped out of the window that overlooked this roof to bring in some forgotten articles that hung on the line.

It had been very warm all day, and as Dexie stood a minute, enjoying the cool breeze that blew in from the harbor, her figure was distinctly outlined to observers from the rear of the house; but her presence might have escaped notice, had she not been softly whistling some little song.

Hugh had just returned from the depot, where he had taken the luggage which was to accompany the young travellers in the morning, and his heart was full of bitter feelings as he thought of his master's son filling the place he coveted so dearly.

As he passed into the yard, Dexie's soft whistle reached his ears. He was too well acquainted with the sound not to recognize the source of it, and, glancing up, he saw her there in the twilight, the breeze gently lifting her wavy hair and fluttering the ribbons around her neck, as if endeavoring to attract his attention. One glance was enough, and before Dexie knew he had returned from the depot, she was startled by his appearance beside her.

She turned to enter the house, but Hugh had not gained this opportunity merely to let it slip by, so he boldly stepped before her and shut the window, and his exultant face was a strong contrast to the expression depicted on Dexie's.

They stood thus face to face for several moments, silently regarding each other—Hugh flushed with triumph, his eyes glowing with a feeling of victory; Dexie, her heart beating fast in her anger, white and defiant as she regarded her audacious companion.

It was Dexie who broke the silence. In a tone of the utmost contempt she said, as she waved him aside:

"Stand back out of my way and let me pass," and she moved towards the window.

"Not yet, Dexie, just hear me for a moment. I want to speak to you."

"Not a word, sir, let me pass at once! How dare you keep me here against my will!"

His tone of entreaty changed to command.

"Because it is my will that you shall hear me," and his face grew paler as he spoke. "For once you shall listen to what I have to say. I can be silent no longer."

"Well, if you must unburden your mind, talk to the chimney there; it will care quite as much for what you have to say as I. It is quite in keeping with the estimate I had formed for you, to keep me here a prisoner on the house-top. Stand aside at once and let me enter the house."

"Dexie," he said more firmly, "I am not going to let you pass until I tell you what I came here to say. Is it not enough that I am to lose the sight of your bright face for such long, weary weeks, that I must be refused these few moments—moments that I must perforce steal from you if I am to get them at all? Do I need to tell you what a blank my life will be while you are away; and not only a blank, but a fearful dream of blasted hopes and weary longing? Oh, Dexie, take away some of the bitterness that your absence will cause, by giving me, at least, the promise that you will not forget me while you are away."

"Not forget you, indeed!" she said in a rising voice. "I may forgive you this insult, but you may be sure that I will do my best to forget you, just as quickly as I can. I am not given to remembering unpleasant things."

"Dexie, do not talk so bitterly; you do not mean it; say you do not, Dexie?" he said, entreatingly. "You are vexed at being kept here against your will; come, then, let us go inside and talk it over quietly," he added, persuasively, and he reached for her hand.

"But I *do* mean every word of it," and she stepped back out of his reach, "and if you do not wish to hear me express myself more plainly, I'd advise you to open the window at once."

"Hear me a moment, Dexie. I know you are prejudiced against me on account of Gussie; but give me time to prove that I am in earnest when I say that it is you that I love," and her hands were instantly imprisoned in his strong clasp, "and I love you, Dexie, with the intense love that a strong man feels for the one woman who is all the world to him, a love that is not to be compared with the boyish feeling that Lancy Gurney has for you. Give me some hope, Dexie, that sometime in the future, when you have rightly considered the matter, you will look on me with a more kindly feeling in your heart than you are willing to own to tonight."

Dexie freed her hands by a great effort. His words had flowed like a torrent from his lips, and she took a step back from him, as she replied,

"Mr. McNeil, I will *never* regard you in the light you are thinking of, so all this talk is worse than folly."

"Have I spoken too late?" he almost hissed.

His eyes seemed to burn as he looked into her face.

"Have you already promised yourself to Lancy? Tell me!"

"I will not!" came the defiant answer. "You have no right to ask such a question, and I will not answer it!"

Her defiant air and scornful words angered him. He had buoyed himself up with the hope that if he once declared his love she would be touched with the declaration, and, if she did refuse him, would do it in a kindly way that would bid him hope for better luck by and by; but to have his love flung back in his teeth, as it were, was more than his passionate nature could bear.

"Oh! so you love him, do you, and spurn me. Tell me, is it so?"

Again she stepped back from him as he was speaking, and was unaware how very near she was to the edge of the roof; but Hugh observed it, and thinking he could force a confession from her lips through fear, if by no other means, he quickly grasped her arm, saying in a voice trembling with passion:

"Do you love him? Tell me, or I'll throw you over!"

Dexie turned her head, and for one awful moment, as she realized her peril, her face blanched to her very lips; but instead of the answer Hugh expected, she raised her eyes to his, and he quailed beneath their terrible glance, as she cried:

"Throw me over then, you coward, for I'll never tell you!"

An instant they stood thus face to face, on the very edge of the roof, when Hugh's better nature asserted itself, and he quickly drew her back to safety, exclaiming hoarsely:

"Forgive me, Dexie, I never meant to do it, indeed I did not; I would not harm a hair of your dear head for a thousand worlds!"

He felt weak and small before the girl whom he had thought to bend to his will, and made no effort now to keep her from entering the house, but stepped to the window beside her and raised it, endeavoring all the while to get a word of forgiveness from her close-shut lips. She never even turned her head in his direction, but entered the house and into her own room, and Hugh was obliged to descend with a more uncomfortable feeling in his breast than he had felt there when he sought Dexie's presence on the roof. "Baffled, after all," was his silent comment; "a coward, she called me; yes, it was a cowardly thing to do, and I might have known she would resent it. But how handsome she looked as she defied me on the very edge of the roof! I believe she would not have opened her lips and answered that question, even to save her life, after she had once refused to speak! But I'll win her yet, and she will be doubly dear when conquered at last, my brave Dexie!" and with feelings that were only intensified by this interview, he returned to the yard to prepare the carriage for the drive to the depot next morning.

It was some satisfaction to be able to see that everything possible was done for the comfort of his darling, though it was bitterness itself to think of her going away under the escort of Lancy Gurney.

When he re-entered the house, his unusual pallor was quickly noticed by Mrs. Gurney, and she kindly asked:

"Are you very tired, Hugh?"

Without lifting his eyes, he replied:

"No, not tired, but heart-sick."

"What is it, Hugh? What is the trouble?" she asked, in her kind, motherly tone.

"Do not ask me, please! it is nothing that can be remedied, believe me," and he raised his eyes a moment and met her inquiring gaze.

"Well, my boy, you, like the rest of us, I suppose, have just so much pain and trouble to bear in this world. Do not let it bear too heavily on your young heart; all is for the best in the end, you know," and her hand was laid on his shoulder with a sympathetic pressure, as she passed on.

All for the best! when in all the hasty preparations that are of necessity left till the last few hours before a journey, no one even thought of the fierce heart-struggle that was his, or would have cared about it had they known it! There seemed to be no kind word of remembrance for him, amidst the bustle and confusion that reigned around him. He felt as if he stood apart from those who, up to this time, seemed as near to him as kith and kin.

CHAPTER XIX.

Both families were early astir the next morning, but the hour soon arrived that the last "good-byes" must be said, and Mrs. Gurney had reason to be thankful that Dexie was one of the party, otherwise it would have been impossible to have started Elsie on her journey without seeming to be harsh. As it was, Elsie clung to each of the family in turn, as if her journey were to extend to the Cape of Good Hope, and the length of her stay to be indefinite. She was lifted into the carriage at last, her hat pulled back on her head, and her disordered apparel otherwise smoothed out by Dexie, and Hugh was bidden by Mr. Gurney to "drive on quickly," amidst the shrill choruses of "good-byes" from the little ones of the family who had gathered on the steps to see them off. Seeing that Elsie still kept looking back and waving her handkerchief in token of farewell, Mrs. Gurney drew the children into the house, and then went away to her own room, where, for a short time, she remained. When she appeared among them again, her face had regained its usual calm and placid expression. She had left her burden with the Great Burden-bearer, and though her heart would go after her daughter in loving solicitude, she felt that Elsie was in safe-keeping, and so could rest content.

During the drive to the depot, Dexie was all life and animation. She plied Lancy with questions which she gave little chance to answer, until she succeeded in getting Elsie's attention turned to outward things, and as they drove rapidly along the road, they began to speculate whether any of the occupants of the cabs that were going in the same direction were to be fellow-travellers.

Hugh was unusually silent—perhaps it was just as well that he was—but the rest of the party kept up such a stream of talk that his want of speech was not remarked.

His heart was too sore for speech, for Dexie's cold, indifferent look cut deeper than she knew. He had not been able to get a word with her since the unfortunate interview on the roof, but he felt that he *must* have one parting word, and he kept revolving in his mind what he could say that would likely win for him one word of forgiveness for his unguarded words.

But it was not easy to obtain even the smallest speech amidst the bustle and distraction of the moving crowd at the depot. Lancy hurried the girls into the car that they might have a choice of seats, then, leaving them comfortably seated, he left the car to secure their tickets and checks.

Had it not been for the fact that amidst the hurry of gathering up the wraps, etc., from the carriage, they had forgotten that ever-welcome addition to one's travelling paraphernalia, the lunch-basket, Hugh might have been unable to get a word from Dexie beyond the curt "good-bye" that she had already cut and dried, as it were, and ready to fling out the window at him at the last moment.

But Hugh's keen eyes observed the forgotten basket, that had been packed with such care, and seizing it he entered the car, just as Lancy was leaving it at the opposite door.

Lancy had wisely chosen the centre seats as being the most comfortable, and Dexie sat chatting gaily to Elsie lest the home-parting should again come before her mental vision, when she saw Hugh enter the car.

She had just time to compose her face into a look of solemn indifference, when Hugh reached her side.

"You forgot the lunch-basket, Elsie," he said, looking across at Dexie who sat facing her. "You left it in the carriage."

"Oh! so we did," said Elsie. "Whatever should we have done if you had not seen it in time! Wasn't it lucky, Dexie, that he noticed it?"

"Oh! I suppose so," was her indifferent reply, "but we could easily have bought something when we felt hungry. I hope, Elsie, that you do not think we are going into a wilderness where people live on grass roots!" and she coolly leaned back in her seat, rearranged the pretty tie at her throat, then pulled a book from the strap, as if ready for the perusal of it when Hugh would be kind enough to relieve them of his presence.

But Hugh was not to be dismissed by hints. Taking the seat by Elsie's side, and opposite Dexie, he said: "Still, I am sure you would have felt sorry to have forgotten it; you know it is the last home-cooking you will eat for some time, Elsie."

Whereupon Elsie's lip began to quiver, and a suspicion of moisture to appear in her eyes; a word more of home matters would cause the drops to fall into the handkerchief that Elsie was already pulling out of her pocket, in readiness to catch the coming shower. Dexie could have boxed Hugh's ears with a good grace, but she refrained.

"Don't be a goose, Elsie," was her flattering remark. "Just as if no one else in the country could make a decent cake but your Susan! Don't, for goodness' sake, get sentimental over eatables just because Mr. McNeil happens to be struck that way."

The tears forgot to fall, the handkerchief was left in a crumpled heap, hanging half out of her pocket; and as soon as the lump that was in her throat could be disposed of, Elsie ventured meekly to remark that she "was sure Lancy would be late if he did not hurry in."

This recalled Hugh to the fact that unless he made good use of the few remaining minutes, his words to Dexie would be left unsaid; and as Elsie leaned out the window in hopes of seeing Lancy, he bent forward to Dexie, saying in a low voice,

"Say that you forgive me, Dexie, before you go. I was wild with pain at the thought of you leaving me so long with nothing to hope for. I cannot let you go without a word of forgiveness for my hasty words; you know I never meant to do it, Dexie, for I would die to save you from harm."

"Very kind of you, I am sure! but pray do not have any funeral on my account. I feel quite capable of looking after myself, and I hope you will not make it necessary for me to repeat this assertion in the future. Say no more about forgiveness; the occurrence is too recent for that, but I will try to forget it."

"Dexie, do not speak so cruelly. How can I prove that I love you, and that it was the thought of losing you that drove me to madness! You can't believe that I meant to carry out my murderous threat—no! I cannot think it, when my own heart aches with love and longing for you. If I write to you, Dexie, and lay my heart open before you, surely you will believe me!"

"Do not trouble yourself to write, Mr. McNeil," was the scornful reply. "If you have any heart-trouble, you will find me a poor physician, for I have not the slightest interest in your condition."

"Dexie, are you going to leave me with no kinder remembrance of you than those cruel words? I *must* write, Dexie; say that you will answer my letter," and a look of entreaty beamed from the dark eyes raised to her face.

"Couldn't think of it! I am going away to enjoy myself, and am not going to bother writing to every Tom, Dick and Harry, so I'll have to *throw you over*!" and a pair of defiant eyes met his gaze.

Hugh's passionate nature was raised to the utmost, but he choked back the words that rose to his lips, and giving her one long, earnest look, said in a hoarse voice:

"You repeat my words! May you never have a happy moment until you are as sorry for saying them as I am!" and he rose and left the car, meeting Lancy on the steps.

"Well, Hugh, we are away at last," said Lancy, gaily. "Good-bye, old fellow!"

But Hugh merely raised his eyes and hurried past, and before Elsie knew he had left the car she saw him driving furiously down the road, past cabs and trucks, escaping collision as if by a miracle, and the speed never slacked until he had covered more ground than was necessary to take him home.

"What is the matter with Hugh?" said Lancy, as he seated himself beside his sister. "I do think he might keep his temper occasionally. What has gone wrong, now?" and he looked over at Dexie for his answer.

"I fear I am the wicked person that has gone wrong and as his eloquence prevailed not in turning me from my evil ways he feels heart-sick."

"Heart-sick!" cried Elsie, in surprise; "that would not put him in a temper, surely."

"Love-sick, then," said Dexie, with a smile; "that might account for it." "Well," said Elsie, in a tone of disgust, "he must be awfully in love with your Gussie, if he can't leave her long enough to drive us to the depot without pining for her," whereupon Dexie forgot her surroundings and burst into such a rippling laugh that Lancy felt forced to join her. The infection spread to their fellow-travellers, and caused a smile to pass around, although the cause of the merriment was unknown beyond the little group from which it started.

"I fancy I can guess the cause of the trouble," said Lancy. "I daresay Hugh found the parting painful. Am I right?"

Just then the starting-signal sounded, and the train sped away across the country, and our travellers settled down to whatever comfort there is to be obtained in a railroad car.

As soon as Lancy could get a word with Dexie, he asked her again what Hugh had said to her, and she, willing to put his mind at ease, replied:

"He wanted me to promise that I would answer a letter he wished to write to me, and I gave him to understand that I wanted no correspondence with my sister's lover, so we had a few words over it and then parted—*not* friends, I fear!"

Lancy knew that Hugh was only waiting his opportunity to oust him from his favored position, and it delighted him to hear Dexie speak of him in that strain.

"Thank you, Dexie; I guess Hugh can hear all he needs to know of you second-hand."

Dexie smiled, and she did not pull away her hand when, for a moment, Lancy laid his own shapely one across it. Lancy was her good friend; why should he not feel sure of it? And a warm pressure of the hand goes a great way towards proving friendship, to say nothing of a stronger feeling.

We must go back to Hugh, whom we left driving furiously along the road, his heart full of bitter, angry feelings. He reproached Dexie for her cold, heartless words, and himself for his ungovernable temper. He would give worlds to recall those hasty words spoken on the roof, but it was too late; he doubted if ever Dexie would forgive them. He felt that he could not meet Mrs. Gurney's searching glance while in such a mood, so he kept on, seeing nothing and hearing nothing of what was passing around him, his only thought being to get away from human sight until the heat of the battle had somewhat passed away.

It was not until some hours later that he made his appearance at Mrs. Gurney's. She was becoming quite anxious at his long absence, as she wished to hear the latest news of Elsie. Even when Hugh did return, he lingered so long in the stable that she had to send a message to him before he made his appearance.

He felt glad to find her alone in the room; he could not hide his feelings from her, but others need not know of his weakness.

"How did she keep up, Hugh? Is she all right?"

"Elsie, you mean? Oh, yes. I think she is all right. She did not get a chance to fret after she left the house."

"But what detained you? I suppose you stayed to see them off, but the train must have gone hours ago."

"Yes, I know it, Mrs. Gurney; but I—I didn't stay to see them off—I couldn't," he added, seeing her look of surprise. "I'm a fool, I suppose, but I couldn't stand there and see her go away without giving me one kind word, so I drove off down the road until I could hide my folly from others' eyes. I have driven Bob pretty hard, I'm afraid, but I have rubbed him down well, and he will be the first to recover from this day's work."

He spoke bitterly, but openly, as any loved son might speak to a tender, sympathizing mother, and he had found her all that during the long years he had lived with them; and though her own son had gained, as he thought, the one thing he longed for, he knew she would feel for his disappointment.

"It is Dexie you mean. You do not like her to be going away with Lancy. Is that it, Hugh?"

"Yes, but that is not all. She has treated me so scornfully, while Lancy—." He broke off abruptly, with a gesture that finished the sentence for him.

"But, Hugh, think a minute! Lancy's tastes are similar to her own. How can she help showing the preference, when their very music seems to draw them together? I would not have thought, Hugh, that you would be so willing to give up Gussie as you seem to be. You are not trifling with both girls, I hope, Hugh?"

"No, indeed! You do not understand, and I cannot explain; but Gussie is not what I thought her at first, and Dexie—well, she is so much more. It does not make it easier to bear to know that I have placed a barrier between us with my own hands. Oh, my temper! my hateful temper! it has done me more harm during the last twenty-four hours than during all my life long," and he laid his arms across the table and bent his head upon them.

"Perhaps it is not so, after all; the last burst of temper always looks the worst. Don't you think so, my boy? Forget it for a few moments, and tell me about Elsie. Has she gone off in good spirits?"

"Yes, I believe so, but to tell the truth I had no thought for anyone but Dexie. Elsie will not get a chance to fret, I feel sure, but I wish Dexie felt half as bad about leaving home as *she* does. It would be a comfort to think about."

"I am quite surprised, Hugh! Surely you can see that Dexie's feelings for you are far from encouraging, and how can you think that two such firebrands—yes, you must excuse the term, if you do not like it, but it suits you both—do you think you two *could* be happy together? Have you thought of this matter seriously, Hugh? I am afraid not. Yet one should study well the character of the one whom we would choose to walk with along life's road. We all know something of Dexie's temper, for she has not tried to hide even her worst faults from us. With your own high temper, Hugh, it would be a great risk to link your life with hers. There is nothing so beautiful and complete as a happy married life, but there can be nothing so unutterably miserable as an unhappy marriage."

"Well, it may be as you say, and Dexie may not be suitable in some ways for me, but I can never care for anyone else as I care for her. If I could only win her, I would make her so happy that there would never be any cause for her to get angry with me."

But the memory of the words he had spoken on the roof a few short hours before stung him at this moment, and sharply reminded him of his inability to control himself as her lover. Would he be more likely to govern himself as her husband?

Seeing that Mrs. Gurney was regarding him closely, he hastily rose to his feet, saying:

"You are right, Mrs. Gurney, as you always are. I should not succeed in controlling my temper in the future any better than I have done in the past. I will try to overcome this foolishness. I love Dexie Sherwood too well to wish to bring one moment of sorrow into her life."

He left the room and sought his own chamber, and during the hour he sat there in silence he fancied he had buried forever every thought of tender regard for Dexie Sherwood. He even imagined that he could look with favor on Lancy, or anyone else, who would make her as happy as she deserved to be.

His magnanimous feelings were even puffed up to that degree that he was mentally witnessing her marriage ceremony, with Lancy as chief actor, when the sound of the dinner-bell recalled him to his senses. Yet, when he sat down to the table and beheld Lancy's empty seat, he ground his heel into the rug under the table, as if it were his enemy, for the thought occurred that Lancy, at this present moment, might be bending over the head so precious to him, or whispering words in her ears which he never wished her to hear, unless spoken by himself. Truly he did not know himself, and as the nature of his thoughts occurred to him he almost despised himself for his weakness. Surely he needed another grave than that he had dug while in the privacy of his own room; a grave that would keep entombed that which he wished to put forever out of his memory! It was only by bringing up to his mind his own imperfections that he could keep Dexie out of his thoughts.

But as days went by, and other matters of importance intervened, he was kept so busy, mentally as well as bodily, that his love was put back out of sight; he felt her absence less keenly, and his love for Dexie was thought of as a thing of the past.

CHAPTER XX.

We must now return to the young travellers, whom we left in the car, expecting to reach their destination by nightfall. In this they were disappointed, for when the train was within a few miles of Truro it came to a sudden standstill, throwing some of the passengers out of their seats, but seriously injuring no one.

"Something wrong with the engine!" was the explanation, when heads were thrust from the windows to inquire the cause of the trouble.

This explanation was received with due submission by those accustomed to railway travelling, but Elsie, her nerves unstrung by other causes, sat crying hysterically, and would give no heed to Lancy's repeated declaration that nothing serious was the matter.

"We will be detained here for a while, Elsie, but that is all," he added.

Elsie, though, seemed unable to control her sobs, and Dexie began to feel anxious, for these crying fits invariably brought on a nervous headache, and when at last the train started, Elsie was hardly in a fit state to continue the journey.

Under the circumstances Lancy deemed it best to stop over at Truro until the next trip of the Island boat. This would give Elsie time to recover, and they would have an opportunity to see something of the pretty town they had heard so highly praised.

Elsie felt relieved at this decision. She was unused to travelling, and found the short journey tiresome in the extreme; indeed her throbbing temples called imperatively for quietness and rest.

The train steamed into the dark, tunnel-like depot, and stepping out on the platform, they found, after some difficulty, the little room that was designated "The Waiting-Room," where Lancy left the girls to inquire for hotel accommodations.

While in semi-darkness they waited his return, Dexie tried to ascertain if there was not a pleasanter outlook than could be obtained from the door, but the one dust-encrusted window gave a dim and indistinct view from that quarter.

As if in answer to their wishes, Lancy speedily returned, and as they gathered up their wraps Dexie asked:

"Do you know why they call this room the 'waiting-room,' Lancy? Give a guess."

"Can't! I give it up," giving a glance around him.

"Well, I'll just tell you. This room has been 'waiting' for years for someone to clean it, and that is how it has earned its name. Even the rusty old stove has taken on the look of dejection that seems to haunt the place."

Lancy was beginning to think that the little town had been very much overpraised, as unfortunately the worst-looking part of it was situated near the depot, and he felt disappointed and vexed that they had not been able to continue their journey. His annoyance was increased when he learned that there had been an excursion to the town the day before, crowding the hotels, which had not yet recovered from the effects of the many disturbances that had taken place inside their doors.

It was a new experience to the girls, this seeking a temporary home at a public hotel, and the unpleasant features of hotel life, to which older travellers shut their eyes, were to them unbearable.

Entering the parlor of the hotel to which he had been directed, Lancy told the girls to be seated while he saw the proprietor; but the expression on the faces of both girls gave Lancy some uneasy feelings, and Dexie's uplifted nose told the cause of her disapproval.

"It will be no use for you to engage rooms here, Lancy," said she, "for if all smells like this we won't stay."

"Well, I will just order a lunch, and we can decide about rooms later on."

This was found to have been a wise precaution, as the disgusting fumes of stale tobacco-smoke and liquor, seemed to pervade every corner.

"It's no use being too particular, girls," said Lancy, as they rose from the table, and re-entered the parlor, "we will not be here but a day or two, you know."

"Well, but surely we can find some other place to stay in while we are here. We don't want to appear at Mrs. Fremont's with our clothes smelling like a bar-room!" said Dexie, rather sharply.

"Well, no doubt the next hotel will suit us better," and a few minutes later they entered its door.

But it was quite evident, even to Lancy, that they had not bettered their condition by going farther. The house had probably been very popular the day before, and there was an air of confusion about the place that added its unpleasantness to the atmosphere that must be breathed by those that sought the hospitality of the house. Elsie looked timidly around the parlor as she entered, as if expecting to see the ghosts of those who had offered up so much incense; but the room was vacant, all having departed, leaving behind a disagreeable reminder of their presence.

"We are just as badly off as ever," Elsie whispered timidly to Dexie. "It is not very much better, is it, Dexie?"

"No, I should say not. The very curtains are full of it. How can people bear it! Tobacco-smoke and rum! Do let us get out of here, Lancy, before anyone comes in!"

"Hush, Dexie! Someone will hear you."

"No danger! but do let us run before they see us here."

"But we must stay somewhere, Dexie," said Lancy. "What shall we do?"

Dexie felt provoked at their unpleasant position, and she replied in no gentle tone.

"Do! Well, I think if nothing better is to be obtained in the town, we will do as some of our ancient ancestors have done before us, we will 'lodge without, in the streets,'" and gathering up the wraps she walked out of the house, closely followed by Elsie, and more uncertainly by Lancy.

The case was becoming serious, but it had its ludicrous side as well, which reached its height when Dexie stood on the sidewalk in front of the hotel. Throwing the wraps over her left arm, she raised her right hand high toward heaven, and exclaimed in dramatic tones:

> "Tell me, ye wingèd winds, that round my pathway roam,
> Is there no hotel in Truro where the landlord sells no rum?"

And the answer came, not from the winds she had apostrophized, but from an open window that she had not observed; and the answer was:

"Fair lady, there is none."

"There! I told you that someone would hear you, Dexie," said Lancy, vexed, yet amused at her behavior.

But Dexie stood as if unable to move, and gazed at the open window in astonishment.

But the owner of the voice now appeared at the door, and Dexie drew a sigh of relief as she saw what a good-natured, smiling face it was that looked into her own. He never belonged to that house, she felt sure, though it was nothing to his credit to be lounging inside its doors. However, it was not likely he would consider her remarks as personal, so she slowly regained her composure.

With a profound bow, the gentleman at the window said:

"There are no hotels such as you speak of in the town, but there are several private boarding-houses where travellers can be made comfortable. May I have the pleasure of directing you to one?" This to Lancy.

"If it would not be too much trouble, we would be very much obliged," and Lancy's natural state of mind slowly returned.

"Oh! no trouble at all," said the affable stranger; then turning to Dexie he relieved her of her armful of wraps, with a simple "Allow me, please," and started away with Lancy, who was carrying the so far unused lunch-basket, leaving the girls to follow at their own pace.

"Oh, Dexie! weren't you startled when that man spoke from the window?" said Elsie. "I thought I should faint away with fright."

"It is a good thing that you thought better of it, then, for they would have carried you right back into the hotel, and there would have been no escaping after that."

"Where do you suppose he will take us?" Elsie asked as they turned a corner.

"Couldn't say," was the unconcerned reply; "but as the place looks nicer the farther we go, there is no need to be alarmed. I hope we will be fortunate enough to secure lodgings on this pretty, tree-shaded street, for flower-gardens are as thick as houses. Oh, see! he is going into that house with the nice lawn in front of it."

A moment later they stepped through the gate that Lancy held open for them, while their new friend went briskly up the walk and entered the house in a manner that showed he was quite familiar with the place.

He had told Lancy as they walked along that he could recommend the house where he boarded, and as he gave such a good account of the place, Lancy determined to seek accommodation there.

"But there is one thing I must tell you," said the smiling stranger. "Mrs. Morris is pretty sharp of tongue, and may make very strict inquiries as to who was your grandmother, and what calling your great-grandfather followed, before she will allow you to engage rooms. But do not mind it. I fancy you can satisfy her on those points. She is as clean as a new pin and an excellent cook—two good recommendations, you will allow."

"Well, I hope my ancestors will please her, for my sister is much in need of rest. Is her husband of the same turn of mind as herself?" Lancy smilingly asked.

"She is a widow, as is also her sister, who lives with her. It is the latter who owns the place, but it is the younger and sharper one who keeps it in running order. But here we are. I'll go ahead and prepare the way for you," and he left Lancy to follow with the girls.

As they appeared at the door, Mrs. Morris was just coming towards it, saying in no gentle tone:

"Don't you know any better, sir, than to rush into the house like that, leaving all the doors wide open behind you! Do you suppose people will want rooms here if they are swarming with flies?"

"On my honor, madam, there were only two that ventured through the door! I counted them!" was the positive reply.

"Come in quickly, sir," to Lancy; "and you women—girls, I mean," taking a second look, and shutting the door the moment they were inside of it. "You want rooms and board," she added sharply, looking them well over. "And how comes it that young people like you are travelling around without your parents? Not running away, are you?"

"Oh, no, madam!" replied Lancy, keeping a straight face by a great effort. "We were on our way to Charlottetown, but the train was delayed by an accident, so we thought we would stay over in Truro and wait for the next boat."

"Didn't get hurt by the accident, did you? for this ain't no hospital, no way; only a plain boarding house for respectable people."

"We not hurt in the least, madam, but we are very tired, and hope you will allow us to stay here for a day or two," Lancy hastened to explain, for her many objections began to alarm him.

"You come from Halifax, do you? Bad place that. Thieves and robbers thrive there, I'm told. How long have you lived there?"

This was addressed to Dexie, but she dared not open her mouth to answer lest she should laugh outright; and Elsie, fearing she might make some unfortunate speech that would send them to the right-about, hastened to reply: "For some years, ma'am; we used to live in England before we moved to Halifax."

"Oh! English, are you? I was afraid you were Irish. You resemble some I have seen. What trade does your father work at?"

"He has a store on Granville Street; but do let us stay here, please," Elsie replied, fearing that this catechising would result disastrously.

"Well, you seem proper enough. I guess you can stay." Then turning suddenly around to where their guide stood, biting his moustache, "This is Mr. Maxwell."

The two girls bowed, and Mr. Maxwell replied: "And I believe this gentleman's name is Gurney. Mr. Gurney, Mrs. Morris."

And Lancy, not to be outdone by all this formality, added: "Allow me to introduce my sister, Miss Gurney, and her friend, Miss Sherwood."

"What! you are not sisters! I thought you were, though you don't look it, sure enough," said Mrs. Morris.

"I hope it don't matter, Mrs. Morris," said Dexie, who actually thought the woman might refuse to keep her. "We are very dear friends, Miss Gurney and I, and will gladly occupy the one room while we are here."

"Very well. Step into the parlor. I will bring my sister to see you," and she disappeared in a twinkling, but returned a few moments later in a quiet, dignified manner with her sister, saying:

"These young people want to stay here a few days. Shall we keep them?"

"Why, to be sure, Matilda. Take off your hats, my dears; you look warm. So you are only going to make a short visit, my sister tells me."

"Yes; we are going on to Charlottetown in a day or two," Dexie replied.

"Perhaps you would like to go to your room at once? Matilda, let them have the pink room; it will be the most pleasant. I will try and entertain the young man while they are gone," said Mrs. Gleason, whose manner was as quiet and pleasant as her sister's was sharp and abrupt.

But Maxwell had decided to see to the young man himself—long enough, at least, to find out something about his companion; so, as soon as Mrs. Morris left the room, he turned to the good-natured sister, saying:

"Let me take him to my room for awhile, Mrs. Gleason; then you will not be bothered with either of us," and, reading permission in her smiling face, he led the way upstairs.

The room Maxwell occupied was really worth visiting, and it told at a glance the character of the owner. Its walls were decorated with articles that would not have been allowed inside the doors had Mrs. Morris beheld them in time to utter a protest, for she was as timid about some things as she was sharp in others. For instance, there was a fine breech-loading rifle, dear to the heart of Maxwell, that hung on the wall above a brace of handsome revolvers. These were the cause of constant terror and alarm to Mrs. Morris, for she never entered the room without a look of fear in their direction. She fully expected them to "blaze away at her," notwithstanding the fact that Maxwell had repeatedly assured her that they were not loaded.

Then there were several stuffed animals that had been deprived of life by these very weapons, and Maxwell had their forms preserved in as natural an attitude as possible. While these added to the adornment of the room, they likewise served to increase Mrs. Morris' terror, and she could not get over the idea that they might "jump at her, for they always looked just ready to do it."

These, among other things, gave Mrs. Morris a particular aversion to the owner of the articles, for it was no trifling thing to keep this room well dusted and in proper order, with one's body in a quiver of fright all the time, not knowing from what direction she might be assailed.

But the treasure that took Lancy's eyes directly he entered the room was the display of fishing-rods that hung on the opposite wall, and he stepped up at once to examine them.

"That is a fine rod you have there," he remarked to Maxwell.

"Yes, rather; fishing is my favorite sport. I have caught a five-pounder with this light one," and in the discussion of flies, reels, etc., they were fast forgetting that they were utter strangers but two short hours ago.

Presently Maxwell asked, as if it had just occurred to him:

"Who is this young friend of yours, this Miss Sherwood? She is very amusing; quite an original, is she not?"

"Well, she is something different from the average young lady, if that is what you mean. She is an American."

"Ah! I thought as much; and your *sister's* particular friend, is she?" giving a sly look at Lancy.

"Yes," not heeding the look, but aware of the hint conveyed in the words. "My sister's health is not good, and Miss Sherwood accompanies her to Charlottetown, as she was not willing to go alone. They have been very intimate ever since Miss Sherwood moved to Halifax. I am sure they are both well pleased that we did not stay at the hotel, seeing that through your kindness we have secured such comfortable quarters here."

"Don't mention it! that appeal to the winds would have moved the hardest heart. I guess she got a start when I spoke from the window. Ha, ha! I fancy I see her yet. She would make a fine actress."

"You had better not make that remark to the lady in question. She would not consider it a compliment, I can tell you," said Lancy.

"No? Then what sort of a speech would your Miss Sherwood call complimentary?"

"Better try and find out for yourself," said Lancy, smiling. "It has been too hard a thing for me to discover for myself to give it away."

A few minutes later, hearing the voices of the young ladies in conversation with Mrs. Gleason downstairs, the young men joined them.

But the entrance of the gentlemen seemed to put a bridle on the tongues of the little party, for Dexie was not slow in perceiving that Maxwell was trying to quiz her, and it was very hard to withstand the good-humored banter of this young gentleman. She stood the teasing as long as she thought necessary, then her ready tongue made Maxwell confess that for once he had met his match, and the laughable occurrence of their first meeting was allowed to drop. Dexie was well aware that her snubbing was not relished, for Maxwell sat regarding her silently as she conversed in low tones to Elsie, pulling at his moustache with a restless movement that was quite annoying, if he only knew it.

Why is it that gentlemen who possess this ornamental appendage to their upper lip persist in using it so unkindly? You see it at all times and in all places, at home by their own fireside, in church, when the sermon is supposed to be occupying their attention, on the streets, in fact everywhere you will see the moustache undergoing torture at the hands of its possessor. Some merely smooth it out, or daintily curl the ends of it, if it happens to be long enough; some lick at it, like an animal at a lump of salt: some chew it savagely, till you wonder there is a hair of it left; in fact it is badly misused by the majority of men, for few leave it to serve its legitimate purpose.

After tea, at Mr. Maxwell's suggestion, the party went out for a walk. They strolled up and down the principal streets until twilight was almost over, and their first impression of the place was happily dispelled. They were willing to accord the same praise to the town as did others who had visited it. Cleanliness and thrift seemed the characteristics of the majority of the inhabitants, and the beautiful grounds and gardens that surrounded most of the houses spoke well for the taste of the owners.

When the time came for them to continue their journey, more than one member of the family regretted their departure, for their presence had quite brightened the household, and Dexie had won the approval of Mrs. Morris herself by her quick movements and practical remarks, and for the decided manner that refused all attentions from Maxwell.

"If you ever pass this way again you must come and see us," said Mrs. Morris at parting, "and if any of your friends ever visit the town we will be happy to accommodate them."

"Thank you, Mrs. Morris," said Dexie; "I will not forget it. We could hardly advise anyone to make an extended stay in your pretty town if they were obliged to patronize your hotels," looking up with a smile at Mr. Maxwell, who was waiting to accompany them to the depot.

"I am afraid our hotels have given you a poor opinion of the place, Miss Sherwood," said Mr. Maxwell, as he fingered his moustache; "but you must remember that they are not intended for fastidious young ladies, but for the accommodation of the general travelling public."

"Then it does not speak well for the tastes of the 'general travelling public,'" replied Dexie, as they turned towards the depot, "and it is a pity that the one blot on your pretty town is just where it falls under the notice of strangers who enter it by the railway."

Years after, when Dexie made her next visit to the town, she was surprised to see the change that had taken place in the vicinity of the railway station. The gloomy, dingy depot had given place to one that was light, airy and commodious, and the unsightly buildings in the neighborhood were replaced by better and worthier structures.

The hotels she had so justly condemned were either obliterated or so improved upon as to be unrecognizable; and if the objectionable bar-rooms were not suppressed, public opinion had caused them to be placed in a more obscure corner of the building, and the respectable stranger was no longer insulted by their immediate presence. But of this more anon.

CHAPTER XXI.

The rest of the journey was made without mishap, and when the travellers arrived at the wharf at Charlottetown, they found Mrs. Fremont waiting to receive them, Lancy having informed her by telegraph of their detention.

Mrs. Fremont's residence was situated in the suburbs of the city, amidst a parklike grove that gave it a very English look in Lancy's eyes. The house was large and roomy, and furnished in a solid, comfortable style, that would make modern parlors look frivolous in comparison.

Dexie had no fault to find with her reception, for the whole party were so warmly welcomed that they felt "at home" at once. Mrs. Fremont's two daughters proved very pleasant companions. Beatrice, the eldest, was of a gentle, quiet disposition, and her very presence held in check her frolicsome younger sister; for Gertrude, who was fat, fair and seventeen, saw too much of the bright side of life to be anything else than good-natured and jolly, and finding her counterpart in Dexie Sherwood the days flew by on gladsome wings.

An enjoyable garden party was held a few days after the young people arrived, and by that means they became acquainted with a number of the young people in the city, and Elsie forgot her shyness in the pleasant bustle that made the days pass so swiftly. The daily drives in the low, comfortable carriage soon began to tell favorably on her health, and she did not find it at all hard to enter into the amusements planned for her benefit; but among all the pleasures that were attainable, one alone stood out above all others, one that neither Elsie nor Dexie ever cared to miss, and that was—to go marketing.

Twice a week, on Tuesdays and Fridays, the country people for miles around drove into Charlottetown, bringing with them whatever farm produce they had to dispose of. Great carts bearing vegetables, eggs, butter, berries and "garden truck" beyond mentioning, might be seen wending their way along the roads leading to the city in the early mornings on market days, and the products of the field, garden, poultry yard, etc., were offered for sale in and around the large market-house that was situated in the centre of the city. Here the people of the city came by hundreds to purchase whatever fancy dictated or needs demanded, making a scene that was worth coming far to see.

To educate her daughters into the difficult part of household management, Mrs. Fremont had given over to them the task of buying the supplies for the family. A sum, ample for a week, was given them, and at the end of the week the accounts were made up under the mother's supervision. If the daughters had planned wisely there was always a surplus, which was added to their pocket-money.

When Dexie learned of this, and realized the responsibility which these young girls took upon themselves as a part of their education, she was anxious to acquire the same accomplishment, and it became quite amusing to hear the prices of different articles discussed in such business-like tones, for Dexie and Elsie were often drawn into these discussions before they were aware of it.

In consequence of this, when market days came round, there was quite an important air about the four young ladies who drove towards the market-house, and there seemed to be a good deal of fun as well as business going on, if one might judge by their eager, happy faces, and the way the task was often unnecessarily prolonged.

One evening, when a party of young people were visiting at Mrs. Fremont's, a remark was made that brought about a discussion of a sect which are known in Prince Edward Island as McDonaldites or "Jerkers;" and after a description of the remarkable character of their meetings, there was much curiosity raised concerning them.

"You ought not to go home without attending a meeting, Mr. Gurney," said Mr. Holbrook, "for I do not think the like is to be seen anywhere else in the world. One visit is generally enough to satisfy most people, but to those who have good nerves one visit only whets the curiosity. For my part, I like to go and watch them whenever I find the opportunity."

"Well, I went once," said Gertrude Fremont, "and that was quite enough for me, and I do not call myself nervous or timid either. Still I would not have missed seeing them *once* for anything, but that experience is enough to last me a lifetime."

"I used to think that the people exaggerated when talking about the actions of the Jerkers," said Beatrice, "but I had to believe my own eyesight; it certainly is a very strange thing."

"I wonder if it is anything like what the slaves down South used to be affected with," said Dexie. "I have heard my grandma tell of prayer meetings in the negro quarters, where some of the slaves would act in the same way you describe, but I suppose it is not the same thing except in name. I should like very much to attend a meeting."

After much persuasion, Mrs. Fremont consented to allow the young people under her charge to attend a meeting of this peculiar sect, under the escort of Mr. Holbrook, but the consent was given reluctantly.

"I quite understand the curiosity you have to witness such a mode of worship," she said, smiling kindly at Dexie, "but I fear the result for Elsie. I am afraid it would quite unnerve her."

"But if she is the least frightened she need not stay in the church to watch them," said Lancy, who was eager to visit a McDonaldite church. "It must be a wonderful sight indeed, if the people go through such contortions as Mr. Holbrook speaks of."

A few days later the little party drove off in the comfortable covered carriage on a visit to Uigg. As they crossed the river to Southport they found several other carriages going in the same direction, so they followed on, journeying by the beautiful Vernon River road towards their destination.

There was but one thing that marred the enjoyment of the drive to Elsie, and that was that the day was Sunday; but her conscientious scruples were overpowered by those who voted that it was "no harm, surely, to drive to church on Sunday."

But Elsie felt that they were not going to church for a worthy motive, but only as sightseers, and, judging by the accounts they had heard, a visit to a McDonaldite or Jerkers' church was similar to going to a play or circus. Still her scruples were not strong enough to allow Lancy and Dexie to go without her, but the beautiful scenery through which they passed had for her no charm, for she felt, for the first time in her life, that she was a Sabbath-breaker.

Dexie had no such pangs of conscience, but enjoyed the drive to the utmost, and Elsie's oft-repeated remark that they "ought not to have come" found no response in the hearts of the rest. Happily for Elsie, a Sunday feeling soon possessed her, for Dexie, in the fulness of her heart, could not be silent, and as ordinary talk seemed out of place in the Sabbath stillness, she began to sing.

Elsie's voice soon joined the rest, and the sound of harmony rolled along with the carriage, and before they reached the church of the Jerkers, Elsie felt more at ease with herself and her surroundings.

It seems passing strange that while the Shakers, Quakers and other peculiar sects have all come in for a share of newspaper discussion, this most peculiar sect called McDonaldites, or Jerkers, have escaped the pen of the reporter. This may be due to the fact that, during the life of the great McDonald, Prince Edward Island was considered by travellers to be rather an out-of-the-way place and not worth visiting. But year by year the army of tourists is increasing, as the Garden of the St. Lawrence becomes better known, and a visit to a McDonaldite church may yet be one of the sights in store for my reader, for it is doubtful if such a sight can be witnessed in any other civilized community.

McDonald, the leader of the sect, has been dead many years. He was a man of powerful physique, and his mind must have corresponded to his large and vigorous body, for the power or influence which he had over his followers was something extraordinary, if not alarming. As his presence was not necessary to set the members of his Church in motion, and the "jerks" are kept up even to the present day, there may be some other explanation for the singular behavior of his followers; but the memory of their leader is held in reverence, and by many the "jerks" are still attributed to his power.

The writer has attended but one meeting where the great McDonald presided, and, being then young in years, the dress, or rather the undress, of the man was itself awe-inspiring. It was something unusual to see a man in the pulpit with his coat and vest laid aside and his shirt open, laying bare his brawny neck. The man himself was enough to create fear, but when the activity of the members began, discretion seemed the better part of valor, and we escaped without ceremony. It would be impossible to convey to the reader an idea of the awful excitement that always prevailed among his followers, when under the direct leadership of McDonald himself. Even the attempt to do so would be called exaggerated and untrue; but after witnessing through the open window the surprising actions of the congregation, we turned away, feeling that the half *could* not be told, for words would fail to portray the scene. The reader must be content with a meagre description of a visit to the church made many years after the death of the leader, when the excitement was less intense, to which meeting Lancy Gurney and his party are hastening.

There are several churches of this sect in different parts of the Island, but the principal church is in a country place called Uigg. The yearly sacrament is held at this church, and on these occasions the multitudes of worshippers who come from a long distance to attend this ceremony are almost doubled by the number of sightseers who flock to witness the sight. At such times the adjacent fences are lined with vehicles of every description, giving the place the appearance of a fair or horse market. These yearly meetings cannot begin to compare with those held during the lifetime of the leader, but those who never witnessed a meeting conducted by the Rev. Mr. McDonald could scarcely believe they were ever more startling than those held in later years.

With this digression we will return to our young travellers, who, having secured their horse under the sheltering trees by the roadside, and fortified their courage by doing justice to the lunch Mrs. Fremont had prepared for them, now entered the crowded church and stood among the number of observers in the aisle.

The inside of the edifice had an unfinished look, and the arrangement of the seats was uncommon, but to most people the seats themselves formed a most unusual sight, for they were all without backs, the reason of which soon became apparent.

The meeting had commenced, and the minister was preaching, but it must be confessed that there was little heed given to his words, for the attention of the people was attracted to the centre of the church, where a number of people were already under the peculiar influence; but our little party, being at a distance, watched the proceedings with a feeling of safety, yet not unmixed with fear and dread.

Presently a young girl about seventeen or twenty, who sat in a seat quite near, began to be affected, and all eyes were turned in her direction. She was dressed in what was probably called in her neighborhood the "height of style." On her head was a saucerlike bonnet of the "gypsy style," covered with large artificial flowers, which drooped over a chignon of such remarkable dimensions that it must have required a multitude of hairpins to keep it together; but her bonnet helped to keep it in place, as strings of ribbon were placed at the back, then brought forward under her chin in a flaring knot.

The peculiar actions of these people are well named "the jerks." In this instance the hands seemed to be the first part affected; a slight twitching was soon followed by a quicker movement, then her feet jerked about as if she were dancing a jig; a moment more and she flung her arms around wildly, while her head began to shake in quick time to the movements of the hands and feet. This soon loosened her chignon, the ingredients of which flew in as many directions, and her hair swept wildly about her face. Her bonnet fell at the back of her neck, but being held by the strings it bobbed up and down her back like an animated nosegay. She accompanied her movements with shrieks and screams that were better suited to a madhouse than a place of worship, and when exhausted nature finally succumbed, she fell back against those seated behind, who, very good-naturedly, it must be confessed, for she weighed more than a trifle, helped her to regain her senses and her seat. When she was able to sit up, her neighbors on either side handed back the articles of wearing apparel and pieces of headgear that she had scattered about, and the girl made a fresh toilet, as well as the limited stock of hairpins allowed.

A number of other cases equally startling were taking place in different parts of the church, and the backless seats were explained. It certainly was less dangerous for the "jerkers" to throw themselves back into the laps of those behind them than against the hard back of a seat. But the feelings of those who received the form of the exhausted enthusiast we do not profess to explain. It is probable, however, that those in the near vicinity of one who had the "jerks" would prepare themselves for the backward throw that so many execute at the last moment of their paroxysm. But to those who looked on, it seemed like a game of "give-and-take," as if each did not know what moment he might be under the same obligation to someone else.

While standing in the aisle Dexie passed her arm around Elsie's waist, lest they should be separated in the crowd. Dexie had become so engrossed in watching the worshippers that she had forgotten how the sight might affect her friend, but glancing into her face she saw that this was no place for one of Elsie's temperament. But the aisles were blocked; they seemed standing in a vice, with no power to move front or backwards. The *enthusiasm* seemed increasing every moment, and as almost every seat held an active member, the excitement in the church was appalling.

One young girl, quite near where Dexie stood, sprang to her feet with a shriek that caused Elsie to scream with fright, and Dexie bade her hide her face from the sight. But Elsie felt she must watch what was going on or else scream again, so great was her terror. The sight was indeed alarming, for the girl beat the air with her hands while she jumped up and down, until her movements appeared actually dangerous to those near her. Her head was thrown backward and forward with such violence and rapidity that it seemed a marvel how she escaped dislocation, and her whole body was in violent motion. At last she fell to the floor with a final shriek, where she struggled about for several minutes, much to the alarm of those in her immediate vicinity.

On all sides shrieks and cries mingled with the quick movements of those who had the "jerks," and Elsie could bear it no longer.

"Take me out, Dexie; I can't stay here another minute!" she cried.

Lancy was some distance away, but he pressed to her side, regardless of the bruised toes and sides he left behind him, and lifting Elsie in his arms pressed to the door, with Dexie closely following. They hurried away to where the noise of the worshippers was not quite so audible, and by degrees Elsie grew quiet and calm. Leaving them seated on the grass by the roadside, Lancy re-entered the church, the strange doings having a certain fascination which he could neither explain nor resist.

In a short time Elsie recovered sufficiently to walk around, but curiosity drew her again to the church, and they watched through the windows the peculiar actions of the people. But the excitement had now somewhat subsided, and Elsie urged that they enter the church again. Dexie was afraid of the effect which another such scene might have upon her friend, so she tried to persuade Elsie to stay and watch at a safe distance. Elsie felt sure she would not be alarmed again, so they entered the church and obtained a seat that had just been made vacant.

A few minutes later, the movements of an old woman attracted notice. They had watched her as she entered the church a short time before, and had pitied the poor, feeble creature, as she dragged herself up the aisle by the aid of a pair of crutches; but all pity left Dexie's heart as she saw the crippled creature thump the floor with her crutches, and bring them together over her head with a crash that rivalled the noise made by many of the hard-handed sons of toil, who had taken the "jerks" during the service.

"What makes them do it, Dexie?" said Elsie, in a whisper. "'And there was in the synagogue many people possessed of the devil;' that is the only solution of the mystery that I can see," was the reply.

"Oh, Dexie! do you really think that is what ails them? How awful!"

"'And there was one woman among them who had seven devils,' and that is she with the crutches, I think. Are you afraid? Shall we go out, Elsie?"

"It does scare me, but I cannot help looking at them," was the answer.

But the "jerks" now spread from one to the other, until pandemonium let loose could not be much more alarming. Elsie turned white with fear, but it was impossible to get out at the moment, as the aisles were blocked by terrified sightseers, their screams of fright mingling with the shrieks of those who had the "jerks." It is safe to say that no madhouse ever held a more excited crowd.

At this moment a heavy woman, who sat on the same seat that held Dexie and Elsie, began to be affected, and as the seats were only supported at each end, this one began to spring up and down, setting all those who were upon it in motion.

The two girls were on their feet in an instant, feeling for one awful moment that they were taking the "jerks" themselves; but finding the floor steady under her feet, Dexie soon regained her composure, and endeavored to quiet Elsie, who was now sobbing without restraint.

Out of this they must get at any hazard, and, drawing Elsie after her, she crossed to the door by stepping on the knees of the people who intervened, giving no thought to the outraged feelings of those she had used as stepping-stones to freedom.

As they reached the doorstep, they saw Mr. Holbrook at a distance, and were soon at his side.

"How soon can we get away from this awful place?" Dexie hurriedly asked.

"Well, I do not know, Miss Sherwood. Are you in a hurry to go?"

"Yes, that I am; I have had enough of this kind of worship, and Elsie must not go near the church again. Where is Lancy?"

"I believe he is inside the church; I saw him there a short time ago. He is much interested, I believe. I hope, Miss Gurney, that these excitable people have not seriously alarmed you."

"Oh, I don't want to see them any more!" cried Elsie. "I wish we could find Lancy, so we could start for Charlottetown."

"Do you know, I believe he wants you to stay overnight at some place near, so that he can stay to the evening service. Could you agree to that plan, do you think?" he asked.

"Certainly; if the place we have to stay is a good piece away from this church, out of sight and hearing of these people," replied Dexie, feeling that a drive back to town would be very tiresome after the exciting day they had spent.

"Well, suppose we start now? The drive will do you good," said Mr. Holbrook, as he turned towards their carriage; and as he led the horse on the road, he proposed that they start for Montague Bridge at once, describing it as a pretty hamlet about two miles from the church.

"But if Lancy should come and find the carriage gone, he would be anxious," said Dexie.

"Oh! I'll pin a note to the tree, so if he comes here it will explain our absence; but I will be back before the service is ended; and I fancy he will not leave the church till then. You are quite sure you have no objections to leaving him behind you, Miss Gurney?" he asked.

"Oh, no! But are you quite sure you can get us a nice place to stay? I suppose you know the place around here very well," she added.

"Yes, indeed; I have spent my life on the Island, Miss Gurney, and I know my fellow Islanders pretty well. I will leave you quite comfortable, never fear."

They were soon driving along at a rapid pace, and Dexie hoped that the scene in the church had passed from Elsie's mind, till her question to Mr. Holbrook proved the contrary. "Do tell us, Mr. Holbrook, what *is* it makes those people act so? Is it the talk of the minister that does it? I'm sure I could only hear a word now and then, though his lips kept moving even when the noise was the worst."

"That is a hard question to answer, Miss Gurney," was the reply. "Some say it is the Heavenly Spirit working within them; others think the spirit is not of a heavenly origin; others, again, say they are getting relief from the bondage of sin."

"Well, if that is the way they show their relief, I think it would be better to stay in bondage," said Dexie. "I wonder if it can be the same craze that used to affect the colored people down South. Grandma's people kept slaves, and I have heard of such actions amongst them, but if I ever heard the explanation of them I have completely forgotten it. Still one would hardly think that a superstitious negro craze would affect the clear-headed Scotch people in the same manner. It is a mystery to me how they live through it."

Mr. Holbrook laid back his head and laughed.

"But they are human, like other people, Mr. Holbrook," she urged; "and how is it that they do not hurt themselves? There was a man with a shock of red hair, sitting near the chimney, who took the 'jerks.' I daresay you noticed him. Now, unless his head is made of something different than ours, it must be smashed in on one side, for he struck the chimney with such rapidity and force that it sounded quite sickening from where we sat. Really, I should not have been surprised had he fallen dead to the floor."

"I daresay he never felt it," said Mr. Holbrook, smiling. "I do not believe that any of them know what they are about when they take the 'jerks,' or else some of the women are very careless of appearances."

"Oh! well, don't let us talk about them any more," said Elsie. "Papa often says that everyone has a right to his own belief, and these people seem to believe *something*, and they really *must* believe it without merely saying so, as so many of us do, or else they could not act out their belief in such a dreadful manner; but whatever their belief is, it must be awful!"

In a short time they entered the village, which was situated on both sides of a river, connected by the bridge that gave the place its name. Mr. Holbrook drove at once to a house where he knew the girls would have every attention, and the pleasant face of the woman who welcomed them at the door seemed to speak of rest and security to be found beneath her roof.

With a few words of explanation Mr. Holbrook left them, promising to be back in good season with Lancy. He then returned with all speed to the church of the McDonalds, where he found the energetic members still in active motion.

CHAPTER XXII.

"What a relief to find ourselves safe and quiet once more!" said Elsie, as she leaned back in her chair with a sigh of content. "I did not know I was so tired."

"A visit to the McDonaldite church is apt to fatigue both body and mind," said their hostess, Mrs. Gardner. "It does not seem right, does it, for people to leave their own church to witness such doings?" she added seriously. There was a mild rebuke in her words, and Elsie remembered with a pang that it was Sunday. She had given little thought to the fact during the last few hours.

"No, I am sure it can't be right, Mrs. Gardner," said Elsie, "but we were so interested when we heard about these 'Jerkers' that we wished to see them before we went home."

"Then you do not belong on the Island. Where is your home, my dears?" she asked, as she stepped briskly about preparing the tea.

"We are from Halifax," Dexie answered.

"And is it possible that you are the daughter of Mr. Sherwood, who buys horses on the Island? Why, we know him well. He always stays here when he comes this way. Well, well; many's the time he has told us about his twin girls, but I never expected to see one of them here. Are you the beauty or the singer?" she smilingly asked.

"Now, Mrs. Gardner," said Dexie, laughing, "I am sure you can see for yourself that I am not the beauty."

"Then you are the singer; but your looks will do very well. Uncommon beauty is often a snare to its possessor, and the ability to sing God's praises is worth far more. Are you too tired to do so tonight?"

Dexie looked up with a question in her eyes, and Mrs. Gardner added,

"There is a service in our meeting-house tonight. Would you like to attend it with me?" turning to Elsie.

"Yes, indeed; I would love to go. The day will not seem all lost if we spend a short time of it properly. But do tell us, Mrs. Gardner, what makes those people take the 'jerks'? It seems such a queer kind of religion."

"My dear, I have lived in these parts for more than twelve years, and I am acquainted with several families of McDonaldites, but I never yet learned why they take the 'jerks,' or what they signify, but I know that there are many good religious people belonging to the sect."

"But they might be good people on *account* of their religion or in *spite* of it," said Dexie.

Mrs. Gardner looked over at Dexie with a serious face.

"I wonder if you can repeat the first verse of the first Psalm. Try it, my dear," she said.

"I do not think I can say it word for word, Mrs. Gardner," said

Dexie, presently; "but it is something like this, 'Blessed is the person who never goes where he knows he ought not to be, and who never sits down in the seat of the scornful.' Thank you, Mrs. Gardner, I see the application," she added, smiling. "I fear I have been on that seat today, and I have no right to be scornful when I am such a heathen myself. Yet I never attend an impressive service that I do not wish I were a good member of that particular church, no matter what denomination it happens to be. But today, although I have witnessed the most impressive service of my life, I never wished I was a good McDonaldite; no, not once. Now, you needn't laugh, Elsie, for you know yourself I can jump around just as lively as most people, and I am sure I could go through some of the most surprising movements if I tried, but I never once felt the least desire to emulate the members of that church, so I conclude that I have not been benefited by attending that wonderful gathering; yet I have always thought that any religious service that does not inspire you with a desire to join heart and soul in it, is a miserable failure. I am afraid if I had to choose between the two, I would rather be a dancing dervish than a McDonaldite. However, perhaps if I understood the doctrines of each I might choose the other way. But that brings me back to the beginning again, and makes me wonder how it is that no one seems to really know why they take the 'jerks,'" turning to Mrs. Gardner.

"Well, since none of us *do* know, let us try to forget about them for the rest of the evening," said she. "It is a comfort to know that there is a religion which the simplest can understand, and a service in which we can all unite without committing any impropriety."

A few preparations followed, and they were soon on their way to the Methodist chapel, where the reverential feeling that always filled Elsie's heart when inside a place of worship was not now wanting, as it had been while inside the church of the McDonalds, and she followed the example of Mrs. Gardner and bowed her head in silent prayer.

The service was opened by singing a hymn—one of those good old-fashioned, heartfelt songs that are dear to the hearts of all Christian people, whatever may be their Church or creed—and a feeling of strong emotion filled Dexie's heart as it rolled from the throats of the people around her, then her own clear, full notes rose above the assembled voices.

The minister lifted his eyes, and rested them a moment on the owner of the voice; but, thinking that he supposed she was just singing for effect, Dexie remained silent while the next verse was sung. A look of disappointment was reflected on the faces of those around her; but Dexie was not prepared for the pointed rebuke that was given as the minister read out the next verse.

"When the Lord gives a good voice, He expects the owner to use it for His glory; so let all sing who can sing, and do not be afraid to praise God in His own house."

Dexie felt that the words were directed to her, and wisely obeyed, fearing a more open command might be given her from the pulpit, and she detected the nod of approval that was given as she lifted her eyes to the preacher.

When the service was over, Mrs. Gardner introduced her young charges to those near her, and as the minister came down among his congregation he was presented to the strangers also.

A few pleasant words followed the introduction; then, drawing Dexie aside, he said:

"I felt sorry to have to reprove you before the whole congregation, seeing that you were a stranger here; but after showing us that you *could* sing, it was very wrong and unkind to be silent. You know, the verse says, 'Let those refuse to sing who never knew our Lord,' and I would be sorry to place you on the left hand when you are so well able to sing God's praises."

Dexie did not know whether to be amused, hurt or vexed. The words uttered were words of rebuke, but the odd manner in which they were said and the humorous twinkle in the minister's eyes did not well agree. He waited a moment for her answer, still holding her hand and looking down into her face with a serio-comic expression quite unlike a clergyman, until Dexie answered, in a low tone,

"I will remember what you said, and will always sing when I can, though I should not like to be spoken to right out in church very often."

"That's right," said Mr. Barkly. "I am glad to know that I have made an impression on one of my congregation, at least, and that your sin of omission will not be repeated. There is nothing like a personal remark to bring people to a sense of their shortcomings; so let this be a warning to you, Miss Sherwood," and he walked down the aisle at her side. "I hope, Miss Sherwood," he added, "that your stay amongst us will allow us the privilege of hearing your voice again. With a good preacher and a fine singer as inducements, we ought to bring out a large congregation, eh?"

Dexie looked up quickly, but the ministerial air could not hide the rich vein of humor in the man, and she smilingly replied,

"I should not like to be reproved before a larger audience than was here this evening, Mr. Barkly, and I might unintentionally do something that would bring it upon me; so I think the preacher must depend on himself, as we expect to return to Charlottetown tomorrow."

A few parting words, and the group separated, and Dexie found herself by Elsie's side, walking towards their temporary home.

As they were very tired, they decided not to await Lancy's arrival, so at an early hour they asked to be shown to their room, and its spotless purity spoke well for the housekeeper.

"However shall we get into that bed, Dexie?" said Elsie, as the footsteps of Mrs. Gardner were no longer audible.

"That is just what I was wondering myself," and Dexie stood regarding the high, old-fashioned four-poster. "Do you suppose they use a step-ladder, or jump into it from the table? Why," lifting up the counterpane and sheets, "it's just a mountain of feathers; we must spring into it from this chair." A little later her smothered laughter camp from its depths, and the laugh was repeated when Elsie sank beside her.

When they came downstairs next morning they found Lancy waiting for them, and a few minutes later Mr. Holbrook put in an appearance, making a merry little party as they sat round the cosy breakfast table.

At the earnest solicitation of Mrs. Gardner, they consented to stay a few days longer at Montague Bridge, and visit the places of interest in the vicinity.

"I will leave the horse and carriage, and return to town with a friend, and report to Mrs. Fremont," said Mr. Holbrook, "so you can drive around the country here; and when you are ready for home just follow the telegraph poles, and you'll not miss your road. You have made a good thing of it by visiting Montague Bridge."

A few days later the new friends they had made were left behind, and they were again in sight of Charlottetown.

When they arrived at Mrs. Fremont's they were received with delight, as there had been a picnic planned, and they were waiting the return of the little party from Montague, in order to announce the day.

After the pleasant bustle of preparation had resulted in hampers of delicacies, a lively procession of vehicles, filled with happy people, started for Stanhope Bay, a lovely spot on the north shore of the Island.

The high sandbanks that here border the waters of the Gulf of St. Lawrence were a source of wonder and amusement to those of the party who were strangers to the place, but woe to the one who stepped unwittingly near the edge of the bank! for the yielding sand gave no foothold, and an awkward slide down the face of the bank was always the result. But the shore below was as firm and smooth as a sanded floor, and soon every member of the party had thrown dignity aside and let themselves down through the warm dry sand to the beach, where they sought for treasures of the deep in the shape of pretty shells and other sea beauties, that were thrown up by the mighty waves that here dash on the shore in thundering tones when tempests rule the waters of the Gulf.

It was only when a sense of hunger brought to mind the full baskets awaiting them in the grove at the top of the bank, that they turned their backs on the restless waves, and essayed to climb the steep sandbanks.

But a complete knowledge of mountain-climbing was of little use here; it was each one for himself in the scramble for the top, for there could be little help given either in front or rear.

A mad rush up the bank, at an angle that offered some slight foot-hold, brought Dexie, hot and panting, to the top, and she turned to give a word of instruction to Elsie, who was trying to climb the steep face of the bank only to find that she slipped back almost as fast as she ascended.

"Go back to the bottom, Elsie, and make a run for that bunch of grass where I came up; you will never get up there; watch Gertrude Fremont. Now, Elsie, run for it!"

After a few minutes' hard climbing, Elsie reached the top, and the next few minutes were spent in shaking their skirts, and emptying their shoes from the accumulation of sand that filled every crevice. A smooth spot was then found to do duty as a table, and the snowy cloths were spread, when the contents of the heavy baskets revealed themselves, and all the delights of a picnic in the woods were present in abundance.

Even the long-legged spiders, who invariably invite themselves to such gatherings, and persist in walking over and around the various viands, were here represented by members of the family who seemed to be great grandfathers of their tribe, judging by their size; and the dexterity shown by some of the young gentlemen in picking up these wandering vagrants and sending them back into oblivion, called forth much praise from the female portion of the party.

After a day of delightful enjoyment, the hour arrived for them to return home, and having so much less to pack up than there was at starting, they were soon on the journey homeward.

Before the picnickers separated, there was a driving party arranged to go to Rustico Beach, Brackly Point or Cove Head, for another day's outing, and the day was set for the drive.

CHAPTER XXIII.

The next morning, when the mail was opened, Dexie received a letter from home, in which, beside the commonplace news, there were pages devoted to a startling and amusing announcement.

"Just think," Gussie wrote, "there is a man at the Gurney's who has come all the way from Australia to find Hugh, and to tell him about the fortune left him by his father. It amounts to a very large sum, and will make Hugh one of the wealthiest men in the Province, so, of course, he is now quite a different person in my eyes than when he was a mere clerk. Unfortunately for me, he is not so agreeable and friendly as he used to be, and he does not come in to see me nearly so often as formerly, but I manage to meet him frequently, and treat him with so much favor that I am quite sure I will have no difficulty in securing him. I have been teasing mamma to buy me some more new dresses, for I feel quite shabby now that there is a prospect of possessing so much wealth. I am sure we will be a fine-looking couple, for Hugh looks particularly handsome lately, but rich men always look well in the eyes of a young lady. If you are asked to stay for a long visit, I would advise you to do so, as it is much more convenient for me to have you away just now."

Dexie smiled at this, but turned over the page and read on: "I shall send you word as soon as I am engaged, for then I shall want your help on my trousseau. As you are visiting among fashionable people, I wish you would keep in mind whatever dressy garments you see that would suit my style. Hugh wished to be remembered to you, and was anxious to know when you would return, but I do not see that your movements concern him."

There were more pages in the same strain, and Dexie smiled at the many things Gussie had disclosed without being aware of it. She could read between the lines, and the reason of Hugh's inquiries on her behalf were not hard to guess. But Dexie knew it would be a great disappointment to Gussie if she failed in her schemes, and she was willing enough to prolong her visit if it favored Gussie's future prospects, but she knew that Hugh's pocket-book was far dearer to Gussie than Hugh himself.

Lancy had received a letter also, and Hugh's unexpected good fortune was told at length. Hugh's father had not died during the journey to the Australian gold diggings, as had been reported, but he had changed his name, and so was lost sight of, until he had accumulated the fortune that now fell to his son. Lancy wondered if Hugh's better prospects would have any influence on Dexie; he knew well that Hugh would use his money as a stepping-stone to Dexie's favor. Perhaps Dexie surmised what was going on in his mind, for she passed him her letter with permission to read it. After they retired from the breakfast room, they discussed the news together. Lancy felt ashamed to think he could not feel as pleased about it as he ought, and Dexie listened with heightened color as he told his fear of being set aside for Hugh.

"Lancy, you must remember I am free to do as I like with my future," she said, with flushed cheeks, "for I have not given you the least word of a promise; but let me tell you once and for all, that Hugh cannot buy my favor, and he has not been able to obtain it by coaxing, or brute force either."

"Dexie, what do you mean?" was the quick reply. "What has he said or done that you speak like this?"

"Let us go to the summer-house, Lancy, and I think I can satisfy your mind on one point, and that is, if I fail to appreciate your attentions as you think they deserve, you need not lay the blame on Hugh McNeil," and, standing under the shadow of the swinging vines, Dexie related the substance of the interview on the kitchen roof the evening before they left Halifax.

"The scoundrel! and he dared to threaten you, and was actually going to throw you from the roof! Why did you not tell me, Dexie, and I would have horsewhipped him if it had cost me my life!" And he dug his heel into the gravel, as if he had his enemy beneath it.

"Don't, Lancy; it is all over, so try to forget it. I know that Hugh felt sorry for his burst of temper the moment after, but he could not unsay the words, and I would not forgive them—that is why he felt so badly when we parted on the train. I did not intend to tell you of it, Lancy; so do not look so vexed."

"Oh! if I only could lay my hands on him, I would pay him for his impudence and brutality! but, Dexie, were you not very frightened?" and he clasped her hands in his own, and looked earnestly into her face.

"For the moment, when I turned my head and saw the stones beneath me, I was almost sick with fear, but I think my temper saved my life just then, for I turned on him and dared him! Oh! I could have torn him limb from limb, I was that angry! I broke the commandment a dozen times as I stood there before him—I mean the one that says 'Thou shalt do no murder.' I killed him in my heart, I mean. However, I feel real pleased to hear of his good fortune, so I think I must have repented; but I'm not quite sure," she laughingly added.

"My brave Dexie! that is no easy matter to forgive!" said Lancy earnestly.

"Oh, well! I am going to forgive everything, and be as amiable as possible to my future brother-in-law. You see, Gussie has claimed him already. Now, you must keep this to yourself, Lancy, or I will never tell you anything again; but you see how foolish it is to hold up Hugh as my possible lover. Are you satisfied now?"

"No, not quite, Dexie, but if you will tell me what you refused to tell Hugh, then I will be," and he drew nearer her side.

"Then I guess you can remain unsatisfied, Sir Launcelot, for I will not confess to a feeling I am not sure of possessing."

"But you will confess that no one else holds the first place—that you love no one else? You will tell me that much, surely, Dexie?" and he tried to read the answer in her dark eyes.

"Well, yes, Lancy. I can safely concede that much without committing myself, but you need not begin to build air castles on that!"

A step sounded on the gravel walk, and Elsie's head appeared through the swinging vines at the door.

"Here I have been searching for you for half an hour! Whatever have you two been doing here, all by yourselves? Not love-making, surely; but your face looks guilty, Dexie," and she looked keenly at her brother, to see what his earnest tones might have meant.

"Well! you little Paul Pry! we were love-making and love-breaking, both. You came just in time to hear that my engagement to Lancy is—not a settled thing," and she laughed at the surprise in Elsie's eyes. "So please unsay what you told Mrs. Fremont in the parlor last evening. But what are your wishes, Miss Gurney?"

Elsie returned her bow with great formality and replied "Miss Beatrice Fremont sends her compliments, and will Mr. Gurney be kind enough to drive us to the market this morning, as Miss Gertrude is otherwise engaged."

"With pleasure, but such dignity ill becomes your youthful brow, sister mine. Did mother tell you the news about Hugh?"

"No! She said you would tell me the news your letter contained."

"Well, just think! Hugh's father has been alive for years, long enough to lay by a big fortune for Hugh. But he took a fever and died, just when he was almost ready to return to England. He managed to get a trusty man to see after his business, who has arrived in Halifax, and Hugh is rich enough to buy us all out if he wants to. Mother says he has made no plans for the future yet, but frequently asks when we are expected home, though why he is anxious about us, I can't see."

Something caused him to glance at Dexie, and the peculiar smile on her face made Lancy understand at once the reason of the frequent inquiries. Hugh did not care to make plans for the future until Dexie had returned, when her acceptance or refusal of his suit would have something to do with his future plans. But after hearing Dexie's story, Hugh's anxiety on their account did not trouble him further.

As they walked towards the house, Elsie expressed a hope "that Hugh and Gussie would soon get married, and would give them a good party to celebrate the event," and Dexie heartily seconded her wish.

But even Hugh's good fortune was set aside, for this was market day, and on no account would they miss the drive to the crowded mart. They were soon speeding along the level road, past cartloads of farm products of every kind, which were slowly making their way towards the same goal. While Beatrice was making her purchases the two girls wandered about to view the busy scene, but they soon became aware that the attention of a broad-shouldered countryman was directed to themselves. Dexie wondered where she had seen the man before, as his face looked familiar, but her memory was refreshed by the outspoken and hearty greeting that met her ears.

"Bless yer bonnie face! If this aren't Mr. Sherrud's dochter, I'm mista'en! What! dinna ye ken the auld farmer McDonald, that was seein' ye in Halifax? Oh, I thocht ye'd ken me! An' whan did ye come owre?" and her hand was grasped and given a hearty shake as she tried to answer his many questions, for the pleasure of the meeting was easily read in the open countenance before her.

"Weel, weel! but it's pleased I am to hae met ye the day, an' is yer faither as smart as ever?" and seeing him glance towards Elsie she remembered herself and introduced her friend.

"She is our next-door neighbor in Halifax," Dexie explained.

"An' ye are both owre for a visit? Weel, weel, an' ye never telt me ye were comin' at a', at a'. But whaur are ye stayin', if I may ask?"

"At Mrs. Fremont's. I am here at Miss Gurney's invitation, and her friends have been very kind to me. We have been here a little more than three weeks."

"An' ye never sent me word! If I had kent ye were here, I wad hae sent doon for ye afore."

"You are very kind, indeed, Mr. McDonald, but I am here with friends this time, and I am afraid I cannot leave them."

"Hoot, noo! ye needna leave them; there's room at the farm for ye a'. Hoo mony is there besides this ane?"

"One young man."

And catching sight of Lancy, a short distance away, she called his name and he stepped at once to her side.

"This is Mr. Gurney, a brother to my friend here."

"Ay, ay; I remember him," greeting Lancy heartily. "An' hoo dae ye like the look o' the Islan'?"

"Very much, indeed!" Lancy replied. "It is a fine place, and we have been enjoying ourselves immensely."

"But ye haena been up oor way yet! If I'd only kent ye were here I wad hae had ye up afore this," he repeated.

"Thank you kindly, Mr. McDonald, but we could hardly impose on your good-nature as far as that."

"Impose, is't? Ma dear sir, it's prood an' happy we wad be to hae ye come to see us. You maun gie me yer promise to come afore ye gang back to Halifax. The gran'mother wad be sair hurt at no seein' ye. Whan could ye come, noo?" turning to Dexie.

Just then Beatrice Fremont came towards them, and her smile of recognition told Dexie that the farmer was well known to her.

"I did not know you were acquainted with my friends, Mr. McDonald," and she extended her hand.

"I ken her faither weel, an' I met the dochter whan I was abroad," he replied with a smile, "but I never expected to meet ony Halifax folk the day. It's her faither that did me the kindness whan I was in Halifax that I'll never forget, an' it's weel pleased I am to meet them. Is't at your place they are staying, Miss Fremont?"

"Yes," replied Beatrice, smiling, "but I think I heard you trying to coax them away from us, Mr. McDonald."

He looked up into the bright face and replied:

"Ay, I want to show them that I dinna forget their kindness to me when I was a stranger in a strange land, an' no wishin' to rob ye o' yer visitors at a', I was tryin' to hae them say whan they wad come up to the farm, for it's masel' that'll come efter them, whanever they say the word."

"You need not be afraid to accept the invitation, girls," said Beatrice, as the farmer turned to say a few words to Lancy. "Your presence would cause no trouble; they are always so glad to have visitors that it is a pleasure to go. I spent several weeks there last summer, and I know they would all be glad to see you."

"It is well enough for Dexie to go," said Elsie, "but it would be very rude for me to go on such short acquaintance."

"There, Elsie, I stand condemned. Behold me, a visitor at Mrs. Fremont's, and we never knew of each other's existence before the visit was planned," said Dexie.

"But this is different, Dexie," Elsie hurried to explain.

"The difference is in your favor, Elsie."

"I think I can promise that they will be as glad to see you both at the farm as we were to have you here, and you know your being no relation does not matter to us."

"Well, I would dearly love to go," Dexie said. "It will be such a chance to see that part of the country, and by the way papa speaks of the McDonald homestead we would like it very much."

"Then you cannot do better than spend a few days at the seaside with him. There is a fine beach near, and chances for sea-bathing and all the rest of the delights of a seaside farm. If you like, Gertrude will go with you and stay for the first day or two."

"Is there a beach and sandhills like Stanhope Bay?" Dexie asked.

"Yes, only better, I think; and they have boats and go fishing sometimes. I am sure you would enjoy yourselves."

Lancy had been talking to Mr. McDonald during this conversation, but he now turned to them, saying:

"What do you say, girls, to accepting this kind invitation? Shall we go in a body?"

"They would all like to go, Mr. McDonald, but they are afraid they will crowd you," said Beatrice, smiling; "but I know so much better than that, that I am going to send Gertrude along with them. You will give her house-room, I know."

"Hoose-room, is't; there's plenty o' that; but hoo shune can ye a' come up?" he anxiously inquired.

"Well, not till next week, Mr. McDonald. We have planned to go for a picnic to Brackly Point, but you can tell the girls at home to look out for them next Wednesday; you need not take the trouble to come in for them, Mr. McDonald; I know how busy you are on the farm, and Gertrude knows the road. You must not let them run wild," she laughingly said, "but keep them well in order. But I must hurry home or I shall not be in time to give cook these vegetables for dinner. You must call in and see us on your way out of town, Mr. McDonald," and promising to do so he walked with them to where the carriage was waiting, and they drove home discussing the proposed visit as they went. Dexie then explained how she became acquainted with the farmer, and gave them a short account of the troubles he had experienced while visiting Nova Scotia.

"He shows to better advantage when he is at home on his own farm," said Beatrice. "He told us how he fell among thieves when he was in Halifax, and how a kind gentleman befriended him, but I did not expect I would ever know any of the family that he praised so highly when he told us the story. He supplies us with winter vegetables, and we are quite friendly, I assure you."

"How strange things do happen! I never expected to set eyes on the man again, and here we are planning to visit his home. A chain of circumstances, linked together, stretches a long way, even though the links are small and insignificant in themselves."

"Yes; it would have been a great disappointment to him had you refused his invitation. He loves to have visitors in the house. I can speak from experience, for I have been there with Gertrude. I expect Mr. McDonald did not impress you favorably when he was in Halifax, but in his own place you will not find a finer man anywhere."

"I can well believe it, but—oh! Beatrice, what is that?"

As they turned a corner they came upon a man standing in the centre of the street ringing a bell which he held in his hand, and instantly the doors and windows in the neighborhood were peopled, and pedestrians within earshot all stopped at the sound.

"Oh! who is it? What is he saying?" cried the girls.

"Listen," and she checked the horse. "It is old Hatch, the town-crier; something is lost."

The bell stopped, and in a loud voice the man read from a paper:

"Oh, yes! Oh, yes! Lost, lost! On market square, a tin box, containing papers. The finder will be rewarded by leaving it with the city marshal at the court-house. Oh, yes! Oh, yes!"

The bell rang again at the conclusion of the proclamation, and the man hurried on to the next street-crossing, where the loss was again set forth, his voice coming back in waves of sound as the carriage rolled farther away.

"The 'town-crier,'—that means a crier hired by the town, does it?" said Lancy. "I thought there was not such a thing this side the Atlantic. Why do not people advertise their losses?"

"That is the way they do it," said Beatrice, smiling, "and it pays better, particularly on market days, than to put it in all the city papers.

It is the quickest way to make a loss known, or to advertise a sale, for everybody listens to old Hatch, or Mr. Hatch, I should say. It is very old-fashioned to have a town-crier, I suppose, but we should miss him very much, though I daresay the office will die with the present crier."

"I think it is an old English custom," said Lancy. "I have read of criers going through the streets to announce great events, such as battles and other public matters, but I thought they were out of date long ago."

The events of the morning were duly discussed with Mrs. Fremont when they arrived at the house, and she assured them that no thought of inconvenience need cause them to shrink from accepting Mr. McDonald's invitation. Their visit would bring pleasure to all the members of the family.

"You will not find the family rude and rough, as some country people are. The girls are bright and intelligent, though full of fun and frolic," she added. "You will be sure to enjoy yourselves, and should there come a rainy day you will find plenty to amuse you in their quaint though comfortable farmhouse."

CHAPTER XXIV.

The same comfortable carriage that carried them to Montague Bridge was now travelling in an opposite direction, and the young strangers viewed with pleasure the luxuriant fields that surrounded the many farmhouses, and which promise such abundant harvest to their owners. The drive proved a very delightful one indeed. In consequence of the many stoppings they made to regale themselves with the sweet wild berries that grew in abundance by the roadside, the afternoon was drawing to a close when the little party reached the McDonald farmhouse.

The hardy pioneer who had first settled on the land that was owned and tilled by his descendants, must have selected the site on which he built his first log-house with an eye to the picturesque and beautiful, for no other spot for miles around had such a far reaching and delightful prospect. As time went by, and the land gave forth its increase, the log-house was supplemented by a more pretentious structure, that was "built on," the original apartments serving for kitchens, outhouses and other necessary buildings; and as this process of erection went on at later periods, the farmhouse was large and many sided, and possessed many conveniences that farmers are apt to consider unnecessary. But the honest pride that the present owner had in the well-tilled acres extended to the buildings upon it, and neatness and thrift were everywhere present. No hingeless gates propped with sticks met the eye; no broken-down doors were to be seen on his barns; a master hand ruled the land, and his rule brought prosperity and happiness.

The inmates of the farmhouse were such as you would expect to find amidst such surroundings—active and intelligent, and not wholly given up to the pursuit of the things which perish with the using, for the young people, at least, found time for intellectual pleasures that would have been considered in some farmhouses a wilful waste of time and means.

The family consisted of two young girls well up in their teens; Tom, a lively boy of twelve, and Dora, a plump little miss of six; and coming after these, in her own estimation, was the mother, a model of neatness and good-nature, a fine dairy woman, whose interests were, of course, centred in her cows and poultry yard, and she was generally found somewhere near the vicinity of her particular treasures.

Then there was Phebe, the strong-armed. A very important member of the family was she, as you would soon learn if you made any stay in the farmhouse. She it was who solved problems by the aid of washboard and scrubbing-brush, and the tempting meals she sent out of the kitchen would have delighted the heart of an epicure. But to see Phebe at her best, one should be at the farm during the busy haying season. It was her pride and delight to be considered "as good as any man," and she could "pitch a load" with a dexterity that even the two farm hands could not equal. These latter were brothers, and lived in a snug cottage a few rods away, said cottage being kept, like everything else on the farm, as "neat as a new pin," by Joe's wife, a brisk little woman, whose head scarcely reached to her husband's shoulder.

Another inmate of the farmhouse should have a paragraph all to herself, for "the grandmother" cannot be described in one brief line. Although she had long since passed the allotted span of life, yet age had not dimmed the lustre of her keen grey eyes nor dulled her faculties; and though she could no longer take an active part in the management of the household, yet from her corner in the pleasant room a potent spell reached out and overshadowed the members of the household. No crowned monarch on his throne ever ruled over such deferential and loyal subjects as those that here yielded to her benign sway. Not that she required it of them—it was graciously accorded her as to the patriarchs of old, and she seemed to belong to a holier age. Her soft white hair fell over her brow, and was drawn back under a large white frilled cap that surrounded her head like a halo, and the placid countenance that beamed beneath it inspired a feeling of reverence. She was called by all the household "the grandmother," and was dearly loved by them all; but the filial love of her son was far above that usually accorded to aged mothers, and it was easy to see how it warmed her heart.

Such was the household into which our young travellers were ushered about five o'clock on a beautiful summer day.

Mr. McDonald had been watching for their appearance for some hours, and his hearty greetings were repeated by the rest of the family. The farmer's daughters, Maggie and Lizzie, received Gertrude with the cordiality of an old friend, and though at first they seemed a little shy with the strangers from "abroad" this soon wore away, and they found their visitors quite as amiable as if they had been born on the same soil as themselves.

As soon as they had been refreshed, outwardly and inwardly, they were taken into the room where "the grandmother" sat in her large, comfortable chair, and were introduced to her with much solemnity; but they only waited for the few words of welcome to each, and then passed into the pleasant sitting-room adjoining.

"You must go in tomorrow and see the grandmother, one at a time," said Lizzie, as she drew a chair near the rest. "She does not see many strangers, and more than one confuses her. It seemed necessary to introduce you in a body, but she will be better pleased to become acquainted with you separately."

"I have something for her," said Gertrude. "She seems to remember me as well as if I were here only last week."

"I have something for her, too," said Dexie, smiling, "but it is only a soft foot-rest, and I see she has one now."

"That is kind of you to think of her," said Maggie. "Let me know when you are going to give it to her, and I will slip in beforehand and pull away her old one. She will be so delighted to think that you remembered her."

But the beautiful prospect from the windows claimed a closer inspection, and they went for their hats and started for the beach.

Lancy followed Mr. McDonald to inspect the premises with the happy owner, promising to join the rest later on. The girls walked along the path that led across a waving field of grain, and then stood for a few minutes looking off at the white-topped waves that extended as far as the eye could reach. The high sandbanks here raised their barriers against the waters of the Gulf, and shrill screams of laughter, such as only come from girlish throats, accompanied their descent through the dry, yielding sand to the beach below. The little white-washed building that served the double purpose of bathing and boat-house was duly inspected; and when Dexie admitted her ability to handle an oar, it raised her very much in the estimation of the bright country lasses, as they were under the impression that her soft hands were not put to much energetic labor, but one who had sufficient muscle to handle an oar could surely do other things as well. While they were on the beach Lancy joined them, and after he had inspected the boat-house, under Dexie's enthusiastic guidance, they agreed that on the morrow they would sail across to the distant point, and view the prospect from that quarter.

"We will take a lunch and have a private picnic," said Lizzie. "I hope the day will be fine. You have no idea how rough it is here when the wind is high; the breakers come rolling in so high and grand that it is quite fascinating to watch them, but dangerous in the extreme to be on the shore. Vessels have to keep out to sea when there is a storm, for this is considered a dangerous coast, but there have not been any wrecks along here for some years."

They returned by a different route, entering the house by a side-door, and the visitors were surprised to see the display of flowers that bloomed in the outer porch, making it, indeed, a bower of beauty.

"Why! you have made quite an addition to the house since I was here last," said Gertrude, as she stood to admire the blossoms.

"No, not an addition, only a little alteration," said Maggie. "Don't you remember this old porch where father used to smoke his pipe of an evening? Well, in the spring, when Joe was making the glass frames to force the early vegetables for market, we got him to put a glass frame on each side of the porch. They are not very neatly done, I admit, but they answer the purpose very well. Then these few shelves were easily fitted up, and this is the result," she added.

"I missed your flowers, from the window seats, and wondered if you had found them too much trouble," said Gertrude, fingering some sweet-smelling leaves near her. "Well, you see, there were so many of them that it was quite a task to look after them when they were spread over the house. In the winter we don't mind the trouble so much, as there is so little left of 'green things growing' to rest the eyes upon that we find them quite a pleasure. In the bright days of spring there is so much to see and do out-of doors that we thought we would collect them here. Of course, we still keep the grandmother's window full of blossoms, for she loves them so dearly."

"It is a pity that the porch is not on the south side of the house," said Dexie. "I should think it would be quite chilly here when the wind blows."

"So it is," said Lizzie, with a smile, "and I suppose you think we might have chosen a better situation for our little conservatory when this many-sided house has better spots to select from, but it was not the flowers alone we were thinking of."

"Well, what else were you thinking of, if I may ask?" said Gertrude.

Lizzie blushed slightly as she replied:

"This is the door that mother uses to go in and out when about her dairy work—that is the dairy under the trees at the end of the path—and father likes to sit here and watch her about her work of an evening while he smokes his pipe; and when she has done her work she will often sit here and rest a few minutes with him; but there is not much of a prospect from this door, except the waters of the Gulf, so we thought we would put our flowers here and she could see and smell them when she went in and out. She might be too busy to stop and notice them particularly, but they are something pleasant to rest her eyes on when she is through with the milk. I always thought that the restless waves made her think of my brother who was lost at sea, but now I fancy that the flowers rest her, though perhaps it is only fancy, after all."

Dexie's thoughts flew back to her own mother lying listlessly on her sofa so much of the time. How much had she ever done to change the current of her mother's thought? She made a mental memorandum to try the effect of a few bright blooms in her mother's window as soon as she returned home.

As they talked, Maggie had taken up her father's pipe that had lain on a shelf near, and emptying its contents she took from a pouch hanging on the wall a piece of tobacco and a jack-knife, and, with a practised hand, she refilled the pipe afresh, then laid it gently on a little shelf within easy reach of the cosy seat that her father occupied during the warm summer evenings. It was done so quietly that it was almost unnoticed, but Dexie saw it and understood the kindly act. She wondered if she loved her own father enough to perform such an act for him. She felt glad that her father did not use tobacco, for she would not care to be outdone by these Prince Edward Island girls; yet in her case she felt that even lovingkindness had its limit, and that she would have to draw the line *this* side of the tobacco pipe.

Maggie felt, rather than saw, that Dexie was watching her, and as she laid the pipe in readiness for her father's evening smoke she looked up and said with a smile:

"You never saw a girl do that before, confess now? Well, I don't care for it, but father likes to find his pipe all ready for him, so I try to overcome my dislike, and his tobacco-smoke helps to keep my flowers free from vermin, you know."

As twilight deepened into evening the members of the family all assembled in the grandmother's room, and a homelike feeling came over Elsie as she saw Mr. McDonald open the big Bible that rested on a small table near the grandmother's chair, and read, in his rich Scotch accents, the evening psalms. Then they quietly knelt, all except the grandmother, who, rising slowly to her feet and leaning on her staff, offered up the evening prayer. It made Dexie think of the patriarchs of old, who blessed their families "leaning on their staffs for very age." Then the family said good-night to the grandmother, and the polished candlesticks that decorated the mantle shelf were taken down by the farmer's wife and a lighted candle set in each; these were then handed to the different members of the family, who passed out of the room in single file, very much after the manner of a diminutive torch-light procession.

The family were supposed to retire to their own rooms at once, as "early to bed" was the rule of the farmhouse, but the laughing group of girls all assembled in one room for a friendly chat before retiring.

As Lancy sat by his open window enjoying the quiet scene without, the sound of their voices reached his ears. He would have preferred a walk, or a short *tete-a-tete* with Dexie, instead of this early-to-bed arrangement, but he respected the rule of the house and blew out his candle at an early hour. He was rewarded for his good behavior by a long refreshing sleep, and Dexie appearing to him in his dreams was more gracious than ever she had been during his waking hours.

But, as everyone knows, when young ladies get talking together of an evening, sleep "comes slowly up that way," and the shortness of their candles alone warned them that it was time they sought the pillow. But the short candles were unheeded, for Gertrude was relating reminiscences of a former visit, and the fun and frolic that prevailed at the farm during their stay. At last, when one of the candles flared up, then subsided in smoke, the girls rose to leave the room, but Gertrude turned at the door, saying:

"Take good care, girls, and sleep well over to the back of the bed, or you may repeat the performance that took place the first night that Beatrice and I slept in the house."

"Oh, do tell them about it, Gertrude," said Maggie, laughing. "Our candles will hold out that long, I think."

Gertrude seated herself on the foot of the bed, while the rest waited for the story.

"Well, we slept that night in the room that Lancy occupies, at the head of the stairs, and, do you know, I never enter it but I feel cold shivers running up my back as I think of that night. You see, Mrs. McDonald's feather-beds are wonderful for size; they are her pride and joy; but we were not used to them, so, during the night, we rolled over too near the front of the bed, when suddenly out we both went, and the feather-bed fell out on top of us! I thought there had been an earthquake, and so laid quiet for the next shock. By and by Beatrice crawled out from under the ruins and tried to lift the feather-bed back on the mattress, but instead of doing so she fell back on the floor with it in her arms. Over went the table, and this upset the whole contents of the water-pitcher over my back. Good gracious! how it scared me! It was pitch dark and I could not tell what had happened, so I screamed—screamed as if I was being murdered. Imagine our feelings when the door opened, and in walked Mr. and Mrs. McDonald, carrying a candle and a poker. Oh! I thought I should die with shame. They thought that robbers had broken into the house and were carrying us off, so they ran with the poker to our rescue. It took them some time to comprehend the true state of affairs, then Mr. McDonald disappeared in a twinkling. The girls here came running up to see what was the matter, and they soon tossed the bed and bed-clothes out of the way, and got some dry garments for poor shivering me. Beatrice escaped with a lump on her head as big as an egg. I had no outward bruises to speak of, but I felt bad enough without any; but the water-pitcher had the handle broken off, and the bed-clothes and feather-bed had to be dried out-of-doors for days after. Oh, dear! I did feel so ashamed; such a scrape I never got into before or since. So take my story to heart, and do not lose your senses if you do fall out of bed," and Gertrude laughed as she took up her candle and followed the rest from the room, leaving Dexie and Elsie to the mercy or comfort of their big feather-bed.

CHAPTER XXV.

There was a full breakfast table the next morning, for the young visitors determined to fall into the ways of the family as much as possible, so decided to be "early birds" along with the rest.

During the meal, Mr. McDonald suggested the various ways they might pass the day enjoyably; but when he had exhausted the resources of pleasure that occurred to his mind, Dexie smilingly said,

"You are very kind, Mr. McDonald, to place so many pleasures within our reach, but it would not be right to spend the whole day in that way."

"What way would you prefer to pass the day?" said Lizzie, with a smile.

"Well, first, I should like to help wash the dishes, then I should like to be set to work at anything else that I can do in a passable manner."

"Dear me! is that what you call enjoying yourself, Miss Dexie?" said Maggie. "I fancy you would not like dish-washing, if you had to do it all the time."

"Well, perhaps a full day's task of dish-washing would be rather tedious," said Dexie, laughing; "but I was only bidding for the breakfast dishes, you know."

"But there is no need to trouble yourselves about anything," said Mrs. McDonald. "Enjoy yourselves all you can while you are here; Phebe can manage the work nicely. Put on your hats, and have a walk through the fields; it will give you a fine appetite for your dinner."

"But I have a remarkable appetite already, Mrs. McDonald; I shall be alarmed if it increases much more," was the smiling reply, "and you know the Bible says, 'If one will not work, neither should he eat,' or words to that effect, so you must have pity on me, and not keep me idle. Lancy, your appetite is wonderful too, for that is your second cup of coffee; you had better hunt up some work also," she laughingly added.

"I will give him some now," said Lizzie. "Before the tide comes in he can go down to the boat-house and get out the boat. We want to be off by ten o'clock; the tide will be about right then, and since you are so anxious for work, Miss Dexie, you may help Maggie pack the baskets. I hope, Gertrude, you won't ask for something to do, for I want you to take Miss Gurney around, and show her the poultry yard. Mother will be too busy to protect her from our feathered enemies."

"Enemies! are they very savage?" Elsie asked in alarm.

"No; the trouble is in the opposite direction," said Maggie. "The creatures are that tame they are quite a nuisance; you can scarcely step for them. The greedy things look for something to eat from everybody who ventures inside the yard, and will fly on your shoulders for the first chance at the pan. Gertrude knows how to protect herself, so you can put yourself under her care with safety."

How pleasant it is when one goes visiting to feel as if you are one of the family; but the expression "Making yourself at home" is more often made than really experienced. While at the farmhouse our young people did truly realize the feeling.

It would take too long to tell of the many excursions by water, and drives by land, that were enjoyed daily, but the vicinity for miles around was thoroughly explored. Every night Gertrude would say she ought to return home, but the next day would seem so full of pleasure that it seemed a pity to miss it.

One evening, when they were seated and idly swinging among the boughs of a low-limbed tree that stood near the house—a favorite spot with the girls—Dexie suddenly remarked,

"Lancy, I am just hungry for a 'sing;' do start up something."

"Bless you for the thought," Lancy replied, from a distant limb. "I have been wondering these few days back what it was I was missing. Take the first choice yourself, and start away."

But they found it was easier to start the singing than it was to end it, for they soon had all the household within hearing distance, and "just one more" was asked for from so many different quarters that their song-hunger was fully satisfied before they were allowed to stop.

They seemed to sing like the birds, from "lightness of heart, and very joy of living." After a few moments' silence, a bird-song was whistled by the "mates in the tree," eliciting strong words of praise, as well as surprise, from the delighted listeners.

"Oh, that's nothing to what we have to endure at home," said Elsie. "Those two are always hooting away like a pair of owls. It is a wonder their throats are not split before this. I almost hope that the piano at home will be mouldy when we get back."

"We will soon knock the mould out of it, hey, Dexie?" Lancy laughingly replied, as he lifted his mate down from her perch.

"Oh, how I should love to have a piano, and be able to play on it," said Maggie, with a long-drawn sigh. "Perhaps we will have one sometime."

"Why, Maggie, how can you say such a thing? A deep sorrow comes before that joy; and how can you wish for it?" was the stern reproof of her sister.

"Oh, dear! what have I said! I forgot that for the moment!" and there was such a tone of regret in her words that Dexie's eyes asked an explanation.

"We can't have a piano while the grandmother is alive. She thinks that all music, except the bagpipes, perhaps, is positively wicked; so we try not to think about it. We spoke about it to father once, and he felt so badly that he could not please us and the grandmother too. Of course she comes first; but he has put the money in the bank to buy an instrument—sometime. I hate to think about it, though I long for it more than I can tell. It makes me feel as if I was such a wicked creature; for just think of wishing for a thing that can only be had over the grandmother's coffin! Oh, dear! I wish I had never heard the sound of music!" and to the surprise and dismay of the little group she burst into tears.

"Oh, do forgive me! I am to blame for this, I fear," said Dexie, her face showing her distress. "I did not know—"

"Don't think of such a thing, Miss Dexie," said Lizzie, putting her arm around her. "It was not your fault; Maggie has her cry over this same thing every few weeks, and feels the better for it, too, I believe. We have many pleasures that few girls on a farm ever think of, and we ought to be content. But I really do believe that if the grandmother could walk around the house, and should come across the books and other things that we girls have brought into it since she was confined to her room, she would die with the shock. She thinks that everything remains about the same as it was in her day, and we are careful not to disturb her opinion; for in this case a little deceit seems wise, or, at least, necessary."

In a few minutes the sunshine again appeared on Maggie's face; but the feeling that was brought out by the sudden tears seemed to draw Dexie nearer to this young girl who had such a love of music, yet could not give it expression until the shadow of death had first walked before her.

The next morning brought a letter from home, and by its tone Lancy felt he must be needed; so it was decided they should return to Charlottetown, finish their visit at Mrs. Fremont's, and then return home.

When Mr. McDonald learned that the young people were preparing to leave for the city, he called Dexie to his side, and turning to a small cupboard brought out a tin box, saying:

"Someane left this box in ma kairt that day I saw ye in the toon. I jaloose the owner was buyin' somethin' an' laid it there an' forgot aboot it, but I never saw it till I got hame. I opened it to see if I could fin' the name o' the owner, an' I found some papers wi' yer faither's name on them. Can ye mak' oot whit it means, ma lassie? Somethin' is no richt, I tak' it."

Dexie sat down beside him and read several of the letters and papers, and their contents filled her with surprise. She was well acquainted with her father's business, as she wrote many of his letters, and she saw at once that something was indeed wrong.

"How strange that I should come across this!" she said. "This letter is written by a man named Plaisted; he does business with papa. He has been on the Island with him, and knows the people that have had dealings with papa, before he joined him. What are you going to do with the box, Mr. McDonald?"

"I was gaun to ask Mr. Gurney to return it to the lawyer whase name is on the inside o' the cover. He's considered an honest man, though he is a lawyer. Maybe if ye wad tell him aboot this man Plaisted, it micht keep him frae daein' yer faither ony mischief. It wad dae nae harm, ony way."

"May I copy this letter written by Plaisted? I would like to show papa what kind of a man this Plaisted is, for I think he trusts him too much."

"Weel, it canna be ony harm, shurely, jist to *copy* the letter, but ye needna mention the maitter to onyane; there's nae kennin' whit they wad mak' o't."

Dexie soon had a copy of the letter and a general knowledge of a few others in Plaisted's peculiar handwriting, and this proved of much value in establishing certain facts that came up at a future time, the copied letter proving the missing link in a chain of evidence that brought Plaisted's misdoings to judgment.

Lancy was consulted about the box, and promised to see it safe into the hands of the owner. Soon after they learned that this was the very box that they had heard the town-crier proclaim as *lost* when driving home from the market-house.

With many regrets at leave-taking, both on the part of visitors and entertainers, the little party drove away, unconscious of the fact that under the seat of the carriage there were several substantial tokens of regard, which were, however, discovered, when they arrived at Mrs. Fremont's.

Mrs. Fremont congratulated them all on the benefit they had undoubtedly received from their visit, particularly Elsie, who seemed to be a new creature. Her pale cheeks had been painted by the sun a warm brown, and the pure sea-air had created an appetite that told its story in rounded limbs and wide-awake appearance that contrasted greatly with the languid movements she had brought with her from Halifax.

Lancy sent word to his parents that they would return the following week, and promised to telegraph the day of starting.

This was glad news to Hugh, who was present when the letter was read, and heard its contents discussed.

Ever since Hugh had come into possession of his fortune he had looked forward to the return of the party with much impatience. There were times when he felt almost tempted to seek Dexie's presence, and try again to win a word that would give him some hope. All his future plans seemed to depend on the way Dexie treated him, and he waited her coming, uplifted sometimes by hope, but more often depressed by fear, and with a restlessness that made him almost irritable at times. He insisted on filling his usual place in the store, glad enough to keep his mind occupied and his thoughts away from himself.

At last one morning the telegraph messenger knocked at the door, and brought the welcome message.

A broad smile passed over Mr. Gurney's face as he read the telegram, and he handed it to his wife, saying:

"Dexie sent that telegram or wrote it, or I'm very much mistaken."

Whereupon Hugh was very anxious to read it, and to his great delight Mrs. Gurney passed it over to him, and this is what he read:

"Kill the prodigal; the fatted calves are on the way."

For the first time in many weeks, Hugh burst into a hearty laugh, and he read the words over until he could almost fancy he heard Dexie's laughing voice beside him.

"Well, that message may have seemed incomprehensible to the transmitter of it, but it tells us a long story," said Mrs. Gurney, a smile lighting up her face. "It says they are well and in good spirits, that they are glad to be coming home again, but will be very hungry when they get here, so I had better bestir myself and 'kill the prodigal,'" and she rose to visit the kitchen.

"Well, she has told the story within the limit of ten words, too," said Hugh, making some excuse for keeping the bit of paper so long before him.

"What prodigal are you going to kill, mamma?" said Gracie, following her mother into the kitchen.

"Oh! that is what we will call the big fat chicken that eats so much oats, and picks the little ones on the back when they try to get a mouthful. He will do for a prodigal, so we will have him cooked for Elsie's supper."

Gracie sat down on a low stool, her face wearing a puzzled expression, and she began to repeat to herself the parable of the prodigal son. Suddenly a bright look came over her face, for she had solved the troublesome riddle, and she joyfully exclaimed:

"Oh, mamma! Dexie didn't learn it right; they didn't kill the prodigal, it was the fatted calf that was cooked! Oh, dear! how funny to make such a mistake, and she such a big girl! Say, Hugh," as he passed through the room, "Dexie is the prodigal, and not the fatted calf, isn't she?"

And with more earnestness than the subject demanded he replied: "I hope so."

It was Mr. Gurney who drove to the depot in the evening to meet the travellers, much to the disappointment of Hugh, who hoped to be the first to receive Dexie's greetings; but the excitement of their arrival had somewhat subsided by the time he made his appearance in the house.

It is needless to say there was great rejoicing in the Gurney household that evening. Elsie was petted and caressed to her heart's content, and she listened with a smiling face to the oft-repeated remark that she "looked so much better."

Hugh's unexpected good fortune came in for a share of the discussion which took place round the tea-table, and the well-cooked *prodigal* was the butt of many jokes. Dexie was asked to come in and get her share of the "fatted calf," as Gracie persisted in calling it, but she begged to be excused, feeling that she would prefer to spend her first evening at home.

Gussie lost no time in telling Dexie all her hopes and plans, and she gave the impression that everything was settled. She could talk of nothing but the splendid time she expected to have in the future.

"Hugh does not say much to me, but I know I can do just as I like with him after we are married, so I don't mind if he is rather cool and short occasionally. Of course he means to marry me, or why did he talk so long to papa about it?" said Gussie, as she followed Dexie downstairs.

"Did papa tell you about it?" a suspicion of the true state of affairs entering her mind for a moment.

"No—but—well, to tell the truth, I was listening at the door, but I heard enough to let me know the nature of the interview, for I heard papa say quite distinctly, 'I don't think she cares enough for you, and she must marry to suit herself,' so what else could he have meant? Now, I do not care so very much about Hugh, I must confess—or I did not, I mean, when he was merely Mr. Gurney's clerk, but with a fortune in his pocket who could refuse such a fine-looking man?"

"Well, I could, for one," said Dexie, trying to hide a laugh. "He would need something more than riches to be attractive to me, for all his fine looks; but I congratulate you, Gussie. I hope you will be happy."

"Of course I will be happy, so long as the money holds out, anyway," said she, with a laugh that grated harshly on her sister's ears. "Did you see any brides when you were away, Dexie, and how were they dressed?"

"I wasn't searching for brides, Gussie. I confined my attention to pollywogs, crabs, and things of that ilk."

Gussie's remarks jarred on her feelings, in spite of her efforts to seem careless, but she smiled, as Gussie scornfully replied:

"Well, did I ever! I guess if you searched for a sunburnt face and a blistered nose, you found *them* fast enough."

"Yes, unfortunately, one can find those sort of things without searching for them; they are thrown in with the pollywogs for good measure; but my nose is not half so ornamental as Lancy's. Don't be cross, Gussie. Let us go into the parlor and wait for the trunks. I have a lot of nice new patterns in fancywork for you."

They entered the parlor together, where Aunt Jennie followed them, and they talked about the many events that had transpired during Dexie's absence. The room was almost dark. It seemed pleasanter to talk in the twilight, but a bar of light shone from the sitting-room door, and relieved it from any sombre appearance. Dexie kept wondering why the expressman did not appear; she was anxious to see if the little treasures she had collected for distribution had borne the journey safely. She rose at last and went to the window to see if there was anyone in sight, but she was disappointed. Not so Hugh, who was just entering the house, and caught sight of her outline against the window-pane, and, thinking the unlighted parlor vacant but for Dexie's presence, he softly opened the door and stepped to her side. All her cold repulses were forgotten, her curt words of dismissal faded from his memory, his heart was yearning for her presence, she was there before him, and in a moment he had her in his arms.

"My darling! my love! do I see you at last. How I have longed for this moment!"

It was so sudden that for a moment Dexie was powerless to move, but she freed herself quickly, saying, as she stepped back:

"How dare you! How *dare* you touch me! It is I; not Gussie," she added, thinking he might have mistaken the person, though his words belied the thought. "I was watching for the expressman, and did not notice you had come in; you made a mistake," came the quick-spoken words.

"Well, I should say it was a mistake, and an odd one too," said Gussie, coming forward. "How could you mistake that mop of a head for mine, Hugh?"

She had seen the embrace, but the whispered words had not reached her. Naturally, Hugh was much taken back when he realized that Dexie was not alone, but he anathematized Gussie in his heart, and bit his lips to keep back the words that sprang up in reply. If Gussie had known how precious that "mop of a head" was to her quondam lover, she would not have been so ready to "give herself away," as the trite saying has it.

CHAPTER XXVI.

The embarrassing silence that followed Hugh's entrance was broken at last by Aunt Jennie, who made some commonplace remark that allowed free speech to resume itself again. She saw at once the position of affairs; the reason of Hugh's coolness when in Gussie's society was no longer any secret. She thought he had lacked the loverlike eagerness that one might expect, judging the matter from the standpoint of Gussie's frequent remarks.

But believing that Lancy Gurney had more than a friendly feeling for Dexie, she felt uneasy for the result of the struggle between the rivals. Dexie would surely suffer between them.

It was impossible for Dexie to feel at ease after Hugh's extraordinary greeting. She felt vexed at the thought of the spectacle she must have presented to those who had witnessed it. Did Hugh really know her, or were his words meant for Gussie alone? The hope that it was the latter made her decide that it must be; but if she had noticed how carelessly he replied to Gussie's entertaining chatter, or observed his eager looks in her own direction, she might have guessed that his heart was not in Gussie's keeping.

The arrival of the trunks brought a grateful respite to all, and Dexie disappeared the moment the expressman arrived, but with the excuse of helping to lift the trunks into the hall, Hugh followed her. Gussie, however, was close behind; not for a moment would she leave those two together. After what she had seen in the parlor there should be no chance of further *mistakes*, if her vigilance could prevent it.

Dexie was so anxious to show her treasures that she opened her trunk as soon as Hugh deposited it in the hall.

"Here, Georgie," as her brother came running down the stairs, "take this parcel to mamma, carefully, mind, and ask her if she is too tired to see me again tonight. When you come back I will give you the box of something that I heard you wishing for," and looking up to her sister, who was bending over to watch her, she added, "Here is your parcel, Gussie, and this is for auntie. Where is she, I wonder?"

"Oh! do let me see what you brought for auntie?" and Gussie caught the parcel from Dexie's hands and began to inspect the contents.

Hugh was for the moment forgotten, but he still lingered near the door, hoping that some chance would favor him. He had so much to say, so much that had been crowded back into his heart during her long absence, that he felt he must seize the first opportunity to speak of his hopes, and he wished to assure her that there had been no mistake on his part when he met her in the parlor. Just then Gussie stepped over to the lamp for a closer inspection of some fancy patterns, and Hugh turned to Dexie, saying:

"You seem to have remembered everyone but me, Dexie. You have not even a kind word to give me."

"Well, I have not an *unkind* word either, Mr. McNeil, so that ought to count for something, I think," and she stooped to pick up some paper from the floor, "but I think you deserve a good many for the ridiculous mistake you made when you came in."

"I made no mistake, except that of thinking the room held no one but yourself. Give me a chance to prove it, Dexie."

Dexie pretended not to hear, but turned the conversation by saying:

"I have not congratulated you on the good fortune you have met while we were away."

"Well! I think it is time you did," Gussie answered, awake to the fact that a low conversation was being held near her. "I am sure it is no everyday affair to fall heir to a fortune. Weren't you surprised when I wrote to you about it?"

"Yes, very," and the memory of the letter brought a smile with it. "And if the possession of money means happiness, I presume Mr. McNeil feels raised to the seventh heaven of bliss."

"Not yet, Dexie, but I am looking forward to the 'seventh heaven' you speak of."

"Mrs. Gurney mentioned that you thought of going abroad. I hope Lancy's absence has not interfered with your plans, Mr. McNeil?" and she made a move to ascend the stairs.

"Would you like to go abroad, Dexie?"

There was an eagerness in his tone that Dexie did not understand, so she answered:

"Well, if going *abroad* means a visit to Great Britain, I say no, most decidedly! What do I care for the English, Scotch or Irish—as a race, I mean? My definition of the term abroad is, a tour through Europe, ending with Egypt and the Holy Land, and farther still if the pocket-book held out."

"Dexie, will you go abroad with me?"

Gussie looked from Hugh to Dexie in open-eyed surprise. This invitation might mean much or little.

"Why, Hugh, it would be improper for Dexie to accept such an invitation," she hastily said.

"There would be nothing improper about it, if she went as my wife."

"You are carrying your jokes too far, Mr. McNeil," said Dexie, coldly. "If you want to turn Mormon you had better 'go West, young man,' for when I go on *my* wedding tour I want a husband who will be content with *one* wife, and, when he and I go abroad, we will go alone. No offence meant; but two is company, while three is a crowd. So good-night to you both," and she turned and ran up the stairs, leaving Hugh looking after her with a beating heart.

"Well, I hope I have been plain enough this time," was her inward comment. "Can he really care for Gussie and expect to marry her, as she thinks, or does he want to turn Mormon and marry the both of us? But whatever he has said to Gussie don't count, so long as he makes eyes at me. I'm willing to be pleasant and agreeable, if he is to be my brother-in-law; but he shall not call me 'his darling' and 'his love,' as if it were me he was engaged to. I wish I had slapped his face for him."

But, figuratively speaking, she had just done so, and if she had seen the grieved look on Hugh's face as he groped his way out the front door, she would have realized that her slap had struck home.

Gussie felt indignant, as she stood in the hall recalling the scene just passed. Hugh had left her without a word, but she could plainly see that the blame was not on Dexie's shoulders this time.

"I do believe he cares for Dexie, after all; what else could his words imply? But she does not care for him, that is plain; and it will be a strange thing if I cannot arrange matters so that he cannot help but offer himself. After what he said to papa, I know he wants to marry one of us, and I will see that it shall be myself."

The next day Dexie had a long talk with her father. She had called him aside to give him the letter she had copied from the one in Plaisted's handwriting, and when she had explained the circumstances Mr. Sherwood was much astonished, and praised her for her thoughtfulness in securing an exact copy.

"I will write to the parties in question and forbid the payment of any money to him, but I will say nothing to Plaisted about the matter at present. I will keep a sharp lookout, and directly he tries to put his plans into execution I will bring him up short. Thank you, my little woman, you have done a lucky stroke of business for me; but stay a minute," as Dexie rose to leave the room, "I want to ask you something. How much do you care for Hugh McNeil?" said he, as she came over to his side.

"Why, papa, what makes you ask such a question? Didn't you make a mistake in the name?" she said, archly. "Didn't you mean to say—Lancy Gurney?"

"No; I have a guess that way. But how about Hugh? Come, I have a reason for asking," and he drew her down to his knee. "Think a minute, and tell me."

"But, papa, I don't need to think a moment in order to answer that question. I don't like him at all. You should ask Gussie that question."

"I need not, for I think I know what her answer would be; but I have a little story to tell you, and I want you to give it serious consideration. As soon as Hugh McNeil knew about the money coming to him, he asked me for a private interview. From what Gussie said, I expected that he intended to ask for her. But Hugh was very straightforward, and made the whole matter plain, and, Dexie, he asked for the liberty of making you his wife. He said he was willing to wait any reasonable time for you, if only he had the promise of your hand in the end."

"Papa! you never told him *yes*! say you did not!" cried Dexie, springing to her feet and regarding him with beseeching eyes. "My dear, I could not; so do not look so frightened about it," and he drew her back to his side again. "I am not willing to give my little girl to anyone yet, but I am not insensible to the fact that a man who loves my daughter as Hugh professes to love you, and can provide for her so handsomely, is worthy of some consideration."

"Why couldn't he take Gussie? She wants him and I don't," she answered with a frown. "I am sure Gussie told me she was all but engaged to him. He doesn't want the both of us, I hope."

"Dexie, I am sorry to say that Gussie has not acted so well about this matter as I could wish. She makes no secret of the fact that she would gladly accept the position he offers you, and it annoys him. Hugh confessed to me that at one time he did think he cared for Gussie, but found his mistake, and he has been so open with me about it that I cannot blame him for the change. Think it well over, Dexie, before he talks to you himself. A handsome man like Hugh, with a good bank account, will not come in your way very often. He offered to make a handsome settlement on you, directly you promised him your hand."

"Dear papa, would you like your poor Dexie to be unhappy for life?" throwing her arms around his neck. "I am sure you would not," as he drew her closer to him. "I could never marry Hugh; his very presence makes me feel pugnacious, and I feel like picking a quarrel with him every time I speak to him, and I enjoy doing it, too."

"Well, in that case it would not be pleasant to live your life with him, would it? but still it seems a pity to lose the money when he seems so anxious to put it into your hands. Your life would be so different with money at your command. If it were only Gussie, now."

"Yes, if it were only Gussie everything would go smoothly while the money lasted; but you did not tell me the result of the interview, papa."

"I told him I would leave the matter for you to settle, but I gave my consent, if he gained yours. I think he would be good to you, Dexie."

"Well! I guess he would have to, if he once got me, or I would know the reason why! What does mamma say about it, for I suppose she knows?"

"She seems much put out that it is not Gussie he asks for, but she hopes you will not be so foolish as to throw the chance away. That is the opinion of the both of us, you see, so do not decide hastily, Dexie."

"Dear me, how provoking it is! Mamma will be vexed, and I cannot help it, for I really cannot *say* I consent when I feel such a dislike to the man. Some young ladies would see nothing but his fortune; but think, papa, we might live for fifty years! and I can't look forward to fifty years of life spent with Hugh McNeil. So tell him for me, papa, that it cannot be."

"Take time to think it over, Dexie, before he gets *any* answer, for

Hugh will be much disappointed if you refuse him. I promised to plead his cause for him, but I cannot do so against your inclinations, since it will be you alone who must live your life with him. But, Dexie, many people live happily together without loving each other overmuch, so do not think it impossible for you to do the same. Do you care so very much for Lancy Gurney?" he asked, after a pause.

Dexie did not feel so embarrassed over this question as her father expected. She was pleased to have her father take such an interest in her little affairs of the heart, and show his sympathy in things that are usually left to the mother and daughter to talk over together.

"I do not know if I can explain it to you, papa," she replied with a smile. "I don't think I should care to marry Lancy—indeed, I am quite sure I never shall, but I like him very much for all that; but you need not tell anyone I said so, will you, papa?" she added, seeing a smile in her father's eyes. "Lancy has been very kind to me ever since we came to Halifax. You know yourself he has added very much to my pleasure by his thoughtful attentions, but I do not think it will end as Lancy expects," and a pretty blush spread over her face.

"Then you have not given him any promise!" smiling at her red cheeks.

"No, but he seems to think everything will be as he hopes, and is so pleasant over it that it is a pity to undeceive him. I'll promise not to allow any love-making, for he knows very well it is useless to become sentimental with me. Please don't tell my little secrets, not even to mamma, for she is sure to tell Gussie."

"Do not be afraid to trust me with your little affairs, Dexie," he said, kissing her cheek. "I am only too glad to be your confidant and adviser. I am sorry that your mother feels so little inclined to take the same interest in your affairs; you need her more now than when you were a child."

Mr. Sherwood watched his daughter with loving eyes as she tripped away from his side, and he wished for the power to look into the future and see how matters would end. He sighed as he realized how much depended on her own judgment; but his daughters must each settle for herself the question that would make or mar their future lives.

A change took place in the Sherwood household a few weeks later, for Aunt Jennie was obliged to return to her old home in Vermont, which was such an unlooked for event to Mrs. Sherwood that it quite upset her. They had all become so used to looking to Aunt Jennie for everything, that the house would seem to be without its head if she were gone.

When Dexie told her aunt how the Fremont girls managed the household expenditure and took the oversight of much of the housekeeping arrangements, Aunt Jennie replied that she thought her niece quite as capable as the Fremont girls, and asked Dexie if she could not undertake to fill her place after she was gone, as she knew

Mrs. Sherwood would be glad to be relieved of the charge. When Dexie broached the matter to her mother, she found her quite willing to let anyone step into the gap, so Dexie determined to learn as much as she could while her aunt was present to advise her.

The little account books were brought out and studied, until Dexie felt sure she understood what ought to be done, though she doubted her ability to put the knowledge into practice. But her doubts soon gave way to a feeling of confidence in herself as, day by day, she mastered new difficulties.

"I think I will make a wonderful housekeeper, by and by, mamma," Dexie said, as they were all seated in her mother's room, and Mrs. Sherwood was regretting Aunt Jennie's approaching departure. "I am learning fast. Even Nancy gives me encouragement. The only thing that troubles me is the fact that Nancy thinks I am playing at housekeeping, and I am afraid she will resent my authority after auntie goes away. I shall have to wear a cap and spectacles to add dignity to my new position," she laughingly added.

"How absurd you are, Dexie," said her mother, with a frown. "If you intend to act as housekeeper I hope you will try and be less childish; and to go through the house whistling like a boy, as you did today, is far from ladylike. Will you ever learn to be genteel like your sister Gussie?"

"I think Dexie should be given her full name in the future," Gussie added, "if she intends to rush through the house like her namesake round the race course."

"But I will not be called after Bonner's trotting-horse! I will not!" said Dexie, angrily. "I fancy this would soon be a queer house if there was no one in it with more energy about them than you possess! However, let us return to the matter under discussion," said she, more mildly. "I want to know, in case I make any savings from the month's allowance, if I can pocket the remainder."

"I am afraid, Dexie, that you will not find much left over, for the first few months," her aunt said smilingly. "You must allow something for your inexperience, you know."

"Oh! I know that, auntie. But can I have it, mamma, much or little? Make the bargain with me, mamma."

"Certainly, Dexie; but you cannot expect to save much out of the usual month's allowance unless you scrimp us."

"Oh, I'll promise not to scrimp," was the laughing reply. "But I am going to begin my reign while auntie is here; then my inexperience will not cost me so much. I kept my eyes and ears open when I was at Mrs. Fremont's, and I didn't peep and listen either; but I learned a few things that I think will be a great help to me in my future sphere."

"I think Gussie had better join you in this branch of study," said Mr. Sherwood, laying down his paper. "It will be as much benefit to her as to you."

"Thanks, papa. I beg to decline the honor! I have no wish to shine as a domestic; it is not in my line," said Gussie, in a lofty tone.

"Well, I do not expect to run the house as smoothly as Aunt Jennie—I am sure you will not expect it of me, mamma—but I will do my best, and it will be nice to learn just how to do things."

"That is right, Dexie. Every girl should learn how, even though she may never have to put her own hands to the work itself. But do not be too particular about keeping within the monthly allowance; I am quite as willing to pay for housekeeping lessons as for music lessons."

How Dexie prized the weeks that followed! In after years she looked back to them with a thankful heart, for Aunt Jennie did not confine her teaching to the art of housekeeping alone. The inward culture of the heart was not forgotten. The good seed was sown with no sparing hand, and though some lay weeks, months and even years without bearing fruit, yet few were altogether lost.

What a blank her absence caused in the household! She had filled a mother's place among them, for the loving tact that bridged over the little jars that are apt to occur in every household was not one of Mrs. Sherwood's accomplishments.

The first few weeks after her aunt's departure were very trying ones to Dexie. There seemed much fault-finding that was really unnecessary, but Dexie honestly tried to do her best. She could see her own failures as well as her successes, and when she found that much of Nancy's ill-temper was due to Gussie's interference in the kitchen, she laid the matter before her father, and that put an end to many petty annoyances.

Dexie had much to bear from her mother also, for Mrs. Sherwood felt aggrieved that Dexie did not appreciate Hugh McNeil's attentions as she thought they deserved. His visits were a daily occurrence, and it was vexing to see Dexie refuse what would have been so acceptable to Gussie.

"If you do not intend to marry him, why do you not tell him so plainly?" she said one day, when Dexie had shut herself up in her room to avoid meeting Hugh. "What is the use of keeping out of his way, when you know what he wants to see you for?"

"Why should I put myself in his way, when I do not want what he has to offer? He shall not talk to me about it, either, unless he does so before a third party. I will not see him alone! I sent him a decided answer through papa, so why can he not be satisfied with that? I declare, I almost hate the man!"

"Tell him so, plainly; then, and give Gussie a chance. She is not so foolish as to allow any sentimentality to come between her and a fortune."

"I have already told him so, as plainly as I can, mamma. But if you think I am standing in Gussie's way, just give Hugh McNeil this message from me. Tell him that I will *never* marry him; that I hate the very sound of his footsteps; that if his fortune were four times multiplied, I would not have him; that I want him to cease persecuting me with his hateful attentions, and leave me alone! Now, is that plain enough for any sensible man to understand, do you think?"

"Dexie! take care! See that you do not repent those words, for I shall see that they are repeated to him, word for word."

"Thank you, mamma, and if you can make the words sound any stronger, I hope you will do so. I will be well pleased to see Gussie occupy the position she craves. When she does, my congratulations will be most sincere and you will not know me—it will make me so wonderfully good-tempered," and she put her arm across her mother's shoulder and kissed her cheek. "Dear mamma, do not be vexed with me; but if I cannot endure Hugh for one hour, how can I think of spending my whole life with him?"

Mrs. Sherwood gave Hugh the message at her earliest opportunity, but it did not have the same effect on Hugh as she expected.

Hugh had no intention of accepting Dexie's refusal at second-hand; he would hear it from her own lips before he would give up hope. It might be an easy matter to remove the cause of her dislike, if he once found out what it was.

But Dexie knew her message had been delivered, and so felt herself free; and as Gussie was in excellent spirits, there seemed no reason why she should be glum when Hugh was near. She no longer slipped out of the room as Hugh appeared, though she was just as careful not to allow him to find her alone; but as Lancy's visits were as frequent as ever, Hugh was supposed to have given up the fight.

But Hugh had discovered that there was one way left him in which he could win a smile from Dexie, and he did not scruple to use it, though he was well aware that by doing so he was giving Gussie a false hope.

He had only to take a seat by Gussie's side, and say a few words to her, even the most commonplace, and Dexie's reserve would melt at once, so he spent many pleasant evenings in the parlor by this little scheme. He knew very well that Gussie was spreading her net, but if he found Dexie entangled in the meshes instead, Gussie's injured feelings would not trouble him. All stratagems are fair in love and war, so he smiled to himself and took courage.

Good fortune did not spoil Hugh. It made his good qualities shine out all the more brightly, and his friends admired as well as envied him. Dexie heard his praises sung from so many different quarters that her dislike to him was fast melting away, and seated by Gussie's side she could look on him with favor. But Hugh was merely biding his time, and was constantly on the watch for a favorable opportunity to press his suit personally and alone, in spite of the fact that Dexie considered the matter forever settled between them.

CHAPTER XXVII.

The auction rooms on Barrington Street were full to overflowing. A stock of goods was going under the hammer at ridiculously low prices, and among the bidders Hugh McNeil was conspicuous. As he turned to speak to a friend, he was much surprised to see Dexie Sherwood among the crowd. She was alone and not a little frightened at finding herself jostled about, and she welcomed Hugh with a smile as he made his way to her side.

"I am so glad to see you, Mr. McNeil. I was just wondering if I should be able to get out of this alive."

"How did you happen to come here at all; curiosity, I suppose?" and he smiled down into her face.

"Oh, no, indeed; I came on business, but I did not know what a hard time I was going to have of it. I heard Mr. Gurney talking about this sale last night, so I thought I might take advantage of it as well as the rest. I am Commissary-General now, you know, so I am on the lookout for bargains in my line," and she laughed softly.

"You want to bid for something, then; come and show me. Take my arm, so we will not get separated in the crowd," and for the first time in her life she placed her hand on Hugh's arm and followed his leading, and this thought came to Dexie with added force as Hugh pressed the hand in token of the pleasure granted him.

More than one person noted the bright young face that eagerly watched the several assortments fall under the hammer, and the light that shone in Hugh's dark eyes was not all caused by the excitement of the sale.

"I feel quite proud of my bargains," said Dexie, as they left the building and turned towards home. "I am ever so much obliged for your help; it will make such a difference in my accounts. Oh, you can't think how economical I am getting to be," said she, with a rippling laugh.

Then Dexie found herself telling her companion how she had gone with the Fremont girls to purchase household supplies, how they all enjoyed the excitement of the sales, and how sometimes no one would bid against them, much to the auctioneer's chagrin; how she was profiting by the Fremont girls' experience, and was accumulating such a nice little sum, to buy something very nice for her mother by and by.

Hugh listened with a beating heart. He had known for a long time what a busy life she led. It had formed the foundation of many excuses when he had asked her to accompany him to places of amusement; but just now all her former coolness was forgotten in her present kindness. She had never talked to him so freely before, and Hugh was lifted up with hope at this unexpected friendliness.

When they reached home, Hugh detained her at the door.

"Will you grant me a favor, Dexie?" he asked. "Do not go into an auction room alone again; without me, I mean. You know I am always at your service, and will only be too happy to help you at any time. You will grant me this, Dexie?" and he looked earnestly into her face for an answer.

A number of expressions passed over Dexie's face as he spoke. Had she done a bold, imprudent thing in attending the sale without an escort? She had not given it a thought. Surely one might go about a matter of business without a gentleman's escort? The Fremont girls did so. That it might be improper had not occurred to her, and it vexed her to be reminded of it by Hugh, so his well-meant offer failed to soften her.

"Yes, and no," Dexie coldly replied. "I will promise not to go again alone, but I won't promise to go in your company again," and she turned and entered the house.

Why had he spoken and lifted again the barrier of reserve that had broken down during their morning's intercourse? was Hugh's thought as he entered his own door. Might he not have brought about his wishes without exacting a promise?

The next evening, several young ladies, with their gentlemen friends, met in the Sherwood parlor to discuss a proposed family picnic, and Hugh came in during the discussion, and was pressed to join them.

"Where is the picnic to be?" he asked.

"Oh, down the coast towards Cow Bay; we'll pick out a place when we come to it. The trouble is, to find out how many teams we can get up," said George Desbrasy.

"Well, the Gurneys are all going, but they cannot take any but their own crowd, and there are several ladies we must find room for amongst us somehow," said Fred Beverly.

"Well, I have to drive mother and sis, but I have one spare seat. Will you accept the seat beside me, Miss Gussie?" said young Desbrasy.

Gussie wished he had not made the offer, as she hoped Hugh would ask her to drive with him, for Hugh had a fine team of his own now.

But as Gussie hesitated about accepting, she saw Hugh turn to Dexie, and with the air of a Chesterfield ask, "May I have the pleasure of your company for the drive down, Miss Dexie?"

"Thank you, Mr. McNeil, but I daresay I am already engaged."

"No chance for you there, McNeil," said Fred Beverly, with a laugh; "Miss Dexie is spoken for already."

"Did I understand you to say that you were *already* engaged for the drive, Miss Dexie?" said Hugh, persistently.

"Well, Lancy has not asked me yet, but since he has promised to go, my invitation will come all in good time."

"But his team will be full. You had better take your chance with Hugh," said Fred.

"There will be room enough for me, never fear," said Dexie, smiling, "so Mr. McNeil is free to offer his services to some other forlorn damsel."

"First come, first served, Miss Dexie," said Hugh. "I asked you first; come with me," he added, bending over her chair.

"Couldn't think of it. We would be sure to quarrel all the way, and when I go to a picnic I want to enjoy every minute."

"It takes two to make a quarrel, and I'll not be one of the pair," persisted Hugh. "Come with me, and let me prove to you how much I can add to your pleasure, when you will let me."

"Prove it now by asking Fanny Beverly or Maud Seeton to drive with you, for I decline the honor."

"Are you so wrapped up, heart and soul, in Lancy Gurney, that you cannot spare a moment to anybody else?" said Hugh, angrily.

"Certainly!" Dexie replied, with flashing eyes, "and since you are going to be so disagreeable, Mr. McNeil, I guess I will leave you," and she joined a group near the table.

"Where is Lancy, that he is not here to arrange about this picnic, said Fred Beverly to Cora Gurney, who was sitting by the table.

"Couldn't say. He promised to come in tonight."

"Listen! isn't that Lancy at the piano?" said Maud Harrington, as a sound of music in staccato style reached their ears. "How plainly you can hear it through the walls!"

There was a hush for a minute, when Dexie said as naturally as if it were the most ordinary thing in the world,

"Yes, that is Lancy's call; he wants me for something. Will you excuse me, friends, for a little while, till I see what is wanted?"

Looks were interchanged amongst some of the young people, and, hoping to make Dexie feel vexed, Gussie said, "Lancy Gurney has only to whistle, and Dexie will run like a dog at a call."

But Dexie took it all in good part, saying, with a smile: "Well, even a faithful dog is not a despised creature, you know, and it is something to know that Lancy will not whistle for anyone else while I am around," and turning at the door she added, "In case I do not come back, let me say you can count on me for anything I can do towards the success of the picnic. Good evening, ladies and gentlemen," and, as Hugh lifted his eyes, she swept him an elaborate courtesy.

Hugh was too vexed to take any further part in the discussion, and he soon withdrew, intending to find out what it was that drew Dexie away from the pleasant gathering.

When Dexie entered the parlor next door, she found Lancy seated at the piano, looking quite unlike himself.

"What is it, Lancy?" going over to his side. "Why did you not come into our house tonight?"

"I have come across something unusual, Dexie, and I could not leave the piano until I mastered it. Sit here and listen."

Lancy's hands moved across the keys, drawing forth such

thrilling chords that her heart was stirred to its lowest depths.

"Stop, Lancy, I cannot bear it," said she at last, laying her hand on Lancy's arm before he had finished a page.

Lancy looked up into the agitated face so near him, saying in a tremulous voice:

"Then I am not mistaken about it, since it affects you the same as myself. What is there about those chords that thrills our hearts so painfully? It is the only piece of music that has ever so affected me. I have not been able to play it through yet without a break. Sit down and try how far you can play, Dexie."

Dexie took the offered seat, and her hands swept the keys; but her firm touch seemed wanting. Wherein was that peculiar power that thrilled her with such exquisite pain; her hands fluttered, tears rose unbidden to her eyes, then, with a sudden break in the chords, she bowed her face in her hands.

Lancy was bending over her in a moment, and drawing her hands gently down, held them in a firm clasp.

"What is the matter with that music?" she said, at last, in a low tone. "I do not think I am nervous, but it sets my heart throbbing so that I cannot bear it."

"I think it is the keynote of our hearts that is struck by those chords, and gives back such answering thrills. I never came across anything before that affected me like it."

"Well, whatever it is, it is painfully sweet. I will try it again, but don't stand looking at me, there's a good fellow, but go away by the window and look out at—nothing."

Again those wondrous chords filled the room, but the masterful touch that usually accompanied Dexie's fingering was now wanting, for it was a trembling hand that followed the printed notes. More the once she faltered, but after a period of waiting she would repeat the passage and go on. But presently a longer silence occurred, and Lancy turned from the window to look at her. Tears were standing in her eyes, and she sat with her hands clasped tightly before her. Drawing her away from the piano, he led her to the sofa, and the silent sympathy in his manner was more eloquent than any flow of words could have been.

"It seems foolish, does it not, Lancy?" she said at last, "but it is no common piece of music, and I shall never be able to play it before strangers."

"No; neither shall I, Dexie. That music speaks to your heart and mine alike. Let it be for ourselves alone, will you, Dexie?" and the grey eyes looked very dark in their earnestness.

"Well, have it so, Lancy. I will be able to play it properly by and by, I expect. But I never noticed the name of it."

"It is simply called 'A Song Without Words.' Let us name it again to suit ourselves."

"Very well. I came in to ask you into our side of the house. The picnic is being discussed; but I don't feel a bit like going back myself now—that music has almost upset me."

"Well, stay with me and let us have a quiet 'sing' by ourselves here; that will be pleasanter than discussing a picnic—shall we?"

When Hugh looked into the door a short time afterwards, he saw nothing that need have caused such a frown to wrinkle up his manly brow, for Lancy was only playing a simple ballad, and Dexie was seated in a low rocker some distance from the piano, her hands clasped behind her head, singing softly, her whole appearance seeming to suggest rest and contentment. Perhaps that very suggestion goaded him to bitterness, for why couldn't Dexie be as contented and happy in his society as in Lancy's?

The picnic came off as planned, and was enjoyed by all excepting Hugh, who, finding he could not have the companion of his choice, coaxed little Gracie and Ruth Gurney to go with him, and they willingly consented. But Gussie looked with angry eyes on the fine turnout, "just wasted on those little torments," as the light buggy flew past the more sober-going horses that were bringing up the rear.

She forgot her anger, however, when she returned home and found that Mr. Plaisted had arrived during their absence.

Bless us! how very amiable we can be when we want to make a deep impression on someone's soft heart!

Gussie's face was now all smiles. Her words were all sweet when Mr. Plaisted was by anyway, and as it is an ill wind that blows nobody good, Dexie felt grateful enough for anything that would cause Gussie to be a little better-natured than she had been during the last few weeks, and Gussie's very unexpected offer, to "keep the parlor dusted while Plaisted is here," touched Dexie to the heart.

But his presence made Dexie's task much harder than usual. Such a "lie-a-bed" as he was in the mornings, and he expected to be served with a hot breakfast whatever might be the hour of his appearance.

Nancy remembered him of old, and resented the added work, and Dexie tried almost in vain to pour oil on the troubled waters.

One evening, when Plaisted was about to retire, Dexie handed him his lamp, saying:

"Our breakfast hour is eight o'clock, Mr. Plaisted, and if you will rise at the first bell you will have plenty of time to curl your hair before the breakfast bell rings."

"Dexie, don't let your tongue run away with you," her father said, reprovingly. "Plaisted will surely be up in good time tomorrow, as we have much work ahead of us if we intend to catch the train."

"Yes, I'll be up tomorrow morning without fail," he replied. "I don't see how it is that I oversleep myself so often when I am here; I fully intended to get up to breakfast this morning, but missed it. However, you will see me tomorrow morning at the breakfast table, Miss Dexie, if I am alive," he added jokingly, as he waved a good-night to Gussie.

"Very well; but if you are not up in time we shan't wait for you," said Dexie, smiling, "for dead men need no breakfast."

"Oh! you'll see, Miss Dexie, I'll be up tomorrow in time, without fail," and he laughed as he disappeared up the stairs.

But when eight o'clock came next morning, it brought no Plaisted with it, and Dexie horrified them by asking if they had better go up and view the remains.

Breakfast was eaten in silence. Mr. Sherwood was vexed at Plaisted's laziness when there was so much need of energetic work to make up for time lost and wasted.

"Perhaps he did not hear the bell," said Gussie, as the clock struck nine. "I'll ring it again," which she did, vigorously.

But another hour slipped by, and still he did not appear, much to Dexie's disgust and annoyance.

While standing by the window waiting his appearance, she became aware of a great event that was taking place in the backyard. It happened that a pet cat had met with some accident that had deprived it of life, and the children were indulging in a funeral. A grave had been dug at the back corner of the yard, and the procession of mourners was marching back and forth across the yard with many twists and turns, to make it last longer, until it at last reached the open grave. Georgie Sherwood, who marched in the front of the procession, with the remains in a raisin-box, now deposited it in its last resting-place, while the little Gurneys, who were sedately following, wailed aloud.

When the grave was covered to their satisfaction, Frankie Gurney came into the house with Georgie, holding a piece of smooth, white marble, and asked Dexie if she would write something on it, for it was to be the cat's tombstone.

"Say that she was the prettiest and best-behaved cat in Halifax, and that she left a large family of sorrowing kittens behind her."

"Yes, and children, too. Be sure and say that, Dexie," added Georgie.

The inscription was soon written in Dexie's largest and clearest hand, and it delighted the eyes of the little ones, who could easily read every word.

"Where did you get such a nice stone, Frankie?" she asked.

"Oh, down in the grave-stone shop. The man told me I could have it."

A sudden thought came into her mind, and she smiled as she asked:

"Could you get another piece as big as that, do you think?"

"Oh, yes; there is another piece like this. Someone broke a foot-stone, and it is no good, the man said. I'll go and get it, if you want it."

"Oh, will you? then run quickly. I'll make you a new kite, if you will hurry."

In a very short time Frankie was back with the stone, Georgie, meanwhile, being engaged in setting up the cat's monument.

"What do you want with the stone, Dexie?" he asked, as he regarded her attentively.

"Come with me, Frankie, and I will show you," and she led him upstairs to the upper hall.

"I want to play a trick on Mr. Plaisted; but I can't, unless you will help me."

"Oh, I'll do anything you tell me," his eyes eager for any fun.

"You see, he is a fearful hand to sleep in the mornings. He is not up yet, and the morning is half gone. He said last night that he would be up in time for breakfast, if he was alive. Well, you can hear him snoring in the next room; but, since he is not up, I am going to consider him dead, and I want you to put up his tombstone. Now, do you think that you can go carefully and put this at the head of his bed without waking him?"

Laying the stone on her knee, she soon had it written over in large, plain letters, and hoping that Plaisted might sleep till noon, as he often did, she slipped downstairs to await results.

It is not often that a man is roused from sleep by his own tombstone falling on him, but that is how was at last awakened. Quite likely Frankie, fearing to awaken him, did not place it very securely. However, as Plaisted was about to turn over for another snooze, down came the marble slab on his papered head! It almost stunned him for a moment, but curiosity roused him enough to find out what had struck him.

Lifting his arms above his head, he grasped the object, but not calculating on its weight, it slipped out of his hands and bruised his head in another spot. Raising on his elbow, he gazed in bewilderment on the thing, but turning it over he quickly grasped its meaning, for the words thereon were plain enough for the dullest man to understand, and read as follows:

"Sacred to the memory of
D.S. Plaisted,
who departed this life while in full health and curl papers.
His death was sudden,
but quite expected.
This monument was erected by one who fully realized his
WORTH-LESS-NESS.
Peace to his ashes."

A few moments of awful silence followed the reading of this inscription, then curses both loud and deep were heard in the room. With a bound he was out of bed, and opening the door he flung his tombstone over the baluster to the bottom of the stairs, with a crash that startled the family from their seats as if a thunderbolt had shaken the house.

Dexie disappeared instantly, knowing what the noise meant, but feeling thankful that there was no one near the stairs when the crash came, or she would have had to seriously repent her joke. As it was, the stairs were dinged and marred, and the fragments of the tombstone were strewn over the hall.

It did not take Plaisted long to dress that morning, and he soon appeared before the assembled family, his brow dark and his eyes flashing.

"Who did that?" he demanded as he made his appearance.

"That is just what we have been trying to find out," replied Mr. Sherwood, who thought he was referring to the noise.

"I mean, who put that stone in my room?"

"What stone? I hardly think you are awake yet, Plaisted," and he regarded him severely. "Do you know what time it is?"

Plaisted glanced at the clock, and his angry feelings were swallowed up in the feeling of shame that spread a flush over his face.

"Heavens! I never thought it was so late as that! So we have lost the train again by my carelessness. Too bad, Sherwood. But that joke was no light one. Did you put up that stone?"

"What stone? I don't understand," replied Sherwood, angrily.

Plaisted turned back into the hall, and gathered up the pieces he had flung down in his anger, then piecing it together on the table pointed to the inscription.

A roar of laughter came from Mr. Sherwood's throat, as he took in the joke. Dexie, hearing the laughter and knowing its cause, came boldly into the room, ready enough to confess her share of it, now that she knew her father would not scold very much about it.

"Dexie, did you do that?" he asked, as she appeared. "That writing looks very familiar."

"Well, I wrote the inscription," her face never changing expression, "but I hired another person to set the stone up. Has there been a miracle that you have come to life again?" she added, turning to Plaisted.

"Well, I'll have to own that you have got the best of me this time, Miss Dexie; but I'll pay you for that tombstone yet, see if I don't," and he seated himself to his late breakfast.

There was no need to set up a monument to Plaisted's memory the next morning, as he was down before the breakfast bell rang, and as Mr. Sherwood kept him confined to the business they had before them, he found no time to pay Dexie back for the trick she had played him.

During the day something occurred that referred to business matters in Prince Edward Island; and becoming annoyed at Plaisted's equivocal answers, Mr. Sherwood took the copy of the letter Dexie had brought home with her, and laid it before his eyes. Plaisted read it with a puzzled brow and shamefaced cheeks.

"Where did you get this?" he asked, in embarrassment.

"No matter; but can you deny it is yours?"

"By thunder! I guess I can! that is not my handwriting," he replied, trying to bluff it off.

"No, the handwriting is not yours, I know. But dare you say that that is not an exact copy of a letter that was written by your hand?"

"Well, you have me there, Sherwood, so I may as well own up. I was going to do a bit of shrewd business for myself, but someone seems to have got ahead of me. Now I look at this writing, it is singularly like the writing on my tombstone," he added, as he studied the letter before him; "but, of course, it isn't possible."

Receiving no answer, he looked up at Mr. Sherwood and seemed to read the truth in his face.

"You don't mean to say that my conjecture is right?"

"Yes, Dexie's thoughtfulness and quick perception have saved me a good thousand. Your doings on Prince Edward Island were made known to her in a singular manner, and she was sharp enough to see the advantage that an exact copy of your letter would be to me; and as your letter was placed in her hands quite unexpectedly, she copied it. You and I must part. I'll have no schemer like you for a partner any longer. I'll not have my name mixed up with such doubtful dealings."

High words followed, but as Mr. Sherwood had the upper hand, Plaisted was obliged to submit to his decision, and he soon left the room to collect his belongings, having received a peremptory dismissal.

"There is one satisfaction that I wish you would grant me, Sherwood," he said, turning as he reached the door, "Tell me how your daughter chanced upon that letter." "No, that you need not know; but it was by the merest accident, and was as great a surprise to her as it has been to me. But she was sharp enough to see how important her information was, and knew that a copy of your letter was the best guarantee she could bring me of your craftiness."

"Sharp! yes, that is just the word for her. She is like a bunch of nettles, stinging you if you but touch her. She has contrived to give me an unpleasant memory of her every time I have been here. And so it is to her I owe this break in our business intercourse;" and with flushed face and flashing eyes he left the room, and before night he was journeying toward the "land of the free," a sadder, and, let us hope, a wiser man.

CHAPTER XXVIII.

"Hope long deferred maketh the heart sick," and Hugh became dull and morose; the happiness he hoped for seemed as far off as ever, and the continued disappointment was making his life bitter. Mrs. Gurney saw the change, and tried to persuade Hugh to go abroad. This he longed to do, but waited; he might yet go abroad with Dexie as his travelling companion. He would not take the message sent him as final; surely if he could see her alone, face to face, he would compel her to give her reasons for refusing him, and he might explain away her objections.

But Dexie considered the matter settled, and feeling herself free she thought it right to drop her stiff, reserved manner, and be once more friendly. This change made Hugh think that there was still hope for him, and he determined to take a lover's privilege, and press his suit face to face.

With this end in view, he called on the Sherwoods one afternoon, and finding Mr. Sherwood alone, he asked permission to take Dexie out for a sail, adding that there seemed no other way of seeing her alone.

"I doubt if she will go with you, Mr. McNeil," said Mr. Sherwood. "Why not let the matter rest as it is? I don't think you are making much headway; better not press it any further."

"She has not given me fair play," was the reply. "If I am to be refused, why must I take it from another's lips? Give me the chance to open my heart to her, and I will be satisfied."

"Well, Mr. McNeil, I wish you well; but she must choose as she likes. What is the water like today?"

"Smooth as a mill-pond; scarcely a ripple," was the reply, as he followed Mr. Sherwood into the next room.

"I have called to see if you will go for a sail, Miss Dexie," said Mr. McNeil, as he entered the room and seated himself beside her. "You have not been on the water for some time; it is a pity to miss this fine afternoon."

Gussie knew very well that she was not included in the invitation; but she had no intention of being left out, so she eagerly answered:

"Oh, yes, of course we will go; it will be lovely and cool on the water this hot afternoon."

Hugh knew it would be useless to hint that it was Dexie alone he wanted, but he meant to get rid of her society somehow.

"You have not said if you would go, Dexie," said Hugh, looking intently into her face.

"Oh, yes! certainly. I shall be delighted to go, if Gussie thinks she will not get sick."

"I don't think Gussie was included in the invitation," said Mr. Sherwood, looking up from his paper as he became aware of the situation.

"But of course it was understood; I would not go without her," said Dexie. "What time shall we be ready?"

"I will call in half an hour," and Hugh left the room with his heavy brow drawn into a decided frown.

During the walk to the wharf Hugh was so silent that Gussie began to banter him on his gloomy countenance.

"You don't look as if you enjoyed the prospect of an afternoon on the water, after all!" she said, laughing.

Hugh took no notice of her remarks, but handed the girls into the boat, threw the shawls on a seat, and shoved off.

"I hope the wind will rise a little," said Dexie, as they seated themselves. "You will find it rather tiresome to row all the time."

"We will catch a slight breeze after we get out a bit," replied Hugh.

But Gussie no sooner felt the motion of the boat than she repented her decision in coming. She was a veritable coward on the water; the least ripple made her shrink with fear, and nothing but her anxiety to keep Hugh and Dexie apart would have allowed her to overcome her dread. But once on the water, fear and sickness overmastered all else.

"Oh! do be careful!" she cried in alarm, as Hugh stepped forward to adjust the sail, causing the little craft to dip slightly on one side.

"No danger, Gussie," said Dexie; "the boat will not tip as easily as you suppose."

"But do you not think it is getting rough?" she asked, as a slight ripple came towards them. "Oh! I wish I had not come. Do let us go back."

"The idea! Why, we have not been out ten minutes," said Dexie, who thoroughly enjoyed the motion that sent the color from Gussie's face. "Gussie, are you frightened, or sick?" she added, looking into her sister's face.

"Both. Do ask Hugh to return; I am in misery."

Hugh lost no time in doing as he was requested, and they soon reached the wharf. Gussie stepped ashore at once, glad to reach *terra firma* again; but as Dexie stepped forward to join her, Hugh turned sharply:

"Are you frightened, too? I thought you were made of something better."

The taunt aroused Dexie, and she replied:

"No, I'm not afraid. It was not I that asked to return."

Instantly Hugh stepped into the boat and, gave it a shove that sent it several rods, saying:

"Then we'll not lose our sail on Gussie's account," and he bent to the oars, sending the little boat far out into the stream.

Gussie stood on the wharf until she saw that they really meant to leave her there, and then walked thoughtfully home.

"I wonder what this means?" was Dexie's inward comment when

she found herself alone with Hugh. "There is some method in this madness, for I see it in his eyes."

She did not offer to begin the conversation until she saw Hugh hoist the sail and turn towards Point Pleasant.

"Where are you going, Mr. McNeil? I thought we were going up the Basin."

"I think we will try the Arm; there will not be so many crafts about."

"Why this wish for seclusion?" said Dexie, forcing a smile. "Surely there will be room for us as well."

Hugh paid no attention to this remark until they had turned up the Arm; then dropping the sail and changing his seat to one opposite Dexie, he let the boat drift with the tide.

Looking at her earnestly he said,

"It was a lucky thought that made me bring you out on the water. I thought Gussie would soon get enough of it. We are not likely to be interrupted here, and you cannot run away from me. Now, do you want me to tell you why I have brought you here?"

"No; I have not the least curiosity about it," was the seemingly indifferent reply.

"You know what I wish to say, Dexie, though you do not care to acknowledge it," he said, in a low tone. "Believe me, Dexie, I have not been playing at love-making all this time. I never was more in earnest in anything than I am in this. Tell me, what is it that you have against me?"

"Mr. McNeil, I thought this matter was settled. You received the message I sent you. Why bring up the subject again? I do not wish to hear another word."

"You cannot help yourself, Dexie. You have had your own way in this all along, and have not allowed me to say a word. Now it is my turn, and I will not be put off. Remember all is fair in love and war."

Dexie was silent. She was a little afraid of Hugh in this mood, but no sign of her fear appeared outwardly.

"I have reached the limit of torture that I can bear," said Hugh, after a pause. "I have had harsh words and cold looks for a long time, and you have slighted me on every possible occasion; but it has made no difference in my love for you. It has grown until it has taken possession of me, and my life seems to hold nothing worth living for with you left out of my future. Dexie, have pity! Is my life of no account to you that you can toss it aside without a thought?"

Dexie raised her eyes to the earnest face before her as she replied:

"I must think of my own self. Why should I make my life unhappy to please a passing fancy of yours?"

"A passing fancy! I understand that remark; you mean it as a sneer. It was a passing fancy with Gussie, I will admit. But, Dexie, it is a strong man's love that now burns in my heart. Think of all that it is in my power to give you, if you will only receive it. But the fact that I possess a fortune gives me no pleasure unless I can share it with you. Say the word, Dexie, and your every wish shall be gratified, if it is in the power of a man or money to do so, and my whole life shall be spent in making you happy. You need never have a care. What more could you ask of me, Dexie?" His eager eyes seemed to burn into her very soul as he waited her reply.

"I ask you for nothing; but if you will take all this and lay it before someone who could and would gladly accept it, you would be far happier in the end. It is a waste of time to try and persuade me to do what my whole soul refuses to consider, even for a moment."

"But why? Tell me why, Dexie? What have you against me? Is it on Gussie's account, or is it Lancy Gurney that comes between us?"

"What matters the reason? Call it what you like, it stands between us, and always will," she answered with rising color.

"You will not say! Can it be possible that you are so much in love with Lancy Gurney that there is no room for a thought of me? He will never make you happy; he knows nothing of love as I feel it—a schoolboy attachment, that will soon be forgotten!"

"Be kind enough to leave Lancy's name out of this discussion altogether," said Dexie coldly, "and as there is nothing to be gained by prolonging this unpleasant interview, we had better return home."

"You are mistaken if you think I am going to end this little excursion without gaining my end. Do you remember the time Lancy took you to drive, on purpose to gain your consent to whistle at the concert? Well, he kept you out until you gave him your promise, and I intend to profit by that idea of his, and keep you here until you give me a promise also."

"Why! Mr. McNeil, are you crazy?" said Dexie, in alarm. "What parallel do you see in the case? What good would a promise do you which you know I would break the moment I reached the shore?"

"You will not break any promise you make. I am not afraid of that. I think I know you better than you do yourself, Dexie."

Dexie flushed angrily, and turned her eyes to see the position of their boat. They had been drifting at the will of the tide, and she had given little thought to it in her excitement. But now, understanding what might be in store for her, it was necessary to think of some way of escape.

Could she keep Hugh from regarding her movements, and draw his attention from their boat's course?

After a few minutes' silence she asked, a smile twitching the corners of her mouth:

"I suppose there is not a piece of paper anywhere about," and she looked into her pocket and beneath the seat in a vain search; and there was a gleam of mischief in her eyes as she added: "I suppose you could not accommodate me with a piece of paper, could you, Mr. McNeil? Oh, thanks. And a pencil? Much obliged. Now, if there is only an empty bottle around some place, with a tight cork, I'll not despise the shipwrecked mariner's post office." "What are you going to do?" said Hugh, looking at her in surprise.

"Well, if I am to be detained here indefinitely, I would like to send a few parting words to Lancy. I am sure it would be *such* a comfort to him, in case the letter ever reached him, to know that I cared enough for him to remain true under such trying circumstances."

Was she making fun of him or not? Hugh could not tell, but he snatched the piece of paper from her hand and flung it over the side of the boat.

"Poor Lancy! how he will grieve for me!" she added in a commiserating tone, as she watched the receding scrap of paper. "You might have allowed me that one bit of consolation, I am sure, Mr. McNeil."

"Do you really love Lancy so much? I cannot believe it, Dexie."

"You might, nevertheless; for believe me, Mr. McNeil, if I had but one last wish granted me, it would be that I might be transported to his side. Ah me! I do not think I ever cared for him so much as I do at this present moment," and Dexie began to sing in a minor tone and in the high, cracked voice of an old woman:

> "Why—do—we—mourn—departed—friends
> Or—"

"Dexie, stop that!" and Hugh's' voice was sharp with pain and annoyance. "I do believe you are the most vexatious creature that ever lived."

"It makes me happy to hear you acknowledge that, Mr. McNeil; and I think you are far too sensible to want to spend your whole life with such a vexatious creature as you know me to be. Put a stop to all this nonsense, and let us return home."

"Never! You are trifling with a matter that is more than life and death to me, and you make jokes while I suffer. Do you think I cannot see through all this professed love for Lancy? Do girls in love confess it to a third party so freely and openly? No! Lancy has no place in your heart at all. I have watched you too closely to be mistaken," and before she was aware of his intention her hands were seized in his strong grasp as he poured out his heart in a torrent of passionate words.

Dexie was moved in spite of herself. She looked into the face so near her, and asked herself the question, "Why could she not love him?" He surely loved her truly, or he would not speak so earnestly. A future such as he could give her would be eagerly grasped by many young girls. She had never thought his face half so expressive as it now appeared to her. Yes, he was very handsome after all; his very soul seemed shining through his eyes, and as he talked she dropped hers before his earnest gaze.

"It is no use," she said at last, in a low tone. "I cannot, I cannot—

> *'I do not love you, Dr. Fell,*
> *The reason why I cannot tell.'"*

But, low as the words were, Hugh heard them.

"Never mind the love, Dexie; marry me, and the love will come afterwards."

"No, Mr. McNeil, I will not risk it," was her low reply, as she pulled her hands from his close grasp. "I am quite sure we could not live a week in peace and happiness. There is something in your very presence that raises up the worst feelings in me, and why should I knowingly spoil all my life?"

"It is no risk, Dexie; you shall never have any reason to be vexed with me. Your father is quite ready to accept me as a son-in-law; he trusts me, why cannot you? My darling, you have had time to think it over. Give me your promise; it need not be fulfilled until you wish it."

"I cannot give a promise I have no wish or intention of keeping, and how can you ask such a thing? How can you want an unwilling bride?"

"Never mind me, Dexie. Say you will be my wife sometime, and that will be enough. You will never regret it."

Dexie covered her face with her hands, and thought it over. The few minutes' silence was broken by Hugh, who hoarsely asked:

"Will you give me your promise, Dexie?"

"No, I will not!"

"But you shall! I swear it! Do you think I am not in earnest?" and the love-light in his eyes was dimmed by a harder and fiercer look. "You will return home my promised wife, or not at all!"

CHAPTER XXIX.

They had drifted on and on.

A little to the left a vessel was riding at anchor, and Dexie felt sure there must be someone on board who would help her. If she could only alter the course of the boat and get into the current, it might bring them near enough to attract attention, then she would shout for help.

There was a long silence between them. Hugh regarded her earnestly, feeling sure she would give in at last. Dexie had no thought of doing so, but was striving to think of some way to escape him. As she sat, her hands folded in her lap, she studied well the position of the vessel; noting also the ladders that hung over the side, and a daring thought entered her mind.

"Dear me!" she said at last, "this is getting very monotonous. I am tired doing nothing. I think I might learn how to use an oar, even though I may never have the chance to put my knowledge into practice."

She reached forward and grasped a light oar, handling it rather awkwardly, as a novice might, but succeeded at last in getting the blade over the side, more by chance than good management, apparently.

"I thought you knew how to use an oar already," said Hugh, his mind turned a moment from the subject that had been absorbing him. He watched the spasmodic dabs that Dexie was making, not thinking there was any purpose in the seemingly awkward efforts at rowing.

"Well, no—I'm not much of a hand at it—I must confess, but I think—I could learn—in time," and she glanced up to see if they were nearing the vessel; but Hugh followed her look and instantly surmised her intention.

"Ha! I see your scheme! Let me warn you not to make any outcry in hope of getting assistance from that vessel, for I tell you it would come too late."

"I am not afraid of your threats, sir, as you might know by this time," said Dexie, in a firm voice. "I do not forget the time you were going to throw me from the roof, if I did not say the words you wished to hear. I am a good swimmer, let me tell you, so you will not find me so easy to drown as you may imagine; however, accidents will happen, and I would fain die a dry death, so take up the oars and turn back to the city, or I shall jump overboard, and try and make for that vessel."

"Sit down, Dexie," said Hugh, fiercely. "Do you think I am such a fool as to let you escape me, after all? Let me tell you, I planned for all emergencies before I asked you to come out with me, and yesterday I made my will and settled up my affairs by writing a letter for your father, in case we do not return. So take care, it remains with you if there shall be a tragedy. There shall be no risk of a separation, for if you make any effort to escape, it will be stopped by this," and a bright revolver gleamed in the rays of the setting sun.

Dexie shuddered in spite of herself. The dread of firearms was as strong in her as in most of her sex, and she shrank back in her seat with a horrified look.

"A fine proof of your regard, I must say, to carry a loaded revolver on purpose to shoot me!" was the scornful reply.

"I prepared it for myself alone. Don't drive me to use it against either of us. Will you promise not to call for help?"

And looking at the murderous toy she gave the promise; and Hugh, knowing she would keep it, laid it on the seat beside him.

"Alone, and with a madman! Heaven help me!" was Dexie's thought. Her heart beat wildly. She dared not take her eyes from his face. But there was something in her glance that had power to subdue him, and, feeling this, she met his gaze unflinchingly. The oar still lay across her lap. Gently, with an almost imperceptible motion, its blade reached the water, and slowly, very slowly, the distance between the boat and vessel was shortened. She sat back in her seat so still that the slight movement of her wrists was not observed, for Hugh's eyes seemed riveted to her face; there seemed a mesmeric power in the depths of her eyes that held him, and obliterated all else from his mind.

Dexie's heart gave a great throb as the shadow of the vessel fell across the boat; but still he saw nothing till Dexie bent forward to give the strong pull to the oar that would give her freedom or death. The boat answered the touch and gave a sideward lurch that sent it broadside against the vessel, and Hugh woke as from a trance. One upward glance, and he sprang forward to thrust the boat aside and keep her off. But as he turned his back Dexie sprang up, and it was but the work of an instant to slip the revolver into her pocket, and as the boat swept past she grasped the rope ladder that hung from the vessel's side.

Terror seemed to lend her wings, for she found herself on the vessel's deck before she had time to draw a breath, where half fainting she lay for some moments, thanking Heaven for her safety.

But was she yet safe? No sign of life appeared on deck; but might there not be a number of sailors, drunk, below? Would she be any safer in their company than with Hugh? She shut her teeth hard at the thought, and slipping her hand into her pocket, with fear and trembling, she pulled out the revolver, and laid it at her side. How had she dared to touch it? Yet, while facing Hugh, the possession of that revolver seemed the one thing to be desired; but now that she had it she dreaded to touch it, though it was her only protector in this, her awful position.

When the boat slipped clear of the vessel, and Hugh turned about and realized that he was alone, he sank down on the seat as if powerless to move.

Where was Dexie? How had she escaped? No cry had reached his ears, no sound of splashing water warned him that she had gone over the side. Yet he was alone, Alone!

His terrified glance swept the water around him, as if he expected to see her upturned face in the waves that mocked his misery by their ceaseless motion.

Merciful Heaven, had he lost her, after all; lost the life that was dearer to him than his own? It could not be. A few rapid strokes, and he was again at the vessel's side, intending to summon assistance from those on board to aid him in his search. Had either of them known that the two men on board the vessel were hopelessly drunk in their berths below, and that the rest of the crew were about returning from Halifax charged with hell-fire in the shape of Water Street whiskey, it might have made some difference in the actions of both.

Dexie watched Hugh's movements with interest, but when she saw him approaching the vessel her fear of him again increased, and she rose and confronted him.

"Don't come any nearer, I warn you!" she cried. "I hold the revolver now, and I shall not scruple to use it for my own safety."

"Dexie, how did you get there?" was the relieved reply. "Put down that revolver before you do harm with it. You must come back in the boat! Do you think you are safe among a lot of sailors!"

Hugh seemed perfectly sane how, whatever may have been the condition of his mind previously, and he shuddered as her unprotected condition flashed over him.

"Keep off, McNeil! don't come any nearer at your own peril! I will trust myself among a shipload of drunken sailors before I will put myself in your power again."

"Dexie, I'll give you my word of honor to take you home at once, if you will leave the vessel. Come, you need not fear me any more; I think I must have been mad."

"Keep off, I tell you! I am not so foolish as you think! I don't forget you prepared that revolver in your sober senses, whatever may have been your state of mind awhile ago. Keep back, or you shall have the bullet you prepared for me!"

What could he do? She seemed terribly in earnest, yet, if she did not come back with him, how should she be able to return at all? Should he make a dash and rescue her against her will? She seemed to define his thoughts, for she leaned over the side, saying:

"Go at once, and send someone for me, for if I ever reach Halifax again it won't be under your care! Go, I say! I hate you! I *hate* you! You need not try to reach me," as Hugh rowed nearer. "You just touch that ladder, and you will find my bleeding body here, not a living person!"

Hugh sat in the boat irresolute, not knowing what to do.

"I cannot leave you there, Dexie; you *must* come back to me, and come quickly before you are discovered. I swear I will row you home at once, and not trouble you with a word," and the boat almost touched the vessel's side. It was heavily laden, and sat low in the water, and Dexie felt the distance between them was very short indeed. If Hugh insisted on reaching her, the struggle would be short and soon over, for nothing would persuade her to go back in the boat with Hugh again. She raised her arm; and the sound of a shot was sent over the water, followed simultaneously with a sharp, splintering sound, as the little leaden missile tore its way along the stern of the little boat.

Dexie look around, expecting the sound would surely bring someone from below, and if that someone was not sober, Hugh was still near enough to help her. But no one appeared; she seemed the only living person on board. She looked back at Hugh. She had not hurt him, nor had she intended to do so, but she struck much nearer than she knew, and Hugh went back a stroke or two.

"Do you believe I am in earnest now?" she asked, as she still held the revolver in her hand. "Go and bring someone for me while there is time, for I will never go back with you!"

But as Hugh bent to the oars, sending the little craft so swiftly to do her bidding, the courage that had hitherto sustained her suddenly vanished. Alone and unprotected, what might not happen to her? But it was too late to call Hugh back now, so she must face whatever fate there was in store for her. What if Hugh had no intention of sending help to her, and should leave her there? Oh, for some chance to get away!

Dexie had almost given up in despair when the muffled sound of oars was borne on her ears. She sprang quickly to the other side of the vessel and looked anxiously in the direction of the sound. Soon the rower came in sight, and by the stripes and epaulets of the wearer she recognized him as a military officer, whose strong, rapid strokes were rapidly taking him citywards. Oh, if he would only take her with him! Dare she ask him? The hitherto-despised soldier seemed an angel of mercy, as the hope of rescue sprang up again in her heart. But he is coming near, and she must not let the chance slip. How should she hail him? In what words make known her peril? She felt stupid, just when she needed her readiest wit. He was almost abreast the vessel before Dexie found her voice, and then in frightened tones came the cry:

"Help, soldier! Help!"

The soldier turned his head, and rested on his oars as he listened.

"Help, soldier! Save me, I beg of you!"

The pleading tones told that the cry was from someone in trouble, and a few strokes brought him to the vessel's side.

"What's the matter, miss? What's wrong that you are calling for help? What can I do for you?"

"Oh, take me away from this vessel! You are going to the city, are you not?"

"Yes; but perhaps I shall get myself into some scrape if I take you away," and a smile lit up his face for a moment. "How came you here? Are you here against your will?"

"Yes, and no. Take me off quickly, and I'll explain," she replied, hurriedly, for a movement below reached her ears.

She was soon seated opposite her deliverer, who looked at her curiously, but said nothing till they were quite a distance from the vessel; then, resting on his oars, he said:

"Now, tell me how you came to be on that vessel; but, first, will you tell me your name?"

"Oh! must I—" and Dexie dropped her head.

"Well, you need not if you do not wish to. I know you, all the same, though I have not heard your name. You are the 'American Warbler.' Now, tell me your story."

"I hardly know how to tell it, though I don't mind you knowing about it. There is so much to tell before you will understand how I came to be on the vessel."

"Well, if it is all a secret, I'll promise not to tell anyone except my wife. She might hear that I have been on the harbor with a young lady, so I had better tell her myself," and he smilingly waited Dexie's explanation.

"Oh! since you are married, it will not be so hard to tell."

There was quite a pause. Where would she begin?

"Come, now, how did you come to be aboard the vessel?" he repeated.

"But I can't tell you *how* until I have told you *why*," said she, trying to control her voice, "so I must tell you all that happened this afternoon," and, beginning from the time that Hugh prevented her from joining her sister on the wharf, she told the story of the afternoon, though not without skilful questionings that made the matter clear, though hardly comprehensible. She gave no names, but mentioned Hugh as "the young gentleman."

"You have had quite an adventure, Miss—," and he looked up thinking she would supply the name, but she smiled and shook her head.

"Miss Jonathan, then; you must have some name for my wife to know you by," he added, smilingly. "Now, I don't think you did a very wise thing when you got on a strange craft for safety. It was all right as it happened, but it might not have happened all right. However, you are safely out of the scrape; still, if I am not mistaken in the young man, he thinks too much of you to really harm you."

"Do you think you know who it was?" and she looked up with a flushed face.

"Well, I suppose it was the same chap that whistled with you at the concert, wasn't it!"

"No, indeed! I suppose I must tell you more, after all. You don't understand the half of it yet. It was one who was, at one time, my sister's lover, or so I thought, but he—"

"He changed his mind, I see," and there was a twinkle of fun in the eyes that watched the face before him. "I begin to see the point now. That is why he did not want your sister with you. May I hazard a guess and say that perhaps it was the dark young man who was glowering at you the night of the concert? Oh, I saw it all," as she looked up in surprise. "So it was he?"

"Yes, he was out of temper that night, I remember."

"Well, he did not look very amiable, I must say; but, for all that, you were safer with him than on the vessel, for, if I am not mistaken, that is the crew going aboard now," and the shouts and songs of the sailors reached their ears as they rowed towards the vessel.

"Oh! thank you, thank you a thousand times, for coming along just when you did! What should I have done? But I had this," and she drew forth the revolver from her pocket.

"Great Scott! have you got that yet? What were you going to do with it?"

"I would have turned it on myself if there was no other way. Would you mind accepting it? McNeil shall never have it back," and she laid it by his side.

The oars were poised in the air as he caught the name. "McNeil, you said! Not the McNeil that has had the fortune left him lately, and is considered such a great catch?"

"Yes, he has had a fortune left him; as for being a great catch"—and the shrug of her shoulders finished her answer.

"Well, I don't think he will have to force his attentions on the rest of the young ladies around Halifax by the aid of a revolver anyway, if all they say of the young man is true. He is well liked, I hear, by all who know him. And so you won't have him?"

"No, I won't promise to marry any man, however rich he is, who would ask it with a revolver in his possession to enforce it. I should hate him for it."

"There spoke the woman's heart; a loaded revolver is hardly a lover's weapon, I'll admit. What a bit of romance this will be for my wife! Have I your permission to tell it?"

"Just as you like; but please do not tell anyone else—your soldier friends, I mean."

"Certainly not, if you wish it; but young ladies usually like to boast of their conquests."

"Well, on all other points McNeil is sensible, and, as he will probably marry someone else some day, it will not be pleasant to have this affair become known."

CHAPTER XXX.

It was quite dark when they reached the wharf, and Dexie was wondering if Lancy knew of her absence when she saw his well-known figure outlined against the sky.

He did not know that the object of his anxious thoughts was so near, as he stood looking seaward, with a dark frown upon his face.

As the soldier moored the little boat, and prepared to help Dexie ashore, she suddenly said: "I gave you the revolver, but will you mind giving me the rest of the bullets in it?"

He looked at her in surprise.

"Certainly," he replied, and he laid them in her hand, "but I think you will find them unpleasant reminders of an incident you would do well to forget. A man in love is often a desperate individual, without realizing his condition; and I have no doubt that, by this time, McNeil would do much to recall what passed this afternoon. So let me ask you, for him, to forgive it."

"I could forgive all but the *revolver* part of it. That was premeditated, and I shall not forget it. Let me thank you again for your kind assistance. I shall always think better of the soldiers for your kindness to me."

"I am amply repaid, my fair warbler," replied the soldier, as they stood at last on the wharf, "and if your excitable lover ever asks for his revolver, here is my address," and he handed her a card; "but, if I mistake not, a friend is waiting for you," and he waved his hand towards Lancy.

At that moment Lancy turned, and seeing the object of his thoughts so near, and in company with a soldier, his face underwent a series of expressions. But it was really Dexie, though he could scarcely believe his own eyesight, and he was at her side in a moment.

"Why, Dexie! where have you been? We were afraid there had been an accident."

A hundred questions were on his lips, but the presence of the soldier kept them back.

"I have been in danger, but there has been no accident, Lancy; and you must thank this gentleman for bringing me safely home."

As the memory of it all passed before her, her self-control gave way, and covering her face with her hands she burst into tears.

This was rather embarrassing to Lancy, who was all in the dark in regard to Dexie's movements. He was told that she had gone off with Hugh, and here she was in company with a soldier, and in tears.

"She will be all right in a few minutes," the officer replied, in answer to Lancy's surprised looks. "She has gone through enough to try a strong woman's nerves. Wait here; I'll get that cab, if it is empty, and you can take her home at once," and he darted up the wharf at a rapid pace.

"Where is Hugh?" said Lancy hurriedly; "not drowned, Dexie?"

"No; not that I know of," she said, choking back her tears.

"Then, what does all this mean? How came you to be out with the soldier, Dexie? I don't know what to think."

"I will tell you presently, but that soldier saved my life. Thank him for me, Lancy, for I cannot say enough."

The arrival of the cab prevented further explanation, and Dexie allowed herself to be seated in it without a word.

"I do not yet know what has happened," said Lancy, holding out his hand to the soldier, "but I thank you very heartily for your kindness. Jump into the cab with us, as far as your way lies, and tell me what this is all about."

As they took their seats, Lancy turned to Dexie, who had almost recovered her composure, saying:

"You have not yet introduced me to your friend. How shall I call him?"

Dexie held up the card she had in her hand, saying: "I do not know myself, and it is too dark to read."

"I am Lieutenant Wilbur, at your service, and I feel happy in being the means of rescuing the 'American Warbler' from a very unpleasant situation."

"I am Launcelot Gurney. Now, will one of you tell me what has happened? You have not been capsized, Dexie, for your clothes are not wet; but you have been gone since early afternoon, and return in unexpected company. I am bewildered by the thoughts and suggestions that crowd into my mind."

"Let me tell the story briefly, and she can relate the details later on. Here it is: Your fair warbler finds herself afloat, and unintentionally alone with a desperate lover, who demands her heart and hand at the point of a revolver, with the alternative of a death in his arms. Choosing neither, said American warbler skilfully guides the boat to a vessel anchored near, hoping to find a rescuer. This failing her, she takes advantage of a moment when the aforesaid lover's back is turned, and escapes to the vessel by aid of a rope ladder, and effectually keeps at bay the aforesaid lover by a judicious use of the revolver, which had previously been turned against herself. Then finding himself worsted, the afore-mentioned desperate lover hies himself away, and your humble servant turns up in the nick of time, and rescues the almost despairing warbler, and returns her to the arms of—well—a waiting friend; quite a romance, my wife will say."

Lancy listened to the story with amazement.

"Dexie, is this possible? or is the lieutenant only joking?"

"It has been no joke to me, Lancy; I can say that," was the reply in a quivering voice. "I was not off the vessel ten minutes, before we met the vessel's crew going towards her. I can't bear to think of it."

"But the revolver; surely that is an exaggeration!"

"It is here," and the lieutenant held it towards Lancy, who drew back with a shudder.

"Heavens! is it possible? I can hardly realize how Hugh was capable of such an act."

"You had better take this Mr. Gurney, and give it to the owner," said the lieutenant, still holding out the weapon.

"No!" said Dexie quickly, "he shall not have it back! If you will not keep it, Lieutenant Wilbur, I will throw it into the harbor the first chance I get!"

"I will keep it then, fair warbler," and he replaced it in his pocket.

"Does he not know your name?" said Lancy, in a low tone.

"No, but he saw us both in the hall, and remembers me."

"Well, it is but fair, lieutenant," said Lancy aloud, "that you should know the name of the lady you rescued. This is Miss Dexie Sherwood."

"Ah! happy to know you at last, Miss Sherwood," was the laughing reply, as he bent over her a moment; "but I must bid you good-bye, as I get off here," and signalling the driver he lifted his cap, and was soon out of sight.

They reached home in a few minutes, and Lancy followed Dexie into the house, saying:

"I must have the story from your lips before I leave you tonight, Dexie."

"Very well; but remember it is long past tea-time, and I am almost famished."

The family had become very much alarmed at Dexie's prolonged absence, and Mr. Sherwood had gone out to inquire if any accident had been reported on the water. As Dexie entered the sitting-room, Gussie looked up in surprise, as she saw who was Dexie's companion; she expected it would be Hugh, and it was easy to see that she was not in the best of tempers.

"It is time you were home, miss," was her caustic remark. "It is a wonder you are not ashamed of yourself to stay out till this hour! Just you wait till papa comes home—he has been almost wild with fright; and you have given mamma one of her nervous headaches, and she is quite ill; so you know just what you may expect from her."

Dexie made no answer, but moved briskly from sideboard to closet, collecting her supper.

"It would have been better for you if you had come home at the proper time to your supper, instead of keeping us waiting for you, as you did," and a torrent of complaints and reproaches were poured out, regardless of Lancy's presence, till he was moved to reply:

"I think, Gussie, if you knew the cause of her detention, and how much she has borne because of it, you would not say another unkind word to her tonight."

"Oh, never mind her, Lancy," said Dexie; "honestly, I rather enjoy it. I was so afraid this afternoon that I should never hear her scold me again that I can bear all she has to say as meekly as a lamb."

Gussie looked up in astonishment, then dropped her eyes for

very shame.

"What has happened? Were you capsized? Is Hugh drowned?" she asked in alarm, noticing for the first time how sober they looked.

Her unceremonious exit from the boat had put her out of temper. She felt angry and mortified when she remembered how glad Hugh seemed to be to get rid of her. Was the day to end in a tragedy?

Where was Hugh, sure enough?

After leaving Dexie, he rowed across the harbor to some small fishing-boats that were riding at anchor, and tried to hire the occupants of one of them to accompany him to the vessel. But the story he told them seemed so improbable they would pay no attention to him for some time. Hugh was almost beside himself with fear on Dexie's account; but he at last succeeded in persuading a crafty old fellow to accompany him, by promising him more money for his services than the fisherman had ever, at one time, seen in his life, and finally he accompanied Hugh back to the vessel.

But, by the time they arrived, Dexie had disappeared past George's Island with the soldier, and Hugh found the vessel's deck alive with a set of men capable of the darkest deeds that drunken sailors ever perpetrated. Hugh's inquiries were not understood, of course; but believing the worst, he demanded to be allowed on board the vessel. This the captain, who now appeared, and who was about as drunk as his crew, refused to allow. Hugh urged and argued in vain, the idea of a young lady being aboard the vessel being hailed with uproarious shrieks of merriment by the vessel's crew. Hugh was at last obliged to give up in despair, and he rowed back with all speed towards the city, to secure the aid of the police in his search.

This was the darkest hour Hugh had ever known. The strain on his nerves, coupled with the anxiety of the previous weeks, was more than he could bear, and when, with the assistance of two men armed with authority, he searched the vessel for any trace of Dexie's presence, and found none, his brain seemed to collapse, and the brass-buttoned officers carried him back in their boat to Halifax in a state of unconsciousness.

About midnight, with a doctor in attendance, he was carefully carried to Mr. Gurney's in a state of delirium.

The next morning the startling news was brought into the Sherwood household that Hugh McNeil was down with brain fever, and that the doctor had not left the house since midnight.

Why did they all look at Dexie in such a horrified manner? Was she to blame? Their looks implied as much. She fought against the implication inwardly, but made no remark whatever as the news was being discussed.

But, as the day wore on, the unnatural stillness of the house seemed to weigh her down with its oppressiveness, and she caught herself listening to every sound with strained ears and every nerve on the alert.

She did not dare venture into the next door to make inquiries, not knowing how much they might be blaming her for Hugh's sudden illness; and the added trouble and anxiety his sickness necessarily caused, left no time for the Gurney girls to run in with a report of his condition. Consequently, when Lancy appeared about nine o'clock in the evening, Dexie's eyes asked the question her lips had not power to form.

"Hugh is no better—worse, if possible," and Lancy's face was as white as Dexie's own. "He keeps calling for you in his delirium; he seems to think you are drowned or worse, and reaches out to catch you. It takes two to hold him sometimes."

"Oh, Lancy! am I to blame?" she said, bursting into tears. "I have had such a horrible day with my thoughts. I don't see how I could help it; yet it was my fault, I suppose."

"Well, under the circumstances, I don't see how you could have done differently, Dexie; but don't fret about it. It is an uncomfortable affair all round, to be sure. I can't help feeling proud of you the way you braved it out rather than give your promise; but, of course, it was hard on Hugh."

"Does your mother know anything about my part of the affair?"

"Oh, yes! I told her all about it. Hugh raved so, I had to explain what I knew about the trouble. She guessed quickly enough that something had happened between you."

"And the doctor?"

"Oh! he knows about it too, and he wants to know if you will come in, if they find they cannot quiet him. Oh, Hugh will not know you," he added, looking into her frightened face; "but the doctor thinks you might get him to sleep if you would be willing to try it."

"Oh, dear! I don't want to go near him; but I suppose I must, if there is any chance of convincing him that I am safe, after all."

The doctor looked up in surprise when Dexie appeared in the room with Mrs. Gurney a short time after. Was it this slip of a girl that had wrought such mischief?

"So this is *your* work," and he waved his hand towards the bed.

Dexie flashed an angry look at him, saying in a low voice:

"I beg your pardon, sir, I think Mr. McNeil can blame himself and no one else. What can I do, Mrs. Gurney?"

Hugh was tossing about in restless delirium, muttering broken sentences; and the piteous cry of "Dexie! oh, Dexie!" rang through the room.

"Speak to him; perhaps he will realize you are here," said Mrs. Gurney.

The doctor placed a chair by the bedside for her, then stood by the foot of the bed, watching.

"I never meant it, Dexie; I would not throw you over for worlds; forgive me."

Dexie knew that the memory of the scene on the roof was troubling his mind, and the anguish depicted on Hugh's face brought such a lump into her throat that she could not speak a word.

"Come back into the boat with me; I'll promise to take you home," he cried.

The doctor eyed Dexie sternly.

"Speak to him," he said, sharply.

"I am here, Mr. McNeil. I have come back safe and well. Try to sleep."

Her voice seemed to pierce the troubled brain, and his face lost much of its troubled look.

"Sing something, Dexie," said Mrs. Gurney, "and perhaps he will sleep. He has not been quiet since they brought him home," and, bending down, said softly, "Try, Dexie. I know it is hard for you, but if he will sleep it will be almost the saving of him. You will do this for me, I know."

"Nearer, my God, to Thee; nearer to Thee."

It was almost a whisper, but it soon had a visible effect on Hugh, and in half an hour the doctor's curt words, "You may go now," were more welcome than the sweetest praise.

As the fever ran its course, Dexie was frequently called to Hugh's bedside. How she dreaded those visits, yet stern duty forbade her to refuse, as her heart often prompted.

Dexie soon saw that she was not in the doctor's good graces, for as Hugh revealed the past, in broken and disjointed sentences, it gave him the impression that she had been trifling with Hugh's affections, and she resented the tone he assumed when speaking to her. However, as the days passed, and the doctor learned the real truth of the matter, he began to look at Dexie with less disfavor; but the inquisitive manner with which he now regarded her was not less objectionable.

"You will marry him yet," the doctor said one night as he watched his patient through his wildest hours.

Dexie, who was sitting near the window, turned in surprise at the unlooked-for remark.

"Yes, my word for it, Miss Sherwood, you will marry him yet, after all the fuss you have made over your refusal."

"Never!" The reply was low, but intense. "I know my own mind, I guess! I would not stay in the same room with him, though he is unconscious of my presence, only Mrs. Gurney imagines he is less restless when I am near, and she is anxious about his recovery."

"Oh! you need not tell *me*! I have heard of such cases before now. I have seen your eyes full of pity as you have watched beside him with Mrs. Gurney."

"Perhaps so; but not with the 'pity that is akin to love,' by any means," and as Mrs. Gurney returned to the room, she bowed a stiff good-night to the doctor and went home.

After days of anxiety the fever reached its height, and there was not a more anxious heart in the house that day than Dexie's own.

As she went about her daily household duties, she mentally pictured to herself what might happen in case of the worst. Would she be blamed for his death? and what would become of all Hugh's money?

She speculated as to how he had willed it, and wondered what were the contents of the letter Hugh had written to her father before that afternoon's sail. She hoped she would not be summoned again to the sick-room. But she was not to have that wish, for late in the evening Lancy came in to bring her over at once.

"The doctor says the next hour will decide whether he lives or not, and he wants you to be near in case you are needed in a hurry."

Towards midnight Hugh opened his eyes and recognized Mrs. Gurney, who was bending over him; and as he turned his face and saw the doctor also, he said, in a faint voice:

"What is the matter? Why am I here?"

"You have been sick, Hugh," said Mrs. Gurney, taking his hand; "do not talk."

"But I thought—I thought—I was in a boat," he said, faintly, and a puzzled look came over his face. "I was looking—for someone—or I was dreaming."

"You must not talk; try not to think itself," said the doctor, as he held some medicine to his lips. "You have been dreaming, no doubt; but try not to think about it any more."

Hugh was quiet for some minutes; memory was slowly returning; but at last the past all came back, and, casting an imploring glance into the doctor's face, said:

"Tell me! I remember it all now—I was searching for Dexie—is she safe?"

"Yes, safe and well, so make your mind easy."

"If I could—only feel—sure—"

"Will you bring me that pitcher of water, Miss Sherwood?"

The doctor's voice was low, but distinct, and an eager light came into Hugh's face as he heard the name.

"Pour a little into this glass," the doctor added.

As Dexie came near at the doctor's direction, Hugh looked up, and for one short moment their eyes met.

But that moment assured Hugh that Dexie was safe; that was all he could comprehend at present, for he was too weak to ask any more questions. Dexie could not bear the strain much longer, so, bending over Mrs. Gurney, she whispered:

"Tell me I may go, if only into the next room. I cannot bear it."

"Just a moment more, Miss Sherwood," the doctor whispered, overhearing the request "Help me a moment here," he said aloud, "and then you may retire."

She came towards the bed, and complied with his directions, knowing full well that Hugh's eyes were devouring her face.

"Is it you, Dexie, or your spirit?" the words were low and tremulous, but, in the stillness of the room, sounded clear and distinct.

"It is I, Mr. McNeil, alive, and well as ever I was."

"Thank God!"

His eyes closed, and with a gesture the doctor dismissed her; then taking his seat beside the bed, he watched until he was assured that Hugh had fallen into a natural sleep.

As Dexie left the room, she mentally said a final good-bye to it, feeling thankful enough that her services would not be needed again to hush the despairing cries or still the grasping hands that had clutched at space. It was the last time her eyes rested on Hugh for weeks. She knew he was recovering, and that was enough.

During his convalescence, Dexie never entered the Gurney household, lest by some chance she might come face to face with her enemy.

The occurrence on the boat was tacitly dropped by all parties concerned, and only when Hugh accidentally heard that the Sherwoods were preparing to return to the States did his reserve break down, and it was to Mrs. Gurney alone he expressed his regrets and intentions.

CHAPTER XXXI.

"Here's news, girls; we are going back to Maine!" and Georgie rushed into the sitting-room where his sisters and their girl friends were chatting together. "Papa says we are going back *for sure*, in just a few weeks, too! Isn't that jolly?" and he manifested his delight in a series of handsprings that would have charmed the heart of an acrobat.

"Yes, I heard something of it, but hoped it would not come to pass," said Dexie.

"It is the best news I've heard for a long time, the sooner we leave this horrid place the better I'll be pleased," was Gussie's comment.

Elsie was quite depressed at the thought of parting from her friends; but the intervening weeks were full of pleasure and excitement, and drives and parties seemed to follow one another in quick succession.

One day Dexie came in from a shopping expedition in great excitement, saying:

"Oh, girls, I have met my double; met her down in a store on Granville Street, and I actually followed her until she entered a house on Spring Garden Road. If she had worn one of my suits, I should have expected her to walk home instead of me. I began to think 'this could not be I.' Whom do you think she can be?"

Nobody knew; but a few days after, Lancy related the fact that he had hurried after a lady, supposing her to be Dexie, and found he had been following a stranger.

"I am going to find out who this young person is," said Dexie, laughing. "Who knows, perhaps it is my only chance to 'see myself as others see me.'"

After a few inquiries, it was found that Dexie's double was a Nina Gordon, only daughter of a widow lately arrived in Halifax, and residing with a bachelor brother who was travelling for a city firm.

Cora Gurney happened to meet both mother and daughter while making a round of calls with a friend, and she ran in to tell Dexie of the meeting.

"Your double is not very much like you after all, Dexie," she said. "Her figure and style of walking are remarkably like yours, even to the poise of her head; her hair, too, is almost the same shade; the eyes and upper part of the face are similar: but the mouth and chin are her own—they have no resemblance whatever to the true Dexie. It is the first sight that strikes one. When you look for the resemblance, it really seems slight enough, and when she begins to talk, my! the illusion vanishes at once, for really I do not think I ever met a person who irritated me as she did. She is a girl after the 'china doll' pattern, and can only use her brains at the direction of her mother. I do not think she ventured a remark of her own all the time I was there."

"Perhaps she did not have the chance," said Dexie, eager to

champion the cause of her double. "Some girls are not allowed to have an opinion apart from the maternal idea of the fitness of things, and are kept down."

"Nonsense! If you had heard her talking, Dexie, I'm sure you would have felt like shaking her. It is only when her face is in repose that she resembles you in the least, for the moment she begins to talk, or even listen—or try to listen, one might say—she has the most senseless expression I ever saw on a woman's face."

"Goodness sake! bring me a looking-glass, quick! do, till I see what I look like when I talk. Does my face assume an idiotic expression when I am conversing? Be honest and tell me, for sweet charity's sake."

"Ease your mind, Dexie," said Cora, laughing. "Did I not say that there the resemblance ends? It is only when her face is at rest that the likeness can be seen at all. If you ask her the simplest question, she must refer to her mother for advice before she replies. For instance, I asked her if she liked Halifax. 'Do I like Halifax, mamma, do you think?' and she turned to her mother with such an affected simper. Really, I almost disliked her the moment she opened her mouth."

"I hope I shall get a chance to see her before we leave Halifax," said Dexie.

"Well, I asked her and her mother to call on mamma next week, almost on purpose for your benefit. Hugh is getting along so well I think mamma can receive some friends. I will let you know when they come."

A further acquaintance corroborated Cora's idea of Nina Gordon's brains. She seemed to have no mind of her own; a good thing, perhaps, in some cases, but a more spiritless person to talk to never vexed the heart of man or woman either. She had no answer for the simplest question without first asking it from her mother, and away from her mother's side she was uneasy and almost dumb.

The mother's idiosyncrasy was always to do "the correct thing." The fear of not doing it, or the dread of having done it unknowingly, was constantly before her—the bugbear that troubled her daily. Perhaps the daughter inherited the mother's dread, and her fear of doing or saying something that was not just "the correct thing" made her put all the responsibility of conversation on her mother's shoulder. Dexie was amused, as well as provoked, as she listened to the efforts at conversation which Cora vainly endeavored to sustain with her double, and it was evident that Mrs. Gurney also was surprised as well as amused at Mrs. Gordon's remarks.

"However do you manage with such a large family, Mrs. Gurney?" she was saying. "Why, with only Nina I am wearied to death; for from the time she wakes up I must see to everything for her until she goes to bed again at night. How you manage it for so many, I can't see, I am sure. I should die of fatigue."

"Oh! the children soon get big enough to help themselves, and the younger ones, too," Mrs. Gurney replied, with a smile. "I seldom see my girls in the morning until I meet them at the breakfast table."

"Is it possible! Do you not have to superintend their dressing?" she asked, in surprise.

"Why, no, Mrs. Gordon! Girls of that age," waving her hand toward the group by the window, "are supposed to have judgment of their own in such things, and with some to spare for the little ones."

"Dear me! I should be so afraid they would not do the correct thing if I was not by."

"Perhaps you are by when she ought to rely on herself," was the smiling answer. "My girls are relieving me of much of the burden of household cares."

"Well, well!" and Mrs. Gordon looked across at the girls in surprise. "I wonder you are not in constant dread that some of them might not do the correct thing when you are not near with your instructions. How wonderful that you can trust them alone so much! Nina seems a child in comparison."

Dexie was mentally comparing Nina to a big, useless doll; for she had to conclude that Nina cared for nothing but "to be dressed up and wait in the parlor for callers."

The girls coaxed Nina away from her mother's side while the latter was talking to Mrs. Gurney; but directly she was asked a question she wanted to rush back to her mother, and see how she should answer it.

"But don't you know yourself whether you like music or not?" Dexie asked her, as Nina vainly endeavored to catch her mother's eye. "Do you not play or sing, Miss Gordon?"

Nina picked at her gloves in embarrassment as she replied, with a simper:

"Well, I play scales on the piano sometimes."

"Then you *are* fond of music, I suppose," said Cora, pleasantly.

"Well, I think I am. I will ask mamma; she knows if I like it. Is it quite correct to like music, do you think?"

The silly look which accompanied this speech made Dexie almost disgusted with her, but she turned to Cora and smiled significantly.

"Well," said Dexie, when her double had taken her departure, "she has tired me out; but with that chin what can anyone expect? It tells her character at a glance."

"Tell us your opinion of her," said Cora. "Do *you* see the great difference there is between you?"

"Why, she is different every way. First in importance is temper; there she has the best of me, for she is as mild as milk-and-water, and I own it certainly is not the 'correct thing' to get into such rages as I do. She gives the impression that she is never determined about anything, and anyone can persuade her that this, or that is right, as she has no mind to solve the matter for herself. She will go through life depending on another's conscience to keep her straight; but with that chin what else could she do?"

"What does her chin say?" said Cora, smiling.

"'Unstable as water; unstable as water.' I saw the words every time I glanced at her."

For the next few days Dexie endured much teasing about her intelligent *double*; but she bore it all so good-naturedly that it soon died away.

Much to everyone's surprise, Dexie endeavored to see Nina frequently, and tried to induce her to visit them often; and Dexie laughingly gave as her reason that she would like to knock a little commonsense into her *double* before she left Halifax, for fear people might think that Nina was her exact counterpart in everything.

CHAPTER XXXII.

One day, as Dexie was going to the post office, she met Miss Taylor, and the memory of the adventure in the snowstorm with Lancy and Elsie rose vividly before her mind as she grasped the outstretched hand in friendly greeting.

"I am in such a dilemma, Miss Sherwood!" she exclaimed. "I drove into Halifax with a neighbor, and he was to meet me an hour ago; but I have discovered that his usual absent-mindedness has caused him to forget all about me. I am at my wit's end, for mother will be alarmed at my absence."

"Come home with me, Miss Taylor. Oh! you must," as a refusal rose to her lips, "and if you really *must* return home tonight, it can easily be managed, I know."

After much persuasion, Miss Taylor accompanied Dexie home; and as she explained the necessity of returning that night, Mrs. Gurney told Lancy to order the horse and buggy and drive her out.

Lancy seconded Miss Taylor's request that Dexie should drive out with them, and the gay little party reached the Taylor homestead about sundown, greatly to the surprise and relief of Mrs. Taylor, who feared that Susan might try and walk the distance rather than miss the evening's festivities; for there was to be a marriage in the family that night, and Susan had been obliged to hasten to the city for some necessary trifles that had been forgotten until the last moment. Lancy and Dexie stayed until after the ceremony, but, having a long drive before them, declined the kind invitation to linger.

As they drove homewards the conversation turned on the intending departure of the family from Halifax.

"I have been waiting for a chance to have a good talk with you, Dexie, ever since I heard you were going away; but there has been so much going on that I never seem to see you alone a minute. Are you sorry to go, Dexie?"

"Yes, indeed I am. I have found Halifax so pleasant that I shall always regret leaving it."

"But you are coming back sometime, you know, Dexie? I am sure you know I am constantly looking forward to the time when you will be my wife. We understand each other, do we not?"

"Well, I am not sure that we do, Lancy. I doubt if we look at things in the same light," and she gave a quick glance into the face that was regarding her so earnestly.

"But you know how much I care for you—that I love you, Dexie?" he said, taking her hand. "You have never told me you cared for me in so many words, Dexie, but I am sure you do. They are all pleased with the idea at home, and father has promised to take me into partnership the first of the year. Until then I shall not know just how much of an income I shall have, but I know it will be enough for us to live on quite comfortably; and we could live in the part of the house that you occupy now. But you have not said the word yet that will bind us. Will you be my wife, Dexie?"

"Lancy, I will be honest and plain-spoken; then there will be no misunderstanding. Of course, I care a good deal for you, but I really do not believe I love you as a woman should love the man she marries; and you may meet the one who will give you that love some day, then you will be sorry you put that question to me. Honestly, Lancy, although we have cared very much for each other's society, I don't believe we would be half as happy together as man and wife as we are now. I can't imagine myself living with you day after day, and performing the little daily services for you that come so naturally from your mother, and which goes to make your father's life so comfortable and happy."

"Why need you pattern your future life after that of my mother; your mother does not—" Lancy paused in embarrassment.

"Oh! you need not mind saying it to me; it is only between ourselves. You want to say that my mother does not put herself out to do much for the happiness of the rest of us."

"No, I was not intending to go so far as that, Dexie."

"Well, I hope when I get married that I shall care enough for my husband to feel like exerting myself a little towards making the house comfortable. I want a happier married life than I see at home. I suppose we all have our ideals, but I would sooner take your mother for an example of what a wife should be, rather than mine."

"I believe you and I would live very happily together, Dexie; if you cared for me as much as I care for you, there would be no trouble," and he pressed the hand he held in his.

"Oh! I daresay we might get along quite *passably*, Lancy; but that doesn't seem to me enough, and I do not want to be bound by a promise which, in the future, we might both wish was never made."

"Dexie, I never thought you would put me off like this," said Lancy, in a wounded tone "You have known all this time how much I care for you, and how it was to end, and yet you think I may fall in love with someone else when you have gone away. How can you think such a thing?"

"I have no cause to think so, Lancy, for indeed you have been most kind to me all along; but I cannot help thinking that you may meet someone else who would suit you better, and yet you would feel bound to me if a promise was made between us. Let me go away free, Lancy, and if by the time you are ready to take a wife you find your feelings the same as they are now, ask me your question again; perhaps I will know my own mind by that time, for I must confess I hardly do at present."

"I will never change; but you—you want to leave the way open for yourself, and I thought you cared for me, Dexie."

Dexie felt hurt at his reproachful tone, but she put her hand across his, saying: "Lancy, don't be silly, for I do care for you. I do not know any other person, outside my own family, that I like so well as I do you. Now, will that admission satisfy you? But do not ask a promise from me for a year; give me even six months; by that time we will know whether we are necessary to each other's happiness or not."

"Very well, Dexie, but I shall feel that you are mine, even though you have not given me your promise; so do not let any romantic notions run away with you when I am not near to watch you."

"But, Lancy," said she, laughing, "supposing I should happen to meet some person who inspired me with love such as one reads of in story books, would you care to have me for a wife if my heart were not in the bargain?"

"No, Dexie, I hope you are supposing impossible things. Would you break my heart?"

"Hearts don't break, Lancy," she said, smiling; "they may ache, but I doubt if they ever break."

"Dexie, you make my heart ache already. I have planned and hoped so much, and you give me so little to build on, after all. Is it fair to trifle with me like this?"

There was a few minutes' silence, then Dexie said:

"Lancy, think a minute. Have I ever been guilty of trifling with anyone's feelings? Have I not been open and outspoken to you in everything? I am afraid, Lancy, this very fact has made you think that I care for you more than I really do, but I think that too many young girls jump into matrimony with their eyes blindfolded, and I do not intend to add to the number. There is plenty of time to settle the question, when I know that I really love you. It would not be honest to deceive you in this, Lancy."

"My Dexie, you could not deceive me if you tried. I am perfectly content with the love you have for me already, without waiting for the romantic passion which some story-writers consider necessary before a marriage should take place. But your answer has disappointed me, Dexie, for I expected to present you to mother, on our return, as my promised wife. Indeed I was so sure you would not refuse me, I prepared myself with this," and he took from his pocket a little casket containing a handsome engagement ring.

"Lancy, how could you?" The words seemed to come from the depths of her heart.

"Do let me put it on your finger, Dexie. Think what happiness you will give me by wearing it."

"Lancy, I want to please you, really I do, but don't ask me to put it on. I always think a ring binds the person receiving it the same as it binds the finger, and, once on, is almost a sacred thing; and feeling as I do, I don't want to wear it lightly. Lancy, can't you trust me for six months without a reminder?"

"Yes, but I wish you would wear it as a 'sign between me and thee'; do not refuse me this, Dexie."

"Let me wear it on my chain, then, and I will take it," and she drew from her neck a fine gold chain with a pretty charm attached. Detaching the latter, she held it to him, saying:

"This is my one treasure, Lancy, take it in exchange; if ever you care for another more than for me, send it back to me. I will wear your ring in its place on the same conditions," and she clasped the chain around her neck again, hiding the ring in her bosom.

Lancy placed the precious token in an inside pocket containing some other treasures, and Dexie blushed as she recognized them as some trifles of her own.

"I think I can claim that glove," said she, laughing as Lancy tucked the little parcel in his pocket. "I have missed it for some time."

"You shall have it when the hand is mine that fits it," said he with a bright smile, as he raised her hand to his lips. "I wonder if you realize how much I shall miss you, Dexie. The only ray of comfort I can see is the thought of the pleasure your letters will give me; only for that I would go melancholy, like Hugh."

"Lancy, don't joke about Hugh; I can't bear it. I was so startled when I saw him out last Sunday. He looked so pale and thin I could hardly believe it was he. Does he ever mention my name, Lancy?"

"Never; but if anyone happens to bring it up in connection with anything, he seems that eager to hear every word, that I can't help feeling sorry for him. Be careful and don't make me your second victim."

"I do not believe I am responsible for Hugh's condition, and it is not fair for you to speak as if I was; but now he is able to be about, I am in constant terror lest he will corner me sometime and renew his attack. That is the only thing that makes me feel glad that I am leaving Halifax. I am afraid I could not bear such another scare as he gave me that day in the boat."

"I will make it known to him in some way that you are to be my wife; and when he hears it, I am sure he will never trouble you again. When everything is settled, I will go and claim you; and I fancy Hugh will not stay in Halifax when we are married. How soon do you think you will be going away?"

"Sometime within a month. Papa is weatherwise, and thinks the winter will set in early, so is anxious to hasten our departure."

A few evenings later, there was a small family party at Mrs. Beverly's, to which Mr. and Mrs. Sherwood and the twin girls were invited. Cora and Elsie Gurney were also going with Lancy and Hugh. This being the first time Hugh was able to appear at such a gathering, he was building many air-castles in connection with it, for he would there meet Dexie for the first time since his illness. He had made inquiries as to whether Dexie would be present, and being assured that she intended going, he looked forward to the meeting with a pleasure that was not unmixed with pain.

But when Dexie heard that Hugh intended going, and had been

asking about her intentions also, she thought she would give it up; yet considering that she must of necessity meet him sooner or later, she thought it would be wiser to do so among a number of people.

Everything seemed to go wrong with Gussie that day. She had heard by some chance that Dexie and Lancy were really engaged, and as Dexie would neither admit nor deny the fact, she felt exasperated almost to madness.

As the day wore on, Gussie's incessant bickerings became unbearable, and among other things she charged Dexie with the most heartless behavior in regard to Hugh, until she could not bear the thought of meeting him, so she silently decided to remain at home, but to say nothing about her decision until the last moment; consequently, no one had a chance to tell Hugh that Dexie had changed her mind.

When the guests were assembled in the commodious parlors, Hugh searched in vain among the different groups for a trace of the face he was so anxious to see. Once he gave a start as a face turned towards him—a face that seemed to belong to the form he was seeking—but when the sound of the voice reached his ears he turned in disgust, for it was only Nina Gordon.

Later on he learned from Gussie that Dexie had turned "sulky" at the last moment and refused to come. His face lighted up at the information, and Gussie never knew that her news sent him to make excuses and adieus to his hostess, and drove him homeward at a pace that seemed unnecessary, seeing that he had so much leisure time at his command.

Dexie had gone to the parlor to get a book, and stepping to the bow window to draw the curtains, saw his well-known figure hurrying down the street.

"Goodness! here is Hugh coming back! What has happened, I wonder?"

It took her but a moment to fasten the hall-door, and running to the kitchen, said:

"Nancy, if anyone calls, do not admit them tonight. You can say the family are out. I am going to the upper hall to finish my book." Then, laying her hand on Nancy's arm, she said in a low tone: "Don't let Hugh McNeil come in tonight, Nancy. I have fastened the front door, so he can't come in unless you let him."

"Rest easy, missie; you shan't be troubled if you don't like. But I mind he is off to the party with the rest."

"I have seen him coming back, so I wanted to warn you."

"All right, then. Ye have had a hard day, missie; run off with yer book. It's meself that will see ye are not troubled the night by anybody."

Nancy had been in the family long enough to know something of their affairs, and she took quite an interest in the doings of her favorite. She saw more than she let anyone suppose, and her apparent stupidity was often put on as a "blind."

With a book as a companion, Dexie was soon in her favorite retreat, for she had one cosy little corner which no one cared to dispute with her. The recess at the end of the upper hall she had curtained off, and besides the few blooming plants on the wide windowsill it held an old-fashioned but comfortable sofa, a big chair and a tiny table. It was here Dexie made up her housekeeping accounts, and performed such other duties as she could bring to her snug little corner. It was the one spot in the house which she claimed as her own.

She had no sooner seated herself to read than the sound of the door-bell echoed through the house. It was several times repeated before Nancy appeared to answer the summons, and Dexie's heart seemed to leap up in her throat as she recognized Hugh's voice. But Nancy remembered the injunctions given her, and refused admittance, saying decidedly that the family were out; and when Hugh reminded her that Miss Dexie was at home, Nancy boldly said that Miss Dexie was not going to be disturbed by anybody. Dexie gave a sigh of relief as she heard the door shut and Hugh's step on the pavement below. She turned to her book and was soon lost to all outside influences in her sympathy for the heroine of the story, when a slight movement of the curtain caused her to look up. The book dropped from her fingers and she staggered to her feet, her face white, even to her lips. Terror seemed to rob her of all power to move or speak, as she gazed into the face before her that was almost as colorless as her own.

With a quick movement Hugh dropped the curtain behind him and came forward with outstretched hands.

"You cannot keep me away, Dexie. You refused to let me in at the door, but you forgot the secret passage in the attic. My darling! I did not intend to frighten you!" noticing for the first time how terrified she looked. "I only came to ask your forgiveness."

He reached out his hands to catch her, but he was too late, for, as he spoke, she fell in a heap on the floor in a dead faint. With trembling hands Hugh lifted the unconscious form to the little sofa, and kneeling beside her bent over her, chaffing her hands and calling her by all the tender names which he had only dared to give her in his heart; and the pent-up emotions of weeks found relief in a shower of kisses, which rained on the upturned face and ruffled hair that framed it like a glory. It was very wrong of him, to be sure; but the man who is famishing, and who steals the loaf that will put life into his starving body, should not be severely dealt with, and Hugh's hungry heart was sadly in need of some satisfying food.

Dexie's faint lasted so long that Hugh began to feel alarmed, yet he could not think of calling to Nancy for help. Not for anything would he have her know that he had dared to enter the house in this clandestine manner, and he knew Dexie would feel vexed enough if anyone should find him there with her; so he hastily opened the nearest chamber door, and securing the water-pitcher on the stand, he bathed the white face until the quivering eyelids told that consciousness was returning. A few minutes later Dexie opened her eyes, and seeing Hugh still beside her she tried to raise herself, but sank back again on the sofa.

"Leave me at once!" she said, faintly. "Oh! I feel so sick! Go, I say."

"I cannot leave you until I see you better, Dexie. I will not touch you again, so do not be afraid of me."

Dexie felt too helpless even to object, so she laid back with closed eyes, wondering what had come over her just when she needed to be strong and bold. At last, when the silence was beginning to be unbearable to both of them, she opened her eyes, and Hugh, seeing her efforts to rise, gently helped her to a sitting posture, then seated himself in the chair beside her.

"Why did you come here, Mr. McNeil?" looking at him with offended eyes. "It is unfair to persecute me in this way."

"Forgive me for coming, then, but I had no thought of persecuting you. I heard news today that troubled me, and I was not strong enough to resist the temptation of coming to see you once more, when I found you were not at the party."

Dexie sat with tight-clasped hands, but said not a word, and Hugh saw no relenting look in the dark eyes that looked almost black in their intensity.

"Dexie, you are displeased with me, and justly so, for my mad behavior in the boat, but I have longed for the chance to ask your forgiveness, and I went to Mrs. Beverly's tonight solely to ask it of you. Dexie, your heart is not as hard as you would have me think, for I know whose kind hands helped Mrs. Gurney during my illness, and how you watched beside me when others were too terrified to be of service."

Still no response from the white lips, for Dexie's heart was throbbing too fast to allow of speech.

"I am going away, Dexie—somewhere—it matters little where—so bear with me, for this is the last time I shall see you alone. I cannot stay here, knowing that others have obtained the happiness I longed for," and looking into her face, he added: "Is it really true, Dexie, that you are going to marry Lancy? I heard it today as a fact."

A deep flush spread over the face that before was so deathly white, and not wishing Hugh to think there was any doubt about the matter she drew from her neck the gold chain, and, as she held up the ring, said in a low tone: "Is that enough to convince you?"

"No, Dexie, it is not, for you would not hesitate to wear the ring in its proper place if you felt sure of your own heart."

"If I was not sure before, I am now!" and in an instant the ring was flashing on her finger, and her eyes were lit up by an angry gleam. She wondered how it was that Hugh always seemed to bring up her worst feelings. She was angry, and she did not attempt to hide it.

"You have no right to speak to me like that! You have no right even to seek me here against my will! I have plenty of unpleasant memories of you already, so be kind enough to go home! When I remember that boat sail, your very presence seems an insult."

"Dexie, I did not mean to vex you again, but it is not my fault that your memory is full of unpleasant happenings in connection with me. Fate seems against me," said he, with a sigh, "but, Dexie, let us part friends," and he rose from his seat and stood beside her.

But the firm, closed mouth gave no promise of yielding until Hugh dropped beside her on the sofa, and in a voice choking with emotion made one further appeal.

"Dexie, if you could but picture the anguish of my heart when I returned that day to the vessel with other help than mine, and found no trace of you, I think that even you would admit that I suffered enough for my madness and folly; and since I have been sick, memory has given me many a weary hour and adds many a thrust to wounds that are almost unbearable. It is hard to give up all hope and face the dreary future without you, for you have robbed my life of all happiness. If I must be sent hopeless away, tell me, at least, that the unfortunate past is forgiven; it would make it easier to bear."

His voice had grown soft, and his eager, pleading tone was hard to resist.

Dexie felt her anger giving place to a feeling of pity.

"I do not forgive easily, I fear, Mr. McNeil," said she, in a low tone, "but I will try and think less bitterly of that unpleasant affair in the future. I would be sorry to think that I had, even unintentionally, spoiled your life; but you will not feel so low-spirited when you get stronger. The best years of your life are yet before you, and I will soon drop out of your memory as entirely as if you had never known me. Forget me as soon as you can; that is the best wish I can give you."

"Ah! Dexie, that proves that you do not know what true love really is! When your heart awakens, as it surely will sometime, you will know how cruel you have been to me. Well, you have told me to go, and I suppose I must; but it is hard—hard to leave you so! Do we part friends?" and he held out his hand as he rose to his feet again.

"Yes, I think so," and she gave him her hand, "but I hope you will not come here any more; it is unpleasant for both of us."

"And this is to be our good-bye! It is hard to give you up, my darling!" and he held her hand as if he would never let it go. "I wonder if I shall ever see you again!"

"Mr. McNeil, I have not troubled you with many favors, so I think you might grant me one. Please do not leave the Gurneys just now; on my account, I mean. We are going away from Halifax so soon ourselves, and I know it will be a disappointment to them if you leave just now. I am sure they do not wish you to go away until you are stronger. They have all been so kind to me, I wish you would not make any change until we are gone."

"That is a great temptation, Dexie, coming from you; but a few weeks of your presence, even though I may not see you, will be heaven itself, compared to the life I must spend without you. I may, perhaps, see you again."

"No! Not alone, at least! Let this be good-bye, Mr. McNeil," and she tried to draw away her hands.

But he drew her close to him, and giving one long, earnest look into her eyes, he lifted her hands to his lips and pressed a burning kiss upon them; then the curtain dropped behind him.

Dexie stood where Hugh had left her for some minutes, listening to his retreating footsteps as he disappeared up the attic stairs, then sank down in the chair Hugh had occupied, and buried her face in her hands. There was a tumult in her heart that required some deep thinking before she would feel like herself again. Thoughts had arisen that had disquieted her. Hugh had told her that her heart had not yet awakened; was it so? Why, then, was she wearing Lancy's ring? She blushed as she pulled it hastily off, hiding it on her chain like a guilty thing.

The story she had been reading, and which she had thought so overdrawn, came into her mind; it had pleased her because she had thought it so delightfully unreal. But had there not been passages in her own life quite as romantic in their nature as that which seemed so interesting when read out of a story-book.

Her heart had not yet awakened! How those words seemed to repeat themselves over and over as she sat.

Had she awakened Hugh's heart only to disappoint him? Well, she had not intended nor wished to do it; but he was very much in earnest, and she was sorry. She sighed as she rose from her chair and picked up the book that still lay on the floor, but she had lost all interest in the story; so she threw it carelessly on the table and went downstairs to await the coming of the rest, her thoughts still busy over the problems that Hugh's unexpected visit had aroused.

Dexie found that the party had not improved Gussie's temper, for she came home with many complaints as to how she had been neglected.

"I wish you had gone," she said spitefully to Dexie. "I was sick and tired of hearing people ask where you were, and why you had not come, and there was not a soul there that I cared to talk to, even Mr. McNeil disappeared, no one knows where."

Dexie colored slightly as her father regarded her curiously; no further mention was made of the matter at the time. Mr. Sherwood, however, was not surprised when, a short time after, someone came behind him, and, with arms around his neck, confessed in his ear that "Mr. McNeil had been in to see her, but had come in through the attic, because he was not allowed in by the door, and that they had quarrelled a little, but parted friends," and ended by asking him "not to tell mamma, for fear Gussie might get hold of it."

"Poor little girl, she has quite a time of it among them," her father said as she left him; "yet I think I can safely leave it all with herself."

CHAPTER XXXIII.

"Only one week more and we must say good-bye to dear old Halifax," said Dexie one morning, as she hurriedly made her toilet.

"Well, I am glad of it, for it is cold enough here this morning to freeze a bear," replied Gussie from among the blankets.

"Oh! Gussie, the ground is covered with snow, and it is still snowing," said Dexie, joyfully, as she raised the window curtain. "Oh, I do hope it will last until we can have one more sleigh drive," and she ran downstairs singing like a lark.

All day the snow kept falling in large heavy flakes, but towards evening the weather turned clear and frosty. Then the merry jingle of sleigh-bells could be heard on every side, for everyone who could was taking advantage of this, the first sleighing of the season.

Lancy had no trouble in getting Dexie to promise him her company for a sleigh drive, but he was planning for a private little drive in a single sleigh, with only room for two; while Dexie, not quite so sentimentally inclined, was hoping to make it a jolly sleighing party, in which a number should participate. She had watched Lancy as he drove away to the store in the large open sleigh which was termed "the delivery team," and a few whispered words to Elsie were hint enough.

A short time before Lancy could be expected home, Dexie and Elsie, well wrapped in furs, were making their way towards Mr. Gurney's store on Granville Street; but meeting Maud Harrington and Fanny Beverly, they stopped a moment to speak to them.

"Which way are you going, girls?" Dexie asked, her eyes sparkling with mischief.

"We are on our way home, just now," said Fanny, "but it is a wonder that you girls are not taking advantage of the sleighing, when it will last only a day or two at the most."

"Oh! we expect to have a drive later on," said Elsie. "Be on the lookout for us, and if you are not over-fastidious as to the style of the turnout, there will be a chance for you to have a drive as well."

"Oh! I'll not refuse a sleigh-drive; I would accept a seat on a bob-sled rather than miss the first sleighing," said Fanny, with a laugh.

Lancy was surprised when Dexie and his sister made their appearance in the store; but as Dexie carried some parcels with her, he supposed she had been out to do some shopping.

"I am almost ready to go home, girls, so sit down and wait for me," he said, as he brought forward some seats, "and if you will accept a drive in the delivery, it will save you the walk home."

Of course they would wait and drive back with him; so Lancy went out and placed some temporary seats in the big sleigh, making them soft and comfortable by the aid of rugs and robes.

"Are you coming back with us, Hugh?" as Hugh made his appearance from the booking-room.

"Well—yes—if I may," and he looked over to the window where Dexie was standing, as if to ask her permission.

"Well, there is plenty of room, Mr. McNeil," she said, with a smile, "so you won't crowd us."

Lancy helped Dexie into the seat beside himself, so Hugh and Elsie took the seat behind.

"Really, this is very comfortable, Lancy," said Dexie, as they flew along the street. "I don't see what better accommodation one could ask than this. Don't drive straight home; let us have our drive without changing the sleigh," she added, in a low voice.

"No, I want you alone; there is too much room here to please me," he replied, with a smile.

"Oh! stop a minute, Lancy," cried Elsie, a moment later. "There is Maud Harrington and Fanny Beverly; I want to speak to them. Do ask them to come for a drive."

"Elsie, are you crazy?—in this sleigh? Good evening, ladies" (this to the laughing girls on the sidewalk). "I am delivering some lively freight, you see. Don't you admire my turnout?"

"Yes; it is superb. May we get on board?"

"Well, if you would care to—I don't mind," was the hesitating reply; "but I have nothing but boards for seats, you know."

"Oh! no matter. The first sleigh-drive of the season is always the most enjoyable, no matter what sort of a sleigh carries you along."

Lancy soon had them seated as comfortably as circumstances would permit, and they drove off with many expressions of delight.

"Turn up Spring Garden Road, Lancy," said Hugh, entering into the spirit of the fun; "perhaps we will meet another friend or two who would enjoy a spin."

Presently they came up with Fred Beverly and May Deblois, as they were stepping briskly along the sidewalk, who started in surprise as the sleigh drove up and they recognized the occupants.

"Will you have a drive?" was Lancy's greeting.

"Most willingly," replied Fred, laughing. "Really, this is kind of you, Gurney, to give your friends a drive on the first snow."

"Oh! you need not give *me* any credit, for you had better believe I never intended to form a sleighing party when I started out with *this* team."

"Unexpected blessings thankfully received," said Fred, laughing. "The going is fine, but it won't last long, unfortunately."

On they went, their merry laughter chiming with the jingling of the sleigh bells, and more than one person turned to look after them with a feeling of envy.

"Oh! that was Mrs. Gordon we just passed at the corner," said Elsie, in a whisper. "How horrified she would be if she knew who we were!"

"Do let us call for Nina," said Dexie; "there is room for one more, and I'm sure she would enjoy it."

"But she would not consider it 'the correct thing,'" said Fred, with a laugh, "so you would have your trouble for nothing."

"Oh, I am sure she would *love* to come! do let me run in and ask her!" she urged, as they neared the house. "Ten to one she will not come until her mamma comes home to tell her if it is 'the correct thing' or not," said Fred, teasingly.

"Yes, that will be just it; she will not know what to wear for this special occasion, and it is a pity to lose a moment of this beautiful evening," said Fanny.

"I'll run the risk, and stand responsible for 'the correct thing' this time," said Dexie; "so do let me out, Lancy. Give me three minutes, and I will return with or without her."

Dexie had noticed Nina's wistful face in the window as they drove up, so she ran into the house without ceremony.

"Come, Nina, can you get ready to go for a drive in three minutes? Say, quick!"

"Oh, I would *love* to go, but mamma is out, and I could not get ready so soon without her. Oh, I am so sorry!" and she looked her disappointment.

"Come along; I'll dress you in a jiffy," and she pulled her out into the hall, and from among the clothing which hung in the cloak closet she soon had her muffled to the ears, in spite of Nina's repeated protests that *none* of those articles of clothing belonged to herself, but to her uncle.

"Oh, I am so afraid; indeed, I feel *sure* mamma would say that it is not the correct thing to go like this."

"Oh, no matter; hurry, or they won't wait for us. It won't hurt to be dressed in this rig for a short time," and Dexie hurriedly buttoned the big coat around her, and pulled a fur cap down over her ears, completely concealing her identity.

"My muff and furs are upstairs somewhere. Mamma put them away."

"This will keep your neck warm," and Dexie snatched a fancy woollen afagan from the back of a chair, and wrapped it around Nina's neck. "Put your hands up your sleeves, and you will never miss your muff," and she hurried her *double* out on the sidewalk.

"Time is just up," said Fred, "but you have done it complete. Let me help you in, Miss Gordon," and Nina was soon tucked in among the rest.

"Now, drive on as fast as you like; we must not keep her out long, for fear her mother should see her. I expect she would never hear the last of it. For once the correct thing has been set aside. What do you say, Elsie?" Dexie whispered; "I am sure Nina will enjoy the drive, even though she may be tormented with the thought of her novel wrappings."

Nina did indeed enjoy the drive. It was so seldom that any girlish pleasures came her way that for once she forgot to worry about her appearance.

Dexie's self-reliant manner was doing much to inspire Nina with courage to act on her own responsibility occasionally, and the few weeks' acquaintance with girls of her own age made quite an improvement in her manner, so that she could now laugh with the rest at the harmless jokes which passed back and forth, without waiting to consult her mamma about the propriety of it.

They were driving along pretty fast, for the streets had become hard and smooth by the continual passing of so many teams; but the speed only added to their pleasure, and no one had a thought of a possible mishap. As they turned a corner the sleigh gave a sudden slew, and instantly all hands found themselves on the ground in one grand, promiscuous heap, the shrill screams of the girls adding to the general confusion. Lancy landed on his feet, and quickly brought the horses to a standstill, and it took but an instant to right the sleigh on its runners again. With quick movements Hugh and Fred picked up their scattered belongings, and helped the girls back into their seats, making many anxious inquiries as to whether any of them were hurt, and they drove rapidly away before a crowd had time to gather. The girls were breathless with laughter and excitement; it had all happened so suddenly they had not time to realize their awkward predicament before they were back into their places again. Lancy was the only one who did not laugh over their tumble, and his frequent apologies made them feel that he blamed himself for the catastrophe.

"Lancy," said Fred, at last, "it was not your fault that we spilled over; that corner was as smooth as glass, and we *had* to go, but we are not hurt a bit, so don't take it to heart. Man alive! it was the crowning event of the evening to see Hugh sliding off on his ear! Did you have time to make an observation of my remarkable somersault, Hugh? It was cleverly done; a professional tumbler could not have done it better!" and Lancy was obliged to join in the laugh that followed.

"Well, I have picked up quite an assortment," said Dexie, whose lap was full of articles she had hastily swept from the ground when she rose to her feet. "This is your muff, Maud, and this fur glove must be yours, Mr. McNeil. Now, who claims this silk handkerchief and handbag?"

The handkerchief proved to have come from Nina's pocket, but no one claimed the handbag.

"I have still a fur-lined driving-glove, with a crown on the buttons, a bunch of keys, and a—something in a jewel case. Will the owners please prove property and pay expenses?"

Fred put in a claim for the bunch of keys, but an owner was still wanted for the handbag, driving-glove and jewel case, which, on examination, proved to contain a handsome gold watch.

"Someone else must have been spilled out at the corner besides ourselves, I expect," said Lancy, "and they must have lost these articles. Perhaps we will find some trace of the owner if we search the handbag when we get home. Here we are, Miss Gordon, none the worse for your tumble, I hope," he added, as he drew up to the curbstone, and Hugh helped her up the steps to the door. The rest of the party were then left at their respective door-steps, as they drove along towards home.

At Elsie's request, Dexie followed her into the house, and they were soon searching the contents of the handbag for some clue to its owner, but with little success. Not so, however, with the watch, for as Lancy touched the spring and caused the case to fly open his exclamation of surprise caused Dexie to look up, and a flush of crimson spread over her face as she read the words that revealed its owner, for engraved on the inside of the case were these words:

"Presented to Lieutenant Wilbur by his brother officers, in token of distinguished bravery."

Hugh could not understand the meaning of Dexie's flushed face, even though he stepped forward and read the inscription over Lancy's shoulder, for he had never learned just how Dexie had escaped from the vessel, but supposed that Lancy had in some way brought it about.

"One good turn deserves another, and—gets it this time," said Lancy, with a meaning smile. "I fancy that Lieutenant Wilbur would not care to lose this particular watch."

"Will you send it back to him, Lancy?" said Dexie.

"No, not I; but I will send him word where he will find it. Do you remember his address?"

"Well, I think I have his card somewhere; but I don't want to see him, Lancy," she said, in a low tone.

Hugh heard the whispered conversation, and wondered what connection there could be between Dexie and the lieutenant that caused such a look on her face at the sight of his name.

Dexie left the watch in Lancy's care and went home, but she was present next evening when the lieutenant called to claim his property; and as he brought with him a letter of introduction from Major Gurney, he was well received, and his pleasant and affable manner won golden opinions from all.

Yet not from all, either, for Hugh McNeil watched him with frowning brows, and he scowled darkly as he observed Dexie and the lieutenant in close conversation in a corner by themselves.

When Hugh met the lieutenant in the hall on his way out, he did not hesitate to put the question that had been troubling him all day:

"You seem to have met Miss Sherwood before, Lieutenant Wilbur. May I ask where?"

The lieutenant looked at him steadily for a moment before replying:

"I am not at liberty to tell you that, at present, Mr. McNeil, for that is Miss Sherwood's secret, not mine. She tells me that she will be leaving Halifax in a few days; if you will call on me at this address, one week after she has gone," and he handed Hugh his card, "I will be at liberty to place in your hands a *souvenir* which Miss Sherwood leaves in my care for you. Until that time, I wish you good evening;" and, lifting his hat, the lieutenant departed, leaving Hugh much puzzled over his words.

CHAPTER XXXIV.

The last day in Halifax—Dexie never forgot it. It was engraved so indelibly on her memory that time had no power to obliterate it. It had been a busy day as well as a sad one, and Elsie Gurney spent the most of it by the side of her friend, helping, as well as hindering her, as the household goods were being packed for removal. Lancy claimed one hour in the evening for himself; and as the rooms in the Sherwood household were almost dismantled, the greater part of the time was spent over the piano in the Gurneys' parlor, and their heart's good-bye was spoken through the one piece of music which they called their own.

"Remember, Dexie," and Lancy turned on the piano-stool and took her hands in his own, "you must not play that piece for anyone; it is yours and mine. When you are alone and think of me, let your thoughts be expressed through our own sweet music. Do you know, my Dexie, I believe I shall know when you are playing to me; that invisible power which we have both felt, but cannot express, much less give it a name, will still be between us, and when my heart goes out to you, my darling, it shall be through the same medium. That piece of music shall be sacred to you alone, and I shall play it for no one else until I see your dear face again. Do you agree, Dexie?"

"Yes, but I feel as if I shall never have the heart to play anything again, Lancy," for this parting from her friend hurt her more than she expected.

"Oh! yes, you will;" and he drew her over to the window within the shadow of the curtains. "The time will soon slip by, and when I go to claim you it will seem to you like coming back home again. I shall always be looking forward to that time, Dexie, so remember your promise."

"You must not forget the conditions, Lancy, and if you find your love grows less, instead of more, be honest with your own heart, and do not, in your pride, hide it from me. Absence may not 'make the heart grow fonder' in our case," she added, with a sad smile.

"Do not prophesy evil, but think of the happy present. Are you afraid or ashamed to own the fact to others, that you care for me at the present time?"

"No, I do not think any one who knows us will accuse either of us of bashfulness; the opposite has been laid to my charge until it has become an old story," she replied.

"Well, seeing that we understand each other, why not wear your ring? I particularly want Hugh to see it on your finger; I don't believe he has given you up yet, Dexie. Will you wear it to please me?"

Dexie unclasped the chain from her neck, and Lancy slipped the ring in its place on her finger.

"I think you need not mind what Hugh says or thinks," she said in a low tone. "I did not intend to tell you, Lancy, but I will confess now that Hugh saw that ring on my finger once before," and she told him the substance of the stolen interview in the upper hall.

"That is how it happens that we are on speaking terms again," she added, "but when Hugh gets well enough to travel, and begins to realize that he is a rich man, he will smile at all this foolishness; but if I live a hundred years, I will never forget that dreadful afternoon in the boat. Lieutenant Wilbur is going to give him his revolver after I am gone; that will be a reminder of it which he won't like, I am thinking!"

The next morning the last article was removed from the house, and the last good-bye given to the friends they must leave behind them. The two families met for the last time in Mrs. Gurney's parlor, and as they lingered over the last words, Dexie seated herself at the piano, and there was no quiver in her voice, though there were tears in her eyes, as she sang:

> *"Farewell, farewell, is a lonely sound,*
> *And always brings a sigh;*
> *Then give to me, when loved ones part,*
> *That good old word, 'Good-bye.'"*

Hugh and Lancy, as well as Elsie and Cora, accompanied the family to the boat, which was to sail about noon. Hugh lingered near the group on the steamer, hoping that Dexie would give him some kind word at parting, and at last Lancy, very generously, took her over to his side, saying:

"Don't look so blue, old fellow; Dexie is not taking a final leave of Halifax. Time is most up, I expect," he added hastily, as he took out his watch, then turned aside as he saw Hugh's agitated face.

"It is really settled, then," said Hugh, in a low voice, as he took Dexie's hand. "I wish you had left something that I could do for you, so that my life will not feel quite so empty."

"I have no favor to ask of you, Mr. McNeil, yet if I hear that you have been kind to Nina Gordon it will please me very much. Mind, I do not ask it of you. If someone would have the goodness of heart to save her from her mother, she would make a sensible woman yet. If Cora Gurney would only take a friendly interest in her, I would not be afraid of the future of my *double*. Good-bye, Mr. McNeil, that is the warning-signal, I believe."

Hugh seemed in no hurry to heed the warning, but stood aside where he could watch Dexie's face as she parted from Lancy. He heeded not the few hurried words so earnestly spoken, nor the fervent clasp of their hands, for there was no answering light in Dexie's eyes as they rested on Lancy's face. Friends were hurrying across the gang plank, but Hugh waited till Lancy had disappeared; then stepping to Dexie's side, he hurriedly whispered:

"I was not mistaken! your heart has not yet awakened, as I said! and Lancy's ring binds no heart but his own. All is fair in love and war, and my chance is as good as his, after all! *Au revoir*, my little wife!" and he raised his hat and hurried ashore.

His heart beat rapidly, and though he carried away the memory of Dexie's indignant look, he stepped across the plank with a firm, light step. Lancy wondered at the transformation which seemed to have taken place in Hugh since he had seen him on deck, a few short minutes ago; but they stood together and watched the receding steamer, until the one that was so dear to them both was lost to view.

While Dexie was on deck taking her last look of "dear old Halifax," Gussie hurried below to secure the best accommodation for herself, and she was so long in deciding the matter that she appeared only in time to wave her farewell from the deck.

After the bustle of departure had subsided, the steward came forward bringing a moss-lined basket, filled with choice hothouse flowers, saying:

"A gentleman left this in my care, to be delivered to Miss Dexie Sherwood. I believe it belongs to one of you ladies."

"Oh, Dexie, they can't *all* be for you," said Gussie, eagerly, as she reached out her hand and took the basket from the steward's hands.

"Here is a note directed to me; wait till I see who it is from," and Dexie picked a tiny roll of paper from among the blossoms. One hasty glance over the written lines, and Dexie curled her lip in a disdainful smile.

"You may have everyone of them, Gussie, for I don't want them," and she drew herself away, as if the very touch of the basket were odious to her, at which Gussie looked up in surprise.

"Hugh McNeil sent them, so you are welcome to everyone of them," she said in a low voice, as the steward withdrew. "He is very particular to state that they are for me alone," and her lip curled. "I wish they had been brought to me while he was by, I would have tossed them overboard before his eyes! Thank fortune, I have seen the last of him!"

"You will live to be sorry for your treatment of Hugh McNeil, mark my words! He would not have found me so hard to please," and Gussie placed the flowers tenderly beside her.

Strange, but the first thing that Dexie did when she reached the privacy of her stateroom was to snatch Lancy's ring from her finger, almost angrily, and slipping it again on the chain about her neck she snapped the catch with no easy hand; and her face was far from being tender and loving as she put out of sight the pledge of Lancy's love and fidelity, for she was saying in her heart:

"I will never be so foolish as to put that on my finger again; it was wrong to wear it at all. Hugh is right; it binds no heart but Lancy's, and I doubt if I can truly say that much itself, three months from now."

If we look in upon the Sherwood household a few weeks later, we will find them comfortably settled in the busy town of Lennoxville, a town which is noted throughout New England for its manufacturing industries. The house is pleasantly situated a short distance back from the street, allowing room for a neat lawn in front of the house, which is made more attractive by a few flower-beds set near the front entrance, and beneath the windows.

The former owner had taken much pleasure in designing the house and its surroundings, and everything about the premises was neat, convenient and attractive, but financial difficulties had obliged him to relinquish the property just when he might naturally expect to reap the benefit of his labors. Mr. Sherwood had purchased it at a very reasonable figure, considering the advantages it possessed, and having obtained a permanent and remunerative position in the office of a large manufacturing firm, the family had reason to hope that this was their last move for some years.

Dexie was delighted at the possibilities which the well-laid-out kitchen garden at the rear of the house promised to afford. Everything at present was bare and sere, but when the spring opened it would require but little labor, and that of a pleasant description, to prepare a garden that should delight the heart of any housekeeper; and the flower-beds in the front of the house, which were now covered and protected by branches of fir, would in due season blossom into spots of beauty.

The family-life at this time was very pleasant. Gussie seemed to have forgotten, for the time, all her former jealous and unkind feelings, which had made her so often, while in Halifax, an unpleasant member of the household.

Society in Lennoxville was pleasant and attractive, and the Sherwoods were made right welcome among a choice circle of friends. Invitations to social gatherings were showered upon the twin girls until their popularity was so firmly established that no one thought of questioning it.

Dexie missed her Halifax friends very much. She met with no one in her new home who could fill the place that the Gurney family had held in her heart, and among all her many friends there was none she could make such an intimate companion of as Elsie Gurney. In musical circles, Dexie soon filled an envious position; but so far she had met no one whose sympathies were like Lancy's. Oh, yes, she missed Lancy very much, indeed—she never hesitated to confess it when the matter was alluded to; and very often, when alone in the parlor, the piece of music which had such a strange power over each of them filled the air with unmistakable longing, and seemed to speak of loneliness and sorrow. But her bright face expressed no such sad feeling to others; it seemed only the musical side of her nature that mourned the loss of a kind and sympathetic friend.

She heard quite frequently from Elsie, and Lancy's weekly letters were always bright and chatty; but they left Dexie with a certain uneasy feeling that should have had no place in her heart, if Lancy's expressed regards met with the reciprocation which he had some right to expect.

She would not have cared to confess to the relief she experienced when, some weeks later, Lancy wrote to her of his intended visit to England, where he meant to spend a few months among his relatives in Devonshire; and the thought that the wide ocean would be between them, did not cause the same regretful feeling in her heart as it did in Lancy's. Once since they had left Halifax, Dexie, to her surprise, received a letter from Hugh McNeil, that had come enclosed in one to her father. Mr. Sherwood said little as to the contents of his letter; but the earnest, passionate words in Dexie's left no doubt in her mind that Hugh had small intention of giving up his suit, though for the present he would leave her in peace.

He told her of his intention of making a journey to Australia, to visit the last resting-place of his father; and after an extended journey, he hoped to come back and find all the unpleasantness in the past forgiven and forgotten.

For some time after the letter was received, Dexie fancied that her father regarded her with more attention than was necessary; but it soon passed from her mind without giving her the slightest suspicion that Hugh had placed in her father's hands a substantial and unmistakable proof of the genuineness of his regard.

This was to be unknown to her until such a time as circumstances rendered it necessary to communicate the facts. But if he survived the dangers of the passage, and returned safely and found her still free, he would again endeavor to gain her consent to a closer relationship.

Fortunately for Dexie's peace of mind, Mr. Sherwood kept the matter to himself; but the fact that both Hugh and Lancy intended to put the ocean between them and herself, even for a short time, gave her a sense of relief and security which she would have found it difficult to explain.

CHAPTER XXXV.

One day, a few weeks later, as Mr. Sherwood was returning from his office, he was much surprised to meet Mr. Plaisted on the street, and he stopped and spoke to him cordially.

"Why, Sherwood! is it you? I never expected to meet you here," and Mr. Plaisted shook hands with his former partner.

"I am settled here now," replied Mr. Sherwood. "What are you doing in this part of the country?"

"I am travelling for a New York firm; just arrived in town this morning. Did I understand you to say you were living here?"

"Yes; we removed from Halifax some time ago. Here is the address; drop in and see us before you leave town, if you are not pressed for time," and he handed him a card.

"Thanks! I shall be pleased to call this evening, my kind regards to the family," and raising their hats the men separated, with but a passing thought of their former differences.

The presence of Plaisted in the town was a great surprise to the Sherwood family, and Dexie heard of his intended visit with a frown.

"I am astonished, papa, that you could ask him to call after all that has happened; but it is like his impudence to accept the invitation, which he might know was more an act of courtesy than a desire to renew his acquaintance."

"Let bygones be forgotten, Dexie; it is poor policy to remember old scores too long. It is enough that there will never be any more business relations between us. His stay in town is likely to be short, so there is no fear that he will trouble any of us long."

"Well, I hope you will be careful, and not say anything that he can misconstrue into an invitation to remain with us overnight. But it will be just like him to stay, and stay, and stay, till it is too late to go back to the hotel," said Dexie. "But if he manages, after all, to foist himself upon us, I'll take a cook's privilege and leave the house—until he is out of it in the morning, anyway. So remember, papa, I have 'given warning,'" and she shook her finger at him as she turned to leave the room.

But there was no frown on Gussie's face when she heard of Plaisted's expected visit. She was only anxious to appear at her best, so she retired to her chamber and spent the intervening time over a toilet that was meant to impress Mr. Plaisted afresh. She was ready as ever to turn a listening ear to his flattery, though she had ample opportunity to realize how empty and meaningless were his words.

The family were assembled in the parlor when Mr. Plaisted was announced, and he found no cause to complain of his reception, for even Dexie's cool bow and formal greeting were so much like her former treatment of him that when she ignored his offered hand he did not resent it openly. But in his heart he vowed to "get even" with her. The frigid stare with which she regarded him when he attempted to draw her into conversation reminded him of past discomfitures, and, forgetting that he seldom came off victor when crossing swords with Dexie, he determined to pay off old scores with interest. As his business kept him in town for several days, his calls were quite frequent, but he found no chance of annoying Dexie, save by the one small and spiteful way of addressing her as "Miss Dexter," and the quick, angry glance that was flashed at him as he said it told that she resented it.

One afternoon, when he was in the parlor chatting with Gussie, Dexie came into the room on some errand, and her slight bow of recognition gave him an opportunity to ask, in his sneering manner, if she was "keeping her smiles for the disconsolate lovers she had left behind her in Halifax?"

A sharp retort rose to her lips, but she repressed it, and her lip curled with scorn as she answered his sallies in the coolest terms that common civility allowed. He might as well have tried his cutting speeches on an iceberg for all the satisfaction he received, so he dropped back to the only source of annoyance at his command.

"Can I trouble you for a drink of water, Miss *Dexter*?" he said, with a malicious grin.

Dexie took no notice of this request, knowing it was made only for the purpose of using her detested name.

He repeated his request a second time, and even Gussie flushed at his offensive tone, though she called Dexie's attention to the request.

"Dexie, Mr. Plaisted asks for a drink. Where are your manners?"

"I have sent them away for repairs, Gussie dear," Dexie replied, in her sweetest tone, "and I fear they will not be returned to me until after Mr. Plaisted has taken his departure. Very sorry, but they have experienced such a strain these few days past that they were about worn out."

"Dexie, I am ashamed of you! Bring a drink of water for Mr. Plaisted directly!"

"My dearest Gussie, if Mr. Plaisted wants a drink, pray get it for him yourself," was the soft and sweet reply, "for he will surely die of thirst before Dexter brings him a drop. Allow me to suggest that, as an alternative, you can ring for the servant to wait on him, or lead him to the pump like any other—beast," and unmoved by the looks cast upon her she passed into the next room.

"You brought that upon yourself, Mr. Plaisted, but I am very, very sorry," said Gussie, who felt all the insolence of the words that were spoken with such suavity. "Why will you call her *Dexter* when you know that it makes her throw aside all civility?"

"Well, it *is* too bad, I will allow," replied Plaisted, "but I own that I have only myself to blame when I provoke her into making such stinging retorts; but the temptation to tease her is irresistible, and I owe her for a good many tricks she has played on me."

"Well, were I in your place, I would not call her 'Dexter' any more; though if your experience of her is not warning enough, I need say nothing more."

"Well, I must admit that she has always had the best of it so far; but I will take good care she has no chance to repeat any of her former tactics—though, if I am not mistaken, I have good cause to remember every visit I ever made to your house, thanks to her. However, I ought to take the old proverb to heart, 'Those that live in glass houses should not throw stones,' for I should feel vexed enough if my second name were thrown at me in the same manner. It is quite as odious to me as 'Dexter' is to her."

"What is your second name? 'D.S.' are your initials, are they not?"

"Yes; but you would never guess what the 'S.' stands for. When I was a little shaver my father was particularly interested in the history of the Prophet Daniel and his three friends, Shadrach, Meshach and Abednego, and I believe he fully intended to name me after the four of them; but at my christening mother drew the line at Shadrach. I am just as close regarding my second name as Dexie is about her own—so close, in fact, that not one of my schoolmates ever found it out."

"But did they never ask what the 'S.' stood for?" Gussie asked.

"Of course! but Danuel gave it as Samuel, and had to answer to the name of 'Danuel Samuel'; but that was better than the changes they would have rung on my right name."

Dexie was an unintentional listener to this explanation, and it did not raise Mr. Plaisted in her estimation. It was so like him to treat another in a way he would object to himself; but after awhile the name came back to her, "Shadrach." Where had she seen or heard that name before? "Shadrach; Shadrach," she mused. "I have it!" she said at last; "the 'Widow Bedott'!" and with the thought she flew up the stairs like a whirlwind.

Dexie was soon in the attic kneeling beside an old box filled with books and papers. All housekeepers are apt to know by experience the state and condition of this box, and to possess its counterpart in some out of-the-way corner of the house. After a diligent search Dexie was rewarded by finding a package of loose leaves which once formed a much-loved volume. The very leaf she wanted seemed lost; but to her great joy a leaf, crumpled and torn, proved to be the object of her search. She smoothed it out carefully, glanced over it, and then laughed softly to herself.

"Now it is my turn, 'dear Shadrach, my Shad.' With the help of 'Widow Bedott,' I fancy I can impress this visit upon your mind quite as indelibly as your unwelcome visits in Halifax," and she slipped the loose leaves into her pocket.

Still, as yet she had no definite plan in her mind as to how she would play her game of retaliation; but during the evening she heard her father inquire how long Mr. Plaisted intended to remain in the town.

"I leave the day after tomorrow," Plaisted replied. "I have an appointment in H—— on the fifteenth."

"Oh, tomorrow is St. Valentine's day!" cried Gussie. "I really had forgotten it. You must send me a valentine to remember you by"—this to Plaisted, who had seated himself beside her on the sofa.

"Am I likely to be forgotten without some reminder?" was the low-spoken reply. "I was hoping something quite different."

The mention of valentines gave Dexie an idea, and during the evening she visited several stores where these tokens of sentiment were kept for sale, but found nothing in the shape of a picture that would suit the verses of tender sentiment so touchingly expressed for her beloved Shadrach by the fair widow.

As she was returning home she passed a little shop, the windows of which were decorated with valentines of the one and two cent variety, and one of these caught her attention. It was one of the most common sort, and showed in variegated colors a large fish with two tails for legs, two elongated fins for arms, on one of which was a basket containing some smaller specimens of its own species, while the other held to its mouth the melodious fish-horn that delights our ears every morning.

Purchasing this caricature of a shad, she pasted below it a version of the affectionate lines of Widow Bedott; then enclosing it in an elaborate envelope, she addressed it with many flourishes to:

"Mr. Danuel Shadrach Plaisted,"

and carried it herself to the post office.

As she passed the fish market her attention was attracted by some very fine shad displayed for sale, and they immediately suggested a further means of accomplishing her revenge, so she ordered a supply.

Dexie sought her mother directly she arrived home.

"Don't you think we might ask Mr. Plaisted to dinner tomorrow, mamma?" she asked.

"Please yourself, Dexie; but if he is asked, you must see about the dinner yourself. It will not do to trust Eliza to get up anything extra, you know."

"The dinner shall be well served, but I have a favor to ask, mamma. If Mr. Plaisted is present, will you praise or condemn the fish course—at the table, I mean; praise it highly, or condemn it heartily."

"Well, I cannot see your object in making such a request, Dexie," said her mother in surprise, "but I will not be indifferent, if that is what you mean."

The next morning, when Mr. Sherwood was drawing on his gloves to go to his office, Dexie followed him out to the hall, and as she brushed a few specks from his coat, asked:

"If you see Mr. Plaisted this morning, will you send or bring him up to dinner; but don't say that I told you to ask him?"

"Well, what's in the wind now? I thought you did not care for Mr. Plaisted's society," regarding her intently.

"An invitation to dinner does not mean that I have changed my opinion of him, does it? He has been quite unbearable, so I'm going to 'heap coals of fire on his head.'"

The roguish gleam in her eyes, and the smile she could not conceal, made her father think that there was more in the invitation than he understood, and he surmised that the "coals of fire" were not absolutely figurative.

"All right! I'll see that he gets the invitation. What shall I order for dinner?"

"Nothing, papa; I have everything ready for our expected guest, so don't let him disappoint me."

"Hum-m! there's something up, sure enough; though I can't see through it yet," he said to himself as he walked thoughtfully away.

"So far, so good," said Dexie, *sotto voce*. "How I wish I could have seen Shadrach when he opened his valentine this morning!"

Dexie would have felt satisfied that her shaft had struck home had she seen Plaisted when he had "taken in" the contents of his valentine.

He had stepped into the office to mail Gussie's valentine, and was much surprised when a beautiful envelope was placed in his hands. It held something very sweet and delicate, no doubt, and as he turned aside he pressed it to his lips.

Observing the name of Shadrach, he felt sure it must have come from Gussie; no one else knew his second name, so she must have sent this sweet love-token. It was hardly fair to write out his name in full; but, of course, it was only done to make known the identity of the sender. He thrust it into his pocket and hastened to his hotel, where in the privacy of his own room he could enjoy it without interruption. The loving words he expected to find were certainly there, yet as he read them a dark frown gathered on his brow:

> "*Dear Danuel Shadrach! thy valentine speaks,*
> *While the rosy red blushes surmantle her cheeks;*
> *And the joys of requital brings tears to her eye.*
> *Now, Shadrach! my Shadrach! I'm yours till I die.*
>
> "*The heart that was scornful and cold as a stone,*
> *Rejoices to hear the sweet sound of your name;*
> *Farewell to the miseries and griefs I have had,*
> *But I cannot forget them! dear Shadrach! my Shad!*
>
> "*Dear Shadrach! my Shadrach! my troubles are o'er,*
> *My name in its fulness you'll whisper no more;*
> *Or your own sweet cognomen will make you feel sad,*
> *For I hold the whip-handle! Oh Shadrach! my Shad!*"

Mr. Plaisted read the lines over several times before he comprehended their meaning, or understood what connection the absurd picture had with them; but when the whole force of the matter struck him, his rage was uncontrollable. He crumpled the valentine in his hands and threw it with all his force towards the fire, but in his anger he aimed too high, and it struck against the wall and bounced back at him, as if those hateful words were hurling themselves at him.

"Ha! if I only knew who sent that, I'd—"

Words failed to express the punishment awaiting the author of those insulting verses. But wait! did he know the handwriting? at thought of Dexie Sherwood's previous productions coming to his mind. Ah! that last verse seemed to throw out a hint! He looked at his tormentor closely, and doubted. That envelope, yes, Gussie must have sent it, for she had spelled his name "Danuel." He never would have thought that Gussie would be guilty of such a thing. He would go away on the next train and never look on her face again. Yes, he would go at once, and forget the whole cursed stuff—said "cursed stuff" being the affectionate lines which continued to haunt him after the manner of the mind-destroying craze which Mark Twain inflicted on a later generation, "Punch, brothers, punch with care;" for as he walked down the street the words kept time to his feet, the train bells echoed them, and it was those very words that pealed a warning at the crossing. So intent were his thoughts on the affectionate lines that he was oblivious to everything around him, and Mr. Sherwood spoke his name twice before Plaisted awoke from his reverie.

He felt inclined to refuse the kindly-worded invitation to dinner which Mr. Sherwood extended to him, but, on second thoughts, accepted it; he would satisfy himself as to whether Gussie sent the valentine or not. But it took only a few questions to assure him that Gussie was innocent, after all, and she seemed so offended when he asked if she had told his name to anyone that he felt compelled to believe she knew nothing of the matter. Gussie was too much enraptured with her own valentine to take much note of Plaisted's abstracted manner, for even the sight of Gussie's pretty face did not put aside the memory of those tormenting lines.

But his torture was only begun. Dexie was determined to crowd into a few hours the annoyance he had spread over several days in her case. Her plans were well laid, and she had even studied a book of statistics for his benefit. A few minutes before dinner was announced, while Gussie was adding a few touches to her toilet, Dexie came into her room, and, after a few general remarks, said: "Mr. Plaisted has come to dinner, has he not?"

"Yes, papa sent him up. I hope you have something nice for dinner, Dexie."

This was the very question that Dexie hoped to hear, so she

replied: "Oh! yes, I think it will pass. There is some nicely-cooked shad for the fish course; but if that does not suit Mr. Plaisted's fancy, there is sufficient besides. Say, Gussie, I don't often ask a favor, but I wish today you would praise the shad."

"Praise the shad! Why on earth should I praise the shad! If it is cooked nice, isn't that enough?"

"No, Gussie, not for this occasion; I'm afraid Mr. Plaisted will not be partial to shad, but if the rest of us seem to like it, of course he cannot refuse it."

"Oh! all right. I'll not only praise the shad, but I'll make Mr. Plaisted think there is nothing I like better."

Gussie hastened down to the parlor, where Mr. Plaisted was waiting, while Dexie threw herself into a chair in muffled shrieks of laughter.

"There, now, I guess I can keep a straight face till the time arrives;" and a few minutes later she followed the family to the dining-room.

There was certainly nothing amiss in the manner of the cooking or serving of the shad, and the presence of this particular fish at the table did not strike Plaisted as unusual, until Mr. Sherwood asked if he would be "helped to shad."

His mind by this time had become almost normal, but that one word threw him back into his former state, and brought again that tormenting refrain, "Dear Shadrach! my Shad!" He glared at the dish containing the fish as if he would annihilate it; but, hastily collecting his scattering senses, he took the plate Mr. Sherwood passed him, thinking it a strange coincidence that the never-till-now hated fish should be thrust before him at this moment. He tried to be his natural self, but those haunting lines had full possession of him, and every mouthful seemed to choke him.

Dexie was watching him closely, and felt sure that his abstraction was due to the one cause, and she silently enjoyed his discomfiture.

Gussie, who sat opposite, also noticed it, and remembering her promise to Dexie, began:

"Oh! Mr. Plaisted, I'm afraid you do not care for shad! How unfortunate that we happen to have it for dinner today! We are all very fond of shad, myself especially, and this is very nicely cooked, just to my liking," and she gave Dexie a sideward look.

"Yes, we *all* like shad, even to the cat," said the irrepressible Georgie. "I found her with her nose in the basket the first thing."

"Be quiet, sir!" said the father sternly, and Georgie obediently subsided, while Dexie could hardly repress a giggle.

"Let me help you to another piece, Plaisted," said Mr. Sherwood. "What! not any more? It is not often we get such good shad in an inland town. Halifax is the place for fine shad! In the season, when the catch is fair, you can get your pick for a song almost, but here, I expect, their scarcity makes them of more value."

"Yes," replied Dexie, "they are rather dear, *dear shad*," and she looked intently at her plate, well knowing how Plaisted was glaring at her. "Yes," she added, "I call them dear shad when one has to pick over such a quantity of bones before getting a satisfactory mouthful, don't you, Mr. Plaisted?" But Mr. Plaisted laid down his knife and fork, and returned her look with interest.

"I fear you are not making a dinner at all, Mr. Plaisted," Mrs. Sherwood put in. "You do not seem to care for shad."

"No! I detest them, though I was not aware of the fact till today," he replied.

"They are not cooked to your liking, I fear! I wish, Dexie, you had looked after them a little better. How do you prefer your shad cooked, Mr. Plaisted?" she added, in a concerned voice.

"I do not care for shad in any shape or form," he said, rather shortly, which caused everyone to look up in dismay, all except Dexie, and she seemed intent on finding the minutest bone.

"I am very sorry! You should have spoken about it sooner. Eliza, remove Mr. Plaisted's plate. I hope we have something else you can relish."

He made a show at eating what was set before him, but it was hard work. Could his entertainers talk of nothing else but shad? It appeared not, for when the conversation seemed about to turn to other things a skilfully put question, or a bit of information, brought the fish back to be discussed in another light; consequently, the shad question was pretty well sifted. The method of catching them, the amount caught during the last season, the catch of the previous year compared with other years; in fact, Dexie seemed to have the fishing reports at her finger-ends, or at the end of her tongue, to speak literally, and Mr. Sherwood seemed delighted with the chance to air the knowledge he possessed to such an attentive listener. But Mr. Plaisted's thoughts were elsewhere; he was repeating to himself the lines he had no power to forget, and when dinner was over he was almost a mental wreck.

Dexie was exulting in his misery, and was longing to let him know she was the author of it.

When they entered the parlor, Mr. Sherwood turned to Dexie, saying: "Give us some music, Dexie; something to cheer us up and drive away the blues," and he nodded at Plaisted, who had thrown himself into a chair.

But seated at the piano, Dexie still kept up the torture of the dinner table by selecting songs that suggested fishing, or fishermen's daughters, until Plaisted rose and walked the floor in ill-concealed distress.

Feeling the crisis near at hand, she tried to think of something that would "cap the climax," but as nothing occurred to her, she added a verse impromptu to what she was singing:

> *"Oh! father dear, I've caught a fish; I'm sure it is a shad;*
> *Pray help me take him off the hook; you see he's hurt so bad!"*

This was too much for Plaisted. Taking a sudden turn he faced his tormentor, but she heeded not his angry looks.

"I tell you what, Sherwood!" and he wheeled around angrily, "if I had a daughter who would play such stuff as that, I'd—I'd smash the piano to atoms!" and he brought his fist down on the table with a crash.

"What do you mean, sir!" and Mr. Sherwood was on his feet in a moment. "Your words and actions are insulting!" By this time Dexie was by her father's side, ready to give the finishing stroke to her enemy, and gently pressing her father's arm, said:

"Let me settle this affair, papa. I think, Mr. Plaisted, we can cry quits from today. You have found great delight in calling me 'Dexter.' I hope you are equally delighted to hear your own name repeated in its most obnoxious form. I find there is nothing more effective for a man of your stamp than to treat him as he delights to treat others. It is through my exertions that you have *enjoyed* yourself so much today, and if you ever wish to have the pleasure repeated, just call me 'Dexter,' and I'll do my best to repeat the entertainment."

Everyone looked at Dexie in surprise, and fearing that Plaisted might still have doubts as to her meaning, she swept him an elaborate courtesy, as she said:

"Good-bye, my dear Shadrach! don't forget in the future that 'I hold the whip-handle, dear Shadrach, my Shad!'" and before the family realized what this scene meant, Dexie had left the room and her voice was heard in the hall singing:

> *"Farewell to thee, oh Shadrach! my dearest Shad, adieu;*
> *But Dexter has hereafter the upper hand of you."*

Plaisted was about to spring after her when Mr. Sherwood caught his arm.

"What does all this mean, Plaisted? Explain yourself, sir!"

"It means that I am the victim of the most diabolical practical joke that was ever perpetrated on an individual, and it appears that Miss Dexie is at the bottom of it, though you have all assisted her in carrying it out."

"If there is any joke afloat I am entirely ignorant of it, Plaisted, I assure you," said Mr. Sherwood. "I see that something is amiss, but I have no idea what it is, though apparently Dexie is not so innocent."

"Let me explain," cried Mr. Plaisted. "Miss Dexie has, in some way, found out what my second name is, and that it is as hateful to me as 'Dexter' is to her, and she has made it the subject of a very cruel joke. As I supposed that nobody knew my full name, you can judge of my surprise when I received this from the office," and he held forth the valentine.

"Oh! that's only a valentine, Plaisted. You surely did not allow such a little thing to disturb you?" said Mr. Sherwood.

"But see what the envelope contains," he urged, bringing out the bedecked fish.

But if he expected any sympathy, he was disappointed, for when Mr. Sherwood's eyes rested on the figure and read the lines beneath, shout after shout of laughter rang through the room, and when Gussie stepped over to see what the paper contained her shrill laughter joined the chorus.

"Well, it serves you just right, Mr. Plaisted," said she. "I told you she would make you repent it if you used her name so freely. But I wonder how she found out your name? Could she have been in the back parlor while we were talking?"

"I believe she was!" Plaisted replied. "But the shad for dinner? Need you have added that? The valentine was punishment enough!"

Another shout of laughter from Mr. Sherwood, and Gussie's perplexed looks gave place to an amused smile.

"Dexie planned it herself! Ha! ha! ha! I see it all!" and Mr. Sherwood roared again. "She marked this out as a day of punishment for you, Plaisted, and she has carried it out pretty well! Ha! ha! It was she herself who told me to ask you to dinner, saying she had everything ready for you, and was going to 'heap coals of fire' on your head because you had been treating her badly. Ha! ha! Guess you are pretty well scorched, sure enough!" and he leaned back in his chair and wiped his hot face.

"Yes, she *has* scorched me! Those verses are burnt into my memory and repeat themselves in spite of me. But you seemed to have studied up the whole business of shad-fishing just for the occasion."

"But, on my honor, Plaisted, I was entirely ignorant that my talk was annoying you. Come to think of it, Dexie herself kept me at it. How she must have enjoyed it!" and he laughed again. "I thought it strange that she ordered shad for dinner," said Mrs. Sherwood. "Yet she actually asked me to scold her before you all if they were not cooked satisfactorily."

"You will not have a chance to call her 'Dexter' again," said Gussie, "unless you want to be addressed as Shadrach or Shad. Whichever you dislike the most, you will be sure to get. Now I understand what she meant when she asked me before dinner if I would praise the shad," and she joined her father's laugh; it was so contagious.

"Well, I will be compelled to cry quits, sure enough," said Plaisted; "but I never suspected that she could make such comical verses."

"Oh! that is second-hand poetry, Plaisted. She has been misquoting the 'Widow Bedott' for your benefit," said Mr. Sherwood.

"And who is the 'Widow Bedott'?"

"She is a character in a most amusing book. Let me advise you to take her as a travelling companion with you tomorrow. After you have read about her Shadrach, the poetry won't trouble you as being too personal."

A short time later Mr. Plaisted left the house, but his day's experience still rankled, and he could truthfully say it was the most unpleasant day he had ever spent. He mentally resolved that should he ever spend another hour in the society of Dexie Sherwood he would treat her with the greatest respect, for his day's punishment would be a lasting reminder of her power of retaliation.

CHAPTER XXXVI.

Among the many social gatherings which the "Sherwood twins" attended were the weekly meetings of the Temperance and Benevolent Society, or the "T. and B.," as it was usually styled.

This society included among its members most of the young people connected with the best families in the town.

It was not so aggressive in the temperance cause as some of the other existing societies, but it had its place, as its ever-increasing membership clearly showed. It accepted no one as a member who had at any time been addicted to the use of liquor, and it kept many young men from falling into the pernicious habit of using intoxicants.

Among the number who had lately signed their names to the constitution of the society was Guy Traverse, the young manager of a large furniture establishment in the town. He had but recently been appointed to the position, but his pleasant, affable manners won him friends from all quarters.

He was quite an acquisition to the T. and B. Society: a fine reader, a good declaimer, witty and quick at repartee, the Social Committee of the society soon learned his value, and a smile of welcome greeted him wherever he made his appearance.

Being on the Social Committee, Dexie Sherwood was frequently thrown into his society, but by some mistake or unintentional oversight they had never been introduced, and there was something in Dexie's manner that forbade him to make any advances without this formal introduction.

As it was taken for granted that all the members had been duly presented to each other, no one gave the matter a thought, and though the committee held several meetings, at which both were present, no one noticed the fact that these two were the only ones who did not exchange ideas on the matters before them.

One evening after the usual business matters were disposed of, the society proceeded to elect new officers for the ensuing quarter, and Guy Traverse's popularity was sufficient to place him in the highest office in the gift of the society. When asked if he would like to name his own assistant, he turned to the speaker and smilingly replied:

"I would be happy to have the assistance of the society's organist, but as we have not yet been introduced, perhaps she would prefer that I did not give her name."

"What! do you mean to say that you have never been presented to Miss Sherwood! How did that happen? Come with me at once." There was much merriment over the long delayed introduction, and Dexie smilingly consented to accept the office of assistant, in addition to that of organist. This gave Guy Traverse the chance he had long been looking for, and at the close of the meeting he offered himself as her escort home.

This Dexie politely declined, adding in her kindest tone,

"Our house is just at the corner, Mr. Traverse, so I will not trouble you," and she slipped away.

The distance was short, for as Guy stood at the outer entrance of the T. and B. rooms he could hear the front gate shut after her, yet he would have enjoyed even that short walk with his fair assistant.

"She is not inclined to be friendly, it seems," he soliloquized, as he stroked his long silken moustache. "I must find out the reason."

The next time opportunity offered he again asked permission to escort her home, but again his offer was so pleasantly declined that he could not feel offended, though it put him upon his mettle. He determined to overcome her prejudice, or whatever it was that made her treat him with so much reserve. As he turned to go home, Gussie came down the steps, and with his hand to his hat he said, smilingly,

"I almost fear to risk a second refusal tonight, Miss Sherwood, but will you accept the escort that your sister has declined?"

It was a blow to her pride that Dexie had been asked first, but such an eligible young man could not be snubbed on that account, so Gussie smiled her sweetest as she walked by his side.

"Have I done anything to displease your sister?" he asked, as they stood a few moments at the gate. "I find her very hard to get acquainted with, though I can readily see that it is not her nature to be unfriendly."

"You have not offended her, of that I am sure," Gussie replied.

"Then you think she had no particular reason for refusing my company tonight?"

"She may have some objection to any company, but not yours in particular." "Has someone else a prior claim?" he smilingly asked. "Believe me, Miss Sherwood," he added, in an apologetic tone, "I am not asking out of curiosity alone."

Gussie believed there was someone else, for Dexie had a gentleman correspondent.

"Then she is engaged, I suppose, but if the fortunate man is absent she might allow others the pleasure of her company occasionally."

But the opportunity of meeting Dexie at his own pleasure came with an introduction to Mr. Sherwood, and on learning that Mr. Traverse was a good hand at chess (Mr. Sherwood's one weakness) he was made right welcome and became a frequent visitor.

Mr. Sherwood's residence was so centrally situated that the young people of both sexes found it very convenient to drop in for a few minutes on their way up or down town. Mr. Sherwood loved to see the rooms filled with laughing faces, and encouraged this free-and-easy intercourse, and he looked forward to the evening's pleasure with the ardor of a young man. When Guy Traverse made his appearance he was sure of a hearty greeting, and the weeks flew by very pleasantly until summer was ushered in, and still there was little seeming difference in Dexie's attitude toward her father's friend.

One evening as a number of young ladies were assembled in the pleasant rooms of the T. and B. Society, discussing a coming convention, the society's Vice-President, Miss Edith Wolcott, said in decided tones:

"Before this convention meets, we ought to make some new badges; these are positively disgraceful! Will someone suggest something, or must I take the responsibility of seeing that this society has decent and respectable tokens of membership?"

"There can be but one opinion where the badges are concerned," said Ada Chester, smiling, "so let us draw from the funds of the society sufficient money to purchase the material for new ones, then we can meet somewhere and make them up."

"Capital legislation! Now announce the place of meeting and the matter is settled," and Frank Fenerty joined the group around the table. "Better set the time and place of meeting without delay, for when you ladies begin to realize the amount of work which the making of these badges involves, you will each and all remember that you have a pressing engagement somewhere else."

"That's so," said George Linton, as he drew a chair beside his friend; "but where's Traverse? As President of this society he ought to take the ladies at their word, and set them to work before their ardor has time to cool."

"There is not a house in town so convenient for all as the Sherwoods," said Ada Chester; then turning to Gussie she asked:

"Could we go to your house to make up the badges, Miss Sherwood?"

"Certainly; that is, I think so. Dexie is the acting manager at home, so you had better consult with her," replied Gussie, pleasantly.

"Come here, Dexie," and Edith turned to where Dexie was evoking sweet music from the organ. "May we go to your house to make the badges?"

"That depends on what night you wish to come. If tomorrow evening is too soon to appoint for the meeting, you could come Saturday. You know I have to be at the church on Friday evening."

"To be sure! I forgot about the meeting, and there is to be choir practice afterwards, so I'm engaged for Friday evening as well. How shall we arrange it?" and Edith looked inquiringly around the group.

"Put it to vote," and Frank Fenerty rose to his feet. "Hands up now for tomorrow night at Miss Sherwood's—or not there at all, is that it?"

"No," Dexie laughingly replied; "our latch-string is out every night, but neither Gussie nor I would be at home Friday evening."

"What is to prevent us from accepting Miss Sherwood's invitation for Thursday. I would rather go there than any other place in town," said the truthful fellow, having long admired Gussie from afar.

"We have to buy the material before we can meet to make it up,"

Edith replied. "Great Scott! how much material do you want to buy anyhow," said Fenerty. "I could buy out a store while you ladies were selecting the ribbons for your neck."

While they were speaking, Mr. Traverse made his appearance, and learning the cause of the discussion, presented a cheque for the amount needed to renew the badges, and volunteered his services as "needle-threader" for the evening.

"Come now, Traverse, you can't thread needles for the crowd," said Fred Foster, "but if the ladies will only invite the male members, we will promise to keep them supplied with threaded needles, *ad infinitum*."

"Have you decided to come to our house Thursday? If so, all members of the T. and B. are invited, but we will keep you gentlemen up to your promise in regard to the needle-threading, so let no one imagine he can come and shirk his duty," and the group separated.

The next evening the parlor of the Sherwoods presented a busy scene. Several small tables placed about the room were surrounded by groups, whose nimble fingers cut and sewed the bunches of ribbon that were provided; and as there were several "needle-threaders" for every group, there seemed no reason why the work should not progress with the greatest of despatch. The ever-increasing pile of finished badges which appeared on the several tables gave evidence that their fingers were as nimble as their tongues, and amusement and work were intermingled.

Amidst the fun and merriment that was taking place in the room, Dexie's abstracted and absent-minded manner was not noticed, except by one pair of eyes—and very little that concerned Dexie Sherwood escaped the notice of Guy Traverse.

He was finding it hard to check the feelings with which he had long regarded her, for he had become attached to her from the very first, and his eyes were keen to note her varying moods. His frequent visits to the house gave him opportunity to study her character, and the more he saw of her, the higher grew his respect. A more tender feeling also was growing within his breast, that gave him secret pleasure, though he kept well in check any sign of its existence. He never had found the opportunity of asking the truth of her engagement; but being assured that she had a gentleman correspondent, he felt he had little cause to hope. He had been present on more than one occasion when Dexie had discussed with the rest of the family various extracts from letters which had come from over the sea. To be sure, these extracts were mostly descriptions of places that the writer had visited, or accounts of amusing episodes met with while travelling; but there lingered an undefined impression on Guy Traverse's mind that these letters were not so sacred as one would naturally suppose they should be if the writer were dear to the heart of the recipient.

"Something is troubling Dexie tonight," he said to himself, as he noticed how unusually silent and preoccupied she remained, even when the merriment seemed at its height. "I must be on the alert and see that she is not troubled unnecessarily," for being a frequent visitor, he was aware that Gussie was not always the pleasant person she appeared to be, and he, somehow, connected her with Dexie's present mood.

But in this case he was mistaken. The evening mail had brought Dexie a letter from Hugh McNeil. She had heard so little of him for some time that she began to hope (when she thought of him at all) that he had forgotten her or had found other attractions that had effaced her from his memory. But this unlooked-for letter told a different story, and his half expressed determination to seek her presence and renew his suit filled her with dismay.

She had thrust the letter hastily into her pocket with but a rapid glance at its contents, just as her numerous guests were ushered in; and her time had been so engrossed that the letter itself was forgotten, though the memory of the eager, passionate words therein was bringing up all the unpleasant scenes that had happened in Halifax in connection with Hugh.

During the evening she had, with the help of the cook, set out a dainty repast in the dining-room, and as she made her way into the parlor again to invite the guests to come and partake of it, she wondered at the sound that reached her ears, for instead of the hum of many voices one voice alone was heard, and that was Gussie's.

Now, for some time back the frequent visits of Guy Traverse had aroused suspicions in Gussie's mind. They certainly were not always intended for her father, and he never offered himself as her escort unless Dexie was in her company. She had repeatedly hinted that Dexie was "already spoken for," but the hint was not acted on in the way Gussie expected. Remembering all this, Gussie's conduct this particular evening is seen in its true light, but it brought its own punishment.

In some unaccountable way, Hugh's letter had dropped from Dexie's pocket while she sat sewing at the badges with the rest, and in searching for a spool of thread, it fell into Gussie's hands. She glanced over the letter, but did not notice the signature. Hugh had been thinking more of touching Dexie's heart than of giving his letter the usual appearance, and had left place, date and all tell-tale marks to find room at the bottom of the closely-written sheet. Gussie guessed at once it was Dexie's letter, and thought it would be "fun" to read it before those assembled; it would let Guy Traverse know that he was wasting his time over Dexie. No one in the room had the least idea what she meant when she rose from her chair and said:

"Oh! friends, listen! here is a specimen of true love for you!"

"My dearest love, my heart's one treasure:

"It is no longer any use to try and put you out of my heart. I have tried to do it as you wished, but I cannot. I love you, my darling, and my love will not die, try as I may to kill it. You thought I could forget you if I went among fresh scenes and new faces; but it is not so—your dear face is ever before me. Sleeping or waking, it is the same. I cannot live without you, my dearest—"

"Augusta! Augusta! what are you doing? Is that your own letter you are making public?"

The words cut the air like a flash of steel.

That word "Augusta" was reproof in itself, and Gussie felt it instantly, and she shivered as she looked up and met the flashing eyes of her sister.

"No," she replied, her cheeks aflame, but angry spite dies hard, and she smiled scornfully, as she added, "I was amusing the company with a specimen of love-making that is rare outside of novels. It is your letter, I believe."

Before Dexie could reply, Guy Traverse had risen to his feet, and coming towards the table so that his form partly shielded Dexie from view, said:

"If you have read all you wish of my letter, Miss Gussie, I beg you will return it to me," and he took it from her hand and thrust it into his breast-pocket; then turning a woeful face to the astonished guests, he said:

"Friends, have mercy on a fellow when he is down, and forget what you heard just now. It was too bad of you, Miss Gussie, to expose a poor fellow's feelings in that way. I ought to have posted my broken-hearted appeal before I came in here, but I thought I might be able to think of some stronger language that would touch the hard heart of my lady-love. I am not in luck, as you can guess; but do not, I beg of you, let it go any farther. I appeal to you, as members of T. and B., to keep this matter quiet and not let it be talked about. Boys, you know how it is yourselves," and in seeming embarrassment he turned to the window and remained in the shadow of the curtain.

"Oh! I beg your pardon, Mr. Traverse," Gussie gasped out, properly ashamed for once. "I never imagined the letter was yours," and hiding her burning cheeks in her hands she hurriedly left the room and flew to her chamber, wondering how she could ever look those people again in the face.

Traverse had given Dexie time to recover herself, and in a steadier voice than she could have commanded a few moments before, she asked the friends to drop their work, and come into the next room for refreshments.

This was a welcome interruption to all; everyone felt glad to hide the uncomfortable feeling that Gussie's act had thrown over them, and merry groups formed in the dining-room as Dexie passed among them. The uncomfortable scene in the parlor was put out of sight, if not out of mind, and no one wondered that Guy Traverse did not make his appearance amongst them.

As soon as Dexie saw she would not be missed for a few moments, she ran up to Gussie's room.

"Come down at once, Gussie. You cannot stay away from our guests without making yourself look worse in their eyes. The sooner you make amends for your unpardonable act, the better it will be for yourself."

"Oh! Dexie, I was never so ashamed in my life! I never dreamt it was his letter; I thought it was yours."

"And what business would you have to read out anybody's letter to a company of people? I am glad to hear that you feel ashamed, for well you may! Come downstairs at once, unless you want everyone to cut you forever."

Gussie followed her sister into the dining-room, and she set about her duties as well as she could, but finding that Traverse was not in the room she soon felt more at ease.

Dexie felt that she must see Mr. Traverse before the rest entered the parlor. She had been so astonished at his bold claim of ownership that for a moment she could not understand it, but the truth flashed on her mind that he had done it to shield her, and she blessed him for it.

Guy looked round as the door opened, and coming forward he took the tray she carried in her hands and set it on a small table near, saying:

"Is this for both of us, Miss Dexie? Sit here," and he placed a screen to hide them from the gaze of intruders; then coming over to her side, drew the letter from his pocket, saying: "Forgive me, Miss Dexie, for claiming your property; it is yours, is it not?"

"Unfortunately, yes; and you were more than kind to shield me as you did," and she put the cause of the trouble in the deepest corner of her pocket. "I did not know what to do when I heard Gussie reading it aloud."

"I knew at once it was yours by the way you looked; but I thought I would play the vanquished lover, and crave your pardon for my audacity afterwards," and he looked intently into Dexie's flushed face.

"Believe me, Mr. Traverse, the writer of that letter is not the silly man one would expect, judging by his foolish words. In everything else he is worthy of respect."

"Do you think it foolish for a man to love a woman with such love as he speaks of in the letter?"

"Yes; when the man knows it is useless, he should try and forget her."

"He should try—hum!—well, it seems one does not always succeed in forgetting, even with much trying. Miss Dexie, you owe me a favor; tell me honestly how you stand with this lover from over the sea. Are you engaged to be married to him, yet give him cause to write in such a strain?"

"No, certainly not; I am aware that this letter has given you the impression that I have been corresponding with the writer, but it is not so. This is only the second time I have had a letter from him, though I believe papa hears from him occasionally; but I have never sent him a line."

"How does it happen that he writes to you so appealingly? Have you jilted him, Miss Dexie?" and he looked eagerly into her face, to read her answer. "Will you not tell me?" he added, as he waited some moments for her reply.

"There is very little to tell, Mr. Traverse. I think the part of the letter that you heard tells the story well enough," and she gave a quick look into his face, "but I think I understand what you mean. This is not the one that Gussie refers to so often."

"Miss Dexie, if I have spared your feelings tonight, spare mine now, and tell me what I ask: Is there more than one lover across the sea? Do tell me the truth, Miss Dexie."

His low, earnest tones thrilled her strangely, and she dropped her eyes, as she replied in a low tone:

"Let me first explain about the writer of the letter. I never gave him cause to write to me like that, for I have always disliked him. He has persecuted me shamefully, even so far as to threaten to shoot me if I did not promise to marry him, and the strongest wish that was ever born in my heart is that I may never see his face again." The words ended in a whisper, but so intense were the tones that Guy felt she told the truth, and he asked: "What sort of a young man is he, if I may ask?"

"If he had not made himself an object of dislike to me, I could give you a very favorable account of him," she answered, lifting her eyes an instant, then turning aside as she met his earnest looks. "He is well educated and very good-looking, if you admire the kind of beauty that goes with olive skin, eyes like midnight, and hair to correspond. He has a good bank account also, and would be a good match—for someone else," she added, laughing softly.

"Did your father favor his suit, that they correspond yet?"

"Oh! yes; and everything was arranged, settlements, and all. Nothing was lacking—except my consent."

"Then there was never a promise between you? Forgive me, Miss Dexie, if I seem inquisitive, but I wish very much to know."

"Nothing like a promise! indeed, nothing could be so distasteful as the thought of such a thing; not even from the first. I never liked him."

"But there is someone else, Miss Dexie. Is there not a promise given to someone else?" came the eager tones.

"Not exactly a promise, Mr. Traverse; but there is a mutual understanding that may lead to one. I think you would like my friend, particularly if you heard him once at the piano," she replied, as her cheeks grew pink.

"Then you are not really engaged, Miss Dexie?"

"Now, Mr. Traverse, I think I have told you enough," she replied, beginning to feel embarrassed. "Some things are not easy to tell, even though one may not care if the facts are known."

"But I have not got down to facts yet, Miss Dexie, and I should like to know the truth. 'For favors received, be truly grateful.' I think it is only fair to let me know how matters stand with you and this lover over the sea."

He waited a moment for her answer, then added, in an eager tone:

"Your sister told me several times about your engagement to this young gentleman that writes to you from England. If it is so, why deny it?"

"There is a promise between us to wait a year," came the low-spoken reply. "Then, if we are both of the same mind as when we saw each other last, I expect I shall spend the rest of my days in Halifax; but a year is a long time, and much may happen before then."

What strange power was there in his looks or words that drew this admission from her? She regretted the words the moment after she uttered them, but she did not know that she had removed the barrier that kept Guy from trying to win her himself.

"Do you think he may learn to care for someone else, or that you—"

"I have never met anyone yet that I like better," and she lifted her eyes to his as she said this, but she dropped them at once, and a strange, uneasy feeling possessed her that she could not understand.

"Thank you, Miss Dexie, for your confidence. Now, let the understanding be mutual. Will you give me the privilege you have so long denied me of being your friend and protector *pro tem.*, as it were? Neither you nor I have anyone here to claim our society, and I get very tired of my own company; I would like to have one special lady friend. Will you not hereafter accept my company without that inward protest which I always feel you have for me?"

"You are very kind, Mr. Traverse, but I would prefer matters as they are. I do not mind going about alone in the least."

"Oh! I know that, Miss Independence, but I mind it; so say that I may occupy the place of the absent friend, to some extent at least. I'll write to him and demand permission, if you object," and he laughed pleasantly as he took her hand a moment in his own.

Just then the sound of footsteps warned them that their interview was over, and Guy rose to his feet and stood by the window as the rest entered the room.

"Hello, Traverse! we missed you in the supper-room," and Fenerty came over to his side. "Have you found all your persuasions in vain, Miss Dexie?" pointing to the untasted repast on the tray.

"Man alive! do you think a man's appetite can survive everything?" said Traverse, with a frown.

"Forgive me, Traverse! I did not mean to add to your feelings. I don't wonder you feel cut up," said Fenerty, whispering his apologies.

"Mr. Fenerty, take him out in the dining-room. My presence has prevented him from partaking of the refreshments I brought him. Try and make him forget the unpleasantness that has occurred," and Dexie looked up with a smile at Traverse, as he followed his friend from the room, and then turned to her other guests.

She was glad to see that Gussie was doing all she could to win her way back into favor, for she passed from group to group with a pleasant word and a smile for all. Fingers and needles were soon busy again, and the unfinished badges were attacked with renewed vigor.

"That was a nasty trick of Miss Gussie's, Traverse," young Fenerty was saying, as he waited upon his friend in the dining-room, "but I am sure she never suspected that the letter belonged to you."

"What difference did that make? The act was unpardonable when she knew it was not her own property. I suppose I will never hear the last of it."

"'Pon honor, Traverse, I hope you do not think any of us are mean enough to refer to the matter again. But come away to the rest, if you are through; they are at work again, I believe."

"It is all right, Miss Dexie," nodding to her as she appeared in the door. "He will soon get over it. Is there any objection to a little carpet dance to finish the evening? That will make Traverse forget to be melancholy if anything will," he added, in a low voice.

"Very well; as soon as they finish the badges you can help clear the room."

Dexie cast a backward look at Traverse and saw his amused smile, and it was hard to control her features when his face assumed such a mournful expression directly Fenerty addressed him.

Half an hour later, tables and chairs were set aside, and the sound that came forth from the piano, at Dexie's bidding, set agoing the feet of the dancers. She had played through several dances when Guy came up to her side with Ada Chester.

"I have brought someone to take your place, Miss Dexie. Play a waltz for us, Miss Chester," and Guy took Dexie from her seat.

The couple made the circuit of the room several times before anyone joined them; it was a pleasure to watch the well-matched pair swaying to the delightful music.

"We seem to have the floor to ourselves," Dexie said with a smile.

"If they knew the bliss of a perfect waltz, we would be crowded out, Miss Dexie. I begin to think I never waltzed before; your step is perfect—what, you are not tired?" as Dexie stopped and led the way back to the piano.

"No, but I will relieve Miss Chester; she is very fond of dancing."

Dexie did not care to confess how much she had enjoyed the little dance, but she was beginning to think that there was some strange spell in the voice and manner of her partner that drew her very thoughts from her. She must get away from his presence, so turned to Miss Chester, saying:

"I can recommend Mr. Traverse as a superb waltzer, Ada, so let me give you the pleasure of a few turns around the room with him to the same music. Mr. Traverse, do let Miss Chester know for once what waltzing really is," and she struck the keys and sent them floating from her side.

The evening's pleasure closed all too quickly, and as the last good-byes were spoken Guy lingered to whisper:

"I shall call and take you to choir practice in good season, so do not run away before I come for you. Good-night, Miss Dexie."

The warm clasp of the hand, and the earnest look in his dark grey eyes, lingered in Dexie's memory until sleep had put all thoughts aside and mixed the real with the unreal in troubled dreams.

CHAPTER XXXVII.

One bright summer morning, while the dew still glistened like diamonds on grass blades and flower petals, Dexie and her father were to be seen walking quickly in the direction of the depot, and, on arriving there, were surprised to see Mr. Traverse waiting on the platform.

"What, Traverse, are you off this morning too?" said Mr. Sherwood.

"Yes, I have business in Boston; some machinery to order. And you, Miss Dexie, are you going on a journey as well?"

"Oh, no; I have come to see papa safely on board the train, and to jog his memory about a few trifles I want him to bring me home from the Hub."

"Ha, ha; a few trifles, indeed! If you expect me to bring back half the things you have mentioned, you had better come along with me, for I've forgotten them already," her father laughingly replied.

"I thought that would be the way," Dexie replied with a smile, "but you will not get off so easily as you think. Here is my book, and the list is on the last pages, so you have no excuse to forget one of the articles, papa," and she slipped the little book inside his vest-pocket.

"Glad to have your company, Traverse. How long do you stay?"

"Well, I am not particular to a day or two. I expect to be ready to return on Friday."

"And this is Monday; well, we can arrange to return together, so, Dexie, you can make your mind easy. Your old dad will have someone to look after him both ways."

"That is very nice. Take good care of him, Mr. Traverse," and she gave him her hand as he said good-bye.

Her father bent his head and kissed her, saying playfully:

"Now, don't run off with the gardener, or do any other dreadful thing while I am gone, and I will try and get your commissions filled, even to the box of chocolates."

They stepped on the cars, and with the usual ear-splitting shriek the train moved away, leaving Dexie on the platform looking after them. The two men stood at the rear door and waved a farewell, and Dexie returned home, never thinking that she had seen her father well and strong for the last time.

Mr. Sherwood had not been away from home since they had moved to Lennoxville, and Dexie planned to have a dainty repast awaiting his return, and she was in the kitchen when a telegraph messenger appeared at the door.

"A telegram for Mrs. Sherwood, and one for Miss Dexie Sherwood."

Dexie tore hers open, and her heart seemed to stop beating as she read:

"There has been an accident, and your father is hurt, but not fatally. He cannot be moved at present. Can you come at once?

"Guy Traverse."

Dexie rushed up the stairs, her white face telling of trouble, and as soon as her mother saw her she asked in alarm:

"What is it, Dexie? What has happened?"

"Dear mamma, come back into the room, and I will tell you. There has been an accident, and papa is hurt. Oh, mamma, do not scream so! No, he is not killed; do not say it. Oh, hush! let me open your message. Mine is from Mr. Traverse, and he says papa is hurt and cannot be moved. Oh, mamma! do not scream so. You will terrify the children and make yourself ill."

"Oh, he is dead! My husband is killed!" she cried. "Why has this dreadful calamity come upon me?" and she wrung her hands and wept aloud.

"Oh, mamma, you *must* stop! Listen: this is what your message says, and it is signed by a railroad official:

'There has been a collision, and your husband is injured. It is impossible to move him in his present condition, but everything possible shall be done for his comfort and relief.'"

"Oh, mamma! let us go to him at once."

"Dexie, do you want to kill me? I could not survive the journey in the present state of my nerves; and does not the message say that everything shall be done for him? What could I do more?"

Another peal of the bell, and Dexie flew down to the door, where a brass-buttoned youth presented himself.

"I am sent to say that there is a train starting for the scene of the collision in fifteen minutes. If there is anyone here going down, they will have to hurry."

Dexie rushed back to her mother's side.

"Oh, mamma, I must go to him! Can you go, too? Say quickly, mamma!"

"Oh, I shall die! I shall die!" and Mrs. Sherwood fell back on the sofa in violent hysterics.

This was answer enough, and Dexie rushed to her own room, calling loudly for Eliza.

Gussie ran up the stairs at that moment, saying wildly: "Oh, Dexie, is it true? Is papa hurt?"

"Yes, Gussie, and I am going to him. Run to mamma; I cannot delay a moment. Here, Eliza," as the frightened domestic appeared, "put those things into this travelling-bag while I tell you what you are to do. Papa is hurt, and I have barely time to catch the train. You must run for Mrs. Jarvis as soon as I am done with you, and tell her to come and stay with mamma; then hurry along for the doctor—he will give mamma something to quiet her. Tell Mrs. Jarvis I leave everything in her care till I return, and say that she must fix up the back parlor all ready for papa, in case he can be brought home. She will know what to do. Now, I must go. I am sure I can trust you to do your best, Eliza, till I get back. I do not know when that will be."

She arrived at the depot hot and breathless, but in time to take her place among the number who, with white, sad faces and tear-dimmed eyes, were on their way to claim the forms of loved ones, or to comfort and relieve those whose lives had been spared them. The first tears she shed were those that fell when she recognized Edith Wolcott and her brother among the passengers.

"Dexie, you here, and alone!" was Edith's greeting, and the answer was a flood of relief-giving tears.

"Papa is hurt," she sobbed, as Edith inquired why she was on the train.

"I am so sorry; but perhaps it is not as bad as you fear. We expected Aunt Eunice would arrive by that train. We do not know that she really was a passenger, but I could not rest at home till I knew the truth!" Edith exclaimed. "Mr. Traverse was to have returned today," she added. "Did you hear if he was hurt?"

Dexie did not know, but thought not, as he had sent her the message concerning her father.

They relapsed into silence, except when someone would voice the sentiments in the heart of each and say, with a sigh, "How slowly the train moves along!" Yet they were travelling very rapidly, and in due time they arrived at the scene of the wreck.

Such a spectacle Dexie had never seen. Cars were piled upon one another in a confused mass, and she wondered how anyone had escaped alive from the broken timbers that had formed the cars.

She seemed to know instinctively which way to turn in search of her father, but she had only made a few steps when she met Mr. Traverse looking for her.

"Do not be alarmed, Miss Dexie; I am not so bad as I look," he said, reassuringly, as Dexie started at the sight of his bandaged head and splintered arm. "I have an ugly scalp wound, and that makes the bandages necessary, and my broken arm is nothing. Now, be brave," he said, as they stopped before the door of the house where her father had been taken. "He has been suffering great pain and looks badly, and he will not be able to see you unless you are calm. The doctor is with him now. I will go and see if you can come in."

"Do not keep me waiting, Mr. Traverse. I will be quiet. Indeed, you can trust me," and she lifted a white face, full of entreaty, to his gaze.

"My brave little girl!" was Guy's inward comment. "It is just as well that she came alone, for no one else in the family has self-control enough to bear this."

In a few minutes Guy returned and conducted her to her father's side, and she bent over him and kissed his white face tenderly.

"Dear papa, I have come to stay with you. What can I do to help you?" and she laid her hand in his. "Mamma feels too badly to come just now, dear papa."

The quiet manner in which she removed her hat and cloak and then returned to the bedside to await the doctor's orders impressed the latter favorably, and with a few words of instruction to Mr. Traverse he departed to see his other waiting charges.

They were sad and anxious days that followed, for it was feared that Mr. Sherwood might not, after all, survive the shock; but Dexie never lost heart, and was rewarded, after many days, by hearing the welcome news that her father could safely be moved to his home.

Traverse had proved himself a helpful and faithful friend, and more than one broken-hearted person blessed him for his ready help and sympathy, for the accident had been attended with much loss of life and had spread mourning into many homes.

Dexie had written twice daily to her mother; but having once mentioned the fact that the few houses in the vicinity of the accident were filled with maimed and wounded who were too ill to be sent to their homes, Mrs. Sherwood considered it impossible for her to witness the sight, and Dexie advised her to stay at home. She was well aware that the distressing sights and sounds which were to be witnessed hourly in every house would have such an effect on her mother that her presence would be more hurtful than beneficial to her father in his present condition.

Dexie was very anxious to know if everything was in readiness for her father's arrival, and Mr. Traverse relieved her anxiety by offering to go to the house with the family doctor and make everything sure, and then return and accompany them home.

It was with a feeling of shame that she gave her last message to him as he was about to leave her.

"Will you be kind enough to tell Dr. Brown how necessary it will be for papa to come home to a quiet house; and if mamma is not able to bear the sight of his arrival, will he see that she is not at home just at the time? He will understand and can manage it, I am sure."

Traverse looked at her in surprise.

"Mamma is apt to be hysterical, and papa will be too tired with the journey to bear any unusual excitement. I dread the time of his arrival at the house more than I do the rest of the journey; but it must be managed quietly, somehow. It would take so little to set him back when he is so weak."

"It shall be managed quietly, Miss Dexie, so do not be anxious; I will see that your father has every chance," and he turned away, wondering at the care and tact that could see and overrule the want of thought in others, when age and experience should have given others the self-control that was so wonderful to see in a girl of her years.

Mr. Sherwood bore the journey much better than they expected, and they carried him to the room which, by Dexie's forethought, had been provided with everything that could add to his comfort. The house was quiet and still, and a good hour's rest fortified him for the visit that his wife must soon make to his room.

Mrs. Sherwood had been persuaded into taking a drive with the doctor's wife about the time the train was expected, and she had been kept away long enough for Mr. Sherwood to rally from the fatigue of the journey. Gussie, with the rest of the family, had witnessed his arrival from an upper window, and wept sorely at seeing her father carried into the house on a bed, remembering how well and strong he had walked out of it a few short weeks before.

When Mrs. Sherwood arrived, and found that her husband had been brought home in her absence, she felt very much hurt, and she entered the room subdued and quiet; but when she beheld the change that had taken place in her strong, robust husband since she had last seen him, nothing but the doctor's presence prevented her from throwing herself across the bed. She dropped to her knees by the bed-side, with a wail of despair, and Gussie's sobs were added to the moans that came from the lips of the kneeling wife. Dexie bent over her sister, saying firmly:

"You must either control yourself or leave the room. Can't you see how it distresses papa?"

Guy Traverse led the sobbing girl out of the room at last, and his kind words of comfort did much to help Gussie overcome her violent grief. He was fast recovering from his own wounds, and he made himself very useful in spite of his one-armed condition—for he still wore his broken arm in a sling. Dexie was not blind to the excellent traits of character he had displayed during the trying weeks past, but when she endeavored to express her thanks he stopped her with a word.

Weeks passed, and Mr. Sherwood's progress was so slow as to damp all hopes as to his ultimate recovery.

"I must know the truth," he said one morning, when the doctor made his usual visit; "it is no kindness to keep me in ignorance of my true condition. If I am not likely to rise from this bed a well man, then it is time I settled my business; so tell me what you think, Dr. Brown."

But it is not easy to get a doctor's opinion, and at last it was decided to send for the famous Dr. Jacobs, and have a consultation.

"Well, have the consultation as soon as possible, for this uncertainty is harder to bear than the knowledge of a speedy death," said Mr. Sherwood.

Oh, the agony of that hour, when Dexie waited, with the rest of the family, the verdict of the assembled doctors. As she knelt by her bed, her face buried in the pillows, she felt as if the worst could not be much harder to bear than this dreadful suspense. She dreaded the sound that would summon her to her father's bedside, yet, when it came, she rose to obey with a firm step, though the white face, from which her eyes shone almost black in their intensity, was proof of the anxiety that filled her heart.

"My dear little girl," and her father pressed the hand she laid in his, "it is not so bad as we feared, after all. Dr. Brown, will you go and tell my wife? Dexie, do you think you will get tired waiting on me if I have to lie here a few more months?"

"Oh, papa!" She could not restrain the tears that sprang to her eyes, so she laid her head on the pillow beside him until she could lift a quiet face.

"Don't fret, Dexie, dear!" and he fondly stroked the head so near him.

"I am likely to live for months, and you are such a capital little nurse that it will not be such a hardship to spend the rest of my life on my back."

Yes, that was the verdict. Mr. Sherwood could never hope to walk again or be a well man; but he would probably live for some time, his splendid constitution being in his favor.

This was hard news for the family; but they had feared the worst, and so felt thankful for the extended time that might intervene before the end would come.

Mrs. Sherwood engaged the assistance of Mrs. Jarvis, an excellent nurse, to attend on her husband; and as Dexie shared the nursing and relieved Mrs. Jarvis, Mrs. Sherwood considered she had done her duty well and faithfully. She did not feel strong enough to do very much of the laborious part of nursing, but she was willing to make her appearance in the sick-room when the patient was at his best. She had been present once when her husband had been seized with a paroxysm of pain, and was so terrified and overcome that she felt more than willing to leave her husband to the care of those who were "so hard-hearted that they could witness such suffering," and still be able to administer the necessary relief.

As the weeks passed by and Mr. Sherwood grew no worse, it seemed impossible to think that the "grim messenger" was really lurking in the shadow, for he bore his illness with such patience and cheerfulness that only those who were constantly about him realized how he really suffered.

Mr. Traverse was always a welcome visitor, for Mr. Sherwood could never forget that awful moment when death stared them both in the face, and how Traverse had kept the flying timbers from crashing into his pinioned body, receiving on his own head and arm the blows he might have escaped.

Dexie had listened with averted face and tear-dimmed eyes to the story as it fell from her father's lips, and she found it hard to meet her hero without betraying something of the feeling which his noble conduct had awakened in her heart.

His frequent visits were both a joy and a pain to her, though why she felt glad to hear his step, yet dreaded to meet his glance, she could not have explained.

Gussie was able now to meet Mr. Traverse without that feeling of mortification which she experienced after she had read his love-letter before her guests. His manner to her was as kind and respectful as ever, and she hoped he had almost forgotten the circumstance. How often that thoughtless act had been regretted no one knew but herself. There was no chance of adding his name to her list of admirers, for he kept her at a distance, even when his manner was most kind. She often wondered if his *city girl*, as she styled her, had yet relented, or if he had given up all hope of winning her. How he must have cared for her to write such a letter!

If she had learned the true facts of the case, and found out that the letter was really Dexie's, as she at first supposed, she would have put aside the fact that her conduct was none the less reprehensible, and would have used all her arts to win him to her side. As it was, she was more willing to sit by her father's side during the time Mr. Traverse was present than at any other time during the day.

One evening when Mr. Traverse was sitting by Mr. Sherwood's bedside, Gussie also being in the room, one of those sudden attacks that always came on without a moment's warning seized upon Mr. Sherwood, and Mr. Traverse was so alarmed that for a moment he lost his presence of mind; but Gussie's shrill screams, as she rushed out of the room, aroused him. Something should be done for the sufferer, he knew not what, and reaching for the bell-cord that hung over the head of the bed he gave it a hasty pull, and as he did so Dexie was beside him.

She took in the situation at a glance, her rapid movements relieving Mr. Traverse from the fear and apprehension that had seized him, and the means of relief were soon at hand.

"Raise his head on your arm a moment," she said, coming quickly to the bedside. "Not quite so much; there. I must get this into his mouth somehow. Thank you. Now, lay him down very carefully." A practical knowledge of what was required made her movements swift, though quiet, and she worked about him with a firm, steady hand. She was able to witness her father's agony and still keep her wits about her; but this was positive proof to her mother that Dexie had "no feelings."

Mr. Sherwood was soon able to look the thanks he could not express, and Dexie took a fan that lay near at hand and began, with a gentle motion, to fan her father's flushed face. Guy noticed for the first time that the tears were flowing down her cheeks, though she gave no sign of her distress, nor made any movement to wipe them away lest that act should betray them.

"Let me do that much, Dexie?" was the low, whispered words, as he took the fan from Dexie's fingers.

He drew a chair softly to the bedside, and kept up the gentle motion until Guy felt assured that the sufferer was asleep.

Dexie was kneeling by the bedside, intently watching her father's face through her tears, and she started when Guy laid his hand across her clasped palms, and whispered, "Come away, Dexie; he is sleeping."

She rose at his bidding, and he drew her to the window.

"This has been very hard on you, Dexie, and you have borne it bravely," he whispered softly, holding her trembling hands in his own. "Do not try to hide the tears from me. Am I not your friend?"

The touch of his hand and the tenderness of his voice touched a chord in Dexie's heart and sent a thrill through every nerve, and she raised her eyes to his for one brief moment; but in that short time she read a story that might have filled a volume, and no one could now say of her that "her heart had not yet awakened," for she knew the truth at last.

The appearance of Mrs. Jarvis at this moment was a welcome relief to Dexie, and giving a hasty account of her father's late attack she hurried from the room. She felt she must get away from everyone and face this new thing that had come upon her.

As she passed into the hall she found Guy Traverse waiting for her.

"May I ask for a few minutes, Miss Dexie?" he asked, in a low voice. "I have something I would like to say to you tonight."

"Please excuse me tonight, Mr. Traverse," she replied, without lifting her eyes. "I do not feel able to see anyone just now."

"Some other time, Dexie, then. Good-night," and he held her hand one moment in his, and turned to leave the house.

He did not seem particularly pleased to find Gussie waiting at the parlor door for him; but he intended to pass on and go home.

"Oh! Mr. Traverse you are not going home so soon, surely!" she cried. "I wanted your opinion of a new book that was sent to me today. Is papa not better?" seeing the altered expression on his face.

"Yes, he is better now, I believe, but you must excuse me tonight, Miss Sherwood; your book must wait for some future time. Good evening," and the door closed softly behind him.

As Guy turned the corner of the house, intending to take a short cut to his hotel through the back garden, there issued from an open window such music as Guy had never heard before—so soft, so sad, yet so exquisitely sweet that he stopped for a moment to listen. He had often listened to Dexie's playing; but he never had heard her play a piece like that, and he drew nearer the window.

He could see her through the thin curtain that hid him from view; and as he stood and watched her, he wondered what it was that had the power to call up such an expression to her face. But as he looked the music suddenly ceased, and Dexie's face was buried in her hands, and he could hear the sobs that shook her frame. He longed to speak to her, yet dared not. He knew he had no right even to witness her emotion, and he turned silently and sadly away. Could he have been mistaken, after all? That one brief moment when Dexie had looked into his eyes he felt sure of her love, and his heart had throbbed with joy; and but for that interruption he might even now be holding her against his breast, while he poured into her ears the story of his love.

But her tears and grief seemed a denial of his hopes. Had thoughts of her absent lover given her that glorified look on which he had based his hopes?

If Guy Traverse had been permitted to read a part of the letter which Dexie penned that evening before retiring, he would not have waited so long before testing the value of his hopes, for he would have guessed the meaning of the words sent to "the lover over the sea."

"I have thought several times lately that you are not so open and frank with me as you used to be. Are you keeping something from me, Lancy? I wonder if you have found out the truth of the words I said to you in Halifax. Do not forget that it was to be 'honor bright' between us. I am beginning to hope that my surmises are correct, but I know it is hardly fair to force a confession from you that I shrink from making myself. It may be true that 'open confession is good for the soul,' but I find it is particularly mortifying to the body.

"But I have been talking to you through the piano tonight, Lancy, and I must set down in writing a little of what is in my mind, for I have to confess to you, Lancy, that I can no longer *honestly* keep the ring that has stood 'for a sign between me and thee.' Now, do not mistake me, dear Lancy. I have heard no word of love from any man's lips since I left you, but for all that I have met someone that will always stand between you and me, and I really have little to tell you, only that under the conditions I cannot keep the ring any longer. Will you release me from any promise I may have given you, and tell me truly if you are not pleased that I asked for the release? You must not think that I have ceased to care for you, for there are times, when I am at the piano, that I would give all I ever possessed to have you beside me, and I have missed you more than I can tell. I see now that more than one kind of love can find room in the heart at one and the same time. Now, Lancy, if I have made a mistake in thinking that you may have had the same experience as myself, and this confession of mine grieves you, I will keep my promise still, *if you wish it*. I shall look anxiously for your answer."

But if Guy Traverse had no knowledge of this letter he was present when Gussie held out the answer across the table, with the words:

"Here is an extra heavy letter from over the sea, Dexie, and that bold handwriting tells the identity of the writer at a glance, so there is no use to deny that it is from Lancy Gurney."

Guy saw no hope for him in the flushed face, and Dexie hurried from the room as soon as she had grasped the letter from Gussie's hand.

But Guy Traverse had no need to be so cast down, if he had only known it, for the letter said:

"I begin to fear that you are gifted with second-sight, and it is with shame I confess that I have not kept 'honor bright' with you. I was afraid you would not understand if I began to explain the matter, but your own confession has made it easier. I can hardly tell you what has happened, Dexie—it has all come about so suddenly that I hardly realize it myself; but I was thrown from a vicious horse while visiting at a country-seat, and was taken up insensible, and when I opened my eyes I found a sweet heart bending over me; but believe me, Dexie, I did not know it was so until her own lips confessed it, and she has become very dear to me since. But I have been in misery when I thought how you would despise me, and I feared your scorn. I shall always care for you, Dexie, as you care for me, and I am glad to know that the music still holds us together. I have a request to make, and if you will grant it I shall know that the admission in this letter has not wounded you. Do not send back the ring, but keep it and wear it occasionally. I have had a counterpart made of the little charm which I enclose in this, and I shall always keep it in memory of the happy hours we have spent together."

Dexie read this letter over a good many times before she laid it away under lock and key; but when she did so she took from its hiding-place the ring she had not looked at for months, and slipped it upon her finger.

"Yes, I will keep it and wear it, now that it means only friendship; of course he does not wish to have it back. I am so glad he has found someone else. He will never forget me, I am sure—I know that by my own feelings for him; but if he had kept me to my promise I—" but she finished the sentence in the innermost recesses of her heart.

Dexie's reply gave Lancy a feeling of relief. He must explain to his parents the change in his feelings, and he feared they would consider that he had wronged Dexie Sherwood; but her letters would prove the contrary, for did she not say:

"Your ring is on my finger as I write, and I never wore it with more willingness and pleasure than I do now, when it tells only of freedom and friendship. I have had those words engraved on the inside of the ring. Will you do the same with the token of friendship which you say you possess? I was sorry to hear you had taken the trouble to get one made after the same pattern, and I have a little scold all ready for you. Do not hide from your ladylove till after your marriage the little romance 'between me and thee.' Believe me, it will sound much better if told beforehand. I am pleased to hear that your prospects are so bright, but you did not tell me half enough about your pretty English lassie, or in what direction her talents lie, but I can well believe that I am far in the shade so far as music goes. I cannot tell you what you ask, Lancy, for my love has not been asked for in words; but I am very happy, and if my future holds nothing brighter than my present life, it will be well worth living, for the only shadow is the thought of poor papa's sufferings. And now, dear Lancy, good-bye. This is my last letter to you, but if we ever meet again I think you will find that I am the same old Dexie."

The letter had such a kind, honest ring to it that it quite relieved Lancy's mind, and he wondered what Dexie would say if she knew that his ladylove was only a passable singer, and had no talent for music at all. Truly, he had fallen in love with his opposite.

CHAPTER XXXVIII.

"I say, Traverse! I believe you are getting melancholy," said Mr. Fenerty, as, seated in Guy Traverse's office, he watched Guy bend over the papers on the desk before him, yet seeming to accomplish nothing.

Getting no response to his repeated sallies, he added:

"What's up! out with it! If that pile of papers is in a tangle, say the word, and I'll bring my mighty brain to bear on them, and set them in order for you in no time! No? Are the men going out on a strike, then? or is your great-grandma down with the measles? Then, for Heaven's sake, why such a doleful expression? It is enough to give one the blues to look at you!" and he re-crossed his legs and looked searchingly at his friend.

"That's all your nonsense, Fenerty! I'm all right! What's the news?" and Traverse leaned back in his chair as if to resign himself to the inevitable.

"News! he asks for news, when I have come here expecting to find him boiling over with anxiety to impart news to someone!" and Fenerty rolled up his eyes in astonishment. "However, now that I have looked at you, and seen the settled melancholy of those features, I am obliged to own that you do not look like a man to be congratulated."

"Why should I be congratulated, and for what? What joke are you struggling to get rid of, Fenerty?"

"'Pon honor, Traverse, I believe you are right! The congratulations are due in some other quarter, yet who is he?"

"I am as much in the dark as yourself, Fenerty. I own that I hoped to win her myself, and I feel the disappointment—keenly."

"Traverse, I hope you will not think me a meddling fool; but I would like to know if it is all up with the other one—she of the letter, I mean. You might tell a fellow that much."

Traverse looked at him keenly. He knew that Fenerty had a good heart, with all his bantering, and it was plain enough to all that his attentions to Dexie Sherwood could have but one significance. Yet there must be a feeling in the mind of Fenerty, as well as others, that in the light of that letter he was not "off with the old love before he was on with the new." Should he trust Fenerty with the secret of the letter, and have at least one friend who would not think him dishonorable in the matter?

"Fenerty, how are you at keeping secrets?" he said at last. "I never hear you parting with any, but whether that is owing to the fact that you have none to impart, or whether your secrets really are secrets, I am not able to guess. I would like to tell you about that letter. What are the prospects of it becoming public property?"

"'Pon honor, Traverse, you are a brute! Do you think I would speak of it to my bosom friend, if I had one? and Heaven knows I haven't! But I have often thought of your possible death from unrequited love. You must have been in a desperate way about the time that letter was written, hey, Traverse?"

"Fenerty, you are a great goose, and let me prove my words. But first, while I think of it, never offer yourself as a detective, for the requirements needed are not included in your make-up. Well, I never wrote that letter at all. Miss Gussie was right in thinking the letter was her sister's, but I guessed the truth before anyone had time to catch the horrified look that came into Miss Dexie's face as she heard her letter read out to the crowd. I felt I owed Miss Gussie one for the hateful trick, so claimed it as mine; and I piled on the agony pretty thick, if I remember rightly. How does that solution of the mystery strike you, Fenerty, hey?"

"Traverse, you are right!" and he fell over against the wall, as if the news had been too much for him. "You are right! 'Pon honor, but that was a bright trick of yours to claim that letter! I hope you appreciated the sympathy I expressed for you on that trying occasion. Ha! ha! But the fellow that wrote that letter had it pretty bad, eh, Traverse? By George! I'll bet a hat she has given in at last. That is where the ring came from!"

This referred to a little scene that had taken place in the T. and B. rooms.

Dexie had taken her place at the organ as usual, and in so doing had displayed a ring that was new to the eyes of those standing near. Dexie blushed painfully when attention was called to the ring by her teasing friends; but she would acknowledge nothing when they tried to draw the truth from her lips. When Guy Traverse joined the circle, to see what all the fun and laughter meant, Dexie rose to her feet and slipped away, unable to meet his eyes. But, with the knowledge he had of Dexie's affairs, he thought there could be only one explanation of the ring's appearance; her engagement to the lover over the sea must be a settled fact. But Guy's frequent visits to the Sherwoods made the rest believe there was an engagement between him and Dexie.

Dexie's ring aroused considerable discussion among her friends, and it only made it seem more complicated when Gussie declared to a friend that she believed "Dexie had that ring before she left Halifax, but never wore it."

But it was her sign of freedom, and its glitter and sparkle was like the light of her own eyes when they rested upon it. She was afraid that her secret, that sweet secret of her own, might be surprised from her. Not for worlds would she have *that* person know that her heart had awakened at last. With that ring on her finger, who could charge her with caring for anyone but the giver?

Guy Traverse thought he had every reason to feel sad and gloomy. How was it that he ever supposed she cared for him, for now she was as reserved and cool when in his society as she had before been frank and pleasant, and, of course, that ring was responsible for the change.

Gussie took the opportunity of relating to Guy, as well as to others, many an interesting story concerning Dexie and her Halifax lover, but she neglected to add that most of her stories were creations of her own brain. Guy felt little interest in these stories. He felt that there was something going on that he did not understand, but he intended to ask an explanation from Dexie at his first opportunity, feeling quite sure she would own the truth to him.

But the opportunity did not present itself readily, and even Mr. Sherwood felt the change and wondered what had come between Dexie and his friend. He tried to seek into the trouble, but could find no explanation of it.

Mr. Sherwood was able now to be lifted to a wheeled chair or couch, and as he could be gently wheeled from room to room, he found the change quite agreeable. The time did not seem so long as when he was confined within four walls.

There were times when Dexie thought her father might be spared for years instead of months, but when one of his attacks of pain seized him such hopes as suddenly sank away. His mind was more free from care, since his lawyer, Mr. Hackett, had brought his business matters to a satisfactory state; but his visits to the house were always times of trial. Mrs. Sherwood would listen to no explanations that would bring to her mind the thought of her husband's decease. But someone had to stand in the gap, and, as usual, it was Dexie; she it was to whom Mr. Hackett explained the many papers and the various transactions to which their contents related.

"What is the matter between you and Traverse, Dexie?" said Mr. Sherwood one day, as Dexie sat by his side, writing at his dictation. "Never mind about that story now; I have forgotten how I intended to end the matter. Tell me what has happened between you two."

"Indeed, papa, there is nothing. Mr. Traverse has probably something else to take up his attention, and he has been away to New York, I hear, so I daresay he is too busy to drop in as often as he used to do. Never mind him; it is a pity not to complete this story when it is so nearly finished. Let me read what I have written down, then perhaps you will remember what you were going to do with this singular young lady."

"Oh, no! Put the thing out of sight! I'm sick and tired of her already. I miss Traverse, Dexie, and if you have had a quarrel, make it up for my sake. He brings a world of sunshine with him when he comes."

"We have not quarrelled, papa; that is not the reason he has not been in. But I will tell Gussie to ask him to come in tonight; she will see him at the T. and B. rooms."

"Why can't you ask him yourself, Dexie? Queer that he has not been in lately! There was never a day but he would run in for a few minutes during some part of it; so ask him yourself to come in and see me."

"I am not going out tonight, papa dear, but I will write him a note, if you say so," and she drew some tiny sheets from among the scattered MS. that filled the desk.

"Do so, then, and tell him to come in as early as he can."

"There, how will that do, papa?" and she passed the few lines for his inspection.

"Well, it couldn't be said in fewer words; that's a fact," he said, looking at her curiously. "Look here, Dexie, out with it. What has happened to you? Don't try to hide it; for I'm not stone-blind yet," and he pinched her pink ear, and pulled her face around to look into it. "What has come over you lately? Some new experience, I am quite sure. Matters are not as they used to be. I have noticed the change in you for some time. You go whistling through the house as happy as a bird, and your face is as bright as a new button. Surely it cannot be because Traverse does not visit us so often? Yet, I notice if anyone speaks to you about him, you get as 'mum' as you please. Come, you used to tell me all your little secrets, you know. What's up, Dexie?"

"Dear papa, I don't know what to tell you," and she stooped and kissed his cheek. "You may look at things differently than I do, and news which may be pleasant to me may seem very strange to you."

"Then there is news of some kind, after all? Well, let us have it. I want to hear the news, good, bad or indifferent. I will try to believe it is *good* news, since it has such a happy effect on yourself," and he looked up at the bright face that was bending over his chair. "Well, you know, there was a sort of promise between Lancy and me; but I am free from it. Our last letters have been sent and received, and by and by he is going to take an English lassie home as his wife."

"You don't say so, and you find it a source of rejoicing! Well, you are a queer girl, sure enough. Gussie would say you have been jilted."

"But I have not, because it was I who asked to be released from the promise. If you knew what good friends Lancy and I still remain, you would not fancy I feel jilted."

"Well, I'm blest if I see the point yet," and he looked at Dexie keenly.

"Please, papa, do not look for it," was the laughing reply; "for if there be any point to this story, it is not visible to the naked eye, and I doubt if you could discern it with a microscope itself. But, papa, I do not want this spoken about yet—Lancy's approaching marriage, I mean. I would never hear the last of it if Gussie got hold of it, and there is a reason why I want everyone to suppose that everything is as it used to be."

"Well, you can trust me, little girl; but I say again, I cannot see the point."

"And I hope you will not get particularly sharp-sighted all at once, either, papa," she replied, shaking her finger at him; "so don't you go spying into my little affairs, until I give you liberty. Dear papa, there is nothing to tell; when there is, you shall hear it the first thing," and she stooped again and kissed his cheek.

"But why does not Traverse come here as usual, Dexie?" he asked.

"Perhaps he will tell you if you ask him, papa," and hearing her mother call, she left the room.

During the afternoon, a little note found its way into Guy Traverse's hand; but the smallest word from the hand that penned those lines was very dear, and he raised it to his lips, then put it in a hidden corner of his pocket-book.

Guy felt that he was indeed welcome when he made his appearance in Mr. Sherwood's room that evening, for Mr. Sherwood received him with such expressions of pleasure that it needed but the quick, bright glance that Dexie gave him to assure him that his presence was welcome to both.

"You have been busy, Traverse. What is going on at your establishment these days?" Mr. Sherwood asked, as Dexie left the room to fetch the chess-board.

"Oh! nothing more than usual. We have a good many orders in, and I have been away to New York on business for the firm; but I was only away a week. Your old firm has a new manager. Quite a step up for Rushton, isn't it? I am pleased at his promotion, for he deserved it."

"Yes; he was not expecting it either. He called to see me, and I was well pleased to hear he had stepped into my place. Now, Traverse, play your best, and see if you can beat me tonight," as Dexie laid the board and chess men in order by her father's side.

Mr. Sherwood soon became so engrossed in his favorite pastime, that he failed to notice that the poor play of his opponent was due to the fact that his attention was so taken up with watching Dexie that only a part of his thoughts were given to the game.

"Traverse, I don't believe you are half playing," said Mr. Sherwood, as he removed a captured knight from the board.

"Well, you 'most always beat me, you know, Mr. Sherwood, though not often so badly, I confess," was the smiling reply.

"Well, don't be so easily conquered this time, Traverse, or I shall begin to think you have something on your mind."

Guy laughed and promised better play in the future, and as Dexie was called from the room he redeemed his character and won the next game, and during the few minutes' chat that followed Guy sought for information concerning Dexie's supposed engagement.

Mr. Sherwood did not see the drift of his remarks until Guy asked:

"There is a rumor that Miss Dexie expects to be married shortly. You will miss her very much if the rumor is correct."

"Oh! rumor has it that way, has it? Well, this time Dame Rumor is just a little astray. Strange how things do get twisted round!"

"Are you quite sure there is no foundation for the rumor, Mr. Sherwood?" and Guy held his chessman poised in the air while he waited the answer.

"Oh, well, there are some facts to start from, certainly; yet I do not see how the news could have got abroad. I feel quite sure Dexie never told anyone about it, and the matter is not known to anyone else in the house, except myself. She does not care to have the matter spoken of just at present, lest it be misconstrued."

"Then where is rumor wrong, if I may ask?"

"Well, Traverse, I promised not to speak of it, but I do not think she will mind if I tell you."

Mr. Sherwood did not notice how eagerly Guy waited for the next words, for he was studying his next move and seemed to have forgotten what he was about to communicate.

"If Miss Dexie does not wish the matter spoken of, you may rely on my discretion," Guy remarked, as a reminder.

"To be sure; well, the fact is, she has broken off the engagement, if there was any, between herself and that young Englishman. I daresay you may have heard us speaking of him, and he is soon to be married to a lady from his own country; that leaves her free, contrary to Dame Rumor."

"Is it possible! And Miss Dexie—"

"Is as happy as a lark; do not extend your sympathy, Traverse, or you will find it much misplaced."

If Dexie had guessed that the very one she had hoped to keep in ignorance was the first one to be told the facts of the case, she would never have parted with her *news*, even to her father.

Guy's heart bounded with hope and joy as he heard it, yet his happiness was still overshadowed by the thought of that ring. There was something more yet to learn.

"I expect the rumor of her engagement is due to the fact that she wears a beautiful ring lately, the ring and the rumor go together, I expect," and he looked keenly into Mr. Sherwood's face, as if to read any unexpressed thoughts on the matter.

"Oh! she wears a new ring, does she? That's nothing, Traverse; most young ladies are fond of jewelry, you know. There is nothing in it, depend upon it, for if the ring had come from the other one I would have known it at once—there! lost again, Traverse; I don't believe you are in a playing humor tonight."

"Is there anyone likely to come between Miss Dexie and this young Englishman, anyone who may have sent her the ring, Mr. Sherwood? You spoke just now as if there was."

"Well, there *is* one who would like to bestow his hand and fortune on her, but she will have none of it; surely it can't be that she has changed her mind, after all," and Mr. Sherwood laid down his chessman to consider this new phase of the question. Could it be that the ring was from Hugh, and she not tell of it? The game lost its interest with this new thought, and hearing the sound of the piano through the walls, he said:

"Suppose you wheel me into the sitting-room; I hear Dexie at the piano."

The music suddenly ceased as the door opened, and Guy pushed Mr. Sherwood's couch into the room.

"It is too bad to waste that sweet music on bare walls, Miss Dexie," said Guy smiling, "so I have brought an audience. Go on with what you were playing; the little I heard was very beautiful, so do not let us interrupt you. I am told that I am not a very good judge of music, but I know that the piece you were just playing was something finer than most piano pieces," for he had recognized it as the same piece she had played when he had listened through the window, and it had ended in tears.

Guy came over to the piano, and leaning his elbow on the cover, watched her hands as they flew over the keys, and there was a puzzled look in his eyes as he asked as she finished:

"Is that what you were playing just before we came in, Miss Dexie?"

"No; but do you not think it is a very pretty thing?"

"Oh, yes, very nice; but—"

"Well, here is a new song just out, and if you do not think it is beautiful I will agree at once with the one who told you that you were not a good judge of music," and her clear voice sounded through the room.

"Yes, that is very fine, Miss Dexie. The words are almost too pathetic, or else you make them sound that way. But let us have the first piece; there is something peculiar in it, I fancy," and he picked up some sheet music from the stand and began to look it over.

"Hand it over, if you think you have found it, Mr. Traverse. I will play anything you choose from that untidy mass," and there was an amused look in her eyes as she watched the search. He was not likely to find what he wanted amongst those promiscuous sheets.

"But I do not know it when I see it, Miss Dexie," he replied. "I am sure you know what piece it is I refer to."

Dexie laughed at his bewildered expression; but as he looked at her, she said in a low tone:

"Yes, I know what you mean, Mr. Traverse, but I do not play that piece for everybody."

"Not for me, Miss Dexie?"

"No."

"What's all this about a piece of music, Dexie? I didn't come here to hear you two quarrelling," and her father smiled over at them. "Let us have the piece you were playing first, Dexie. It sounded fairly well, the little I heard of it."

"Choose something else, papa. Shall I play your favorite?" and she struck a few chords.

"No, not that! What is the reason you can't play the one I ask for?"

"That piece of music is only for one pair of ears, and they are not yours, papa, nor do they belong to Mr. Traverse. Name something else."

Her father, looked at her in surprise, and then laughed.

"You have raised my curiosity, Dexie. You will surely play it for me when I ask you?" "No, papa; it is sacred to the memory of someone else."

"But what if I command you to do so?"

"You will not do that, papa dear, I know," and she looked over with a world of entreaty in her eyes.

"Well, well, has it come to this!" he said, with a soft laugh. "Did I ever expect to hear Dexie say such a thing to me! See how badly I am used, Traverse; she actually refuses to obey me, knowing very well I cannot punish her for disobedience. Well, well! who would think it of Dexie?"

"Perhaps it is one of her own compositions that she is trying to keep hidden under a bushel, as it were," said Guy, with a sudden inspiration.

"Oh, now you are wrong! and, to prove it, you shall be made to listen to one of my very own pieces as a punishment," and she turned again to the piano.

"Dexie, is that your own?" when the last chords had died away.

"Yes, papa, all mine, and I have a verse or two composed to suit the music; so be careful, or I'll inflict them upon you as well."

"Now, gentlemen," she added, "what else shall I favor you with—instrumental music, or songs, ballads, whistling choruses, or what? I await your orders. I have an extensive repertoire from which you may select," and her fingers passed softly over the keys as she smilingly waited.

"Then it is no use to ask for that one piece, Miss Dexie?" Guy said, in a low voice.

"No, sir, not at all! I only play that when—well, when I am sentimentally inclined, you know. Did I not say it was sacred to someone else?" and she lifted a saucy face to Guy's gaze.

Then without a moment's pause Dexie began to sing, and she soon charmed away the frown that had gathered over Guy's face on hearing her frank admission. He stood and watched her as she sang, feeling that she had the power to make or mar his life.

"Now, papa, you have heard quite enough, I am sure," she said, at last, going over to his side. "You are looking tired."

"There! that is just the way I am served. Directly I am beginning to enjoy myself, my pleasures are nipped in the bud;" then changing his tone, he added, "Yes, dear child, I do feel a little weary. If Traverse will be kind enough to wheel me back to my room, I guess I will let Jarvis put me to bed; I hear her rummaging about looking for me now," and he smiled as he drew her face down and kissed it.

"Dear papa, I wish it was in your power to escape her search."

Mr. Sherwood understood the wish, and pressed her hand in reply.

Mr. Traverse was soon back by Dexie's side, watching the hands that were evoking such sweet strains, but she seemed hardly aware of his presence until he said, in a low tone:

"Remembering what you told me, Miss Dexie, I was not surprised to hear that you were shortly to be married. May I know the truth from your own lips, Miss Dexie?"

"I do not know why the report, true or otherwise, should trouble any person, Mr. Traverse," and she stooped to pick up some scattered music, and hide her face at the same time.

"It is more to me than you think, Miss Dexie. If you will admit that the report is true, I will not trouble you with further questions; but I understand, from what your father said, that the rumor is not correct."

"Papa had no right to tell you anything, Mr. Traverse, but I fancy you are not much the wiser for any information he may have given you."

Her blushing cheeks and downcast eyes did certainly convey the impression that her father was not aware how matters stood, so he replied:

"No, I am not much wiser, I must admit, for I cannot make what he told me agree with that engagement ring."

"Do all rings have that significance? Gussie frequently wears several without implicating any gentleman," smiling.

"Dexie, you do not know how much this means to me, and I do not know if I have a right to explain. When I remember how much you told me the night that Gussie read your letter, I do not see why you should hesitate to tell me the rest now."

"What was it that papa told you, Mr. Traverse?" Dexie asked, in a low tone.

"Only that you were free. Yet how can I believe that, with this ring on your finger denying the fact, and that music has some connection with the past, that touches your heart, or why is it sacred to one person alone. I do not understand it, Dexie."

"And I do not expect or desire you to understand it, Mr. Traverse," came the hesitating reply, as Guy awaited her answer. "I could not explain about the music, even to papa, but the ring does not tell the story you are thinking of."

"Well, if I may not hear the music, may I know the story of this?" and he took the hand that wore the ring in his own.

Dexie slipped the ring from her finger and held it towards him. "Oh! what a great fire a little ring has kindled!" said she, smiling.

Guy took the ring in his hand, and noticed the words engraved inside, "Freedom and friendship," with the letters L. and D. in monogram.

"That may mean more than the words imply, and be but a part of what the music signifies after all. I am only too willing to believe in the motto engraved here, but I hope the word 'friendship' is called by its right name. Perhaps the writer of that letter has touched your heart at last, Dexie?" he added, looking intently into her blushing face.

"No! oh, no! The ring did not come from him, Mr. Traverse."

"My thoughts have not been pleasant to me since my eyes rested upon this, and heard the rumor connected with it. Dexie, be honest with me and tell me what it means."

Dexie slipped the ring back on her finger, and shook her head.

"It has been discussed enough, Mr. Traverse, please say no more about it," she said, shrinking away from the eager, searching looks that made every moment more embarrassing to her.

"Just a moment, Dexie! Your father said that you asked Mr. Gurney to release you from any promise between you. When speaking of him that evening, you told me that you never had met anyone that you liked better. Tell me, Dexie, have you met anyone *since* then, that you asked to be free?" and he bent nearer and looked intently into her face.

Why had he put such a question to her? If she said "No," it would imply that she still cared for one that was betrothed to another; but she could not say "Yes," for that might betray her secret.

Guy's face was very near her own, as she answered with a beating heart:

"You have no right to put such a question to me, Mr. Traverse, and please to remember that I am 'Dexie' to no man but papa," and there was a touch of anger in her tone, to which, however, Guy gave no heed.

"Excuse me, Miss Dexie, if I have offended you," and a bright smile lit up his face. "I *had* no right to ask that question, but I shall endeavor to find it out all the same," a glow of satisfaction filling his heart.

Gussie entered at this moment and Dexie escaped to her room, but Guy did not think his case quite hopeless as he walked home, thinking it over.

"I believe she does care for me; but shall I ever be able to make her confess it? She must know how I love her. However, I feel free to go to the house as usual, and I may not, after all, repeat the moth-and-candle story, as I feared."

But try as he would, he could not break through the reserve that now surrounded Dexie like a mantle. She welcomed him with the fewest possible words when he called on Mr. Sherwood, and she seemed so cool and stiff that he felt chilled to the heart. It was seldom, indeed, that she addressed a remark to him during an evening. Yet there were times when, suddenly turning his eyes in her direction, he would find her looking at him so intently that his heart would throb with hope and gladness, only to be chilled again at the first word that fell from her lips. For weeks this battle with hope and fear went on, and their friendly intercourse seemed to have come to an end. Her visits to the T. and B. rooms were fewer than ever, and the hour for choir practice was so often changed that he found it almost impossible to see her a moment alone. His visits to the house gave him little pleasure. Mr. Sherwood always brightened up when he arrived, and but for the pleasure these visits gave to the sick man Guy would have hesitated about making them at all.

One evening as he entered the parlor he found the family assembled and busy over various trifles: Gussie, with a basket of colored wools, was picking out some needed shade; Mrs. Sherwood was by the fire with some fleecy knitting work in her hands, while Flossie sat at her feet intent on fitting a brilliant dress on her newest doll.

Traverse stood in the doorway looking at the family group for some moments until Dexie, who was reading the evening paper to her father, lifted her eyes and acknowledged his presence with a bow. She perused the paper silently, while her father and Mr. Traverse entered into a discussion concerning certain charges made in it against one of the public officers of the State, and at her father's request Dexie read again the article that had called forth the discussion.

When she had finished she lifted her eyes, and a wave of color spread to her very brow as she met Guy's earnest gaze. If there was more animation in the remarks that followed, Mr. Sherwood did not guess the cause of the change.

Wishing for a certain volume that had reference to the matter, Dexie rose to get it from the bookcase, but not finding it readily Traverse came over to assist her. The search went on in silence for some time, when Guy said in a low tone:

"Is there any quarrel between us, Miss Dexie, that we so seldom speak to each other?"

"Not that I know of, Mr. Traverse," Dexie replied, dropping her eyes to the lowest shelf.

"Then, why are you so silent when I am near? We used to be good friends, but now you cut me to the heart by your cold looks and cruel speeches. What has come between us?"

"Nothing that I know of, Mr. Traverse, and if my words and looks do not please you there is a way to keep out of the reach of both."

"You are an enigma hard to solve, Miss Dexie," was the smiling reply; "but I intend to find the solution, and until then you will not find it easy to drive me away."

"As you please," and catching sight of the book she was looking for, she turned hastily from him and seated herself by her father's side.

Guy felt in little humor to continue the discussion. He felt that Dexie's manner was but a cloak to hide her true feelings from him, and finding it impossible to draw her into further conversation he rose to leave the room.

"May I speak to you a few moments in the hall?" he quietly asked, as he bent over her chair.

But Dexie shrank from such an interview, and replied:

"Please excuse me; papa needs me just now."

"No, I don't," came the unexpected reply from her father, who had heard the request as well as the refusal.

Dexie rose slowly to her feet, a look of indecision on her face.

"Go at once," said her father; "Mr. Traverse is waiting for you, Dexie," then she followed him out of the room.

Her cheeks were pink with embarrassment as she waited in silence for Mr. Traverse to speak, and her heart beat wildly as he regarded her with earnest eyes.

"Dexie, tell me honestly, do you wish me to cease visiting here?"

"No, Mr. Traverse;" then after a pause, "papa would miss you."

"But I do not come here on purpose to see your father; you know that very well, Dexie," and the tender, reproachful tone made Dexie droop her head still lower.

"Have I offended you, Dexie, that you are so cool and distant with me?"

"No, you have not."

"Then is it because you dislike me that you will not speak a word to me? Is that why you are so silent, Dexie?"

No answer came from Dexie's lips, but she shook her head in reply. "What is it, Dexie that has come between us—there is something, is there not?"

"Did you ask me here on purpose to catechise me?" recovering her voice at last. "Then I wish you 'good evening,'" and she turned to leave him.

But Guy stepped quickly before her and seized the hand that reached for the door.

"Do not dismiss me so curtly, Dexie, but shake hands when you bid me 'good-bye' tonight."

Dexie laid her hand in his, and he held it close, while for one brief moment her eyes were raised to his, then as quickly averted; but that was all Guy needed—the secret was his at last.

CHAPTER XXXIX.

The next afternoon, while "the twins" were out with their mother on a shopping expedition, Mr. Traverse called at the house, and tapped lightly at the door of Mr. Sherwood's room.

"Ah! Traverse, is that you? Glad to see you," said Mr. Sherwood. "I was just wishing that someone would come in. The girls are out, and Jarvis is outside rattling among the dishes, and there is not a soul to speak to. Take a seat and be comfortable; the girls will soon be home, I expect."

"I did not come to see the girls this time, Mr. Sherwood," said Guy, smiling. "I knew they were out, met them in a store down town, so came upon purpose to catch you alone."

"Well, that is good of you, Traverse; it is intolerably slow to be cooped up here all day, not sick enough to stay in bed, and not well enough to be moved about. Any news?"

"I have not read the day's papers yet," and he pulled them out of his pocket, and tossed them on a table near. "You can look up the news yourself by and by. I have come to have a talk with you this afternoon, Mr. Sherwood, and to ask a favor. I hope you are sufficiently acquainted with me by this time to grant me this favor, without taking much time to consider the matter. I presume you have guessed that my frequent visits here are due to something more than the friendship I feel for yourself," and he smiled down at Mr. Sherwood, adding: "I have come to ask for the hand of your daughter."

"Oh! that is what you are after, is it?" and Mr. Sherwood leaned back in his couch and smiled. "I had not given the matter a thought, though I might have known there were other attractions than a sick man in the house. Well, Traverse, I am pleased to hear your request, for I have always had a personal liking for you, and I do not wonder that you have reached my daughter's susceptible heart. My life is not going to last much longer; the doctor may bolster me up for a little while, but the end is coming fast. I feel my strength going daily, and I shall feel relieved to see her settled in a home of her own before I am gone. Gussie is young and inexperienced, but you will make her a good, kind husband, I feel sure."

"Oh! but you mistake me, Mr. Sherwood," said Guy, speaking quickly; "it is not Miss Gussie I am asking for. I admire her beauty and respect her highly, but it is Miss Dexie I want for a wife."

"Dexie! Man alive! what nonsense is this! You don't mean to tell me that it is Dexie you have been making love to all this time?" said he, in surprise.

"Well, I haven't made much love to her yet, I must confess," he replied, laughing at Mr. Sherwood's astonished face; "but that is because she won't let me. She will not give me the chance! indeed, I can hardly get a word from her at all lately. Does it look to you as if I should be asking for Miss Gussie, Mr. Sherwood? Believe me, I have never said a word to her more than has been said in your presence, that would lead to the inference that I had serious intentions in regard to her. I hope you will not refuse to give me the one I want."

"Well, well, I don't know what to say, Traverse; it is so sudden. I never thought of you in connection with Dexie, and upon my word, Traverse, she doesn't appear to be very much in love with you either, if I am any judge!" and Mr. Sherwood looked up at Traverse, who was standing by his couch, his hands clasped behind his back in a waiting attitude. "Now, with Gussie it would be an easy matter."

"Mr. Sherwood, I am happy to know that you are not indifferent to me, apart from the fact that I aspire to be your son-in-law. I am sure you will understand that I mean no offence when I say that while I admire Miss Gussie I should not care to make her my wife; Miss Dexie is different."

"Well, it strikes me, Traverse, that the difference is not in your favor," and Mr. Sherwood smiled as he watched Guy's restless movements, for he was now walking up and down the room.

"Love-making must be done in a different way than when I was a young man, I fancy."

"Give your consent to the wooing, Mr. Sherwood, and I'll do the winning. I will frankly admit that at present she appears to dislike me heartily, but I have grounds to hope that there will be a change very soon. The signs may not be visible to others, but I am not in despair, by any means," and he stopped by the couch and smiled down at Mr. Sherwood's face.

"Well, Traverse, though I ought not to say it, she will make you the better wife of the two. You are not blind, and if a daughter is loving, unselfish and sympathetic to her old father, she will make a good wife. Success to your wooing, though it looks to me as if it might be a tough job. If you win her, you shall have my blessing with her; but do not take her away from me, Traverse. You will not have long to wait, and I should miss her sadly."

"Well, there seems to be no sign of a speedy marriage at present," was the smiling reply, as he took a seat by the window, "but I hope your life will be spared for a long while yet. Do not say anything about my calling here this afternoon. Dexie does not seem in the humor to hear a proposal yet; but I am going to take advantage of the first chance, so you may expect news at any time."

"Well, Traverse, I shall watch the progress you make, *sub rosa*. It will add quite an interest to the monotonous life I spend here on my back."

"You may not have long to wait, for I am going to press the matter at the earliest opportunity, even though I may get a positive refusal for my answer," was the laughing reply. "I have bought the ring, so you see I have some hope."

"Well, upon my word, Traverse! that is taking time by the fore-lock, sure enough. I must be even blinder than I thought, if there are enough signs for you to go that far already. She wears a ring now that has given rise to much gossip, but I cannot get at the truth of the matter. She will not tell me her secrets as she used to do; so take care, Traverse, the giver of that ring may be in your way, after all."

"I'll risk it, Mr. Sherwood," he said, smiling. "But the young ladies have just turned the corner; I shall have to escape by the side-door. Good afternoon, Mr. Sherwood, you have made me very happy," and after a cordial hand-clasp Guy left the house.

"Strange that I never mistrusted that it was Dexie he was after all this time," thought Mr. Sherwood. "Yet I might have guessed, if I had given it a thought, for he never asks after Gussie when he calls, and it is always Dexie he brings home when the girls are out—when she will let him," and he laughed softly, as he remembered the playful account that Traverse had given him of the trouble he had in keeping Dexie in sight, and how she had escaped him sometimes by changing hats with one of her friends at the last moment, and so bewildering him by her changed appearance that it was hard to catch her until she was almost home.

"I must find out if she has anything against him; perhaps I can speed the wooing. She will need a protector soon, brave, independent little woman though she is."

The entrance of his daughters at this moment put an end to his thoughts, and led him to notice once more the difference between the twins. Gussie rushed to her rooms at once to view the purchases afresh, but Dexie quietly slipped to his chair to see if he was asleep.

"Have we been very long, papa? I hope you have not been lonesome or wanted anything. They kept us so long looking at the things in the store that I was getting anxious, fearing Jarvis would be too busy to see after you," and she smoothed back his hair and stooped to kiss his forehead. "What shall I do for you before I go to change my dress?"

"Nothing at all." But noticing that Dexie was regarding the daily papers on the table, added, "Oh, yes! just hand me those papers; I was wishing I could reach them. There, that is all! be off! be off with you and change your gown, if you want to!" playfully shoving her at arm's-length, for he was afraid she was going to ask who had left the papers there.

"They were today's papers," she said to herself, as she went to her room. "Who could have left them? Surely *he* was not here, for we met him down street. Papa would have mentioned it at once if he had called, yet those papers were left here by someone since we went out."

Thus reasoning to herself, Dexie put on her house-dress, intending to return to her father's room and ask who had called during the afternoon, but second thoughts prevented her, and she turned to the kitchen to see what had been provided for her father's supper, or to prepare, if need be, some little extra dainty to tempt his failing appetite.

Mr. Sherwood unfolded the papers Dexie had laid before him, but they failed to claim his attention; the events of the afternoon still had possession of his thoughts.

"Traverse has told on himself by leaving these here, but perhaps she did not notice the date, and there are always papers lying around the room. I will not let her question me about them."

But Dexie acted as if the matter had passed from her mind. She was as gay as a lark, giving him bits of news she had heard while she was out, telling him of the things she had seen during her walk that she thought might interest him, even trifles which seemed hardly worth speaking about; but when one is confined indoors, the veriest trifle of outside life is welcome, so Gussie need not have curled her lip so scornfully when Dexie was relating the sights of the afternoon.

"Just think, papa," Dexie added, taking no heed to these silent objections so plainly visible, "they have put new steps before the door of your old office, and a new 'No admittance' card is tacked on the inside door, and the place is being all spruced up. The painters have got to work at the old Baptist church; it is to be repaired inside and out—quite time, too, for it looks as if it had been exposed to the weather ever since the Flood! Mitchell's tailor shop has two new figures in the window, and, judging by the styles displayed, the latest style of coat is much cut away and would suit you exactly. But if you want to dress in the very latest style, you must also have a gorgeous plaid necktie. Shall I buy you one, papa?"

"Why, Dexie; how silly you talk," said her mother severely. "What does your father need with new neck-ties while he is lying there on his back?"

The tears sprang to Dexie's eyes at once. Why could not her mother let him believe for one half minute that he was *not* "lying there on his back" with no need of fashionable attire? It made Dexie's heart ache to see the changed expression come over her father's face at the thoughtless words, and she turned from the room to hide her tears.

But Dexie had many little devices to amuse her father, who was quick to catch the passing moods of those around him. One little diversion in particular always brought a spice of frolic with it, while it caused Mrs. Sherwood to frown in displeasure. Dexie would set her father's table before him, but bring in his food covered over, and he must guess at the contents of the dishes by sundry whiffs which she would allow him from the corner of the raised napkin, and his many absurd guesses, in response to her efforts, often caused much merriment between them. He always found some little surprise on the table, if nothing more than a new cup to drink his tea from, or a pretty device on the little pat of butter; there was sure to be something to make remarks about. But this "foolishness," as Mrs. Sherwood called it, was kept up, and the harmless sport did much to induce the sick man to eat, and thus kept up his strength. Dexie was glad to find that her mother had left the room when she returned with a covered tray. Setting it on one side, she raised her father and settled his pillows, placed the invalid's table across the couch, set the tray thereon, then whipped off the napkin that covered the dishes.

"Now, papa, what do you think of that for a cup and saucer?"

"Is that a cup and saucer, Dexie? Well, you might call it anything else and not be far astray, I fancy. I'll have to ask, like the little nigger in 'Dred,' 'Which be de handle, and which am de spout?'" and he looked at the cup with interest.

"Why, that is the beauty of it. You can't make a mistake! If you take it this way, why, *this* is the handle and *that* the spout. If you prefer it end for end, why—there, you have it! I saw it down in the store, and thought it would be just the thing to drink out of. Try and see how nice it is. Not a drop spills out, you see, even when you are lying down. When you get tired of it as a cup, then I'll call it a fancy vase, and set it on the mantel for flowers. Handy thing, isn't it? useful or ornamental, just as you like."

Her father set the cup on the table and laughed pleasantly.

"Now, papa," she added, "you will need your Yankee guessing cap tonight, for I have something very nice. What is it?" holding up a dish.

"Well, sure enough, what can it be? It smells like chicken, but there is also a suggestion of oysters. There!—I give it up, Dexie."

"That's right, for I do not know the name of it myself. I saw how to prepare it in a book, but the name is beyond me. There is no English word to express how nice this tastes, so you must eat in French tonight, papa," sitting beside him to assist. "The little book tells how to prepare some lovely little stews and dishes, and I am going to make some of them for you. But don't be alarmed, papa! I'll try all the new inventions on myself first—to see if they are safe, you know! But, between you and me, papa, the author of the little cook book is a fraud! Some of the dishes are quite plebeian. He goes on to say how to prepare some toast, so-and-so, some milk and butter, or cream, so-and-so, put this and that in it, then you dish it up and call it—oh! I can't say *what* he calls it; but, if you will believe me, it is just 'cream toast,' and nothing else, disguised under a high-sounding name to deceive innocent people, and make them believe they are eating something very high-toned. Just a little more tea, papa. But I am up to their tricks and I'll not palm off any old-fashioned dishes on you, under a Frenchified name," and she chatted on, helping him and preparing what was before him, till she had beguiled him into making quite a hearty meal.

That evening Mr. Traverse made his appearance as usual, bringing with him a pretty basket of fruit, and his inquiries after Mr. Sherwood's health were made so earnestly that Dexie felt sure he could not have been in during the afternoon; someone else must have left the papers.

As may be supposed, Traverse was in excellent humor. He seemed bubbling over with good-natured fun, and even Dexie thawed out sufficiently to answer his repartees less caustically than usual.

"Something very pleasant must have happened to you today," said Gussie, looking at him archly, "or else you have been studying a joke-book for our amusement."

"Well, I have good reason to be jolly tonight," he replied, changing his seat so as to watch Dexie's face. "I am going to be married! That fact alone ought to make any reasonable man happy, don't you think?"

This announcement was so unexpected by everyone, that even Mr. Sherwood looked up in surprise, and wondered "what next," and Dexie's eyes flashed in indignation as she said to herself:

"Then he was only trying to get up a flirtation with me, after all, and his tender looks and gallant speeches were only intended to draw me out! How glad I am I never gave him the smallest encouragement! What should I have done if he had guessed my secret? Yet he looked so true—who would believe he was so deceitful? Oh, dear!"

She bent her head lower over her work, and said not a word. No one should ever know how her heart ached at that announcement.

Gussie had always feared that if ever Guy Traverse gave up his "city girl" he would turn to Dexie for consolation, and she was glad to hear this announcement. Dexie was not going to get him, after all. She hoped Dexie would feel disappointed, but she smiled sweetly as she said:

"Ah! you sly thing! How you have deceived us? How long have you been engaged, and when is the event to come off? Do tell us about it."

"Well, I only received her father's permission today—something I was afraid I would never get, so the time has not been set."

"Come, Dexie!" looking up to see how her sister took the news, "you have not congratulated Mr. Traverse yet on his approaching marriage."

"I have not heard your congratulations, either, Gussie; but I believe Mr. Traverse will not doubt the sincerity of mine as I fear he may yours."

The retort struck home, as Dexie intended it should; she felt hurt, and was glad of the chance to say something sharp to relieve her feelings.

"Well, it is to be hoped that the future Mrs. Traverse is a little milder in her manner than you are; he has endured a good deal from your sharp tongue lately, and needs a change. Mr. Traverse seems to be waiting for your congratulations, Dexie," she added, as she noticed how intently Guy was regarding her.

"I hope it is not needful for me to assure Mr. Traverse how glad I am to hear of his approaching marriage," came the cool, stiff words from Dexie's lips. "I hope that hereafter he will see fit to bestow his obnoxious attentions exclusively on the lady of his choice."

"Why, Dexie," said her mother in surprise, "you are forgetting yourself."

"I stand adjudged!" and Guy smiled serenely, as he exchanged looks with Mr. Sherwood. "But I regret to say that the lady in question has not cared to monopolize my attentions so exclusively as I could wish, and they have overflowed, as it were, upon others occasionally. I beg to hope, Miss Dexie, that in the future you will have no cause to consider my attentions obnoxious."

"Well, give *me* your attention just now, Mr. Traverse," said Gussie, lifting up a skein of silk for him to hold, and beginning to wind it off. "Does the future Mrs. Traverse indulge in this work?"

"Well, now, I really don't know, Miss Gussie; but if the knowledge of it is important I am sure she can do it, though I may never have seen her at it."

Dexie was suffering agonies of mind. Who could it be that had won his heart? It must be someone he had known before coming to Lennoxville, and his visits away from town were not always on business matters. She sat listening to every word with a beating heart, but those who were watching her closely could read no word from that quiet, immovable face.

"Do tell us something about this city girl of yours," Gussie said, teasingly. "We have been so intimate that it is only fair to tell us something about her. Is she tall or short, a blonde or brunette, and what kind of work is she usually at when you go to see her? or is she a society lady with nothing to do but dress up and look pretty? Perhaps she paints; that is fashionable now."

"Paints! No, never! 'Her cheeks are like the rose, that in the garden blooms,' and so on, but for all that, I am sure she does not paint!"

"Paint pictures, I mean! You know I did! Of course, I never meant her face! But what sort of work is she fond of? What are her talents? I am sure you must know that!"

"Well, now, I really don't believe I ever asked her what she likes to do best, and she is so unselfish that it would not be fair to judge her by what she is actually doing when I happen to see her, for I am sure that some of her self-imposed tasks are far from pleasant to her. I have heard her called her mother's right hand. I suppose you know what that means, Miss Gussie?"

Dexie raised her eyes for one moment, but dropped them when she saw Traverse looking at her intently. She was glad it was not a fashionable belle he had chosen for his wife, for she knew what a position she must hold if she was "her mother's right hand." That term told a long story to one initiated into its duties.

"But I am not going to let you off with such a general answer, Mr. Traverse," was Gussie's persistent reply, "so tell me at least *one* thing that you have seen her engaged in when you called upon her."

"Well, really, Miss Gussie, you fairly puzzle me, for I can't think of the name of the work which I see her at most frequently," and he looked up as if reflecting on the matter; then glancing over to Dexie, who sat by the side table with a mending basket near, he added, "Oh! now I remember it. It is 'family mending,' I believe you call it. You just put me in mind of it, Miss Dexie," as Dexie raised an astonished pair of eyes to his face.

A sudden thought struck her, though she instantly refuted the idea, and despised herself for entertaining it for a fraction of a moment; but Guy had witnessed the flush that spread over her face as he uttered the words.

"Oh! how poetic!" and Gussie laughed heartily. "She must be, like Dexie, also, the housekeeper of the family, or at least the eldest daughter in it."

"Why, I thought you were twins, Miss Gussie," said Mr. Traverse, in surprise.

"Well, so we are as to age, but Dexie is years older than I am in other things. She has left the vanities and other worldly things behind her years ago."

"I wish you could see the fine affair that Dexie works at when she sits up with me at night. Where is it, Dexie? Bring it out and let us all have a look at it," said Mr. Sherwood, who had listened in silence to the discussion, and did not wish Traverse to think that Dexie was ignorant of this particularly feminine employment.

"Oh! never mind it just now, papa; I would rather not show it," she replied. But seeing that she had somehow disappointed him, she added, with a smile, "Wait till it is done, papa. It is not easy to judge the looks of an unfinished piece of work. Perhaps I will be able to finish it in time to make it a wedding present to Mr. Traverse." Traverse looked at her with such a happy smile on his face that she made some excuse to turn her chair about, and her fingers trembled so she could scarcely guide the needle.

"What is the matter with me, I wonder?" she thought. "Surely I am not so foolish as to be disturbed by his looks, after what he has just told us! Surely I am not so weak and foolish as that!"

Although the day had been a pleasant one to Mr. Sherwood, it had also been a trying one, and he began to feel the effects of it. He was getting uneasy and restless, and Dexie soon observed it.

"You are tired, papa. Shall I wheel you to your room?"

"Yes, I think you had better, and call Jarvis at once," and he leaned back white and weak against his pillows.

Guy was on his feet in a moment, and rolled the chair into the next room with a steady, firm hand; while Dexie hurried past him to summon Jarvis, and to get the hot applications which were always kept in readiness for these sudden attacks.

"I fear you are worse than usual tonight. Has my extra visit today been more than you were able to bear?" Guy asked, as, with the gentleness of a woman, he lifted him across into his bed.

"No, it is not that; I have been up too long, I guess, and my strength is daily growing less. I ought not to be moved out of bed, perhaps, but it is torment enough to be bolstered up in a chair without staying in bed all day," he added savagely, as the pain began to grow fierce. "Oh! this is awful!"

Guy seemed helpless as he stood on one side to let Jarvis approach the bed.

Dexie came in at that moment with several hot cushions, and with their help they soon had the sufferer more at ease; but for the few minutes the sight of his agony was terrible to witness.

"Don't go, Traverse; sit down for awhile; I shall soon be better," he said, as soon as he could speak. "There is more medicine in those hot bags than in all the doctor's bottles—they ease the pain faster than anything else," he presently added.

"How is the pain now, papa?" and Dexie bent over him with anxious face.

"Better, dear; much better, but it was fearful cutting for awhile. Did I frighten you, dear? You must not mind it so. Jarvis might see to me alone, if you would let her."

"Oh! I must help you if I can. I could not bear it if I could not do something to relieve you, dear papa," she whispered, as she bathed his flushed face.

Presently Mrs. Sherwood came in to see if her husband was better, and to ask if there could be anything further done for his relief.

"Nothing more, my dear; do not worry about me. You had better go and rest. Dexie will bring me something hot to drink presently, and that is all I shall want."

"Then I will leave you now with Jarvis, and see about it, papa," and Dexie left the room without saying a word to Mr. Traverse, who had taken a chair and seated himself at the other side of the bed. She was too much taken up with her father's sufferings to remember that her own heart had cause for grief.

She was some time away from the room, and naturally expected that Mr. Traverse had left the house, as Mrs. Jarvis said nothing about his still being in the room when she came out to speak to her.

"It is my turn to sit up the first part of the night, Mrs. Jarvis," said Dexie, "so you had better go at once to bed. I will call you if he should be worse, so do not sleep with one eye open. I will be sure to let you know if you are needed."

"Well, Traverse, you astonished me tonight," said Mr. Sherwood, as soon as they were alone in the room; "that was a strange way of beginning your wooing," and there was a smile on his white face as he looked into the manly one before him.

"Yes, I astonished them all," and he laughed softly. "It was quite amusing to see the effect of the announcement on the whole of you. I thought you were going to jump out of your chair; Miss Gussie was evidently surprised, but was not very much put out at the news; and Dexie—well, she hardly expected it, but she seemed pleased to hear she was likely to get rid of me," and he laughed again.

Just then Dexie came into the room carrying a little alcohol lamp with attachments for keeping hot her father's beef tea, and she stopped abruptly as she saw Traverse, saying almost rudely:

"You here! why I thought you had gone long ago!"

"Come! never mind looking at Traverse; I want my tea. I hope it is strong and hot."

Dexie colored slightly as she poured it out and helped him to raise his head as he drank it, knowing how a pair of eyes were watching her.

"Shall I shake your pillows while you are up, papa?"

"No; they are quite comfortable. Perhaps you don't care to believe that Traverse is almost as handy a nurse as yourself; but there! he can never be quite so good as my own little girl," and he drew her down to his side.

"You look pale yet, papa. Are you sure the pain is gone? There are more hot cushions outside if you would like them. I wish I could bear the pain for you," she said, in a low tone.

"You cannot do that, little woman, but you can do something else that would make me feel better. Be a little less rude to Traverse here; he is my best friend, and there is no need to snap his head off every time you speak to him. I can't think what ails you lately, Dexie; you never used to be so quarrelsome."

Dexie flushed painfully and softly replied:

"As *your* friend, papa, I will try and give him less cause for complaint in the future—if I can help it," she added, without lifting her eyes.

"Well, it is something to have you promise that much itself, but he has not been complaining, Dexie. I am the one who is finding fault, so don't begin to scold him for that. Now, I am going to try and sleep, so go out of the room, the both of you, and don't come disturbing me. I will pull the bell if I want anything," and being thus dismissed, Dexie found herself alone with Guy in the sitting-room.

CHAPTER XL.

The house was silent and still. All had retired, and Dexie moved gently about, placing the room in order, wishing that Traverse would make some move to leave the house; but he seemed in no hurry to depart, as he stood with his elbow on the low mantel, watching her.

At last Dexie broke the silence by asking anxiously:

"Do you think papa is any worse than usual tonight, Mr. Traverse?"

"Well, I hope not, Miss Dexie. Does he take those bad turns very often?" and his eyes were full of pity as he spoke.

"Not often at this hour; the turn of the night is always his worst time. Oh! I hope it will not be severe tonight. He seems so much weaker than usual that I—I'm afraid for him," she said brokenly.

"Let me stay with you tonight, Dexie; I cannot go away and leave you with such a dread on your heart," and he came near to her side. "I can help you if he is worse," he added, gently, "so let me share your watch tonight; indeed I will not leave you like this," for his tender, sympathetic words brought the tears, and she hid her face in her handkerchief.

Presently she grew calmer, but her voice was very low as she answered:

"You are very kind, Mr. Traverse, but I shall not need your help. I can call Mrs. Jarvis if he should be worse. I thank you for your kind offer, but your assistance will not be necessary."

"That is not kind of you, Dexie," said Guy reproachfully. "Your father said I was his best friend, and you ought not to send me away when I might be of service to him; so let me stay, Dexie."

"Well, I suppose it looks rude to refuse your help; but I am sure mamma and Gussie would think it improper, if I allowed you to remain," she answered, with downcast eyes.

"Is that the reason you do not wish me to stay with you?" and he smiled down at the bowed head. "Do you think conventionality should be considered when your father's comfort is in question?" he asked. "You know your father has often asked me to sit with him when he was restless and could not sleep, but you did not seem willing," he added, seeing she had no reply, "and I have been anxious to please you in all things, Dexie."

"There was no need to consult me about it," she replied, feeling vexed at the tone that implied so much more than he had a right to express under the circumstances, and taking her work-basket to the far side of the table she sat down to work.

"Must I go or may I stay, Dexie? at least till the time of your father's usual attack? Be kind this once and say I may stay."

"As you please. There is a new book of poems, and a late New York paper," said she presently, feeling that she must say something. "They will help to pass away the time."

But Guy Traverse had no intention of passing his time over reading-matter, something of a more personal nature was in hand. Dexie was determined she would not be the first to break the silence, and the ticking of the clock was the only sound heard for some time.

"And so my attentions are obnoxious, Miss Dexie? I was grieved to hear that, when I wished them to be the opposite."

The words, low and tender, brought painful heart-throbs to Dexie's bosom, but she hastily answered:

"You said they should not be so in the future; so please say no more on the subject," and glad to escape from his earnest gaze, she rose and looked into her father's room.

Finding him quietly sleeping, she soon returned, and folding up her finished work, laid aside the basket, then brought from a drawer a frame containing the delicate piece of needlework her father referred to, and began to pass the needle back and forth. Presently Guy came over to her side, and stood looking down at the work in her hands; then said with a smile:

"Is this the fine wedding present you are going to give me, Dexie?"

"I was not in earnest when I spoke, but I will not go back from my word, if you think it will be acceptable," was the low reply.

"If that is the only thing you will give me for a wedding present, I think I won't accept it;" then bending over her, said tenderly, "My darling! I want you to give me yourself!"

Dexie was on her feet in a moment, her embroidery forgotten.

"Mr. Traverse! do you wish to insult me? How little you must respect me, to speak to me like that!"

"My little girl, why will you misunderstand me? Don't you know that I love you with my whole heart—will you not let me tell you?" as she shrank away from him.

"Those are strange words to say to me, Mr. Traverse, after telling us about your approaching marriage; and papa thinks you are a gentleman."

"And you do not!" smiling at her indignant look. "Dearest, you must let me explain," and he came nearer.

"No! I will hear no explanation! there can be none after what you have said! Is it honorable to say such things to me while you are looking forward to marriage with another?" and her eyes flashed angrily.

"Dexie, you are mistaken. Surely you do not think me such a villain!"

"What else do your words imply?"

"That I am looking forward to my marriage with you, dearest; that was what I meant tonight," taking a step nearer, and looking at her tenderly.

"Do gentlemen usually announce their approaching marriage before saying a word to the lady in question? I am not so easily deceived as you think, Mr. Traverse."

"But, Dexie, you would not let me say the word, though I have sought an opportunity for weeks past. Dearest, I have loved you since I first knew you, even during the time I thought you were promised to another. I hid it then in my own breast; but lately, since I heard you were free, you have given me no chance to tell you of my love. Sometimes I have felt that you knew it, Dexie, and that you were not indifferent. Today I asked your father's permission to win you, and he gave his consent."

"So I was bargained for and sold like a horse!" and her eyes flashed indignantly, "and I have nothing to say in the matter whatever! How much was I considered worth?" Then overcome by her feelings she sank down on the sofa, and hiding her face in the cushion burst into tears.

Guy was kneeling beside her in a moment, and with one arm thrown around her said tenderly,

"Dexie, you know better. You know your father loves you and would keep you beside him always if he could. But he knows that I love you dearly, and he would give me your hand if you gave me your heart. Do not try to hide it from me any longer, love. Do you not love me already?" and he bent his head beside her own. "Lift up your face and tell me, dearest."

But Dexie could not raise her eyes; she was afraid to believe the sweet words she heard. Did he really love her, after all!

"Think how long I have loved you, Dexie," he added, tenderly, "and yet you have never given me one word to encourage me, but have been so cruel—so cruel! Dexie, have you nothing to say to me after all this waiting?" and he lifted her head to his arm, saying softly, "If I wounded you tonight by my abrupt announcement, it was unintentionally. I thought you would guess my meaning; but you would not even look at me. You will believe me, Dexie, for I did not mean to vex you," he pleaded earnestly.

Still no answer; but Guy seemed to know intuitively what was in her thoughts, and she no longer shrank from him when he stroked her soft hair and drew her closer to his breast.

"Uncover your face and look at me, dearest. Did you not know that I cared for you? Tell me, Dexie."

"I did think so sometimes," was the low reply.

"Then what was the reason you were so cool with me?" smiling down into her blushing face. "Tell me, or I shall believe I know the reason already."

"If you know, why do you ask?" was the shy reply.

"Because I would like to hear you say it yourself. Confess it, now, or must I say it myself?"

She endeavored to release herself from his encircling arm, but he held her close as he whispered:

"You love me already. You know you do; so own it now."

A pair of eyes, glorious with the love-light that shone in them, were raised to his, and as he read his answer in their depths, the happy lover whispered,

"Kiss me, Dexie."

A blushing face was lifted to his, and an arm was raised till it encircled his neck, as Dexie gave her first kiss of love to the man who had won her heart.

"How could you be so cool and short with me when you loved me all the time?" he asked, as he held her in his arms.

"I was not quite sure you cared for me," was the low reply. "But I am forgetting papa. I must go and see if he is all right, Guy."

It was the first time she had used his name, and he smiled fondly into the dark eyes raised so shyly to meet his own.

"I do not want to let you go from my arms for a minute, darling. I have been longing for this hour for so long that I am afraid I shall find it all a dream if I once let you go. Will you come back to me if all is right—back to my arms, I mean?"

"Perhaps—yes, then," and she stepped softly into her father's room.

But it needed only a few minutes to assure her that he was sleeping soundly and peacefully, so she returned to her waiting lover.

"Not beside me, but here, where you promised!" and he held out his arms as she endeavored to take a seat on the sofa beside him. "I wonder how long it will be before you will make my heart glad by coming to my arms of your own accord. It is hard to believe that this is the same little girl that used to send me home with such an aching heart that I walked the floor for hours, instead of going to bed."

"Oh, Guy! I am so sorry. I never thought you cared for me like that," she whispered, as she laid her head on his shoulder.

"I wish I could tell you how much I *do* care, my own darling! but words give so little expression to one's feelings; yet I am longing to hear just three little words from you. Don't you think it would be fair to take away the memory of your unkind words by telling me that you love me?"

"Dear Guy, you know I love you, or I would not be here! I have loved you ever since papa was hurt, but I did not want you to know it. Will that confession do?"

"I knew you cared for me, my darling! yet it is sweet to hear the admission from your own lips. And to think how long we have misunderstood each other! If I had only taken you in my arms that first night I was present when your father was so ill, and made you own to what I felt was true, these unhappy weeks might have been spared us; but it is something to have this joy in the end, my own little wife."

Dexie gave a little start of surprise at this sweet epithet, and a rosy blush spread over her face, at which Guy repeated lovingly:

"My own little wife! Is it not so, Dexie?"

"I had not thought of the future, so much has happened in such a short time," she answered, in a low voice; "but I love you, Guy, and the future shall be as you wish."

"I am glad you have no rings on tonight, Dexie," said Guy, as he took a little parcel from his pocket. "You have one that has troubled my peace of mind for some time, but I have something to take its place," and as he took her hand in his the flash of a ring told Dexie his intention.

"Oh, Guy! wait! I cannot let you put that on yet. I am afraid to trust myself that much tonight; it is all so sudden, Guy!"

"My darling! what do you fear? You are not afraid to trust yourself to my keeping when you know I love you?" and he drew her closer, as he looked down into her eyes.

"No, Guy, but it is all so new and strange that I hardly know myself. You know I accepted a ring once before when I ought not to have done so, but I wore it honestly lately, Guy; I did, truly."

"Tell me about it, Dexie, and clear up the mystery. The ring has a story, one that has given me much trouble of mind."

"I think your trouble was imaginary, Guy," smiling. "The ring, in the first place, did not signify an engagement, though it was the sign of a promise which Lancy Gurney and I made to each other. He was to ask me again to marry him at the end of a year, unless during that time we found there was someone else we liked better. As you know, I did not wait for the year to be up before I asked to be released. Oh, yes, I confessed that I had met someone that had the first place in my heart," she blushingly admitted.

"And you told him what you would not tell me! Oh, Dexie!"

"Yes, for I promised him I would be honest with him. This led to explanations on both sides, and to assure him I still felt kindly towards him I agreed to keep and wear his ring. I wore it gladly, because it reminded me I was free to love where I chose; besides it helped to keep you from guessing that I had given my love without the asking. That is all, Guy, so you see the words engraved inside are honest and true."

"My dear little wife! but how could I guess that the ring meant so much happiness to me. It did indeed deceive me, but this shall tell the truth from the start."

"I do wish you had not bought it—just yet. Everyone will make remarks about it. Something plainer would not proclaim our secret to the world as this will surely do."

"Yet I thought it not good enough for the dear hand that was to wear it. Let me put it on, Dexie. Think how many times I shall see you when there will be no chance to say a word to you, but when I see the ring I can say, 'She is mine! mine!' How sweet to know that it is so!" and he kissed her hand as he slipped the ring on her finger.

"Mine now, dearest; yet you seemed so far away from me only a few hours ago. How surprised your father will be! I wish he could see you here in my arms."

"Oh, hush! that would be dreadful! Was he surprised this after-noon at your errand? I thought it was you who left those papers; but when you announced your coming marriage this evening, then I began to doubt," and she laughed softly.

"It was a surprise at first, but he consented at last to give me his treasure—if I could get her."

"Poor papa, I will never leave him. No one else seems to have time to be with him or amuse him as I can, and it is hard for him to feel so helpless when he has such a restless and energetic disposition."

"I promised not to take you away while he needed you; but, dearest—I do not want to alarm you—I do not think he will have to bear his pain many weeks longer. He is failing, I can see, and he told me today that he felt his strength going fast."

"I know it is so, though I have tried to put the thought aside. Dear papa, how good he has been to me! What news this will be to him! But I hope no one else will find it out—just yet. Everything must go on much as usual, before others anyway," smiling into his happy face.

"That will be very hard, don't you think, little wife? How shall I be able to hide my love from Gussie?"

"Oh! you will be coming here after this just to see papa, you know," looking at him archly, "and I fancy she will find little to interest her in the man that has so openly announced his approaching marriage to a lady who is unknown. I'll not object, per-haps, to let you stay—with papa, you know—on the nights that I take my turn to sit up with him. But there is his bell, and oh! Guy, look at the clock!"

Dexie's heart beat fast as she hurried to her father's room, but she was needlessly alarmed. His unusual sleep had renewed his strength, but Dexie, fearing the worst, asked anxiously:

"Are you in much pain, dear papa?"

"Oh! no, child; I feel first-rate. I guess that bad spell I had at bed-time is going to do me for tonight; but I am thirsty, so when you get me fixed up you can go to bed. You must be tired to death, my dear girl," he added, as Dexie busied herself about him. "What time is it? Not past two, surely? Why, I must be turning over a new leaf, eh, Dexie?"

Guy Traverse stepped to the door as Dexie entered the room, fearing also that Mr. Sherwood was worse, but hearing his cheerful voice he thought he would surprise him by showing himself, and he stepped to the bedside, his hands clasped behind him, and a curious smile played over his face as he waited.

"Bless my soul! Traverse, what are you doing here at this time of night?" was the astonished remark as Mr. Sherwood turned and saw who was beside him.

Traverse laughed pleasantly and drew a chair to the bedside.

"I have been waiting in the next room, fearing you might be ill again at your usual hour and would need my services."

"And a sorry night you have had of it, I expect. Well, you don't seem much the worse of it, after all," and he turned and looked curiously towards Dexie.

"What mischief have you been up to now, Dexie, that you look so guilty? Come here to me directly!"

"Are you going to scold me, papa?" and she stooped over and kissed him.

"I would like to find out first if you deserve it. I hope you have not been quarrelling with Traverse, after what I said to you?"

"Well, not all the time," she blushingly answered. "He would not go home at the proper time, though I tried to turn him out of the house."

"I see! Then it was the first part of the night you did not agree. And what, may I ask, have you been doing since the row was settled? Out with it now," holding her face between his two hands and looking into her eyes.

"Dear papa, that is not fair," as she tried to hide her face in his arms.

Mr. Sherwood felt sure that Guy had come to some understanding with her, and wanted to make her own it, but Guy knew she would not care to be the first to speak of it, so said in a happy voice:

"Give me a chance to tell a part of the story, Mr. Sherwood. Dexie has made me a happy man at last. You will not care to hear all the particulars just now, but she has promised to be my wife."

"Is this really true, Dexie?" looking with loving eyes at his daughter.

Dexie raised her hand, saying softly:

"See, papa," and the flashing ring answered the question.

"Well, well; I can hardly believe it yet. Go and kiss him, Dexie, right before me, if it is really true; seeing is believing, you know."

Guy looked at her smilingly, saying, as he held out his hands, "Come, Dexie."

Dexie put one hand in his, and laying the other across his shoulder bent over and kissed him; and she made no resistance when he put one arm around her and drew her down on his knee.

"Well, this is a pleasant surprise, I'm sure. You have made good use of the time, Traverse," and Mr. Sherwood laughed softly. "You have been rather a perverse young lady, Dexie, but you have fallen into good hands at last. You must not leave me yet, dear child, for what should I do without my little nurse? But, bless my heart! there's three o'clock. You will not get into your hotel at this hour, Traverse, but I expect you would not sleep much if you did, so go back into the sitting-room, the both of you, and finish the night!"

"Thank you, Mr. Sherwood; your liberty adds much to the pleasure. I hope we have not tired you," he added, as he rose from his seat.

"Not at all! Another drink, Dexie, and be off with you!"

"Don't tell on us, papa," she whispered, as she prepared his drink. "Jarvis is sure to sleep till I awaken her, and this is not likely to happen again," laughing.

"Well, better make the most of it, then; so be off with your lover," and he waved her away from his side.

"It was not so dreadful, after all, to come to my arms before your father, was it?" Guy asked, a few minutes later. "I am sure it pleased him to see it, and it was good of him to allow me a little longer bliss."

But time passed swiftly, as it always does with happy lovers, and the grey dawn of early morning warned them that they must separate. As they stood by the window, watching the first rays of light in the east, Dexie said:

"I will have to send you away soon, Guy, or you will be discovered; but I am going to invite you to an early breakfast here with me before you go."

"Never mind breakfast, dearest; I would rather have you here by my side until the last minute. I expect some machinery by the early train, so I think I will go down and see if it has arrived; that will give us forty minutes more together," taking out his watch.

"Then a part of the time will be well spent in preparing you a slight refreshment—nothing elaborate, you know, or Eliza would pounce down on me at the first sound," and she left him at the window, and hurried to the kitchen.

A few minutes later she appeared again, looking as fresh as the morning, with a white ruffled apron clasped round her waist and a dainty muslin cap perched on her head, from beneath which stray curls peeped bewitchingly out, and passing her hand through Guy's arm, said laughingly:

"Will you mind coming to the kitchen, Guy? I am afraid someone will hear us if I take you anywhere else, and I don't want the rattle of dishes to betray us."

"Well, this is enough to make any fellow selfish," as he followed Dexie out to the kitchen, and closed the door softly behind him. "You must be a fairy, to conjure such a dainty breakfast in this short time. No one will hear us here."

The appetizing odor of coffee filled the air, and the most fastidious person could have found no fault with the dainty little table and its appointments, with plates laid for two.

"Now, you really must be quiet, Guy," trying to escape from his arms. "Just see how you have mussed my hair!"

"And you haven't mussed mine at all, I suppose! I say, Dexie, what if Gussie should catch us here?" "Which, fortunately, is not likely; but what *would* she say? The impropriety of our conduct would be shocking," and a musical laugh sounded through the room.

"I should plead extenuating circumstances, dearest. One does not have the delightful experience of last night but once in a lifetime, and why should we not make the most of our pleasures? However, I can thank your father for this extended bliss."

"The extended bliss of eating in the kitchen!" and she smiled mischievously, as she handed him a cup of coffee. "Is this your first peep into my domain?"

"Yes, and I think it the pleasantest room in the house. Who planned it, and invented such contrivances?" glancing approvingly at the adjustable shelves which Dexie disclosed by shoving aside what appeared to be a panel in the wall. "We must have our kitchen just like this."

Ignoring his last remark, except by a blush, Dexie answered:

"I have to thank papa for the liberty I enjoy in this room; but for him I should have had the usual bare walls and no conveniences whatever. If you had seen all the newspaper articles I read up, giving the experience of practical housekeepers, you would not wonder at the change which, with the help of a carpenter, I made in this room. I am monarch of all I survey in this part of the house, as mamma does not care how many experiments go on here as long as everything is satisfactory that comes out of it."

All pleasant things come to an end, and the early breakfast in the kitchen was no exception to the rule; but it remained a bright spot in the memory of both, and in after-years was often referred to.

A few minutes later Guy left the house, and, for the first time, he left it contented and happy, the sweet "Good-bye" in the hall being in strong contrast to the usual curt dismissal that had fallen to his lot hitherto when Dexie showed him out.

CHAPTER XLI.

Dexie stood in the doorway until her lover was out of sight; then, remembering that the little table in the kitchen would tell tales, she was soon stepping briskly about, and quickly removed all traces of the early meal. Going softly into her father's room, she found him awake and feeling very well, and in the best of spirits.

"I heard you in the hall," said he, pretending to scold. "A fine time for a young man to be leaving the house, isn't it, now? I am astonished at you, Dexie!"

"Well, dear papa, I am astonished too!" and they both laughed. "I am sure if anyone had told me such a thing was about to happen, I would have thought him a fit subject for a lunatic asylum."

"You look very happy over it, dear, or your face tells a story! But I thought I smelt coffee when I woke up."

"So you did! My young man stayed to breakfast. What do you think of that? He says he is going to plead 'extenuating circumstances,' if he is brought to the bar. But don't you think you would like a cup of coffee and a nice piece of toast?"

"Yes, I think I would; it is rather early for breakfast, but I feel ready for it."

Dexie was soon beside him with a small tray, and as he drank his coffee he said, as he looked at her keenly:

"I want to know one thing, Dexie, and then I won't question you any more. What was the trouble between you and Traverse these few weeks back? Something was wrong with you, at any rate, but you do not confide in me as you used to do."

"Well, you naughty papa! How could I tell you my little secrets when you let them out the first thing?" she laughingly replied.

Her father looked at her in surprise, and she added,

"I told you not to tell that I broke the engagement with Lancy Gurney, and you told Guy that very first evening."

"Well, where was the harm? He seemed very anxious to know about it, and I am sure you seemed to rejoice over your freedom."

"Yes! but I didn't want Guy to know it, for it made it so much harder for me to meet him."

"Dexie, did you break your promise with Lancy on account of Traverse? Well, well! I understand it now; but who would have thought that you cared for him when you were so cool and short!"

"You surely would not have me make the first advances, papa?" laughing.

"No; but you might have allowed him a chance to make them himself. However, all's well that ends well, and I wish someone would ask to be Gussie's protector before I am gone—someone as trustworthy as Traverse. You are of an age to find life rather hard without someone's sheltering care, and it will not be long before you will both need it, for your mother is not able to see after you as you need."

The rattle of pans and dishes told that the kitchen had an occupant, and with a parting word to her father "not to tell on her," she left the room.

At this moment Jarvis appeared, looking positively frightened.

"Oh! why did you not wake me, Dexie?" she cried. "I cannot see how I slept so heavily. But I depended on you to rouse me, Dexie."

"It is all right, Mrs. Jarvis. Papa passed a splendid night; so you were not needed. But wait a minute, I have something to tell you. I did not want you up, for I had company of my own, and I have news for you this morning." Then with a blushing face she raised her hand to show her ring, adding, "I am engaged to be married."

"My dear, is it possible!" and the motherly creature took the fresh, happy face between her hands and kissed both cheeks. "Is it Mr. Traverse that is going to take you away from us?"

"He will not take me away while papa needs me; but it is to be a secret for the present, Mrs. Jarvis, for under the circumstances we can make no plans for the future."

"Yes, I understand you, dear. You can trust me; and I am well pleased to hear of your good fortune. Mr. Traverse is thoughtful and tender beyond his years, and I have learned to respect him highly. But you will go and lie down now, won't you? I will see to everything, so go to your room and make your mind easy about the work this morning."

When Dexie appeared again in her father's room some hours later, he looked at her with pleasure. Her face seemed to have grown beautiful; love had so glorified it that her happiness seemed to speak from every feature. He did not wonder that Guy Traverse had lost his heart to his little nurse.

"Do you feel well enough today, papa, to dictate those unfinished stories?" she asked, as she wheeled his couch over to the sunshine. "You have left those three fishermen quarrelling about who caught the largest fish, till by this time the fish must be spoiled, to say nothing of the temper of the fishermen. And there is that city belle, who wished to become a second Rosa Bonheur; you have left her in the pasture fleeing for her life, with the vicious bull in full pursuit, her sketch-book flying in the air. Now, surely by this time the brute has killed her, or she has died of fright. Then there are several other characters all left in some dilemma that must be settled by this time in some way or other," and gaily talking, she brought out her writing tablet and set it across her knee.

"Well, it seems to me, Dexie, that as soon as I get my characters into some trouble I lose all interest in them; I wonder what trait that represents in myself," he added, musingly. "Finish the stories yourself, Dexie. I am sick and tired of them, so get them out of the fix they are in the best way you can."

"Well, how would you like to begin something new, papa?" her only idea being to get his mind occupied, and this had been a wonderful means of diversion ever since he was hurt.

"Not today, Dexie. I think I am too full of your little romance to invent anything new. Finish up those old things and let me see how you get on. Give the smallest chap the biggest fish; he told the biggest lies, and will claim it anyway. Let the girl jump the fence. If she can't do that, let her crawl under it, or let the bull toss her over; no matter how she gets out of the field, so long as she gets out alive. She will never want to paint again, I feel sure; so let her escape with her life."

Dexie laughed and began to write, knowing she would get her father interested, and she soon found she had to move her fingers very nimbly in order to keep up with the flow of words that fell from his lips. Page after page fluttered to the floor till Dexie cried, "There, papa, that is enough for today. The house party are happily paired off and are on the way to the supper table; let us hope they will find enough to eat upon it, while we go and see about our own supper."

In the evening, much to Gussie's surprise, Mr. Traverse made his appearance, and her smiles and good-humor rose to the surface at once; this was the more remarkable by reason of their non-appearance throughout the day.

Dexie answered his ring at the door, and if they remained in the hall just a little longer than usual, no one seemed to remark it; and if the blushes which mantled her cheeks were observed, no one guessed the cause.

During the evening Gussie noticed for the first time that Dexie wore a new ring, and the volley of questions she poured forth regarding it was quite astonishing.

"Why, where did you get it, Dexie? It is just a beauty; mine look quite common beside it! That is the second new ring you have worn lately, Dexie, but I hope there is not so much mystery about this one as there was about the other. Lend me your ring for this evening, will you, Dexie?" she added, coming over to her sister's side.

"No, thank you," and Dexie turned away. "You have half a dozen rings of your own, and you know your own motto is 'What's mine is mine,' so I'll neither borrow nor lend," laughing good-naturedly.

"Keep your old ring, you stingy thing!" Then, fearing that Traverse might have heard her, she said sweetly:

"Have you noticed Dexie's new ring, Mr. Traverse? It is a mystery to me where she gets them, for I am sure she would never buy them herself. Perhaps Hugh McNeil sent it, eh, Dexie? It looks just like one he would send," and she regarded her sister closely.

Dexie colored painfully at this interrogation, and Guy, who was amused at Gussie's inquisitiveness, said in feigned surprise:

"Are you really guilty of wearing a new ring, Dexie?" the corners of his mouth twitching suspiciously. "I hope you are as happy in possessing it as the donor was in bestowing it."

"Thank you, Mr. Traverse, I think I can truthfully say that I am."

"Oh, Dexie! was it really given to you by a gentleman? Was it

Lancy Gurney who sent it?"

"Hardly, Gussie, or some other young lady would have a right to complain," smiling at Gussie's look of surprise.

"Then it was Hugh McNeil, as I thought. I always said you would repent your behavior to him. Then I suppose the affair is settled. Where *is* Hugh, Dexie?"

Dexie did not answer at once, but clasped her hands, palms downward, in that convulsive grasp that always told of some mental struggle. Something of the old terror filled her heart at the very mention of Hugh's name, and her answer was evidently uttered with much reluctance, not unmixed with fear:

"He is probably on his way to New York, Gussie. Is there anything else you would like to know?" forcing a smile to her lips.

Guy felt that something unusual had brought that look of alarm to Dexie's face; he would ask the cause at the first opportunity.

Gussie felt sure that she knew all about it now, so began to twit her sister about "giving in at last." She had been in a bad humor all day, and was glad of the chance to get rid of her ill-feelings by teasing Dexie in the presence of Traverse.

"So Hugh's money has bought you, after all! and your high and mighty airs were just put on! I am glad you have come to your senses, for I suppose that ring means a marriage in the future."

"If the latter admission will keep you quiet and make your mind easy, then you shall hear it. I did accept the ring with the understanding that it meant marriage in the future, but Hugh McNeil is no more to me now than he ever was. Now, if you are satisfied, Gussie, will you be kind enough to leave my affairs alone for the rest of the evening?"

"Hum—m, yes; I'm satisfied, since I know the whole of it! An invisible lover! a ring! a promise of marriage! and Hugh coming back! Oh, yes, I'll leave you alone for the rest of the evening, never fear!" and taking a book from the table she drew an easy chair to the light, then turned her back to the rest in the room. If Guy Traverse was soon to be married to his "city girl," and Dexie was going to be Hugh's wife, they could entertain each other, for she would have nothing to say to either of them!

Queer, wasn't it, that neither of them resented this rudeness, but kept up a low conversation at the farthest side of the room!

When Guy was about to leave the house, and the "few" last words were being said in the hall, he asked what had caused her alarm at the mention of her supposed lover's name.

"I forgot until that very minute that Elsie Gurney told me in her last letter that this McNeil would leave England for New York on the coming steamer, and for the moment my heart stopped beating from sheer fright."

"But, dearest, he cannot harm you now. Do you think he is coming here?"

"Indeed, I cannot tell, but I fear that is his intention; and if he should, oh, Guy, I believe I should hide! I own to being rather afraid of him, though, luckily for me, he never found it out."

"But if he knows you are mine, surely, Dexie, he is enough of a gentleman to leave you alone in the future."

"Well, I may be needlessly alarmed, but I feel a presentiment of evil, and should an ill wind blow him this way, you must be extra good to me while he is here—come oftener—and I will feel safe, at least, while you are with me."

About two weeks later, when all thought of Hugh McNeil had been dispelled, Dexie's presentiment of evil took shape. He arrived in Lennoxville on the afternoon train, and a few inquiries soon brought him to Mr. Sherwood's residence.

Mrs. Sherwood and Gussie were out making calls that afternoon, and Dexie was busy in the kitchen making some new dainty, and was much interested in watching the result of her work, when Mrs. Jarvis came in search of her.

"Dexie, there is a gentleman in the parlor asking to see you."

"What a nuisance, when I want to see how this turns out! It is not Mr. Traverse at this hour, of course," she added, carelessly.

"No; it is a stranger. He is a large, dark-complexioned man, with a heavy black moustache and beautiful black eyes—a perfect gentleman, Dexie!"

The dish fell from Dexie's hand with a crash to the floor.

"Heaven preserve me! what shall I do?" and she turned pale to her lips. "I cannot see him, Jarvis; I really cannot! Here, I'll write a line to papa, and you can take the gentleman to his room," and with trembling fingers she wrote a few words and gave them to the nurse; then, throwing off her big apron, she seized a hat, sayings to Eliza, who looked on in astonishment:

"Tell Mrs. Jarvis that I have gone over to Ada Chester's, and I won't be back till tea-time, when I hope that man will be gone; and oh, Eliza! do, like a good girl, clean up that mess for me," pointing to the demolished dish and the contents thereof, "and I'll do something for you sometime. I dare not stop, for I am properly scared for once," and she flew out the back-door, down through the kitchen garden and into a back street, out of sight of the house, before she stopped to regain her breath.

Mrs. Jarvis was thoroughly surprised at Dexie's behavior, but she carried the little note to Mr. Sherwood and waited his direction.

"Yes; show the gentleman here, and I will see him."

"Well, Hugh, so you have found us out," as he appeared behind Mrs. Jarvis. "You find me on my back. Get a chair for yourself."

Hugh was surprised to learn of the seriousness of the accident that rendered this position of his friend necessary, having supposed it a slight affair from which he had long since recovered.

The two men talked for some time on matters in general, when

Hugh said:

"I suppose you know what has brought me here, Mr. Sherwood. My feelings for Dexie have not changed, unless they have become more intense. I heard through the Gurneys that her engagement with Lancy was at an end, and started from Australia at once, on purpose to try again to win her. I have still your permission; have I not?" he eagerly asked.

"I fear then you will be disappointed, Hugh; Dexie is already won."

"Mr. Sherwood, you are not in earnest; you are saying this to try me," and Hugh turned an appealing face to the one that lay back on the pillows.

"Have pity, Mr. Sherwood; I have suffered enough."

"Hugh, my dear fellow, I was hoping you had got over this, and not hearing from you for so long I believed you had. But it is true. You are too late, for Dexie is the promised wife of another."

"She is not yet married, then?" and his face recovered from the despairing look.

"Not yet, but as much lost to you as though she were. How is it that you did not take my last letter to heart and seek a wife abroad? I told you that Dexie had not changed towards you, though I did all I could to influence her in your favor. But she has won the heart of a good man, Hugh; he is everything I could wish for, even in Dexie's husband."

"But I love her so!" The words were low, but seemed wrung from his very soul, and he turned away toward the window, but without seeing anything of the prospect beyond.

"Can I see her?" he asked, at last. "Let me hear from her own lips that she loves another, and, if she really does, I will surely know it. If I find it is so, I will go away and not trouble her any more. Give me this one more chance, Mr. Sherwood."

"It will be of no use, Hugh. I may as well tell you so at once; but I will try and persuade her to see you, though she sent me word just now that she would not come in while you were here. It is fair enough that you should hear the truth from her own lips, but I know the interview will be painful to you both," and Mr. Sherwood pulled the bell-cord that hung above him.

"Tell Dexie I wish to see her here for a few minutes," he said, as Jarvis answered the summons.

"She has gone out, Mr. Sherwood, and she left word that she would not be back till tea-time," and she glanced at the foreign-looking gentleman who made himself so very much at home.

"Very well, that will do," and Jarvis left the room.

"You see how it is, Hugh; she has run out on purpose to get clear of you."

"But that is no sign that I need despair," and there was a happier look in his eyes than there had been since he heard she was lost to him.

"Ask me to stay, Mr. Sherwood, for I cannot go away till I see her. I must learn the truth from herself before I leave the house," and the well-remembered impetuosity of old was visible in his words.

"Certainly, Hugh; stay, of course, but I fear you will not find your refusal as pleasantly spoken as if you had taken it at second-hand," and a feeble smile parted his lips for a moment. "But you know Dexie's ways, Hugh, so you must abide the consequences."

"I have borne much for love of her, and I am still willing to suffer if I may be rewarded in the end by seeing her once again," he answered earnestly. "A sight of her face would have been more welcome than an angel's visit during these long, weary months; to look back on them is like looking into desolation," he added, in a low, serious tone.

There was silence in the room for some moments. Hugh sat listening for the first footfall that would announce Dexie's approach, while Mr. Sherwood lay back, with closed eyes, thinking what an easy solution of the trouble it would be if Hugh would turn to Gussie for the gift that Dexie denied him. Then, rousing himself, he talked to Hugh of his travels and adventures on sea and land.

Meanwhile Dexie had rushed in haste to the house of her friend, and from thence despatched a note that brought Guy Traverse to her side, and her agitation and alarm were so great that Guy was almost unable to soothe her.

"I cannot go home without you, Guy. There can be only one thing brought him here, and I cannot face him unless you are with me."

"I will go with you, certainly, dear, but I cannot understand why you are so frightened, for by your own description of him he is a gentleman."

A few hurried explanations of Hugh's past history in connection with herself were given, and Guy grasped the headlines of it as it poured from Dexie's lips.

"As my promised wife, darling, you need fear no further annoyance from him. I will see to that," he replied. "Give me a few minutes while I go to the hotel and change my suit. I have been putting in shafting with the men, and am hardly presentable in my present condition," he laughingly added.

"I am putting you to great inconvenience, I fear, Guy; but I cannot help it, for it will not do to send word that I will not go back till he is gone."

"No, certainly not. He would put a different construction on your absence. Let me find a more smiling face on my return, darling, for I will take care of you."

Half an hour later Guy and Dexie had entered the house; and finding that Hugh was still with her father, she left Guy in the parlor while she sought Jarvis in the kitchen.

"He is still here, then? Well, tell Eliza she can place *two* extra plates for tonight, as Mr. Traverse will be here also," and giving no time for Jarvis to put the questions she was evidently anxious to have answered, she returned to the parlor.

"How I wish I could peep into the future and understand the programme of the next few hours," she said to Guy, as she stood by his side in the shadow of the window-curtain. "I hope it will be short, but I know by the shiver in my bones that it will not be sweet. Your adversary's weak point is his temper, as you will see at a glance; so, Guy, don't—whatever the provocation—don't lose your own, dear."

Mr. Sherwood's bell sounded through the house, but for the first time it was unheeded by Dexie. She knew what was wanted, but feared to face it, even with Guy at her side. But Mrs. Jarvis was in attendance, and she now appeared in the doorway, saying:

"Your father has found out you are home, and he wishes to see you at once."

With one long look at Guy, Dexie followed her. The excitement had sent a pretty color to her cheeks, and her eyes were brilliant with suppressed feeling, but she crossed the room to her father's side without giving a glance in any direction save on her father's face. Apparently she saw nothing of the dark eyes that brightened so vividly at the sight of her. Hugh was not expecting anyone to follow her, and coming more slowly into the room Guy caught the look on Hugh's face, and his own heart rose up in a protest against it. Guy had time for a good look at Dexie's unwelcome admirer before his presence was discovered, and he wondered how it was that Dexie had not lost her heart long ago to this bold, handsome lover who so openly declared his passion, for the eager, longing gaze that followed Dexie's movements was easily read.

"Dexie, here is an old friend come to see you," and her father waved his hand in Hugh's direction.

Dexie turned herself about, her feelings well under control, and even Guy was surprised at the easy, natural tone in which she replied:

"How do you do, Mr. McNeil? You are like a bit of Halifax, and, as such, an old friend."

As she gave him her hand she turned instantly about, adding,

"Guy, this is Mr. McNeil, a gentleman we used to know in Halifax. Mr. McNeil, Mr. Traverse."

Hugh had not noticed Guy's entrance till Dexie turned to introduce him; consequently he felt slightly embarrassed, but Guy stepped forward with outstretched hand, and greeted him frankly and heartily.

"Any friend of yours, Dexie, is sure to meet a welcome from me. Glad to know you, Mr. McNeil."

It was impossible to resist the pleasant, affable manner in which Guy spoke. There was a magnetism in his winning smile and in the cordial grasp of the hand that attracted Hugh in spite of himself.

As Guy continued speaking, Hugh regarded him intently. Was this the man who had won Dexie from him? The looks interchanged when Dexie spoke said as much, and there was an air of ownership in Guy's manner that sent an arrow through Hugh's heart.

Dexie followed her father's eyes and regarded the two men as they talked, and the fear at her heart sank out of sight. Hugh's recent voyage from Australia and to New York gave ample opportunity to confine the conversation to questions and descriptions concerning the Island Continent and other places he had visited, and there was an amused smile in Dexie's eyes as she listened, for she knew Guy was keeping up the conversation in order to gain time and study his rival.

She contrasted the two men who sat reading each other's faces as they talked. Hugh had regained all his former strength and vigor by his Australian tour. He had also grown stouter and his shoulders broader; but the same masterful manner, the same quick glance were present, that made Dexie's heart beat fast when he turned his gaze upon her.

Guy had more the figure of an athlete, and his quiet, easy manner gave the impression that his passions were well under control. He looked a man to be trusted; there was a firm, yet tender look in his eyes that was not unfelt by the man who sat opposite him. Both were handsome men, though of a different type, but Hugh's face lacked something that could be felt, if not described in the one opposite.

Gussie's shrill voice in the hall gave Dexie an opportunity to leave the room, and she hastened to do so, as something had evidently gone wrong, and Gussie was protesting and scolding in audible tones, though the words were not intelligible.

"Hush! Gussie! someone is with papa. What is the trouble?"

"Who is it? Is it company of yours that Eliza is so flurried over that she cannot attend to me?"

"Mr. McNeil has arrived, Gussie; don't let him hear you talk like that."

"Oh! he has come at last, has he? Well, it's high time! How long is he going to stay, Dexie?"

But her questions remained unanswered, for Dexie was talking to her mother on domestic matters, and presently they all assembled in Mr. Sherwood's room.

Gussie soon noticed how intently Hugh was watching Guy Traverse, and she made up her mind to "tell Hugh a thing or two" regarding Dexie's behavior, for since the night Gussie had decided in her own mind about Dexie's ring she saw there was an unexpected intimacy between her sister and this engaged young man. She wondered how it happened that Guy was present at that hour; it would complicate matters with Dexie, surely, but to her surprise she found herself paired off with Hugh as they went to the supper table.

"You should have returned long ago, Hugh," she whispered. "Dexie has developed into a desperate flirt! Just now it is Mr. Traverse, as you can see for yourself, though she is aware he is engaged to a lady in the city."

"Gussie, are you sure of what you are saying? Is this only a flirtation?"

"Well, I don't see what else you can call it."

"Do you think she has given me up? I have come on purpose to find out."

"Oh! is that all you have come for? Why, I thought it was a settled thing between you. Then she must be going to marry you just for your money! and now that I think of it, she said as much," said Gussie bluntly.

There was no chance for further conversation, but Gussie's words raised all sorts of questions in Hugh's mind, and he watched the couple on the opposite side of the table, his hopes and fears alternately rising.

Dexie's manner bore out her father's statement, but how was it that Gussie looked at the matter so differently.

As they rose from the table Guy stood for a moment talking to Mrs. Sherwood, but Hugh crossed over at once to the window where Dexie was standing, bending over some flowers.

In his quick, eager tone, Hugh asked:

"Will you give me a few minutes alone, Dexie, when I have come so far on purpose to see you?"

"I am sorry to hear that request, Mr. McNeil, as it forces me to seem rude when I would prefer to be cordial. Do not let us renew our old antagonism."

"Dexie, I think, if it ever existed, it has given place to a better feeling. My heart has been starving for a sight of your face, and you have grown so beautiful that it is hard to resist the temptation to take you in my arms."

Dexie shrank away from him, and she gave a quick look at Guy, who was still talking to her mother, but his smile reassured her. She knew he would soon be at her side.

"Don't leave me, Dexie," Hugh entreated. "I will not touch you, so do not he afraid of me. Do you know I have come as fast as I could travel, just to see you face to face as I do now. Yet I have a further hope in my heart, Dexie, for Lancy is not between us now."

Dexie's heart beat too fast to allow of a reply, and Hugh added:

"You can guess how glad I was to hear that you and Lancy were friends only, and from what Gussie tells me there is hope for me yet. Is it so, Dexie?"

"You must not put any faith in Gussie's stories, Mr. McNeil," Dexie managed to reply. "I am aware she is resting under a delusion, but I did not take the trouble to convince her of the fact. I was hoping I should not have to tell you what is surely plain to yourself," blushing as she gave a meaning glance in Guy's direction.

"Then your father was right! I have come too late! Is that what you wish me to believe? Think a minute, Dexie, before you say what will rob me of all hope!" and he bent his head in his eagerness to read her answer in her truthful face.

"If papa told you I was engaged to Mr. Traverse, he told you the truth," Dexie said, in a low tone.

"But do you love him, Dexie? Are you sure your heart is given with your hand? I was right in Lancy's case, you know."

As he spoke, Guy came over to her side, and she laid her hand on his arm, and looked into his face with such trust upon her own that Hugh felt she had answered his question.

"Mr. McNeil, I am not naturally jealous," said Guy, pleasantly, "but if my little wife is making love to you here, I'm afraid there is danger that I shall grow that way," and he laid his arm across Dexie's shoulder, and smiled at them both.

Dexie looked over her shoulder at this declaration, and was surprised to find there was no one in the room except themselves, but Guy had brought this about in order to announce their engagement to Hugh.

"Unfortunately for me, the love-making is only on my side," said Hugh, bitterly. "I cannot win even one word of kindness from Dexie's lips; my very presence seems unwelcome. She has just given me to understand that she belongs to you, and I am expected, I suppose, to offer my congratulations; but I cannot do it—I must get used to the thought first. I am not afraid or ashamed to confess that I have loved Dexie Sherwood for years—loved her madly, blindly, though she has given me nothing but hard words and scornful looks through it all. Months of travel have failed to make me forget her. She has been like a loadstone drawing me back to her, when in my pride I would have rejoiced to feel myself free. I would have plucked her out of my heart if I could, but my love seems a part of my life, and I cannot kill it while I live myself. I believe you are a noble, generous man, or you never would have won her heart. Be good to her, since you have taken her from me, for if I thought there should ever be a time when you would cause a tear to fall or grieve her heart by a word, I would kill you where you stand!"

Dexie hid her face against Guy's breast as Hugh's hot words poured like a torrent from his lips, but Guy drew her protectingly to his side, and his firm, clear voice sounded low and distinct as he replied:

"Have no fear for Dexie, Mr. McNeil! She shall always be my first thought and care. I cannot blame you for loving her, though it is but natural that, under the present circumstances, I should regret to hear you own it. Dexie has given me her love willingly and freely, and I am sure she will be happy as my wife, the present condition of her father being the only obstacle that prevents our immediate marriage."

"Forgive me, Traverse! my words were hasty!" and Hugh held out his hand, "but my heart is sore at the disappointment. I have hastened forward with all possible speed, hoping for something so different from this, that my heart rebels. But I shall go back to Halifax, Dexie, and the day I hear of your marriage I shall propose to Nina Gordon. I wish to my heart she was dumb! I might persuade myself into thinking sometimes that I had you near me, if only she would keep her mouth shut! If I cannot have your love, I may be able to delude myself into thinking that I have your presence near me occasionally."

"Oh, Mr. McNeil! you cannot mean what you are saying! You surely would not do such a thing as that!" said Dexie, in a horrified tone. "Your good sense will prevent you from throwing your life away so needlessly. Oh! I cannot think that you have a thought of such a thing. It would be dreadful!" and the dark eyes met his with an eagerness that was questioning.

"I heard you say once that if she were away from her mother one might make anything they liked of her," said he, more quietly. "I shall make a second Dexie of her if the thing is possible, for I'll see to it that she keeps her tongue quiet till it suits her face!"

This was uttered in such a tone that Dexie shuddered. His outbursts of passion seemed less devilish than this quieter expressed determination, for it was accompanied with a glint in his eyes that reminded her forcibly of that memorable boat sail, and her voice was less firm as she replied:

"I cannot think you are in earnest, Mr. McNeil; you would not wreck another's life for merely an unfortunate resemblance! No! I cannot think it of you; but it is wicked to say it, even in jest!"

"Would you take even that small comfort from me?" he said, almost fiercely. "Do you know what love is, and think that I can bear the burden of solitude that you have laid upon my life; even the solace of your shadow denied me, while you have everything!"

"There! I think you two had better say no more," Guy firmly though smilingly remarked. "You will be quarrelling in earnest the first thing I know. Of course I do not understand what all this means, Mr. McNeil, but I have such confidence in Dexie's judgment that I join her in the request that you will do nothing hasty, and throw the best years of your life away because of this disappointment. Come, shake hands, you two, and make it up, and let us join Mr. Sherwood in his room, or he will think we have shared the fate of the Kilkenny cats."

Dexie held out her hand and Hugh clasped it in both his own, and, looking tenderly into her eyes, said, in a voice so changed that it seemed to come from other lips:

"Forget my hasty words, Dexie, if they have hurt you, and try to think of me kindly sometimes. We would have been better friends if I had loved you less. I give you up, though most unwillingly, for I cannot say now as I did before that your heart has not awakened, for I see that it has, beyond a doubt," and like a courtier of old he stooped and kissed her hand.

Gussie was full of curiosity concerning the interview; but when the little group appeared in the room, their faces told no tales that she could interpret.

Hugh looked more sober than usual, and listened to the conversation rather than joined in it. Guy looked cool and composed and, maybe, a trifle triumphant. Dexie looked rather paler than usual, and remained almost as silent as Hugh. This might mean much or little, but something in the manner of each checked Gussie's light chatter.

When Guy rose to go, Hugh rose also, and asked permission to accompany Guy to his hotel. Then, promising to return the next day to see Mr. Sherwood, Hugh followed Guy from the room.

At a look from Guy, Dexie followed them into the hall, and while Hugh put on his coat and gloves, Guy said, in a tender, reassuring tone, as he smiled into her anxious face, "Do not be alarmed, dearest; there will be no shooting, I promise. You can trust your friend with me, and I will see after his comfort; so good-bye till tomorrow, love."

He bent his head and kissed her, though he was aware that a pair of dark eyes were watching his every movement.

Hugh was very silent as he walked along. The kindly-spoken "Good-night, Mr. McNeil," did not make him feel his disappointment less keenly.

When the hotel was reached and his room engaged, Hugh turned to Guy, saying:

"May I go with you to your room for a little while? I shall go away tomorrow, I think, and I would like to have a talk with you if you have no objection."

"Certainly! I shall be glad of your company," and Guy led the way to his room.

"It is no use, Traverse," he said, as Guy tried to draw him into a conversation on matters in general. "I have no thoughts but for one thing, and am no company for any man, least of all you; but I want to ask a favor of you. Tell me of your plans for the future, and let me help you, even in the smallest way, to bring them about. I coveted wealth at one time, thinking if I had it all else would come easy; but I have found my money a burden, because I could not put it to the one use for which I longed to possess it. Do not be offended, Traverse," for Guy was looking at him intently, and with a puzzled face; "what I want to say, I say with a good heart towards you. In business matters, you know, money alone is power. Is there anything that money could do for you—any position it could procure for you, which would give Dexie pleasure to see you fill? I am sure you are ambitious—in your position I would be myself; so tell me your hopes and plans, and let me help you." "You are most kind, Mr. McNeil, and I thank you for your generous offer," and he held out his hand, which Hugh clasped heartily. "I was not prepared for this, but expected to hear reproaches heaped upon me. I see I did not know you. I am deeply sensible of the kind thought that suggested this; but I have no need of the help you so kindly offer. I own to being ambitious, but it is the want of brains more than money that hampers me at present. Yes," as Hugh looked up inquiringly, "I am of an inventive turn of mind, and if I can work out the problems that are hatching in my brain I will win fame as well as money. Your offer is none the less kind because I cannot accept it. I am sure it will give Dexie much pleasure to hear of your kindness."

"You do not wish me to have any share in your happiness," Hugh said, with downcast features. "Well, I daresay I would feel the same myself were I in your place; but, be generous, Traverse. Think how long I have loved her, before you ever saw her at all, and contrast the blank my life will be with the happiness in store for you in the future. Let me do something for you, Traverse."

"Believe me, McNeil, if there was anything you could do for me I would gladly accept it, if only by way of atonement—not that I think that I alone stood in your way, but for the pleasure I know it would be to you to serve her or hers. My position is better than most men of my age, and since I have won Dexie's hand I have frequently thought there is nothing more I require to make me contented and happy."

There was a few minutes' silence, when Hugh asked, with a perceptible paleness in his dark face,

"When do you expect to be married?"

"She will not leave home while her father lives; whether we shall be married while he is so ill, I cannot say. Much depends on circumstances. Her father is a very sick man, though owing to his cheerfulness the fact is not apparent to everyone."

The conversation was carried on until the clock struck the midnight hour. Hugh seemed to lay bare his heart to his successful rival, and Guy listened in surprise to the account of his many efforts to win Dexie's favor, even so far as to tell of the unfortunate boat sail and its consequences.

Guy's heart was full of pity as he listened. How much Hugh loved her when, in spite of the rebuffs and scornful refusals, he could be so blinded by passion as to dare attempt to win a promise by such rash and desperate means! Dexie's love for himself seemed all the greater since it had stood such a siege from this fierce, passionate man, and Guy wondered no longer that Dexie was alarmed when she heard of his coming.

When Hugh mentioned what Gussie had said of the "city girl," Guy could not help smiling, and explaining the circumstances that gave rise to the story, added:

"I believe it was one of your letters that Gussie captured that night, Mr. McNeil; but as I played the lover and claimed the letter, Gussie felt obliged to believe me, and my imaginary city girl has kept her quiet ever since."

"I can well believe the distress Dexie felt when she heard the letter read aloud. You did a kind act that not one in a hundred would have dared to do. No wonder she loves you. But away so far from her, it seemed that I could not bear my life if I did not tell her, even on paper, what was in my heart. I am glad to know you, Traverse; if I cannot win her myself, it is a comfort to know she is in such good keeping."

At last Hugh rose to go, and the hands of the accepted and the rejected lover met in a warm, friendly grasp.

The next day when Hugh made his appearance at Mr. Sherwood's, and made known the fact that he had spent the forenoon with Guy at his office, Dexie looked her surprise, but she blushed with pleasure to hear his words of praise when speaking of her lover.

Hugh remained several days in Lennoxville, but he seldom made his appearance at the house unless in company with Guy.

Gussie could not understand this at all, but her spiteful remarks were so wide of the mark that they were only amusing.

She needed no one to tell her that Hugh was as much in love with Dexie as ever, yet why he allowed Guy Traverse to monopolize her was a mystery that was incomprehensible.

Hugh spent the last evening of his stay at the Sherwoods', and, in spite of Gussie's raillery, he was silent and sad; even Guy could not rouse him into cheerfulness.

During the evening he obtained a few minutes' conversation with Mr. Sherwood, and his low, earnest words brought a mist to the eyes of the sick man.

"I am truly sorry for your disappointment, Hugh," was the low reply, "but you prove beyond a doubt that her happiness is still dear to you when you propose to do such a thing. But wait awhile, and think it over. You may form other ties, and there may be others who will have a stronger claim on you than the wife of Guy Traverse. Oh, yes! yes! I know the money is your own, and you can do what you like with it, but Dexie would not approve of this, neither would Traverse."

A few minutes before it was time to leave for the train Guy came behind Hugh and whispered a few words in his ear, words that sent a flash of light and joy into his dark, sad face.

"God bless you, Traverse, for this kindness; I was getting desperate; five minutes will suffice," was the reply, and he slipped out of the room, crossed the hall, and a moment more was standing by Dexie's side.

"Traverse told me you were here, Dexie, and that I might come and say good-bye to you alone," and taking her hands in his own, added:

"Dexie, if there should come a time when you need a friend, or if you should ever be in trouble, will you promise to let me know and let me be the one to help you? You know how gladly I would serve you."

"Thank you, Mr. McNeil, you are very kind; I will not forget your offered help. I hope you will have a pleasant journey home," and she drew away her hands and turned away.

"Dexie, when we parted in Halifax you gave me angry looks, even at the moment of parting, but there was a hope in my heart that helped me to bear it. It is different now; do not add to my present misery the memory of your cool, indifferent words. Lift up your face and say, 'Good-bye, Hugh.' Do, Dexie."

Dexie stood irresolute a moment, then, giving him her hand, she lifted her eyes, and said in a low tone:

"Good-bye, Hugh; I did not mean to be cool or indifferent, for you have been kinder than I dared to expect."

Something in her tone and words swept Hugh's self-control to the winds, and he clasped her to his heart.

"My darling! my darling! must I indeed say good-bye forever; it is like parting with you at the grave," and his hot kisses touched cheek and brow. "I cannot bear it, Dexie. Oh! if I could die now with you here in my arms; my darling! my darling!"

A soft knock at the door, and a moment later Guy entered.

"Time is up, McNeil, if we want to catch the train." Then putting his arm across Dexie's shoulders, as he noticed her pale face and quivering lips, said:

"Has it been too much for you, dearest? It was the last time, you know."

"How could you, Guy! How *could* you send him here to me alone!" came the low, trembling words.

"It was no use, Traverse; the first kind word unmanned me, and made me forget that you trusted me. I have held her in my arms and kissed her face; but forgive me, Traverse, if you can, it is the last time," and giving a long, imploring look at Dexie, who stood with her face buried in her hands, added, in a low voice:

"I am ready, Traverse; let us go at once, and may God help me to get over this," and with his arm drawn through Guy's they both walked out into the night.

CHAPTER XLII.

One morning when Dexie was out in the back garden whistling like a bird, and busy about some domestic matters, someone outside the high fence called:

"Georgie! I say, Georgie! come here a minute."

No answer being received, a shower of small pebbles came over the fence, and the call was repeated.

Thinking it was Mark Perrin, a wild young lad with whom Georgie was forbidden to associate, Dexie called out:

"Go away from here at once, you torment, or you'll get your jacket dusted for you," and hastening to the gate as if eager to perform the operation, she found Guy Traverse awaiting the promised punishment.

Astonishment rendered her silent for a moment, when she laughingly exclaimed:

"For pity sake, Guy! was it you threw the pebbles?"

"Yes, and am I to believe that it was you who was whistling?"

"Well, as you took me for Georgie, it must have been well done, so I'll own to the whistling; but what brings you here so early in the morning? I am not dressed for visitors at this hour," and she glanced down at her short frock, that revealed a neat foot and well-turned ankle; then pulling forward the sun-bonnet that had fallen back from her head, added:

"This is the latest style. I hope you admire it."

"I do, indeed," and his face filled the front of it for a moment.

"Oh! do come in till I shut the gate; someone might see us. Now, what do you want with Georgie, if I may ask?" and she lifted a saucy face to his.

"I didn't want him particularly, but I thought it was he who was whistling, and I was going to ask him to look for you, but as it is your own sweet self, so much the better, for I want to speak to you here a minute."

"But why here, at the back gate?"

"I wanted to ask if you would drive into the country with me, as I have to go on a matter of business."

"Then why didn't you go to the front door and ask me properly, sir?"

"Well, I am going to, just as soon as I find out if you can come or not. You were up part of the night with your father, and I did not know but you were resting or too busy to come with me. In that case, Gussie might feel it her duty to accompany me."

"Oh, I see! I shall be most happy to accept your invitation, Mr. Traverse; so go around to the front door and ask me like a gentleman."

Shutting the gate after him, she entered the house, intending to have a little fun over the invitation.

His ring at the door was answered by Gussie, and Mr. Sherwood, who was dozing on his couch, brightened at once as he saw who was the visitor.

"A splendid morning, Traverse," was his greeting. "You are early today."

"Yes, I have called to see if you could spare Dexie for a drive with me this morning."

"Certainly. Gussie, hunt her up."

"Dexie is very busy this morning, papa," Gussie replied, "but I am at leisure, Mr. Traverse, if you are looking for company."

"Busy, is she?" said Mr. Sherwood; "then go and relieve her, Gussie, for she has been up half the night and needs a rest," and raising his voice, called:

"Dexie, Dexie; come here."

Dexie was standing outside the door waiting for this summons, and she entered the room, her head still enveloped in the enormous sun-bonnet, her arms bare to the elbow, and her whole appearance proclaiming her a busy little woman.

"Did you call me, papa?" and she stepped to his side.

The contrast between them was too painful, and Gussie blushed with embarrassment, and hastily exclaimed:

"Leave the room, Dexie, Mr. Traverse is here."

"Where!" and the scooplike bonnet was turned in his direction.

"Oh, good morning, Mr. Traverse. Excuse my toilet, but we wash sometimes at our house, and this is one of the times. Fine morning this for washerwomen. Now, what do you want of me, papa?" and she turned leisurely to her father again, much to Gussie's horror.

"Well, Traverse called to take you for a drive, but I doubt if he will care to ask you after seeing you in such a rig."

"This is not my carriage dress, my dear papa, but my working suit; but seeing that Mr. Traverse has been talking to me at the back gate in this very *rig* and survived the shock, I trust the second sight won't prove disastrous. If you say you can spare me, I'll promise not to appear in this costume in public. Thanks, papa. How soon do you wish to start, Mr. Traverse?"

"In half an hour, if possible," was the smiling answer.

"You will find me waiting your appearance," and making a sweeping, old-fashioned courtesy, she pulled her bonnet forward with a jerk and danced out of the room.

Traverse looked after her with a smile, and with a few pleasant words to Mr. Sherwood, and a polite "good-morning" to Gussie, he bowed himself out.

As soon as Guy was beyond hearing, Gussie's ill-humor found vent. She did not see why Dexie should leave her work to go about the country with young men, and Traverse must have regretted his invitation when he caught sight of Dexie's ridiculous figure, her dress to the top of her boots and a sun-bonnet that would disgrace a countrywoman! But one never knew what Dexie would do next. Awhile ago she could scarcely speak a civil word to Mr. Traverse, but now that she knows he expects to be married, her manner is just the reverse. Reproaches like these fell on Mr. Sherwood's ears unheeded, but a kindly smile lit up his face when Dexie made her appearance, looking as dainty as if right out of a band-box, and as she drew on her gloves a handsome buggy drove up to the door.

Giving her father a hasty kiss, she whispered:

"I wish you were able to go in my place," then ran down the steps, and a few minutes later the high-spirited horse carried them out of sight.

They did not return for some hours, and Dexie enjoyed the little excursion exceedingly; she was grieved to find on her return that her father had spent a very sick day, and she regretted leaving him for her own pleasure.

"You needed the change, my dear," her father assured her. "You are losing your roses by waiting on me so constantly, and this hand is thinner than it was six months ago," and he patted the hand that rested in his own.

Mr. Sherwood was daily growing weaker, and had to keep his bed the greater part of the time. The old pain returned oftener, and was so very severe while it lasted that it kept them all in a constant state of alarm. This so worked on Mrs. Sherwood's nerves that her fancied illness threatened to develop into something not quite so imaginative, and she required almost as much care as her husband. It became necessary for Gussie to spend a part of her time in her mother's room, and this she disliked very much, for Mrs. Sherwood was not a patient sufferer, and Gussie chaffed and fretted against the restraint to her liberty. Her extreme selfishness was so apparent that her mother received her half-hearted services with little thanks.

The constant care and attention which divided Dexie's time between her father's and her mother's room made it very hard to keep domestic matters running smoothly, and Gussie's obstinate refusal to take any part of the labor of the household or care of the children upon her own shoulders, gave Dexie little chance to get the rest she needed. This was telling on her health, and she was fast losing her rounded cheeks, and her eyes began to look so large and black that it made Guy's heart ache to look at her. He wished to tell Mrs. Sherwood of their engagement, and even attempted to persuade Dexie into marrying him at once, so that he would have the right to protect her against some of the needless burdens that were put upon her young shoulders, but Dexie would not hear of it.

"Mother is aware that I expect to be married by and by; if she is making a mistake as to the man let it be for the present. Were the truth known, my life would be unbearable. It is all I can do to keep the true state of affairs from coming to papa's ears, and he has enough to bear without family troubles being put upon him."

"My dear little girl, do you think I am going to let you stay here and be at the beck and call of everyone? Let me claim you at once; that will be the best way to settle the difficulty, and your father would say the same if he knew about it."

"But he must not know it, Guy; think how unhappy it would make him. It would never do, dear; but I have a good mind to write and ask Louie to come home. Surely aunt would let her come for a few weeks. I have written to her about it before, but she would not let her come unless she was positively needed, and I do think she is now. She must be quite a young lady by this time, and would be such a help and comfort. I believe I will write and ask her again."

That night, while Dexie sat up with her father, the letter was written, and Guy dropped it in the letter-box on his way home, and in less than a week, to Dexie's great joy, Louie came rushing into the house, as fresh and strong as any little country lassie.

Her coming did, indeed, make a great difference in the house, as Dexie expected. She brought such a new atmosphere into it with her quick, outspoken criticisms, that she worked quite a revolution.

Then she had so much that was new to tell them all, and it was told in such a breezy way, that her father brightened up as he listened. Her aunt had not sent her empty-handed either, for she had a loving and tender heart under a rather harsh exterior, the cold looks with which all sentiment was frowned down seemed but the rough, hard shell which covered a noble and generous disposition. But this rather severe aunt had refused Louie permission to make many visits at her father's home, on account of the displeasure with which she regarded her mother. She had never been pleased at her brother's marriage, and when Louie had been given over to her care she determined to cut off all connection with the mother's influence. Dexie's letter had revealed more than she was aware to the keen, sharp-sighted woman, and Louie was sent to help wait on her father, with many admonitions as to her conduct at home. She was given a "month's leave of absence," as Louie laughingly expressed it, but when alone with Dexie she admitted that her aunt would extend the time if her father should seem to be near the end.

Louie was very practical in many things, wasting little sentiment on trifles, and Mrs. Sherwood reaped the benefit of Louie's strict bringing up, which she had received at the hands of her aunt.

"Now, mother," she said one day, as she displayed some of the handsome garments her aunt had provided her with, "do try and get well as quickly as you can. I have only a month to stay, and I brought these dresses to wear, and I cannot do that if I am to be a nurse for you. I will get everything, and do everything for you, that you really need, but I cannot run up and down stairs all the time on useless errands. I can't think how Dexie has a foot left to stand on, the way she is called hither and thither. Of course, she must have a rest, now that I am home, or she will be laid up, and that would be a calamity for this house, I fancy. Now, you sit up, and I'll brush your hair and fix you up so nice that you will long to get downstairs to the rest of us, for I am going to spend the next hour with papa," and she bustled about the room and set everything in order to her mother's hand.

To the surprise of the family, Mrs. Sherwood made her appearance downstairs before Louie had been in the house a week; and as she continued to improve, Louie quietly ordered an easy carriage to be at the door at a certain hour, and when that hour arrived she made her appearance in such becoming attire that she had little trouble to induce her mother to step into the carriage with her, and as these outings became quite frequent they soon had a beneficial effect on her mother's health and spirits.

Louie's home-coming made a difference that was quite remarkable in Gussie also. She took so much for granted that Gussie was constrained to exert herself. It was rather amusing to watch Gussie's face when Louie would say, as they rose from the breakfast table:

"Now, Gussie, come on. I'm not going to be a mere visitor, you know; so I'll help you set the rooms in order. You will be no time over them, with my help;" and not wishing it to be known that all such things were left to Dexie, she would follow Louie, and join in the task for very shame sake.

But Dexie enjoyed Louie's visit more than anyone, for she not only kept Gussie's hands employed, but her presence forbade the continual fault-finding which she had hitherto freely indulged in; for Louie was a person of some consequence, being the heiress of considerable property, as well as possessor of a bank book that she was at liberty to use at her own discretion, and this had much influence over Gussie.

Louie soon remarked the frequent visits of Guy Traverse, but was puzzled at first to account for them. Gussie had told her that he was engaged to a young lady in the city, and was only a particular friend of her father's; but this did not prevent Louie from forming her own opinion on the matter.

She asked her mother one day, as she brushed out her hair, how it was that her father had become so attached to such a young man, and if there were not some other reason to account for his frequent visits.

"He was with your father when he was hurt, and your father thinks he saved his life at the risk of his own, so I daresay that may account for the attachment. I did hope at one time that Gussie might be able to secure him; they would make a nice-looking couple. I have thought sometimes that he pays Dexie sufficient attention to warrant her in thinking he means something serious, but Hugh McNeil has some claim on her; he has been to see her lately. You remember he had quite a fortune left him. I expect she will keep a fine establishment when she is married. But I know nothing about her affairs; she was always close-mouthed, and she is sure to do something entirely different from what you expect."

"But, mamma, this Mr. Traverse seems to be more than just friendly to Dexie. I am sure he is with her every chance he gets."

"Oh! that is nothing; he is seldom in her company outside of her father's room. Besides, he is going to be married to someone in the city. He said as much before us all. I am sure Dexie does not care for him in that way. If you had heard the way she used to talk to him, you would see at once that his visits mean nothing to her."

"Nevertheless, mother, I have my suspicions," said the quick-witted girl, as she left the room.

"I'll corner Dexie sometime, see if I don't," she said to herself. "If there is any love-making going on in this house, it will be a funny thing if I do not find it out!"

But Dexie was well aware that there were a sharp pair of eyes about, and it took considerable manœuvring to get a word with Guy without having Louie pounce in upon them at the most unexpected moment.

"Seems to me, Dexie," she said one day, as they were in their chamber dressing for the afternoon, "if I was Mr. Traverse's young lady in the city," and she made a grimace, "I would not care to have my young man visit so much in a house where there are marriageable young ladies. Do you think she is aware of his frequent visits here?"

"What lady do you refer to, Louie?" turning from the mirror, where a blushing face was too freely reflected.

"You know who I mean well enough! The lady that Gussie says he is going to marry. I suppose you know that story as well as Gussie."

"Oh, yes; it is quite an old thing now. I have had it dinned into my ears till I am tired, both of the story and the lady as well," she carelessly replied.

"Oh, indeed!" said the laughing girl. "I suppose he has told you all about her during one of your many interviews. When is the wedding to take place?"

"The exact time was never mentioned, Louie. If you feel very curious about it, why not ask Mr. Traverse yourself. He might give you an invitation to the wedding, you know."

"But, honestly, Dexie, does he ever talk to you about his future wife?"

"Certainly! why shouldn't he? Didn't Gussie tell you that he announced his approaching marriage before the whole family?"

"Well, Dexie Sherwood, you can smile and smile and be—the young lady yourself, after all," said Louie, not yet convinced, "and that ring looks new, and I see no photograph of Hugh McNeil lying inside your favorite book, so there!"

"Well, you might have seen one in the album if you had looked for it, you silly girl. And how many new rings has Gussie had since you were home, and yet I hear no word of her engagement!"

"That may be, my dear sister Dexie; but I have not seen any young man kiss Gussie good-bye at the door, either; therefore I begin to think—"

What her thoughts might be upon the matter, Dexie did not give her time to express, but disappeared from the room as suddenly as if the cry of "Fire" had been raised in the house.

"Well, I may be mistaken; then, again, I may not," said Louie, reflectively, as she found herself alone, "but appearances point to the latter view. However, auntie says that 'circumstantial evidence is not positive proof,' so I will wait for further developments. If it is so—all right; if it is *not* so, well—then I think they should not be *quite* so familiar when Dexie shows him out. He is quite a handsome young gentleman and will make a distinguished-looking brother-in-law, and I am ready with my approval and blessing as soon as they ask for it; but, by the way things look to me, my approval and blessing have not been waited for."

When Dexie entered her father's room, she found Mr. Hackett, the lawyer, present, and she was about to withdraw when her father called her to his side.

"You will have to go over the papers in the desk with Mr. Hackett, Dexie," he said. "There are one or two missing which I know I have put somewhere in safety, so look carefully, dear; the loss of them would be rather serious in a case that Mr. Hackett has yet to settle. In case I have not mentioned it before, Mr. Hackett," and he turned towards the lawyer, "the old desk with all its contents, excepting those bundles relating to business matters, which you will take with you, belong to Dexie, here. There are several unfinished manuscripts which you can easily finish yourself, Dexie, and who knows but the beginning of your fame and fortune may be lying there waiting for you in the old ink-stained desk. There, do not cry, Dexie! It grieves me to see you fretting. You would not like to have your poor father lying here suffering much longer, surely! Now, be my brave, helpful little woman a little while longer, and help Mr. Hackett all you can. I was speaking of the old desk, Dexie; do not part with it to anyone, dear. Keep it as my last gift to you, and, if it ever needs repairing, have it done under your own eyes. Do not forget this, Dexie."

Dexie winked away her tears, and bent over to arrange his pillows more comfortably, saying:

"Do you want me to hunt up the papers now, papa? I will do so at once, if Mr. Hackett will explain what they are about."

"He will help you, then you can get through more quickly. You had better explain to my daughter, Mr. Hackett, about the amount of income there will be in the future. She is the housekeeper here, though I expect she will not remain in that position very long after I am gone. I am glad I purchased this property when we first moved here. It is increasing in value every year, and, if they should ever find it necessary, they can sell it and be comfortable in a smaller place, but this will not be needful for some years, if things are properly managed. There is another thing, Mr. Hackett, which I wish you would see about for them. Look around and find a respectable middle-aged couple that will be capable of giving the necessary help about the house and grounds. The place needs a man around it to keep it in order, and if his wife looked after the work in the house they would give better satisfaction than single people, I fancy. I cannot think what they will do when Dexie has left the house," and he sighed heavily.

When Mr. Hackett departed with the missing papers, Mr. Sherwood called her to his side and explained many things which would have to be seen to after his death, and Dexie sat and listened with quivering lips and hands clasped, palms downwards, across her lap, in an agony of mind, until she fell on her knees beside his couch, crying, "Oh! papa! dear papa! what shall I do without you!"

Her father stroked the ruffled hair and soothed her by his tender words till her tears flowed less freely and her sobs were checked, when he added:

"Now, I want to speak of yourself, Dexie. Do not keep Traverse waiting for you after I am gone. He has been very patient, and it has been on my account that he has waited so long for you. I am not blind to the trouble which you have borne so bravely and quietly these few months back; you have had little time to prepare anything for your new life, as most girls like to do, but this shall be made up to you, my dear. I have thought sometimes I would ask you to have your marriage performed here before me, but I will not be so selfish; that should be the happiest hour of a woman's life, and it would not be so to you under such circumstances. Louie has brightened the house by her coming, but she will soon be returning to her aunt, and then I am afraid you will find it harder than ever, my dear little Dexie."

Mrs. Sherwood came into the room, and finding Dexie sobbing on her father's pillow, was much alarmed.

"What is it? Are you worse, Clarence?" she cried, hysterically.

"No, no, dear wife, not that. But I have been giving Dexie some directions regarding matters after I am gone, and it makes her feel badly, poor little girl! She has been a good daughter to us, wife; so do not forget it when she needs your help and sympathy, and that time may be nearer than you think."

Dexie could bear no more, but she must not grieve her father by her tears; so rose hurriedly, and kissing his brow, left the room. She met Louie in the hall, and alarmed her by her grief.

"Is papa worse, Dexie?"

"I do not think so, but he has been talking to me about things which must be done when he is gone, and it breaks my heart! Poor papa! he is so kind and thoughtful, he seems to remember the smallest thing that we shall need to look after, and advises about them. I am afraid it will not be many days, Louie, before it is all over, and I believe he thinks so himself," and she went to her room to sob away her grief.

It was evident to them all the next day that Mr. Sherwood was rapidly sinking, and Dexie scarcely left his side for a moment.

Once when he woke from a troubled sleep he smiled into her face, and said faintly:

"She sang it very well, didn't she, Dexie? the 'pastures green,' you know. I never have forgotten it. Can you sing it now for me?"

"Try to tell me a little more, dear papa. Where was it you heard it?" trying in vain to think what had called forth this request.

"At Dr. Grant's church that Sunday morning in Halifax. You know—the new singer you wanted to hear. I know all about the 'pastures green' now, Dexie, but sing about it."

Instantly the Sunday morning so long ago flashed back to her mind, and with one arm around her father's neck, as she kneeled by his side, she sang:

> *"The Lord's my Shepherd, I'll not want.*
> *He makes me down to lie*
> *In pastures green; he leadeth me*
> *The quiet waters by."*

Her voice trembled, but there was a happy ring to it withal, and presently she saw that he slept again, his face looking happy and peaceful as it rested on the pillows.

When the doctor made his usual visit, he stayed a long time in the room, and he looked very serious as he called Dexie to the door.

"You realize how ill your father is, do you not, Miss Sherwood?" and he looked earnestly into her face. "Ah! I see you do. I wished to prepare you for the worst. I will come in later in the day and see if I can be of use."

"You think there is immediate danger, Dr. Brown?"

"He may live through the day—not much longer, I fear. You have been expecting this, have you not?"

"I was afraid of it," and she hid her face in her hands.

"Is there anyone I can send for, for you? If I can be of use in any way, Miss Sherwood, command me."

"Someone must tell mamma; she does not believe the end is so very near. Would you do it? Does papa know it himself, doctor?" she added, after a pause.

"Yes, and he wished me to make it known to the rest. Be brave a little while longer. Now, go back to your father. You can rely on Jarvis; she knows what to do, and has been through many trying scenes before today."

"Shall we send for you if—" She could not say it, but the doctor knew what she meant.

"Yes, if you like. I can do little, if anything, more; but he will not suffer any. Now I will see your mother," and he turned and left her to her grief.

It took some time for Mrs. Sherwood to fully realize the truth, for she listened to the doctor as if dazed. It was the first trouble that had ever really touched her, and at the suggestion of Jarvis she went to her room, where by degrees she grew calmer, as the terrible truth came home to heart that she was soon to be left a widow and her children fatherless.

When Louie came into her father's room a few moments later, and learned the truth, she threw her arms around Dexie's neck and wept with her. This was the darkest hour they had ever known. But there was no time to indulge in grief at present—that would come later—and Dexie whispered:

"Take Gussie up to her room, Louie, and tell her there, and do not let her come down till she is quiet. Warn Georgie not to go away from the house; papa may ask for him any minute. I am so thankful the doctor has told mamma! Watch the door, Louie, and when the minister calls today try and persuade mamma to see him. She would not see him the last time he was here. Oh, dear! I shall be so glad when Guy comes in!"

"Give me one little bit of comfort to cheer my heart this sad day, Dexie. Tell me, what is Guy Traverse to you—do, Dexie?"

"Dear Louie, you *shall* know, if you think it will comfort you any. He is my promised husband."

"I thought so all the time, and I am so glad!" and she turned away to prepare Gussie for the dreaded hour.

The time passed heavily and sadly, until the day drew near its close. Mrs. Jarvis was sitting near the bed, watching, with the eyes of an experienced nurse, for any change, and presently she bent over Dexie, who was kneeling by the bedside, and whispered:

"I think I had better bring back your mother. Do you think she can bear it?"

"She *must* bear it!" Dexie answered, with a sob.

As Jarvis left the room, Guy quietly entered it, and saw at a glance that the end was near. Dexie gave him one appealing look as he came beside her.

Bending over, he laid his arm across her shoulder, and whispered:

"Is there anything I can do, darling?"

Dexie shook her head, and the look on her face told of the anguish that was wringing her heart.

Seeing that her father had opened his eyes, she bent nearer.

"Are you in pain, dear papa?"

"No, dear child; and I shall soon be where that question is never asked."

Lifting his eyes, he saw Guy, and his lips parted in a smile.

"So glad you have come, my boy!" and he held out his hand. "You have indeed been like a son to me from the very first. You will be good to my little girl, and do not wait to claim her; take her very soon, and do not let her fret for me. Raise me up, Traverse! Ah! that is easier," as Guy seated himself on the bed, and raised his head and shoulders on a pillow with his arm.

Supported by Guy's arm, and with his head leaning against Guy's shoulder, Mr. Sherwood embraced his wife, who was led to the bed-side by Jarvis, and Dexie bowed her head from the sight of the despair written on her mother's face.

The family were soon assembled around the bed. Mrs. Jarvis lifted Flossie in her arms, and telling her to "kiss papa good-night," laid her on the bed beside him a moment, then carried her from the room, and the few loving words spoken to Georgie did much to make him grow up a true, good man.

Gussie was overcome with grief when she realized that her father was dying, but Louie's loving arm was thrown around her, and she restrained her sobs to hear her father's last few words.

It was a sad scene. The dying father, supported in the arms of Guy Traverse, was looking for the last time on the faces of his family. Dexie, kneeling close to where Guy sat, with one of her father's hands clasped in both her own, was silently weeping. Mrs. Sherwood was kneeling on the opposite side of the bed, her face hidden against her dying husband's breast. Louie and Gussie stood near, their arms around each other's waists; while Mrs. Jarvis stood behind them, her arms extended across their shoulders, as if she would willingly pro-tect them from this anguish if she could. Poor Georgie sobbed at the foot of the bed, a picture of childish woe.

The minister's words of peace and comfort, spoken at this moment, were sorely needed, for the prayer had scarcely ended when Mrs. Sherwood raised her eyes to her husband's face and saw the change that passed over it. A few murmured words fell from his lips as he looked into her face, then his eyes closed and his spirit was gone to the God who gave it.

Guy laid the form gently back on the bed, and something in his face must have told the stricken wife that all was over, for her piercing shriek chilled everyone to the heart.

Guy was just in time to catch Dexie's fainting form and bear her from the room, when the children round the bedside understood that they were fatherless.

CHAPTER XLIII.

Many changes took place in the household during the weeks following Mr. Sherwood's death. It was a sorrowful time to live through, and a most unpleasant memory to look back upon.

These were days of trial to Dexie. There was no one in the house that she could turn to for sympathy, for Louie had returned home the week after the funeral, and the house seemed desolate.

Mrs. Jarvis was called away by a case of sickness in another household, and Gussie, finding herself free from all restraint, made so many unreasonable demands on the patient and willing domestic that she refused to submit to it longer, and left the house; consequently, the actual work of the household, as well as the care and responsibility, rested on Dexie's shoulders.

Mrs. Sherwood had not left her room since the day her husband was buried, and her frequent hysterical attacks were very alarming to the rest of the family. She seemed as fretful and helpless as a child, and quite as unreasonable, almost blaming her husband for dying and leaving her alone in the world.

When Dexie tried to draw her thoughts away from their sad bereavement, she charged her daughter with being hard-hearted and unsympathizing in the extreme, and it seemed as if she did not wish to be comforted.

Lawyer Hackett attended the funeral, but as Mrs. Sherwood was not able to discuss business matters at that unhappy time, he promised to return later on and explain all things necessary.

Dexie awaited his return with much anxiety, for the expenses of the funeral, together with their necessary mourning, left little ready money to meet the daily expenses, and it was only by the strictest economy that she managed at all. Her "scrimping," as Gussie called it, met with no favor from anyone; and though Mrs. Sherwood talked of "ordering" this and that from the store, Dexie positively refused to be the mouthpiece of the order. They could do very well till Mr. Hackett arrived, she said.

Dexie missed her father sorely, and the one bright spot in the long, toilsome day was when Guy came in the evening. Then they would walk out together through the quiet streets to the country beyond, and she always returned refreshed and strengthened to bear the burden of another day.

As yet they had made no definite plans for their future. Dexie wished to see the household matters settled in a more satisfactory state before attempting anything that would benefit her own condition.

When the lawyer had explained to her mother the business matters which she had refused to discuss during her husband's lifetime, then it would be time enough to lay her own plans before her.

The appearance of the couple whom Mr. Hackett had secured to assist in the house and garden was daily expected, and Dexie looked forward to more freedom on their arrival.

One day, as Gussie answered the summons to dinner, she surveyed the table scornfully.

"Is this all that you have for dinner? This is the third day, Dexie, that you have given us no meat. *You* may like a vegetable diet, but I am sure no one else in the house does. We might as well dine at the poorhouse."

"Well, Gussie, you know it is not my fault," Dexie said, sinking into a chair with a tired sigh. "I cannot make things out of nothing, and my housekeeping money has come to an end. If you had not insisted on those extra dresses for yourself, the money would have lasted until Mr. Hackett arrived. I am sure he was not aware how little ready money there was on hand or he would have arranged for the expenses that were necessary. It is no use to fret, Gussie; there is plenty in the house to keep us for weeks yet, if we live plainly. It is a shame to worry and find fault because you have not everything you want when we have such a comfortable home left to us."

"But we can't eat the house or the furniture in it," Gussie snappishly replied, "and I am just tired and sick of the things you have given us to eat lately. I haven't the least appetite for your 'plain dishes' that you spend so much time over."

"Very well, Gussie, if you can prepare something better out of what there is to cook, I wish you would do it. I do not prepare your meals from choice. I have work of my own to do, and would prefer to keep out of the kitchen altogether, if it were possible."

"Well, I guess you'll be pretty hungry before *I'll* go in the kitchen to cook!" said Gussie, with uplifted nose. "I have no intention of messing myself up for other people."

"You do not need to 'mess yourself up.' I don't; and you may have to do more disagreeable things than that yet. I am going away for a rest as soon as the woman comes and gets used to the house, and she will not be able to see after everything without some help. Those starched clothes that you put into the wash every week with so little thought of the extra work they make—she will not be able to do them, if she has to see about everything else. There is a whole basketful there now, waiting for you to iron."

"Waiting for *me* to iron, indeed! Why didn't you do them when you ironed the rest of the clothes?" her temper rising at the bare suggestion that she should do them herself.

"I had too much else to do, Gussie, as you might know if you would give the matter a thought. You must see after them yourself, Gussie—while we are without a girl, anyway."

"We will just see about that! I never had to iron my clothes yet, and I am not going to begin now. I want my tucked skirts tomorrow, so see that you have them ready for me," and she rose to leave the room as if the matter settled.

"You will find your clothes in the basket, Gussie, whenever you choose to iron them," Dexie quietly replied, unmoved by Gussie's insolent manner, "and remember, Gussie, I positively refuse to do them for you again—never once again, remember!"

Glancing out the window she saw Guy Traverse approaching the house, and not wishing him to see Gussie in her present humor she took her hat, intending to meet him at the door and take him to the garden; but her mother called her just then, and when she came downstairs Guy was standing in the hall.

"You are not going out, surely, Dexie?" said Gussie, coming out to see who she was talking to. "Mamma would not let you go if she knew that you refused to do what I told you. It would be better for you to go to the kitchen and finish your work, instead of gadding about with the men."

"My work is done for the day, Gussie; it is your work that is waiting in the kitchen," and she hurried down the steps, with Guy closely following, his face dark with anger at the insulting words he had heard used to his promised wife.

"And this is the way they treat you, my darling!" he said, as he reached her side. "I understand why you never want me to come in and spend an hour with you; you are afraid I shall hear how they talk to you. I have a good mind to take you to the minister's this very afternoon, and make you my wife, so I can look after you."

"Do not mind it, Guy," trying to keep back the tears. "Gussie was vexed because she did not find her clothes done up for her as usual."

"And she is actually imposing on you to such an extent as that, is she? That explains that pale, tired face! My dear little girl, I cannot allow it! Do you love me well enough to come and live in a set of rooms until we can get a decent house ready?" and he looked tenderly into her face.

"I could live happy with you in one room, Guy, if I could leave home, but I cannot do that just yet. I must stay until Mr. Hackett comes back. I know they cannot do without me just now, dear. I would go with you willingly if I could, for I feel so tired and discouraged. Mamma thinks I neglect her if I am not constantly waiting upon her; but there are the children to see to. They are good little things, but they take up the time, you know, and the hours seem to more than fly."

"But if you were not there, dear, perhaps your mother would rouse herself; and I do think that would do her more good than all the doctoring she is getting, and Gussie should be able to be of as much assistance as yourself."

"Perhaps you are right, Guy, but it does not seem right for me to leave them now, and so soon after papa's death, too," and her eyes filled again.

"But you know your father said we were not to let that delay our marriage, dear. I feel quite sure he knew you would not have a happy life, so wished you under my protection."

"Don't tempt me anymore, Guy," said the quivering lips. "You do not know how my heart cries out for the comfort and relief that you offer me. I know very well I am only tolerated at home on account of my usefulness, but they do not understand what it would be like if I were not there. Gussie has not the necessary practice to make her the help she might be, and mamma would be sure to suffer if I left them before the new help arrives. Besides, Guy, I have not had time to prepare a thing for myself yet," she added, in a low, shy voice.

"You have not had time to get the rest you need, darling, and that is of more account than anything else. You must not think I am going to let you stay home and have Gussie abuse you while you make up a lot of finery. Be my little wife in earnest, darling, and whatever you want you can get just as easily after you are married as before. I never could see the sense in women making up such a quantity of new clothes just before their marriage; it always looks to me as if they were afraid their future husbands would not give them what they required when they were married."

"Let me speak to your mother today, Dexie, dear," he added, "and I will tell her that it was your father's wish that we should not delay our marriage; and I must insist that you be used with more consideration. I really cannot let matters go on without some protest; it would not be right for me to allow it, either."

"Very well, Guy, do as you think best; they cannot make it much more uncomfortable than it is at present."

But in this Dexie found she was mistaken.

Mrs. Sherwood listened to Guy's manly and straightforward declaration in silence, though her raised eyebrows showed something of her surprise as well as displeasure. She admitted she had no right to refuse her permission for their marriage if her father approved of it, but it was "quite like Dexie to keep her in ignorance of the true state of affairs." Of course, the marriage must not take place for some months yet. The impropriety of it so soon after her father's death was quite shocking, even to hear it suggested; besides, Dexie could not be spared from home. When Guy reminded her that Dexie should have the rest she evidently needed, her manner became icy at once, though she kept her indignation well in check until Guy had left the house.

"So you have been complaining to Mr. Traverse, have you?" she said angrily to Dexie. "We will see hereafter if you do not have something to complain about! If you are thinking of getting married to Mr. Traverse on purpose to shirk your duties at home, I will see to it that you *earn* your wedding while you *are* home. As for being married in the near future, your father's death will certainly forbid that, and I think Mr. Traverse will find that you are still under my authority, and that I am not quite so fond of him as your father was."

"Do not have any fear, mamma, that I will ever ask for a wedding that would be so grudgingly given," said Dexie, with quiet dignity;

"but I think I have already fairly *earned* my wedding, if that is the way you choose to put it. I hardly think anyone will ever hear you suggest that Gussie must *earn* her wedding before her marriage can take place, and I think I have been as good a daughter to you as Gussie has—I have tried to be, anyway, mamma."

"Gussie will never have the low tastes and plebeian ways that have made you such an eyesore to me. She is too much of a lady to delight in the domestic economy that you always aspired to, and when her time comes I shall see that she has a wedding that shall fill your heart with envy!" said the now thoroughly angry woman.

"I think that will not be possible, mamma," said the low, quiet tones, so unlike the Dexie of old. "It is not to the wedding I am looking forward with so much happiness, but to the loving husband I shall gain thereby, and the future happy life I shall spend with him. I am thankful to say that I do not need a grand wedding to make me perfectly happy," and Dexie left the room, her face white and sad as the result of the interview.

Gussie soon learned the true state of affairs, and Dexie had reason to be thankful that Guy had not spoken at an earlier day.

To most mothers, the few months or weeks previous to a daughter's marriage, the heart is full of loving consideration for her; the new position which her daughter is soon to fill arouses all her tenderness, and she is full of love that is not unmixed with pity. But mothers are not all cast in the same mould, and Mrs. Sherwood thought of Dexie's marriage only in the light in which it affected herself. Dexie was a necessity in the household, and she would see that Dexie had no spare moments; she must make herself doubly useful, and prepare for *their* future comfort; and as Gussie held to the same opinion, only declared it more frequently, Dexie had anything but an easy time of it.

One day when Gussie was harping on the same string, yet found it impossible to get Dexie to tell of her future plans, she retorted:

"Well, I think you have acted shamefully! I wonder what Hugh McNeil will say when he hears you have thrown him over again!—but I warned him! I told him just how you had been flirting with Traverse, and I am quite sure Hugh spoke to him about it, too! But you have been like the dog in the manger—you would neither take Hugh yourself nor give anyone else the chance of getting him. I might have had the benefit of his money if it had not been for you! I suppose you think you are smart to 'cut out' Guy Traverse's city girl, but it just shows how mean you are, though I can't see for the life of me what any man sees in *you* to admire!"

Dexie looked at her sister with flashing eyes. She longed to tell her what a ridiculous mess of mistakes she had got into. But what was the use! she would not give way to her temper if she could help it, though it was a temptation hard to resist.

"Sometime, Gussie, you shall know all about Guy's city girl, if for no other reason than to make you thoroughly ashamed of yourself;

and if you only knew how far from the truth all your surmises are, you would not be so free to talk. You make yourself ridiculous, if you only knew it!"

The next day, much to Dexie's delight, Mr. Hackett made his appearance, and easily explained the cause of his delay; and as he wished to have a final examination of all the papers in her father's desk, he asked Dexie's assistance, giving as a reason that a certain Mr. Plaisted had put in his claims for a large amount as soon as her father's death had been published. After explaining the matter to Dexie, she knew at once where to look for the proof needed to refute such claims, and placing the copy of the letter she had brought home from Prince Edward Island into the hands of the lawyer, she told him all the circumstances connected with it, and the break in the business intercourse with her father in consequence of it.

"Well, that Plaisted is a regular scamp!" said the lawyer. "I will take this letter with me, and with the knowledge I have now of him and his doings I fancy he will not care to face a judge and jury to enforce his claims, as he so boldly announces his intention. If I had known of this, or had taken this bundle of papers with me before, it would have saved me much time and annoyance. However, this time I will leave nothing but what you can claim as your father's gift, Miss Sherwood. The desk and its contents are now yours."

"Now, Miss Sherwood," said he, later, "I am ready to see your mother and have a talk with her; and if you will bring along the bills, which I daresay are rather heavy, I will see to their settlement."

"There are no bills to settle, Mr. Hackett—none, at least, that I know of; everything was paid for as it was ordered. I must confess we are about penniless, though," she smilingly said, "and if you had delayed coming for many more days we would have been like Mother Hubbard, with a bare cupboard."

"Why, you do not mean it, surely! Well, well! I never thought of such a possibility! But, then, I never thought you would try to settle the bills out of the money left for other purposes. Other things might have waited till I came to look after them myself."

"It has not hurt us to practise economy, and I did not want people to think that papa did not leave us enough to pay our expenses, so I paid the bills as long as the money held out. I had a little saved up, and that came in very handy, but I shall be glad to get something on the housekeeping account. They have all been protesting against the lack of variety on the table, till my sister thinks she is boarding at the poor-house."

"Oh, not quite so bad as that! not quite so bad, I hope! But you should have written to me, my dear Miss Sherwood, and told me about it. You have managed wonderfully. I have come prepared to settle all accounts and arrange about the future; but, by the way, I have something here for yourself," taking a package from his breast-pocket, and handing it to her. "Your father directed me to give you this. Oh, it is all right!" as Dexie exposed a roll of bills. "Your father explained it to me the last time I saw him, and I think myself it is only fair that the daughter who watched over him and waited on him so faithfully should be especially remembered. It is all right, and will come in very handy when the wedding comes off. There! don't mind me! Your father told me all about it, and explained many things which I need not have known if there had been any chance of his recovery. But he knew someone must take an interest in you as a family, and I am paid to do it, so it is all right, and the money is justly your own, for you helped to earn it—yes, this was received from his publishers for the work you helped him to do."

"But I have a twin sister, Mr. Hackett," Dexie began, as she counted the bills in her hand, "and I ought to share this with her."

"Not at all! not at all, Miss Sherwood," was the decided answer. "Your mother will supply your sister's wants willingly, which I fear would not be the case with yourself, if you were left to her generosity. Pardon my plain-speaking, Miss Sherwood; it is sometimes necessary, and I know what I am talking about. It is your father's gift—a wedding present, if you like to call it—and is intended for yourself alone, and in my opinion is not half what you deserve, there! I am an old man, comparatively speaking, but my eyes are young yet."

Dexie led the way to Mrs. Sherwood's room, where her mother was anxiously awaiting the appearance of the lawyer. She had become quite alarmed at the want of money, and insisted that Dexie must have been wilfully extravagant. But as Dexie produced all the accounts, and went over them before Mr. Hackett, Mrs. Sherwood was obliged to confess that the blame was not all on Dexie's shoulders, though she thought some of the bills extremely exorbitant, and could not be convinced that the extras which Gussie had ordered made such a difference.

Mrs. Sherwood found the interview with the lawyer very satisfactory, and she viewed with pleasure the roll of bills he left for their immediate use; and, at the sight of it, Gussie made a mental list of various luxurious articles she had long desired to possess.

Dexie was putting the desk in order when Mr. Hackett returned through the room, and he stopped for a few minutes' conversation with her while he drew on his gloves.

"I omitted to tell your mother, Miss Sherwood, that the woman to whom I referred when I was here before, will be ready to engage with you in about two weeks. Both she and her husband have excellent references, and I think they will suit very well. I believe you will find them both very trustworthy and worth waiting for. Do not hesitate to write to me if any difficulty should arise," and bidding her a cordial "Good-bye" he left the house.

Gussie was not pleased over the fact that Dexie had to "waste all the morning over those old papers," though she had not dared to remonstrate in Mr. Hackett's hearing, for she stood very much in awe of the lynx-eyed lawyer, who seemed to read her through and through with his keen grey eyes.

"How much longer are you going to be over those papers, I'd like to know?" she said, as she heard the front door close behind him. "The idea of you sitting there, and the dishes not washed yet!"

"Well, Gussie, you might have washed them before this; you have had plenty of time. I must put away these papers while I have them sorted out; then I will do what I can in the kitchen. Try to manage till I am done, Gussie; I won't be long now," and she looked up with a smile, as she tied a package of MSS. together and laid it away snugly in the drawer.

"You can finish those papers after you see to your work," said Gussie authoritatively. "You need not think you are going to be allowed to sit here all the afternoon, for Mr. Hackett left mamma a lot of money, and I guess we'll see who is going to run the house after this."

"Well, Gussie, that last remark of yours suggests good news," said Dexie, with a good-humored smile. "I will be delighted, indeed, if someone will take my place, for I feel sadly in need of a rest."

"Oh! I did not say you were to give up any part of the work! I guess you'll have to do that, whether you want to or not; but mamma says that I am to be the housekeeper and do the ordering after this," and there was a triumphant ring in her tone.

"Well, I was afraid that you would never care to do that, Gussie, and I am glad to see you are willing to undertake the difficult task; but the woman that Mr. Hackett is sending us cannot come for two weeks, so we must look up someone to do the work until she comes. Janet Robinson goes out by the day; I think we had better send for her."

"Well, the idea! Hire a girl so you can sit in the parlor with Traverse, I suppose! You managed well enough since Eliza left, and I guess you will get no chance to play the lady in this house! The kitchen is your place, and that is all you are fit for!"

"Then I throw up the situation from this moment!" said Dexie, hotly, thoroughly aroused at last. "It is quite time I turned my attention to something higher—to the making of blue or green dogs on canvas, for instance! Hire a servant to wait on you before night, for I will not step my foot into the kitchen again! I'll find something to do in a more congenial latitude," and Dexie thrust the remaining papers into the desk in startling confusion, locking the several drawers with a snap.

As Gussie left the room she rose to her feet, intending to send word to Guy to come and take her away, but, as she turned about, he caught her in his strong arms and held her close to him.

"Oh, Guy! how long have you been here?" and she burst into tears.

"Long enough to make up my mind that Gussie shall never get

the chance to insult you again as she has done in my hearing. Dexie! it makes my blood boil to know that you are treated in this manner! You must come away with me! I cannot leave you in the house after hearing those words said to you. You must not refuse, darling!" and he wiped away her tears and kissed the white face in his arms.

"Oh, Guy! if you only *would* take me," she sobbed. "I was just going to send for you, and beg of you to take me at once."

"I ran in to tell you that I am called to the city on business, and must go on the 5.30 train, so come with me, darling. I have a married sister living in Boston, who will make you right welcome, and we will be married as soon as the ceremony can be performed. Will you agree to this plan, my darling?"

"Yes, and bless you for the chance of getting away so quickly; but oh, Guy! I seem to be all alone since papa died!" and the tears fell afresh.

"You will not be able to say that in a few hours' time, dear; but I must hasten—I have an appointment at my office this minute. I will be back for you in less than an hour, and will see your mother then. Now, go and get ready for your journey, my little wifie," and with a tender embrace he hurried away, and Dexie flew upstairs to her room.

She had barely time to lock the door when Gussie came towards it.

"Open this door at once," she said, as she found it locked. "Mamma says you are to go to the kitchen and finish the work, and if you make any more fuss about it you will be sorry for it."

No answer, for Dexie had swiftly turned the contents of her trunk out on the floor, in one promiscuous heap, and was repacking it with a swift and practised hand.

"Do you hear what I say, Dexter, or shall I repeat it?"

"I have resigned my place in the kitchen, Gussie," came the reply, "and do not intend to enter it again; besides, I have accepted a better situation since I saw you downstairs. I am packing my trunk to leave the house, so you see I cannot be disturbed."

Gussie stood dumb with astonishment at this unexpected announcement, but of course it could not be true!

"Oh! never mind your high tragedy airs just now; open the door at once."

"I fancy that the tragedy part of this performance will be enacted by yourself, Gussie," was the reply. "I shall not open the door till I get my clothes packed; if you choose to wait till I am done, pray do so. I will not be any longer than I can help, as I intend to take the first train for the city."

Gussie applied her eye to the keyhole, and the limited view she had of the room was enough to convince her that Dexie was certainly packing her trunk, and she flew to her mother's room with the news.

Mrs. Sherwood could not believe it. Leave the house just when they needed her the most! Impossible! She sent Gussie back to the door with a peremptory message for Dexie to come to her room immediately.

"Tell mamma I will be there in a few minutes. I am almost through packing, and if I were you, Gussie, I would go at once and see if that Robinson girl will come and stay with you till the new cook arrives; and do have a care how you speak to her, for mamma's sake. Do not imagine that something will happen to prevent me going away, for that is a settled fact!"

Gussie hastened back to her mother in alarm.

"She is really going, mamma, and says she won't come out of her room until she gets her trunk packed. Oh! what shall we do with no one in the house to do a thing for us! I did not mean to vex her when I spoke to her as I did," bursting into tears.

"So it is your fault that, she is going! Are my troubles not heavy enough that you drive the only help I have away from me? What will become of us if Dexie leaves us, for you are as useless as you are extravagant!" And the mother scolded and complained as if Gussie alone were responsible for the trouble. "Go at once and make some amends for your ill-tempered words," she added, "and perhaps Dexie will overlook it, for my sake."

Gussie returned to the closed door, and in contrite tones begged for admittance.

"Do let me come in, Dexie. I am sorry I vexed you, and you are not in earnest about going away, surely, for you know we cannot spare you."

Dexie threw open the door, saying: "Come in and judge for yourself, Gussie. You see I really am going," she said, snapping the catch of her travelling bag. "If my sudden departure puts the rest of the family to inconvenience, you can blame yourself for it, Gussie; but you are just as strong as I am, and should be able to fill my place. However, if you think yourself above being useful, I hope you will not delay in getting someone else here, for you know you could not have driven me out at a more inconvenient time, for there is literally nothing cooked in the house."

"But where are you going? Not to auntie's with Louie, surely?"

"No. I should not like auntie to have a worse opinion of you than she has already. In leaving home I am consulting my own happiness, and I am going where I shall be kindly treated and warmly welcomed."

"Well, I'm sorry now I said anything to vex you, Dexie; so you need not go, after all."

"Your repentance comes too late, Gussie, for my plans are made; but I do not want to go away with any ill-feelings to any one, so here is my hand, Gussie."

"Oh, if you are really going, I'll not shake hands and make up with you! If we only had some help in the house I would be glad to get rid of you. I don't believe mamma will let you go, anyway," and with a toss of her head she left the room, saying to herself: "She'll have to unpack her things when mamma gets hold of her, so why need I humble myself to her."

Dexie was soon in her mother's room, listening to the reproaches that were heaped upon her without stint; but as no reply was given to them, Mrs. Sherwood looked at her intently, and something in the mother's heart brought to her attention the wan, white face of her daughter. She had not noticed that Dexie looked so worn and thin, and for a moment her heart smote her.

"What is this I hear, Dexie?" she said at last. "Do you think I am going to allow you to leave the house like this? You are forgetting that you are still under my authority."

"But you do not use your authority fairly, mamma. You have made my life very hard and unhappy since papa died, and permit Gussie to be impudent to me, even when I am doing everything for her comfort. I would have stayed a few weeks longer, but Gussie has gone too far and made it impossible for me to stay another day, so I am going away to be married."

"Married! Dexie, are you crazy?"

"No, I think no one else will think so, when they know that I am exchanging my present life for one so much happier."

"But, Dexie, I will not allow this! To be married in such haste, and away from home, without any preparations whatever! I forbid you to leave the house with such an absurd intention."

"I am sorry to have to deliberately disobey you, mamma, but I have passed my word and have no wish to take it back. I admit it would have given me much happiness to have been married from home, but it is doubtful if I could live long enough to *earn* a wedding, so it is best as it is."

"And you talk of being married, and your father not dead three months yet! Oh! you heartless girl! And you pretended to care so much for him! You shall not do this shameful thing! Fancy how people would talk!"

Dexie burst into tears at the mention of her father, and turning to leave the room, she heard Guy's voice in the hall below.

"Are you nearly ready, my darling?" as she ran down the stairs to meet him.

"All ready, but mamma is not going to let me go without some trouble, Guy."

"Take me to her at once, dear, and do not be alarmed. She will not forbid our marriage, so dry those pretty eyes."

Mrs. Sherwood found she could not talk to this stern-faced man as she did to Dexie. She felt embarrassed at his replies to her many objections, and the truths that Guy put so plainly she could neither deny nor refute.

"It was Mr. Sherwood's wish that our marriage should not be

delayed," was his answer to this objection, "and according to Dexie's wishes it will be strictly private. As to the unkind remarks which you fear will be made about our rather hasty marriage, I will take it upon myself to silence them, directly they reach my ears, by explaining Dexie's unpleasant position at home since she has been without her father's protection."

Mrs. Sherwood saw it was the best policy to give her sanction to the marriage, seeing she had no power to prevent it; but when she offered, after some hesitation, to give Dexie a sum of money to provide her with an outfit, Guy refused to allow Dexie to accept it.

"It is no matter, mamma," Dexie said through her tears, for the interview had been most distressing. "Papa gave me the money he received from his published sketches, so I will do very well."

Mrs. Sherwood did not care to ask what the sum amounted to; but having a poor opinion of her husband's literary efforts, she considered that it could not be much.

"I hope you will not regret this hasty step, Dexie," as Dexie came to her side to wish her good-bye. "You cannot expect me to think kindly of you when you leave me in such a way as this."

"Well, mamma, you know I am obliged to seek the protection of a husband that has been denied me as a daughter; I hope you will not miss me very much. Will you not kiss me good-bye?"

Her mother turned her cheek, but Dexie waited in vain for the kind parting word she longed for.

"I am sorry to leave you, mamma. Think kindly of me sometimes. Guy takes me because he thinks I need his love and care."

"Go to him, then! You have made your choice!"

With this dismissal, Dexie hurried to the hall where Guy was awaiting her, wiping her eyes as she went.

"Well, for my part, I'm glad to see the last of you," said Gussie, following slowly after her sister. "You have always stood in my way, and your Puritanical notions have spoiled many pleasures for me; so whatever tears *I* shed will be tears of joy."

"Thank you, Gussie; that speech is all that is needed to remove every vestige of regret I may have felt at leaving home," was Dexie's reply, an unusual light in her dark eyes. "Come, Guy, I am quite ready," and without turning her head she passed out the door of her own home to the untried future that she was to share with Guy Traverse.

"My heart aches for you, my darling," and Guy pressed the hand that rested on his arm. "Let Gussie shed her tears of joy while she can, for, if I am not mistaken, they will flow for another cause before the week is out."

CHAPTER XLIV.

A kinder welcome could not be imagined than Dexie received from Guy's sister when they arrived in Boston, for Mrs. Graham had heard so much of Guy's "little girl" that she took Dexie to her heart at once.

The mental disquietude and physical weariness that she had passed through kept Dexie confined to her room for two days, but on the morning of her third day in Boston she stepped out the church-door a willing, happy bride.

"Really, I can hardly believe that I have been turned into a married woman since I entered the church," she said softly, as Guy seated her in the carriage. "Does it seem real to you, Guy?"

"Well, hardly, dearest; but I am going to prove the reality of it, and use the authority just granted to me, by insisting that you put aside the thoughts that have made your face so sad. Let us think of the new, happy life before us, and forget the trials we have passed through. We are going to be very happy together, my little wife."

"Yes, I am sure of that. I believe our quiet and unconventional wedding will bring us quite as much happiness as if we had been married with all the fuss that generally attends affairs of this kind."

(They were driving back to Mrs. Graham's, where a few friends had been invited to meet them before they left for a short trip.)

"Yes, indeed," was the reply; "and I think we will enjoy it in a greater degree than if we were surrounded by a crowd of distracting friends, though I believe it is usually considered the one time in a person's life when friends are most appreciated. Why it should be so I cannot see, if all love is like ours. I have obtained my heart's desire at last. This happy day has been long delayed, but is none the less dear for the waiting, and you can never say again that you feel 'alone' in the world."

Dexie gave him a grateful look, as there was no time for words before the carriage stopped at Mrs. Graham's hospitable doorway, where smiling faces awaited them. Kisses and congratulations were not wanting, and the few friends who had accompanied them to church followed them into the house. A few hours later the happy married pair left for New York, where they spent a pleasant season viewing the sights of the metropolis.

On returning to Boston, Guy was offered a position in a large establishment, the headquarters of the firm, doing business in Lennoxville, in which he was previously engaged. This arrangement proved agreeable to all parties, and made it unnecessary for Dexie to return to the scene of her former trials.

Dexie soon found herself mistress of a charming little house, situated in one of Boston's beautiful suburbs, where her windows looked out on a lovely prospect. Here the time flew by so rapidly in caring for her dainty rooms and blossoming borders that her thoughts seldom dwelt on the unhappy weeks which preceded her marriage.

It was a delightful surprise when the dear old piano came with the rest of her belongings from home, but the grateful letter of thanks which Mrs. Sherwood received was tossed aside without a word, though the letter had not failed to touch the mother's heart.

The piano had been a silent rebuke, and Mrs. Sherwood had been pleased to remove it out of her sight, wishing in her heart that the memories which troubled her could be as easily banished.

But no other piano could have been half so dear to the heart of Dexie, and when she sat down before her beloved instrument the first chords she struck brought happy tears. It was like the greeting of a dear friend long absent. Little wonder her fingers lingered lovingly over the keys as piece followed piece.

"Dexie," said Guy, coming over to her side and leaning one arm on the piano, "do you remember playing for your father and me one evening and refusing us a certain piece? I have often wondered at the reason of that refusal. May I ask if you will play it for me now, darling?"

Dexie dropped her hands into her lap and lifted a flushed face to her husband's gaze.

"Dear Guy, I wish you had not asked me, for I do not think I can."

"What! not for me!" said he, laughing. "Not for your own husband! Come now, Dexie, have I found a cause to be jealous already?"

Dexie's arms were around his neck in a moment.

"Do not say such words, dearest, not even in jest; you do not know how it hurts me. Do you think I would have refused to play that piece for papa for a slight reason, Guy?"

"No, but tell me the reason, wifie. Come, no secrets from your hubby, mind," looking into her eyes with a teasing glance. "You know you told me you only played it when you were sentimentally inclined, and you must only be 'sentimentally inclined' in my direction now, so what is the secret?" kissing the lips so temptingly near.

"You are welcome to the secret, dearest, if I can put it into words, but not to the music, I fear, unless you will stand where I shall not see that you are watching me. There are some things hard to explain, and the effect of that piece of music upon me is one of them. Had I played it for papa, it would have grieved instead of pleased him, for it generally makes me cry; though why it has such power over me I do not quite understand. I have only played it before one person, and he understood it; so I did not mind."

"Now you have made me more curious than ever, little wife. You have played it for one person, and that person a gentleman, and yet you cannot play it for me. Now, Dexie, how could you break my heart by such a confession!" said he, laughing.

"It was only Lancy Gurney, so don't be foolish," leaning her head confidingly on his shoulder.

"*Only* Lancy Gurney! Worse and worse!" laughing gaily, as he held up her face to meet his gaze. "Don't tell me you are 'sentimentally inclined' in *his* direction yet, or I shall do something desperate."

"How can I tell you about it, if you laugh? I am afraid you will not understand it, if you look at it seriously!"

"Well, try me, anyway," and he drew her on to his knee.

"I fear it needs a musician's heart to understand it. I do not mean that the piece is so very difficult, but it has such strange, peculiar chords, which sound so exquisitely sweet, that it makes the tears come, no matter how hard I try to repress them. It affected Lancy the same way, so I did not mind playing it before him, but you see I could not give any reasonable explanation for my tears had I played it for you at papa's request."

"Say no more, little wife. I'll not tease you about it again; but let me confess a little sin. I listened to you one night through the open window when you were playing that piece, and I saw you in tears, too, but I did not rightly guess the cause of them."

"But I have not told you all yet! What will you say when I tell you that I gave Lancy Gurney one promise which I have not been able to break! Possibly, Lancy and I *were* 'sentimentally inclined' when he exacted it of me, but we agreed not to play that piece for other people, and I doubt if he finds that promise any easier to break than I do, for he would not care to let others see his emotion. I have often wondered what was in the heart of the composer, for it touches my heart like no other piece of music has power to do. I fear I have not made it very plain to you, dear, but I wish you understood it as Lancy did."

"Little wife, I believe you care for him yet," lifting her face and kissing her lips.

"Yes, of course I do, but not as I care for you. It is only the musical corner of my heart that he has touched, for apart from music I never give him a thought. My love for you is different; it seems to fill my life."

"You shall not find me exacting, dearest. Lancy is quite welcome to that musical corner, while I have such a heart full of love for my own. I would not have spoken about that music had I known what it was to you. I will remember after this," he added, smiling, "that it is 'sacred to the memory of—Lancy Gurney,' and I am quite willing to have it so," and he drew her close to his side.

"It is kind of you, dear, to respect this, my one bit of private property. I could never tell you what that music has been to me, for though it brings tears to my eyes it has the power to comfort. It seems to soothe and sympathize with me in my little troubles, and during that unhappy time after papa died I do not know what I should have done without the piano to talk to; it seemed the only bit of comfort left to me."

Guy raised the drooping head, and gazing tenderly into her tear-filled eyes said, gently:

"Dearest love! I do not believe that I half know you yet! There seem depths in your nature that I have never reached, and thoughts in your heart that I have never shared; they are so far above me. Trust me as far as you will, darling, and do not think that I wish you to break a promise that seems more sacred than sentimental," and he drew her to his heart again.

A few days later Guy brought home a thick letter to Dexie bearing the postmark of Halifax, and as Dexie read it a troubled look spread over her face, but she said nothing until the lamp had been lit and the curtains drawn; then she drew close to her husband's side, saying:

"Elsie has sent me very unpleasant news, dear."

"Then I wish she had not written; I do not like to see my little wife look sad over anything. May I know what it is, dear? but do not tell me if you had rather not, Dexie," and he drew her down to his knee.

"I do not think Elsie knew that her news would trouble me, for she seldom sees beneath the surface of things. My marriage has given her mother a great deal of trouble, and as she is the dearest little woman that I ever knew, I feel very sorry."

"For your marriage or the 'little woman'?"

"What a tease you are!" joining in his laugh. "But there is a ludicrous side to Elsie's story, too, though it is the unpleasant part of it that strikes me first. Do you remember the threat that Hugh McNeil made when we told him we were going to be married? Well, he has carried it out, and has married Nina Gordon, my double, that I told you about. Oh, it is a shame! a cruel shame! What a life she will lead with that passionate man, with no love between them to soften his feelings! Hugh could never listen to her patiently five minutes at a time; that is why he said he wished she was dumb! Oh, Guy! I feel so grieved. She is so sensitive at heart, for all her silliness, while Hugh is hasty and hot-tempered. How cruel of him to spoil her life, if he only married her for the chance resemblance to me, and it would be just like Hugh to tell her of it in one of his outbursts of temper. It has made me feel so unhappy that I could not finish my letter; I feel as if I were to blame in some way."

"Do not feel so troubled about it, my little wife; perhaps she will so improve under Hugh's tuition that she will be glad that her chance likeness was the means of making her his wife. I have often wondered, Dexie, how you refused him yourself. He seemed so persistent it is a wonder that he did not take you from me," drawing her closer to his side. "He seemed to have every quality that women most admire in a man."

"Well, I did admire him—at a distance—a *long* distance, you know," she laughingly answered, "but directly we were near enough to talk to each other, we were sure to disagree. What a charming married couple we would have made!" and both laughed at the mental picture. "Poor Nina! she has not the spirit to stand the first unkind word. I do hope Hugh will not be rough with her."

"I have a better opinion of Hugh McNeil than to think he will be rough with his own wife. From what I saw of him I rather admired him, and I hope he will be happy in his married life."

"I hope so, too, but—I fear for Nina. Let me read Elsie's letter to you, and you will understand the situation, for she is such an innocent little kitten that she has disclosed more than she is aware of":

"I cannot call you by your new name yet, but I hope you will not mind, for you will always be just 'Dexie' to me. I know that I ought to begin my letter with best wishes and congratulations, but I cannot do it honestly, so it would not be honor bright. Your marriage has made such a disturbance here that I do not know what to think, only that I am sure you are not to blame for it; so I wish you to know the story, even though Cora often says, 'I hope Dexie will never hear about this.'

"When I received the papers you sent me containing the announcement of your marriage, I, very naturally, read it out for the benefit of the rest in the room, never thinking I was doing anything out of the way; but that horrid Hugh McNeil was present, and before I had quite finished reading it he jumped to his feet and glared at me till I screamed with fright. Then he snatched the paper from me, and tore it in a thousand pieces, and stamped and stormed about the room till I felt sure he was crazy, then I ran from the room in terror. Then, as if that were not enough, Cora followed me out and said she had a good mind to box my ears for reading it out before Hugh, and yet I am quite sure that she likes you as much as ever. Well, we had an awful time with Hugh that night. He attempted to shoot himself, and mother cried and father scolded, and Lancy had to come and watch him till daylight. We were getting over our scare, and I was beginning to think it was a 'temporary fit of insanity,' as Cora said, when we were startled by another fit that is anything but 'temporary' this time, for Hugh asked papa to rent him the other half of the house where you lived, stating that he was going to be married immediately! Of course we wanted to know the name of the lady, and you can imagine our surprise and dismay when he said it was Nina Gordon. We all felt badly about it, for no one can imagine for a minute that he cares for her. As soon as he had rented the house he started off to Montreal, taking Mrs. Gordon and her daughter with him, and he returned about a fortnight ago, bringing Nina as his wife. Mrs. Gordon is to live in Montreal, and however Nina will manage without her mother at her elbow, is what puzzles everybody.

"I did not see Mrs. McNeil till a few days ago, for I was huffy at Hugh and would not be friendly with his wife; but when I did call I got such a surprise that for a few minutes I stood still in astonishment, for, if you will believe me, Dexie, they have got the house fixed up just as it used to look when you lived there—the same pattern of carpets and curtains, the pictures on the wall seem to be the very same, even to 'George Washington' that you used to make fun of. A piano occupies the same spot, and in the midst of it all there sat Nina with one of your pretty dresses on. Well, I suppose, the dress *was* her own, but I cannot understand how she happened to get it made so much like yours. Of course I made remarks, how could I help it when everything was so much like old times! but, in the most unexpected moment, in came Hugh, and the way he went on at me was something fearful! I am sure I never hinted that he had not a right to furnish his house to suit himself, but when I went home he followed me and had a long talk to mother about me. Nasty thing, that he is! and now I am forbidden to mention to anyone the astonishing resemblances that I see next door. They have sent me to my room for an hour because I *looked* surprised at a remarkable thing, so I thought I would sit down and tell you how badly I am treated, for I am snubbed at every turn, and no one likes to be continually snubbed.

"We like Lancy's wife very much, though she is different from what we expected. It is quite plain that she is very much in love with Lancy, so he ought to be pleased. I suppose it will not be 'the correct thing,' as Nina says, if I tell you why we felt so disappointed over his marriage, but we all expected his wife would be the dear girl we used to know and love. I often think that Lancy misses her, for his wife is not a bit musical; but everything is contrary here. There! I am called, and my hour is not yet up, so that's odd, too."

"That is only the first part of the letter, but it contains news enough for a dozen," said Dexie, as she laid the closely-written sheets on the table before her. "I am sure you see now what a trouble my marriage has been to dear Mrs. Gurney."

"Yet we imagined it was a very quiet affair, eh, Dexie?" regarding her with an amused smile: "However, do not take it so seriously, darling. Things have, no doubt, quieted down by now, and everyone will not see Hugh's wife and home with Elsie's eyes."

"But I have not finished the letter yet; wait till you hear the rest."

"There is a postscript, I suppose, and like every other woman's letter, it needs to be read first," was the smiling reply. "Well, let us hear the conclusion of the matter."

Taking up the remaining pages, Dexie read:

"I was called downstairs to see Mrs. McNeil, who was in the parlor and had asked to see me especially, and as my eyes rested upon her the word 'Dexie' sprang to my lips. She had on your garnet velvet suit, and looked as well in it as ever you did. I intended to treat her very coolly, for I had not forgiven Hugh, though I have been to church twice since he offended me; but she was so very friendly, and so anxious to make amends for Hugh's behavior, that my coolness melted away. She begged me to try and like her 'for Dexie's sake,' and as Hugh had sent regrets for his hasty words and wished me to run in as freely as I did in the old times, I feel as if I can repeat the responses in church this evening without feeling so terribly wicked over it. I fancy, from what Nina says, that Hugh is often quite stern and cold in his way of speaking to her, and she admitted that he has already made her cry. I feel very sorry for her, for I did not know when I began this letter why Hugh was so put out at your marriage, but I do now, and I think that since you would not have Lancy it is a good thing that you are safely married; but take care that Hugh does not run away with you some day. He is quite equal to it yet."

"There is no danger of that," said Guy, referring to the concluding passage. "I can read another story between the lines of Elsie's letter, and I think, dear, that Hugh's wife will not blame you if her marriage should not prove a happy one."

"I hope you are right, Guy; but how could I bear it if I thought you married me just because I resembled someone that you knew and loved, but could not marry," and she put her arms around his neck and looked into his eyes.

"But you know that my heart has been yours since I first saw you, so why need you borrow trouble, my little wife? There! lie still in my arms and rest content," drawing her close to his breast with a tenderness that gave a fresh assurance of his love.

"Do you know, Dexie, dear," he added presently, "something in that letter tells me that Hugh explained everything to Nina before he married her, and she could have refused him if she objected to the conditions. Hugh's money would overbalance many difficulties, and I have no doubt that Mrs. Gordon urged her daughter to accept him, with a full knowledge of his reasons for wishing to marry her. I feel sure that Nina is willing and anxious to please Hugh, and he may yet find much happiness in the society of your double. Few men would care to do such a thing, I admit, but if he finds any solace in his disappointment in surrounding himself with things that are dear to his memory and in making his wife a second Dexie, it is well."

POSTSCRIPT.

Having happily married my heroine and disposed of her lovers, it occurs to me that I have reached the place where story-writers usually make a big flourish, write "Finis," and then lay down the pen.

But the story of a person's life does not end with marriage, as some would have us think, for marriage generally brings out one's best qualities or develops the worst, and is sure to make or mar the life of every woman; consequently, this story is not yet finished. Yet why should I trouble myself to write out the remainder of it until I have discovered if the reading public are interested in Dexie's life so far as it has been already told? It may be that no one cares to follow her fortunes any further, or feels the least desire to know what the future has in store for her, to say nothing of the friends who have been associated with her; and as I have no wish to bore you, dear reader, gentle or otherwise, it rests with you to say if their married lives shall be laid bare or not.

I am aware that the marriage of my heroine lacked the *eclat* which usually attends events of that kind—in story books—but I fancy the average reader is well acquainted with all the details of an elaborate wedding, and must be surfeited with the various accounts of them by this time. However, if that is the style of wedding you prefer, I can give the names of several volumes which contain everything you can possibly desire in the way of description of gorgeous wedding costumes and all the rest of the paraphernalia that goes along with them, and you can read any account that suits you better, then take up my story further along. See?

Those that take objection to Dexie's home-life—particularly to that immediately preceding her marriage—are reminded that such lives do exist. When death visits a family, and removes the restraining head, the petty faults of the remaining inmates are apt to grow apace, unless the Angel of Death has touched their hearts with divine grace. Lacking this, the development of character has a downward tendency. It does not make pleasant reading, but I have not told an impossible tale. But who knows "how the other half lives?"

The question is—Do you care to know if Dexie has chosen her life as wisely as she might have done? Would her married life have been happier if she had married Lancy Gurney? The affection they had for each other was akin to love; there was a sympathy between them which those who have an intense love for music can alone understand, and which might have proved a source of happiness, even during a life-long existence. They might not have experienced the rapture of heartfelt love, but their lives might have been more peaceful and contented without it, for deep love often means keen sorrow.

Or would it have been better if she had accepted the love as well as the money which Hugh McNeil was so anxious to lay at her feet?

She might have learned to care for him in time, and to have found pleasure in a life surrounded by all the joys that wealth can bestow. To have an abundance of worldly goods, and to be exempt from the petty cares and economies which a limited income necessitates, is a condition much to be desired, even where no love exists to soften the heart of husband and wife, and in this case Hugh McNeil could not be charged with possessing an unloving heart.

Dexie thinks she has made the wisest choice in accepting Guy Traverse and marrying for love, but she has yet to face the question—Is mutual love alone essential to secure a happy married life? or in the language of the world:

"Does it pay to marry for love alone?"

THE END

www.ingramcontent.com/pod-product-compliance
Lightning Source LLC
Chambersburg PA
CBHW060423030726
47495CB00003B/710